Alexandria,

Welcome to ...

The Club!

The Club Trilogy book one

THE CLUB

Lauren Rowe

xo

Lauren Rowe

Chapter 1
Jonas

Name?

I inhale and exhale slowly. Am I really going to do this? Yes, I am. Of course, I am. The minute Josh ever so briefly mentioned "The Club" to me during our climb up Mount Rainier four months ago, I knew it was only a matter of time before I'd be sitting here on my laptop, filling out this application.

"Jonas Faraday," I type onto my keyboard.

With this application, you will be required to submit three separate forms of identification. The Club maintains a strict "No Aliases Policy" for admission. You may, however, use aliases during interactions with other Club members, at your discretion.

Yeah, okay, thanks. But the name's still Jonas Faraday.

Age?

I type in "30."

Provide a brief physical description of yourself.

"Extremely fit. 6'1. 195 lbs."

Wait a minute. I've been working out like a demon this past month. I walk into the bathroom and stand on the scale. I return to my laptop.

"190 lbs."

With this application, you will be required to submit three recent photographs of yourself to your intake agent. Please include the following: one headshot, one full-body shot revealing your physique, and one shot wearing something you'd typically wear out in a public location. These photographs shall be maintained under the strictest confidentiality.

Jesus. Am I really going to send my personal information and three photos of myself to who-knows-where to some unknown "intake agent" for a dating service/sex club I know nothing about?

1

I sigh.

Yes, I am. I sure as hell am. Even if it's against my better judgment, even if doing this flies in the face of rational and analytical thinking, even if my gut is telling me this is probably a horrifically bad idea, I've known I was going to do this since the minute I heard Josh talk about The Club four months ago.

"It's incredible, bro," Josh said to me, getting a foothold on a boulder and stretching his hand toward a nearby crag. "Best money I've spent in my life."

The best money my brother had ever spent—and this coming from a guy who drives a Lamborghini? It was an endorsement I couldn't ignore. In fact, thanks to Josh's intriguing recommendation, I've thought of little else since our climb. Even when I've been smack in the middle of what should be an epic fuck with a hot kindergarten teacher or state prosecutor or barista or flight attendant or personal banker or dog groomer or graphic designer or court reporter or waitress or hairdresser or pediatric nurse or photographer, all I can think about is what I'm probably missing out on by not belonging to The Club.

"It's like a secret society," Josh explained. "You can find members anywhere you go, anywhere in the world, on a moment's notice, and the members matched to you are always ... uncannily *compatible* with you."

It was the "uncannily compatible" part of that sentence that grabbed me and wouldn't let go, not the part about being able to find other members on a moment's notice anywhere in the world. Because God knows I can find a sexual partner virtually any time I want, anywhere I go, on my own.

I hate to be blunt about it, but women throw themselves at me, I guess based on my looks (so they tell me) and money (so I surmise) and, sometimes, thanks to the Faraday name (which, believe me, ain't such a prize). Young, old; married, single; hot, mousy; blonde, brunette; bookish, badass; full-figured, heroin-chic. It doesn't matter. It seems I can have anybody I want, as easily as ordering "fries with that" if I'm so inclined. And, yes, over the past year or so, I've become increasingly, incessantly, obsessively so inclined. And I'm beginning to hate myself for it.

Before anyone gets all up in arms and starts righteously listing off all the women I could never bed—"Well, you could never fuck Oprah or Mother Theresa or Chastity Bono before she became Chaz"—let me be crystal clear about what I'm saying here: I can bed any woman I *want* to. No, not literally every woman on planet earth. I fully acknowledge I couldn't nail a nun or Oprah or an eighty-year-old great-grandmother or a pre-op-transgender-lesbian. Nor would I want to, for Chrissakes.

What I'm saying is that if I, Jonas Faraday, *want* a particular woman to be naked and spread-eagle in my bed, if that's what I *want*, if a woman turns my head and makes me hard, or, hell, makes me laugh, or think about something in a whole new way, or maybe if she can't find her sunglasses and then chuckles because they're sitting on top of her head, or if her ass is particularly round in a snug pair of jeans—oh, yeah, especially if she has an ass I can really sink my teeth into—whoever she is, she will, eventually and most willingly, float onto my bed like the beautiful angel she is, spread open her silky thighs and, after a only a few moments of mutual bliss, beg me to fuck her.

I wish I could say "end of story" right there, but, unfortunately, I can't. Because sex is never the end of the story when it comes to me. And that's why I need The Club. I can't keep going to the same pond with the same fishing rod, dipping my rod into the same waters—no matter how warm and inviting those waters happen to be—and just keep bringing up the same goddamned tilapia, regardless of how moist and delicious. I just cannot do it anymore.

If I keep doing the same thing I've been doing, over and over, the same way I've been doing it, then I'm going to go completely insane—which is something I've already done once, albeit a lifetime ago and under completely different circumstances, and I'm not willing to do it again. What I want is something different. Something brutally honest. Something *real*. And if the only way to get what I want is to ignore my better judgment and shell out an enormous monetary sacrifice to the gods of depravity, then so be it.

Please sign the enclosed waiver describing the requisite background check, medical physical examination, and blood test, which you must complete as a condition of membership.

No problem. I'm relieved to know every member gets rigorously vetted. I sign where indicated.

Lauren Rowe

Sexual orientation? Please choose from the following options: Straight, homosexual, bisexual, pansexual, other?

"Straight." That's an easy one. Just out of curiosity, though, what the fuck does "pansexual" mean? I Google it. "Pansexual: Not limited or inhibited in sexual choice with regard to gender or activity." Ah, okay—anything goes. Interesting concept, solely from a philosophical perspective, but it most definitely doesn't describe me. I know exactly what I want and what I don't.

Do any of your sexual fantasies include violence of any nature? If so, please describe in detail.

"No." Emphatically, categorically, no.

Please note that your inclination toward or fantasies about sexual violence, if any, will not, standing alone, preclude membership. Indeed, we provide highly particularized services for members with a wide variety of proclivities. In the interest of serving your needs to the fullest extent possible, please describe any and all sexual fantasies involving violence of any nature whatsoever.

Hey, assholes, I answered honestly the first time. "None."

Maybe I should move on to the next question, but I feel the need to elaborate. "There is nothing whatsoever I enjoy more than giving a woman intense pleasure—the most outrageously concentrated pleasure she's ever experienced in her life. Now, granted, if I do my job, her pleasure, and therefore mine, is so overwhelming, it blurs indistinguishably with pain. But, no, my fantasies do not tend toward violence or infliction of pain, ever. I find the entire idea repulsive, especially in relation to what should be the most sublimely pleasurable of all human experience." What kind of sick fucks do they let into this club, anyway? My gut is churning.

Are you a current practitioner of BDSM and/or does BDSM interest you? If so, describe in explicit detail.

"Never," I write, my fingers pounding the keyboard for emphasis. A distant memory threatens to rise up from its dark hiding place, but I force it back down. My heart is racing. "My extreme disinterest in bondage and sadomasochism is absolutely non-negotiable."

Payment and Membership Terms. Please choose from the following options: One Year Membership, $250,000 USD; Monthly Membership, $30,000 USD. All payments are non-refundable. No

4

exceptions. Once you've made your selection regarding your membership plan, information for wiring the funds into an escrow account will be immediately forthcoming under separate cover. Membership fees shall be transferred automatically out of escrow to The Club upon approval of your membership.

What did my father always used to say? *"Go big or go home, son."* Oh, how he'd laugh heartily from his grave to know the son he derisively called the "soft" one is harkening back to his father's mantra to choose a sex club membership. *"I guess you're more like your Old Man than I thought,"* he'd say. I can hear his ghost laughing wickedly in my ear right now.

It's not the amount of money that gives me pause. I could buy either membership plan multiple times over and never hear so much as a peep from my accountants—but I don't throw money away, ever, in any sum. Regardless, though, if I'm going to do this, which I am, doesn't it make the most economic sense to join for a full year? My hands hover over the keyboard. My knee is jiggling.

All right, fuck it, yes, I admit it—it's crazy and irresponsible to spend this kind of money on a club, or dating service, whatever the hell this is, especially sight-unseen. I'm Jonas, after all, not Josh. I'm not the twin who buys himself Italian sports cars on every whim or who hired Jay-Z to play his thirtieth birthday party (which would have been our joint birthday party if I'd bothered to attend). And yet ... I sigh. I know damn well what I'm about to do here, no matter the cost or how loudly the voice inside my head is screaming at me to retreat.

"One year membership," I write, exhaling loudly.

Please provide a detailed explanation about what compelled you to seek membership in The Club.

I close my eyes for just a moment, collecting my thoughts.

"I love women," I type. I take a deep breath. "I love *fucking* them. And most of all, I love making them come." I smirk at the stark boldness of the words on my computer screen. There is no other context in which I'd ever make these crude statements to anyone.

"Perhaps what I'm supposed to say is, 'Oh, how I love the smell of a woman's hair, the softness of her skin, the elegant curve of her neck.' And, yeah, all of that's true; I'm not some kind of sociopath. Yes, I've been known to lose my composure over a woman's sharp

5

mind and wit—and that's not sarcasm, by the way; when it comes to women, the smarter the better—or her husky voice or raucous laugh, or, yes, even a flash of genuine kindness in her eyes. Yeah, that's all sexy as hell to me. But in my view, a woman's hair only smells so damned good, and her skin is only so damned soft and inviting, and her laugh is only so infectious all as a delicious prelude to one thing—the most honest and primal and fucking awesome thing our bodies are designed to do. Everything else is just prelude, baby, glorious prelude."

I take a deep breath. I've never articulated these thoughts before. I want to get this exactly right—otherwise, what's the point of filling out this application?

"From as early as I can remember, I've always particularly admired women. As I grew up, that translated into a powerful sexual appetite, but nothing I couldn't control. I could take a woman to an art gallery or concert or movie or candlelit restaurant and pleasantly ask her about her work, her passions, and even her beloved Maltese Kiki over a bottle of pinot noir and not even once feel compelled to blurt out, 'I just want to fuck you in the bathroom.'"

I stare at the screen. I'm pretty sure I sound like an asshole right now. But it can't be helped. The truth is the truth.

"And then, everything changed. About a year ago, I went on a typical date with a very pretty woman, and when I fucked her after dinner—and not in the bathroom, mind you—she did something a woman had never done with me before. *She faked it.*" I grimace. "She fucking faked an orgasm. It was so obvious as to be insulting. And it pissed me the hell off. Sex isn't supposed to be about *humoring* someone or being *polite*—it's not high tea with the goddamned Queen. Sex is supposed to be the *truth*, the most real and raw and honest and primal expression of the human experience. And orgasm, by its very nature, is the height, the very culmination of that honesty."

Jesus, after all this time, I still get riled up about this. My chest is heaving. My cheeks are flushed. I can't think straight. I need music. Music is the thing that calms me when my thoughts are racing and my pulse is raging. As a kid, my therapist taught me to use music as a coping mechanism and it still works for me. I click into the music library on my laptop. I choose "White Lies" by Rx Bandits and listen for a few minutes. Quickly, the song soothes me and clears my head, opening a window for my bottled thoughts and feelings to fly through. I listen for several minutes, until I'm calm again.

"I couldn't understand why she'd lied to me," I continue. "Why would she prematurely and artificially end a damned good fuck (or what I *thought* was a damned good fuck) and thereby exclude even the *possibility* of her actually getting off? Was I that big a hack at fucking her that she preferred ending the intolerable tedium to at least *trying* to come for real? I was beside myself."

I inhale deeply and exhale slowly.

"One night, as I was tossing and turning and thinking about it, the truth grabbed me and wouldn't let go. I suddenly knew she'd lied to me precisely because, yes, indeed, I was just that terrible at fucking her—because she'd thought getting off with me was so hopeless, that *I* was so hopeless, why even bother to try?

"It might have been enough to send me to a very dark place, a place I've been before (and it ain't pretty), except for one thing: I knew down deep that I hadn't really *tried* to get her off, not like I knew I was capable of doing. I'd concentrated solely on my own pleasure, not hers, and assumed that whatever I was experiencing must have been mutual. The more I thought about it, the clearer it became—she'd given me exactly what I deserved. And I was ashamed of myself.

"It was a watershed moment. From that instant, I became a man obsessed, singularly focused on fucking that woman again—only *excellently* the second time around—and making damned sure she came for real and harder than she ever had before. I wanted to teach her a lesson about truth and honesty, yes—but even more than that, I wanted *redemption*.

"Well, of course, she agreed to see me again—she actually seemed excited to accept another invitation from me, despite my apparent hopelessness—but this time, when I fucked her again, I was a new man, a man possessed, a man *enlightened,* you might say, singularly focused on her pleasure and nothing else. And the result was mind-blowing. Her entire body convulsed and undulated against my tongue from the inside out, slamming open and shut violently like a cellar door left open in a tornado. And the noises that came out of that woman were fucking amazing, too, the most primal, desperate sounds I'd ever heard—nothing at all like the hollow bleating she'd

7

tried to pass off the first time around. She was a fucking symphony. Of course, women had come with me before then—but never like that. No, no, no, never, ever like that. I'd held her in the palm of my hand and pushed her over the edge, at my will, and into another realm."

My heart is racing. My cock is hard.

"And the best part—the true epiphany—was that getting *her* off like that got *me* off. Holy fuck, did it ever. In fact, pushing that beautiful liar into untethered ecstasy, making her surrender to the truth, to me, to her pleasure, turned out to be the most epic fuck of my life—a high like nothing I'd experienced before. After that, I wanted that high again and again (though not with her, of course—never again with her)—and ever since, I've been chasing that high like a horse running to the barn with blinders on."

I take a deep breath.

Has any of this babbling answered the question? Shit. I don't know. But this is the best I can do.

"And that's what's brought me to The Club."

I stare at my screen. I shrug. That's all I got.

Please provide a detailed statement regarding your sexual preferences. To maximize your experience in The Club, please be as explicit, detailed, and honest as possible. Please do not self-censor, in any fashion.

My hands are trembling over the keyboard. The question I've been waiting for.

"Some guys say fucking a beautiful woman brings them closer to God. But, really, they should aim higher. Because when I make a woman come like she's never come before, when I make her surrender and leap into the dark abyss, I don't just get closer to God, I *become* God. *Her* god, anyway, for one, all-powerful, fucking awesome moment."

I stare at the screen. My dick is straining painfully inside my jeans.

"Making a woman come, at least the way I'm talking about, is an art form. Every woman's orgasm is a unique puzzle, a treasure locked away by a secret code. Almost always, the best and most reliable way to crack a particular woman's code starts with licking and kissing and sucking her sweet spot, but even that seemingly 'sure thing' only

8

works if, as I do it, I pay close attention to her body's special cues and adjust accordingly as I go. I can't just lick her—I have to *learn* her. Usually, after only a few minutes, though, I've got her figured out.

"I always know I'm on the right track when she suddenly and involuntarily arches her back, thrusts her hips reflexively into my mouth, and spreads her legs as wide as they'll go. That's when I know her body's preparing to give in to me, that I'm breaking down her defenses—that she desperately *wants* me to unlock her secret code."

I'm rock hard. God, I love that moment. I lick my lips again.

"When she thrusts herself into me and begins to open herself, I become ravenous, myopic, relentless. I lick her and kiss her and suck her with increased fervor, and maybe even nibble and gnaw at her, too, depending on what her body's telling me to do, and she continues rapidly opening and unlocking, spreading and unfurling, untethering and breaking down. It's fucking incredible.

"She's a beautiful, blooming flower. The trick, of course, is to catch her the exact moment before her petals fall off, and not a second before or after, because what I'm aiming for—the holy grail, if you will—is to plunge myself into her at the very instant when doing so will push her over the edge. It's tricky. Too early, and she might not come at all. Too late, and she'll go off without me."

I unbutton my fly and my cock springs out. I want to jerk myself off right now, but I want to get these thoughts onto my computer screen even more.

"She's on the verge—so fucking close—and I'm out of my mind, a shark in a frenzy. Finally, she reflexively *shudders* in my mouth—a feeling so delicious, I often dream about it—and I know her body's teetering right on the very edge, hanging by a thread, aching to give in, but her mind is keeping her from what she wants, usually thanks to daddy issues or a raging good girl complex or low self esteem (take your pick, it's always something). Whatever it is, her mind is getting in the way of her body surrendering utterly and completely to the intense pleasure she yearns to experience.

"But I won't be denied. She claws at me, gulps for air, her pleasure mounting and morphing into an agony she increasingly cannot contain. She whimpers, groans, writhes—and I'm so fucking turned on, too, I can barely contain myself. 'Fuck me now, *please, please,*' she often says, or some variation thereof, but I won't do it, even though I'm losing my fucking mind, because I know she's not maxed out just yet."

I breathe deeply.

"Finally, like a key turning in a lock, something inside her clicks. She opens. Her mind detaches from her body. She becomes untethered. She *surrenders.*"

I let out a shaky breath.

"That's when I plunge into her like a knife in warm butter and fuck her with almost religious zeal—sometimes pulling her on top of me to do it, sometimes turning her around, sometimes slamming into her the good old fashioned way—by then, any which way is equally effective—and the moment I enter her, her body releases completely, reflexively shuddering and constricting and undulating all around my cock, over and over again. Sure, she's come before, of course. But never like this. No, never like this. It's pure *ecstasy* in the way the ancient Greeks defined that word: *the culmination of human possibility.* For both of us."

I let out a long, controlled exhale and shift in my seat. Holy shit, I've really gotten myself worked up. I breathe in and out deeply several times. I'm trembling. I take a moment to compose myself.

"I should be clear about something, in the interest of full disclosure. What I've described here is the ideal. The *aspiration.* Sometimes the timing works out exactly this way, and sometimes it doesn't. Sometimes, especially when I'm still learning a woman, or if she's particularly hard-to-read for some reason, she might come like a freight train before I manage to get inside her. And if that happens, it's nothing to complain about, believe me—fucking a beautiful woman immediately *after* she comes is also a delicious privilege, no doubt about it. But the pinnacle, the peak, the perfection to which I aspire—the holy grail—is and always will be bringing a woman right to the edge of ecstasy and pushing her over it from the inside out."

I shift in my seat again, but my erection is too intense to ignore. I have to stop typing. How could anyone fill out this application without having to jerk off? I grip my shaft and pump up and down until a staggering wave of pleasure wells up inside of me and finally releases in fitful spurts. I go into the bathroom and pull off my jeans.

I hop into the shower and let the steaming hot water rain over me, relaxing me, cleansing me.

Getting women into my bed isn't my problem. The problem occurs right after a woman has had the best sex of her life, when her body has finally functioned at full-tilt capacity for the first time. That's when a woman invariably confuses discovering the full extent of her sexual power with the ridiculous notion that she's found her soul mate. Thanks to a lifetime of brainwashing by Disney and Lifetime and Hallmark, she naively believes glimpsing God during an epic fuck somehow translates into some kind of happily ever after with her Prince Charming. No matter what I've said beforehand, no matter how clearly I've presented myself and the limits of what I'm willing to give, she's suddenly convinced she's found The One. *"He just doesn't know it yet,"* she tells herself.

And that's when I hurt her, whoever she is—whether she's a librarian or tax accountant or personal trainer or pediatrician or makeup artist or singer or bioengineer or therapist or paralegal. Whether she's funny or sweet or shy. Whether she's serious or sexy or smart. Whether she's a tree hugger or a Sunday school teacher. I hurt her, whoever she is. Because I'm too fucked up to be The One. Not for her, not for anybody. She can't change that fact. No one can. *I* can't even change that fact—and believe me, I've tried.

Damn. How am I going to accurately convey all this information in my application? I get out of the shower, throw a towel around my waist, and get right back to my laptop. I stare at my computer screen for a brief moment, trying to find the right words to succinctly express my thoughts.

"No matter how honest I am right from the start about how little I'm willing to give outside the four walls of my bedroom, women always seem to get hurt by me, nonetheless," I type. "Either they don't believe me when I tell them what I really want, or they think they can change me. And they can't."

I sigh.

"I'm not out to hurt anyone." And it's the truth. "All I want to do is give a woman pleasure like nothing she's experienced before—which leads to my own ultimate pleasure. After I taste her and fuck her and teach her what true satisfaction feels like, I might want to lie in bed and talk and laugh with her, too—because, believe it or not, I

11

enjoy talking and laughing quite a bit, as long as everyone understands it's not going to lead to a heart-shaped box of chocolates and a weekend shopping trip to IKEA. Maybe I'll want to get into a hot shower with her and lather her up, running my soapy hands over her entire, beautiful body. Maybe I'll want to dry her off with a soft, white towel and then fuck her again, maybe the second time so intensely, so deeply, so expertly, we'll come together, both of us gasping for air and shuddering simultaneously as our bodies discover the culmination of human possibility together.

"After all's said and done, I'll surely want to tell her how beautiful she is and how much I've enjoyed our time together. I'll want to kiss her goodbye, gently and gratefully, thanking her for our glorious time together. And then, almost certainly, I'll never want to see her again."

My hands hover over the keyboard for a brief moment.

"And I don't want to feel like an asshole for any of it." I sigh. "Because I'm sick and fucking tired of feeling like a complete asshole."

I pause again.

"You've asked me to state my *preferences*, but clearly what I've described here transcends preference. I *need* smart, sexy women who *honestly* want what I do—no lies—and who, most importantly, can clearly and rationally distinguish physical rapture from some kind of romantic fairytale."

I stare at my computer screen, a sense of hopelessness threatening to descend on me. Am I kidding myself here? Do women like this even exist?

I type again. "If I could find even one woman, just one, whose 'sexual preferences' are uncannily and genuinely compatible with mine, I'd be ... " What would I be? *Elated.* That's what I was about to write. *Elated.*

Jesus. I quickly delete that entire last sentence. It's a non sequitur, for Chrissakes. I mean, shit, I'm either a sexual sniper with a rampant God complex or I'm fucking Nicholas Sparks. I can't be both. I have no idea what bizarre place in my brain that last ridiculous sentence came from. I guess that's what happens when a guy like me tries to articulate his deepest, darkest needs without a filter—the thoughts come out in a jumbled, desperate, douche-y mess, inexplicably intertwined with all the fucked up shit I've tried unsuccessfully to fix with years of useless therapy.

What the hell is this mysterious "intake agent" going to think of all my incoherent rambling? I cock my head to the side, an epiphany slamming me upside the head. An "intake agent" is going to read my application—yes, of course—and that intake agent's going to be a woman. *Of course.* And not the eighty-year-old pre-op-transgender-lesbian variety, either. They can't let assholes like me, or, worse, crazy fucks with violent fantasies or bondage fetishes or some other latent form of psychopathy into The Club without first passing a woman's gut check. Right? *Right.*

I grin broadly and place my fingers back on my keyboard.

"And now a message directly to you, My Beautiful Intake Agent." I lick my lips again. "Have you enjoyed reading my brutally honest thoughts—my deep, dark secrets? I've enjoyed writing about them. I've never expressed these truths to anyone else—never even thought about them quite like this. It's been enlightening to arrange the bare truth so clearly on the page and confess it to you—and therefore confess it to myself, too. In fact, telling you the brutal truth turned me on so much, I had to take a break midway through writing this to jack off."

I smile again. I'm such a bastard.

"So, tell me, My Beautiful Intake Agent, are you surprised at how wet your panties are right now, considering the fact that you've been brainwashed your whole life by Lifetime and Hallmark to think you want flowers and candy and a candlelit dinner followed by silent missionary sex, a chaste kiss goodnight, and a trip to IKEA the following morning to shop for a mutually agreeable couch? And yet, despite a lifetime of conditioning about what you're supposed to want, here you are, anyway, aren't you, My Beautiful Intake Agent, imagining my warm, wet tongue swirling around and around your sweet button, wishing I were there to lick and kiss and suck you 'til you were jolting and jerking like you'd gripped an electric fence? You're a unique puzzle, My Beautiful Intake Agent, yes you are—a rare treasure locked down by a padlock. But guess what? My words have already begun to *unlock* you, as surely as if I were there to turn the key myself.

"So what are you going to do about the dark urges clanging

around deep inside you right now, My Beautiful Intake Agent? Are you going to ignore them, or are you going to let them rise up and eventually untether your body from your mind? Perhaps you should use this opportunity, as I have just done, to touch yourself and think honestly about your deepest desires, to think about what *actually* turns you on, as opposed to what's *supposed* to. Touch yourself, My Beautiful Intake Agent, and go to the deepest, darkest places inside you, the places you never allow yourself to go—and embrace the brutal truth about your wants and needs. Your whole life, you've been taught to chase all the Valentine's Day bullshit, haven't you? But that's not really what you want. Tell the truth—to me and to yourself. You'd ditch all the Valentine's Day bullshit in a heartbeat to howl like a rabid monkey for the first time in your life, wouldn't you?"

I'm smiling from ear to ear, imagining some frazzled, middle-aged woman sitting in a cubicle in Dallas or Des Moines or Mumbai, reading my words with wide eyes and a throbbing clit.

"I know what you're thinking: *Cocky bastard! Asshole! A legend in his own mind!* All true exclamations, my dear. But guess what? Cocky bastard or not, if I were there to lick you, nice and slow, right on your sweet button, the way you deserve to be licked, the way you've only ever dreamed of being licked, the way no man has ever done for you before, I guarantee it'd take me less than four minutes to deliver you unto pure ecstasy that would make you surrender to me, totally and completely." I smile to myself.

"Yes, My Beautiful Intake Agent, if I were there to teach you what your body's divinely designed to do, you'd be forced to admit an immutable truth, whether you wanted to or not: In addition to me being one cocky-bastard-asshole-son-of-a-bitch motherfucker, I'm also the man of your dreams."

Chapter 2
Sarah

I'm stunned. Like, mouth hanging open, eyes bugging out of my head, I've turned into a strand of wet spaghetti stunned. I can't believe *this* is the first application I've been assigned to review and process all by myself after three months of supervised intake training.

What an asshole. What a flaming, unparalleled, self-absorbed, self-righteous, egomaniacal, self-important asshole. I don't know whether to laugh or scream or cry or throw up. Talk about emotionally stunted. Pathetic. Delusional. Narcissistic. And maybe even a little bit scary. He wants to lick my "sweet button" 'til I howl like a monkey? It'd take him less than four minutes to "deliver me unto pure ecstasy that would make me surrender to him, totally and completely?" What the hell? Who talks like that? Who *thinks* like that? Freak.

Oh, and the best part of all, he'd make me come harder than I ever have in my entire life? Ha! That one made me laugh, considering the situation. I'm sure he'd be shocked, and oh so titillated, to find out that making me come *at all* would *de facto* qualify as making me come harder than ever before. Yeah, I'm sure that little nugget would make his head explode into a million tiny pieces.

Maybe the woman who faked it with him wasn't the devil incarnate, after all—maybe she just knew she wasn't capable of having an orgasm, no matter what he did. Did he ever think of that? Maybe she pulled the chord on her parachute when it became clear things were going to end the way they always did for her—with a big, fat nothing. Sure, he *says* he made her climax the second time around, but can he be sure? Maybe she faked it again. Maybe she just wasn't wired to have an orgasm. Maybe she was wired like me.

15

Jerk.

But if he's such a jerk then why am I squirming in my chair right now, trying to relieve the pounding ache between my legs? Dang it, despite my brain's firm desire to be disgusted by what he wrote, his words, and especially his message to me personally, lit my body up like a Roman candle. Wow, just sitting here, staring at my laptop in my little student apartment, I want to reach down past the waistband of my pajama bottoms and touch myself—and I *never* have that urge, ever.

I need to get a grip.

But when I close my eyes to clear my thoughts, all I can think about is his warm, wet, flickering tongue on my skin—between my legs—right where I'm pulsing mercilessly right now. I feel my face flushing crimson.

What the heck has gotten into me? I'm not some kind of sex-addicted nympho. I mean, I'm no virgin, either. I lost my virginity during my freshman year of college to a guy I thought was hot (who then promptly turned into a cling-on), and in the five and a half years since then, I've had two long-term-ish boyfriends (both of whom were cute and sweet, even though things eventually got too boring to continue), one fairly forgettable one-night-stand (thanks to my best friend, Kat, who lured my guy over by flirting with his friend), and, to top it all off, a second one-night-stand six months ago I can barely remember (thanks to a fourth cosmo that pushed me well past Fun-and-Confident-Sarah and right into Hot-Mess-What-Were-You-Thinking-Sarah—something I swore to myself I'd never let happen again).

So, yes, even if I'm not a sex fiend, *per se,* I've definitely had my share of sex, including oral, by the way—both giving and receiving—so it's not as though I'm some kind of squeaky clean fairytale princess who blushes at the sight of a penis. I'm certainly not gonna swoon and pass out just because some jerk refers to my clit as my "sweet button," for the love of Pete. And, anyway, even if I'd had any hang-ups about words that begin with the letter "c" before I started this bizarre "intake agent" job three months ago, they're long gone now.

But I digress. Big deal if my body's not wired to have an orgasm. I'm not alone in this predicament, or, situation, rather—it's not a *predicament*. I've done my research. Seventy-five percent of women never reach orgasm through intercourse alone and a full *ten to fifteen percent* of women like me never reach climax at all, ever, under any circumstance, no matter the tongue or toys or position or emotions involved.

So, okay, I'll never suffer a horrible backache after having a mind-blowing orgasm like Kat "complains" about. Big deal. It certainly doesn't mean I can't experience sexual pleasure at all, because believe me, I do. I thoroughly enjoy the physical sensation of sex, especially when there's an emotional connection with the guy (or, occasionally, when alcohol creates the *illusion* of an emotional connection with the guy).

The more I think about it, I can totally relate to what this Jonas Faraday guy is saying because, much like him, I get most turned on when I'm pushing my partner over the edge hard and fast— particularly when he's trying desperately to hang on. Getting a guy off, especially when he's like "no, wait, not yet, I wanna hang on," makes me feel powerful, like I've got a superpower. So, yeah, I totally get it.

But *understanding* the guy certainly doesn't explain why I'm so frickin' *turned on* by him. I mean, seriously, why the heck do I feel like touching myself right now? I *never* want to touch myself. What's the point? I've tried in the past, and all it does is make me feel defective in the end.

And it's the same regarding a guy going down on me. Getting licked to death by some well-intentioned guy with a frenetic tongue might be pleasant at first, sure, but it can only do so much for me when I know I'm not going to come. The whole exercise inevitably begins to feel kind of pointless—and, honestly, kind of embarrassing and anxiety-producing, too. And if he keeps going and going with no success, the whole situation becomes soul-crushing, actually— especially if it's obvious he's frustrated or, worse, disappointed.

That's why, almost every time sex heads down the whole "oh let me make you come, baby" path, I wind up faking it, usually right off the bat, so he won't wind up feeling disappointed and I won't wind up feeling like a flaming failure. It's not his fault I'm a ten-percenter—and it's not mine, either. It's just the way it is.

But I'm sidetracked. All I'm saying is I'm not the kind of girl

17

who's going to get hot and bothered by some guy talking about licking a woman's "sweet button" or "fucking her brains out" or making her "come like a freight train." So why the heck is this guy's application turning me on like this? Wow, I mean, I'm really, really turned on. This is a first. In my three months on the job, I've had all kinds of reactions to the twenty or so applications I've processed, but never once before now have I been close to feeling like my panties are on fire—not even when the applications are a little bit sexy or kind of sweet.

Often, the applicants are just normal (rich) men searching for true love in an overwhelming world who are hoping The Club will curate their search. I have no problem with that. I mean, if you have a particular sexual quirk—whether it's a foot fetish, wearing women's lingerie, or being whipped while dressed in a bunny suit—it must be kind of difficult finding women (or, men, or both) who'll accept, and maybe even enjoy your freaky thing, whatever it is.

The way I see it, most of these guys are just diehard romantics who, yes, happen to have some kind of sexual peccadillo. Sometimes, I read their heartfelt confessions and yearnings and desires and I actually think, "Aw." But I never, ever think, "Oh, pick me, Mr. Bunny Suit Guy." Hellz no.

In addition to the diehard romantics (as I prefer to think of them), the second largest contingency of applicants consists of globetrotting tycoons and celebrities and professional athletes who apparently want to find compatible companions wherever their global travels might take them. Again, I have no problem with this. Some of the guys in this category are pretty hot, actually, and not particularly weird or anything—some are even sexy as hell—but even the hottest globetrotter/athlete guy has never once made me want to slide my fingers into my pajama bottoms. So why now?

The third category of applicants, the group I call "the wack jobs," not only *doesn't* turn me on, the whole lot of them makes me want to shower in Lysol. They're the ones who, without exception, apply for a full year's membership, apparently seeking to indulge their every depraved fantasy without the pressure of a ticking clock. These guys aren't interested in finding true love like the diehard romantics, and they're not looking for love despite a hectic travel schedule like the globetrotters and pro athletes. They're simply not looking for love, period—or else they'd never pay for a full year's membership up front.

Who in their right mind, *if* they were looking for love, would commit to paying a year's membership fee if there were even the *possibility* of finding someone special after only a few months? That's the thing I hate about the wack jobs the most—that they're motivated solely by their hedonism and demons, and not even a little bit by their hearts. They're all diehard cynics, every last one of them, led uncontrollably to their next nameless, faceless sexual encounter by their gigantic, throbbing dicks—without even an ounce of hope or romanticism coursing through their horny veins.

Reading the wack jobs' sexual preferences is like driving past a horrible car wreck. Disgusting. Horrifying. Shocking. But you can't look away. These guys are the ones who want to tie a woman up and shove steel balls up her cooch (what?) or dress a woman in a Goldie Locks costume and make her do unthinkable things with porridge (I almost quit after reading that one).

My least favorite wack job so far was a guy who wanted a secret gay life on the down low, concealed from his wife and four kids, even though he was a politician who'd recently campaigned vigorously based on his vehement opposition to gay rights. (I flagged that application as "do not approve," but my recommendation was ignored.) It wasn't the secret gay life part that got me so riled up—I figure half these guys are joining The Club to cheat on *someone*—it was his disgusting and inexcusable hypocrisy, his self-loathing disguised as moral superiority that got me seething. That guy almost made me throw my hands up and quit—but then, after I cooled down a bit, I decided not to throw the baby out with the bathwater.

True, twenty percent of the applications are revolting, but eighty percent of them are semi-titillating, or at least fascinating or amusing or even sweet; the pay is fantastic; and the work schedule is pretty easy. So, all things considered, it's an ideal part-time job for a first-year law student who needs the money but also needs time to attend classes and study. If I quit, I'd have to find something else, anyway—I'm drowning in student loans as it is, and the law job I've committed to take after graduation doesn't come with a lawyer-sized paycheck.

But, anyway, the point is that even the most appealing applications haven't made me fantasize about having monkey-sex with the applicant. And yet, here I am now, after reading a certain megalomaniac's application, doing just that. What the hell?

Jonas Faraday.

Who is this guy? I mean, really? Despite all The Club's warnings and demands for complete honesty, most applicants lie about *something*—hence the reason The Club hires law students like me to rigorously vet applications. Sometimes, the guy shaves years off his age, or says he's single when he's married, or describes himself as "extremely fit and 190 pounds" when his pictures tell another story.

So what's "Jonas Faraday" lying about? That he's some kind of woman wizard who can have any woman he wants and make them come as easily as shooting ducks in a barrel? *Puh-lease.* No man can have any woman he wants—no matter how rich or good looking he might be—and I'm living proof the second part is impossible, too. But what else is he lying about?

Let's find out.

I put my curser over the first photo attached to the application and click on it. This ought to blow an icy frost into my blazing panties pretty damned quick.

Oh. My. Gawd.

I'm looking at a picture of the most exquisite male specimen I've ever seen, dressed to perfection in a meticulously tailored suit. Holy crappola. His eyes. His lips. His jawline. Did I say "his lips" yet? Okay, let me say it again. *His lips.* Wow, I'd give anything to kiss them, even once. I just want to run my fingertip over those lips. I want to lick those lips. Holy moly.

The photo is from some sort of professional photo shoot. I can tell by the quality of the image and the lighting. Obviously, whoever this guy is, he's a male model. I sigh. Okay, that's a relief. I might have had a stroke if the guy who wrote about licking my "sweet button" until my "mind detached from my body" actually looked like this.

Damn. If this alleged "Jonas Faraday" guy looked even remotely like this male model he's pretending to be, I'd believe he was some kind of pied piper for women. I mean, a guy who looked like this could certainly bed *me* any time he pleased, thank you very much (assuming I didn't know he was a narcissistic asshole, of course). But it's a moot point because there's no way he looks like this. No effing way. This is a blatant "catfish" attempt if I've ever seen one—where the applicant tries to pass himself off as some ridiculously perfect human specimen, as if nobody's ever going to discover the discrepancy between the Greek god he's claiming to be and the elf from *The Lord of the Rings* he actually looks like.

I click on the next picture and, this time, I practically black out.

"Wow," I say out loud.

The bastard attached a bathroom-mirror-selfie, wearing nothing but tight briefs and a cocky grin. Oh man, there are muscled cuts above his hips, and his stomach is rock hard and chiseled. His nipples are small, perfect little circles. There are tattooed inscriptions running down the inside lengths of both forearms. I can't make out the phrases, but I'm drawn to them. I touch them on my screen with my fingertip.

I suddenly imagine this Adonis' naked body pressed against mine, and every drop of blood in my brain whooshes directly into my crotch. What the hell is happening to me right now? I'm like a frickin' cat in heat. This is so unlike me I want to slap myself silly right now. And, anyway, I don't know what I'm getting so worked up about. This Greek god is not the one flirting with me—the one flirting with me is some normal-looking guy who swiped these images off a European ad for condoms.

I click on the third picture. Another selfie. A headshot this time, as instructed. He's staring into the camera, unsmiling. His gaze is matter-of-fact. Unapologetic. Intense. Magnetic. Confident. I can't look away. He's stunning. Well, the *male model* is stunning. I'm transfixed. I'd really like to have sex with a man that looks like this just once before I exit this planet. I'd really like to feel someone like this touching me, kissing me, making love to me—and, wow, imagine if he did it all expertly, like this Jonas Faraday claims to do. Talk about a perfect storm.

I close my eyes.

Maybe that's the thing that's got me so hot and bothered about this guy's application—I'm realizing I desperately want to have sex, just once, with a guy who knows exactly what he's doing.

The guys I've been with have been cute and well-intentioned but just sort of ... I don't even know how to put it. Functional? Clumsy?

Clueless? Or maybe it's just been so long I'm just not remembering it right. I haven't had sex in six months—and that was a drunken one-night stand I don't even remember in any detail. But reading "Jonas Faraday's" words, and now looking at the photos of this male model, I just can't help thinking—what if I were to have sex with a guy who was masterful at it *and* looked like this, too? Yeah, that'd be *my* holy grail.

I sigh.

I'm really veering off task here. I've got a job to do. I force myself to click out of Mr. Perfect's photos. Okay, no more ridiculousness. Time to work. Job, job, job. Do, do, do.

I load the three photos onto my Google images software to run them against all the existing images on the Internet. I don't normally start my research this way, but, more than anything, I'm dying to find out the true origin of these photos. After I press the "go" button, I grab myself a glass of wine in the kitchenette and put on some music. I linger for a moment against the counter, sipping my wine and listening to Sarah Bareilles sing me a happy song, trying to distract myself from the tingling inside my body that won't go away.

I shake my head and take a big swig of wine. And then another. I can't believe I'm getting turned on by a wack job who signed up for a *year's* membership in a sex club. I mean, come on, he admits explicitly he can't form any kind of emotional connection with a woman to save his life. So why is my body reacting this way? Even before I saw those three mesmerizing photos, I'd already physically reacted to his application exactly as he predicted, and quite emphatically. As I lean against the counter, thinking about those photos again—his body, his eyes—an insistent ache keeps tugging at me. A throbbing I can't ignore.

Damn, I can't resist.

I take another big swig of wine and slide my fingers inside my pajama bottoms, just for the hell of it. When my fingers reach their target, I close my eyes and let out a low moan. Wow, I've never been so wet in my life. If he were here, he could enter me like a hot knife in warm butter, just like he said, without needing to do a damned thing first.

My laptop beeps and my eyes pop open. There's a result window on my computer screen. I pull my hand out of my pants and lurch over to my kitchen table. "No matches" is the message on my screen. What? Surely, if this guy took those images off some gay porn site, or a Facebook profile, or an ad for ass-less chaps, there'd be a frickin' match. How can these photos not be posted *anywhere* on the Internet? Where'd he get them, then? My heart's thumping in my chest. He couldn't possibly look like this, could he? No way. He couldn't turn me on with his bare words and then turn out to look like a Greek god, too—could he?

All right, I'll start at the beginning, like I usually do. I Google "Jonas Faraday," even though I'm sure he's using an alias (despite The Club's strict instruction against it). Much to my surprise, the search instantly calls up countless links for a "Jonas Faraday" in Seattle. I click the link at the top—a website for Faraday & Sons, Global Investments, LLC, based in Seattle with satellite offices in Los Angeles and New York, and much to my shock, there he is, boom, right on the homepage. *Jonas Faraday.* The Adonis himself. The most beautiful creature I've ever beheld. Ever, ever, ever. Like, seriously, ever. He's standing next to another very good-looking guy with darker hair but similar looks, both of them in sleek suits. The caption under the photo says, "Brothers Joshua and Jonas Faraday carry on the legacy of their late father, company founder Joseph Faraday."

So, there you go. He really looks like this. Oh my God.

I scrutinize the photo. The other guy, his brother, seems authentically happy, smiling with what appears to be genuine glee. Jonas, on the other hand, stares at the camera with such burning intensity, it's not clear if he wants to murder or devour whoever's behind the lens. I smirk. The photographer must have been a woman—which, of course, would make the answer to my question "devour." I bet he took that photographer home after the photo shoot, whoever she was, and "delivered her unto the culmination of human possibility."

I feel a pang of envy.

His muscled torso flashes across my mind. His abs. His eyes. His sculpted arms with those elegant tattoos along his forearms. His lips. I imagine those lips whispering "Sarah" in my ear as he makes love to me—or, ha! Who am I kidding?—as he *fucks* me, as he so clearly stated was his predilection. I imagine those lips smiling up at me from between my open thighs. I shiver. Another swig of wine. I'm losing my mind here. Have I had a brain transplant recently and I just don't remember? These thoughts are not normal. At least not for me. My heart is racing.

I click onto the selfie-headshot he submitted and stare into his smoldering eyes. In this shot, unlike the one in the suit, there's a sadness behind his eyes. Is that loneliness? Exhaustion? Whatever it is, I can't resist it. He looks totally different here than in the suit and tie photos—bare, somehow. Vulnerable. The more I stare at his mournful face, the more I'm sure: This is the money shot for me, the one that makes me want to touch him and kiss him the most, even more so than his almost-nude selfie. It's just so disarming. Beautiful, really. It makes me ache all over, and not just in my panties. In my heart.

A nagging realization begins washing over me, nipping at me, threatening to consume me—a slow but steady drip, drip, drip of a deep and secret truth. I want to feel the sensation of losing myself completely to someone. I want to know what it's like for my body to detach from my mind, just once. I want to convulse and shudder and whimper and shriek the way other women do—the way he describes it. I want to experience the kind of pleasure that blurs into pain. Yes, I admit it—I want to howl like a rabid monkey. *I do.* And something tells me Mr. Jonas Faraday, the cockiest and most self-aggrandizing human being on planet earth—and yet the most physically alluring creature I've ever seen, too—with the saddest and most captivating eyes—just might be the man for the job. In fact, if I'm being honest here, I'm ardently hoping he is.

But why am I wasting time fantasizing about him? This is a man who just applied to The Club—*for a year*—and I'm his frickin' intake agent. It's a non-starter. I need this job more than I need to howl like a monkey.

Damn.

He told me to touch myself and think about what turns me on. Well, there's no harm in doing that, job or no job. I grunt with exasperation, grab the bottle of wine off the kitchen counter, and stomp into my bedroom, slamming the door emphatically behind me. If I can't have him in real life, then I'll just have to crank up the music, close my eyes, and imagine a world where I can.

24

Chapter 3
Jonas

My entire morning was hijacked, stranding me in a conference room with my management team, half listening to a phone call with Josh in Los Angeles and my uncle in New York and their respective teams. "That new acquisition isn't performing as projected." "Yeah, but the question is whether that's a trend or a blip?" "Can someone put that into a spreadsheet?" Blah, blah, fucking blah.

Ever since I submitted my application to The Club the night before last, I can't concentrate worth a shit. Even when the checkout girl at Whole Foods last night smiled and asked me what I was doing later, I just grabbed my bags off the conveyor belt and said, "I've got a busy night." And she had piercings, too—which means she had major daddy issues. I can't remember the last time I passed on a woman with daddy issues—they're usually my Achilles heel. But my head's just not in the game right now.

Within minutes of sending in my application, I received an automated email from a "no reply" address, informing me that my application had been received by my intake agent and would be queued up for immediate processing. "The review process takes up to two weeks and is designed to ensure maximum protection, privacy, and satisfaction," the email said. "Thank you for your patience."

I was pissed as hell to find out things would take so long. I'd hoped to get a warm and quick welcome from The Club—like how a Hawaiian hotel hands you a mai tai as you walk into the lobby. What could possibly hold things up for two weeks? I'd answered every question honestly and followed all directions to a tee; I'm not a serial killer or felon or druggie; and God knows they've got my full membership fee, in cash, sitting in the bank earning interest. So what the hell could possibly take two weeks? I can't stop checking my private email account, hoping things will somehow go faster than expected.

Now that I'm finally in my office alone, I close my door and quickly open my private email account, even though I know nothing will be there. My heart stops. There's a message in my inbox time-stamped at 2:12 a.m.—about an hour after I went to sleep last night. My breathing constricts just thinking about this message sitting here all morning while I've been trapped on a conference call about "projections" and "action items."

The email is from a sender identified as "Your Beautiful Intake Agent." Holy fuck. When I click on the sender name, the actual email address is "Your_Beautiful_Intake_Agent@gmail.com." Oh my God. My pulse is racing. My mouth is dry. I click open the email.

"My Brutally Honest Mr. Faraday:

"This email is not an official Club communication. In fact, if anyone at The Club ever found out about it, I'd lose my job faster than I could say 'my sweet button' or 'petals falling off a flower' or 'plunging into me like a hot knife in warm butter,' or, perhaps, my favorite, 'cocky-bastard-asshole-son-of-a-bitch motherfucker.' So, in the interest of me being able to make my next rent payment, I'm hoping you'll keep this message just between us—you know, our little secret. *Gracias*.

"I went back and forth and round and round, trying to get up the nerve to send you this note, and then trying to convince myself not to send it (because it's obviously a horrible idea), and then trying to stop myself from obsessively reading and re-reading what you wrote to me (I wasn't successful), and then trying to figure out exactly what to say to you if and when I actually sent you a note (which, of course, I knew was inevitable). So, here I am, after consuming a significant amount of two-buck chuck for some liquid courage (or maybe liquid stupidity?), finally writing this note to you and swearing to press 'send' when I'm done—even if doing so qualifies as felony stupid.

"I think I've finally figured out exactly what's so freaking important to say that I'm willing to risk the best-paying job I've ever had to say it. It's the thing you value the most, Mr. Faraday—the truth. You so kindly showed me yours, right? Well, then, I think it's only right I show you mine. Yes, Mr. Faraday, I'll give you my tit— in exchange for your tat, of course. (What did you think I meant?)

"But the truth is like an octopus when you start trying to pin it down—it's got lots of moving parts. So for starters, let's just start with pinning down the easiest parts—the parts I think you'll like the most.

"Yes, Mr. Faraday, I am indeed a woman. You're so damned smart. But you already knew that.

"Yes, Mr. Faraday, I thoroughly enjoyed reading your application, just as you predicted I would, particularly your personal note to me at the end. Given the fact that I've been raised on Lifetime and Disney and Hallmark, and since I do, no doubt, have a raging good girl complex (among other self-sabotaging complexes, some of which are none of your business), I really wanted to hate your message. Actually, I just wanted to hate you, you cocky bastard asshole motherfucker. But my body had a different idea.

"As I read your note to me, despite my mind's unyielding desire to hate you, my body went rogue on me and *ached* for you. It *throbbed* for you, Mr. Faraday. Yes, my body had the exact physical reaction you predicted it would have. I won't go into too much detail, because I'm a fancy lady and all, but, yes, a change of panties was most definitely in order. Or, if we're being honest, the minute I started touching myself, just like you told me to do, I just tossed them on the bedroom floor.

"And, now, goddamn you, Mr. Faraday, I'm having that very same unmistakable physical reaction to you, yet again, just from typing this email to you. And, shoot, I'm all out of clean panties in my pretties drawer, too—and I don't have quarters for the laundry room downstairs! You really are a bastard, aren't you?

"That's a nice segue for another truth. Yes, I think you're a cocky bastard, as I've already mentioned. And worse, you're a cocky bastard with a raging God complex. Your God complex is so big, in fact, it rivals the size of your raging hard-on, if you can believe it.

"But you've also got honest eyes, Mr. Faraday. And they're sad, too—which is something I apparently cannot resist. And damn, you've got some effing kissable lips. And you make me laugh, too (though not intentionally). Oh, yeah, and you've got smokin' hot abs, by the way—but I probably don't need to tell you that. I mean, you've got a mirror, right?

"Yes, Mr. Faraday, it's true. I wanted to touch myself after reading your note to me, long before I even saw your photos, in fact.

Your words alone—your crass and cocky and self-congratulating but honest and confident and insightful and spot-on words—made me want to slide my hand inside my panties. But I resisted because I don't touch myself, Mr. Faraday. Ever. There's never been any point.

"However, when I saw your photos, I must admit my self-restraint and 'not seeing the point' flew right out the window along with my brain. Suddenly, I was spread out on my bed next to an almost empty bottle of wine, music blaring—and I was touching myself and wishing your warm, wet tongue was doing the touching instead of my fingers. I imagined your gorgeous face smiling up at me from between my open thighs, your lips slick and shiny with my wetness. And then, Mr. Faraday, I touched myself some more and imagined you inside me, whispering in my ear. And for the first time in my life, I felt the promise of incredible pleasure simmering and bubbling inside me. No, it didn't erupt, of course, because it never has and probably never will—but for the first time, I believed it *could.* Or, hell, maybe I'd just had too much wine.

"Now, before you start gloating or jacking off or doing whatever it is a cocky bastard like you does to celebrate your sexual godliness, let me tell you a few more truths—the ones you might not like quite as much as the above entries. Brace yourself, Mr. Faraday.

"Despite what you think, you haven't made every single woman you've ever graced with your godliness come harder than she ever has. The unpleasant truth is that some of them didn't come at all. Perhaps every single woman you've ever been with has *appeared* to come during sex with the Magical Fuck Wizard himself, but, statistically speaking, at least ten percent of them are lying to you. Why? To enhance your pleasure. To spare you from feeling like a failure (considering how much effort you undoubtedly exert). To convince you she's worthy of an invitation to dinner or some other "Valentine's Day bullshit" you so abhor. Or, most likely, to avoid her own feelings of inadequacy and shame at not being able to perform what her body is apparently designed for, despite her desperate desire to do so. You think that first faker who inspired your current odyssey of box-lunch-munching is the only woman who's ever faked it with you or who ever will again? Maybe. But I highly doubt it—statistically speaking.

"Think back on some of those allegedly epic fucks of yours, Mr. Faraday. Really think about them. Could I be right?

28

"Or, hey, okay, okay, don't get all worked up about it. Maybe I'm dead wrong. Maybe you really are lighting up each and every one of your sexual conquests like Christmas trees. It's not a statistical probability, but I suppose it's *possible*. There are documented cases of people being struck by lightning on three separate occasions, after all; and I just heard about some guy in Chicago winning the lottery three different times in the same week. So I guess it's *possible* you've somehow managed to randomly avoid ten percent of the female population during your apparently many, many, many sexual exploits over the past year. It could happen. If that's the case, though, there's no way to know if you're as good as you think you are, is there? Think about it—if you've somehow been so lucky as to avoid the really tough nuts to crack, then you really haven't tested the limits of your skills, have you? I mean, I'm sure you'll agree that being able to climb *Mount Rainier* doesn't guarantee a successful climb of *Mount Everest*. (Speaking of which, that article about you and your brother in *Climbing Magazine* was excellent. I particularly liked it when they referred to you as 'enigmatic.')

"Of course, there's also a third possibility. Perhaps you have some kind of innate radar that kicks in subconsciously during your selection process? Perhaps the women you instinctively *want* in your bed happen to be those women who are innately disposed to go off like bottle rockets at the slightest flicker of your golden tongue—because you can sense it. If so, it doesn't necessarily prove your alleged sexual prowess, really, it just means you've got a handy talent for spotting and plucking low-hanging fruit (which, in and of itself is a dandy talent, indeed). It also makes a girl like me a little bit annoyed, if you want to know the truth. I mean, if you really are that good in the sack, where's your spirit of charity? Why not use your superpowers to help the less fortunate occasionally? Throw us ten-percenters a bone, will ya? Look at it this way: Is it really fair for you to pass right by a homeless shelter and waltz into the Ritz Carlton next door in order to serve some rich, fat lady a free turkey dinner smothered in gravy? And on top of that, once you've done that, should you really go back to the homeless shelter and saunter right up to the poor, starving girl in the corner and *brag* to her about how expertly you just served turkey to a fancy lady? Really, Mr. Faraday, how rude. (And just to be clear, the poor, starving, homeless girl in this elaborate metaphor is lil ol' me.)

29

"I'm not sure which of these three scenarios is The Truth. But it doesn't matter. Whichever one it is, the result is the same: Despite your alleged hunger for brutal honesty, you clearly haven't experienced it like you think you have. Why? Because *honesty* is just the flipside of a little thing called *humility*. (This word is pronounced 'hyoo-míl-uh-tee.' It's a noun. Look it up.) Without having one, you simply cannot have the other.

"Well, my Brutally Honest Mr. Faraday, have you enjoyed reading *my* secrets and confessions and wine-induced thoughts? Because I've enjoyed sharing them with you. In fact, I've enjoyed writing this note to you so much, I took a break midway through to touch myself (again)—all the while thinking of you and your warm, wet tongue and your beautiful, sad eyes and your luscious lips. I'll leave it to your active imagination as to exactly where in my narrative that pleasantness occurred.

"Well, Mr. Faraday. Perhaps this is goodbye. Probably so. I hope you find everything you're looking for in The Club, especially the honesty you so desperately crave. And don't worry—despite the horrific lapse in judgment I've displayed by sending this email to you, I'll diligently process your application according to all protocols and standards of professionalism going forward.

"Oh, yeah, and one last thing (in the interest of brutal honesty, of course)—yes, Mr. Faraday, I would indeed ditch all the Valentine's Day bullshit to howl like a monkey for the first time in my entire life. Hellz yeah, I would. I'm already apparently willing to risk my job to send you this email, so why not throw a little Valentine's Day bullshit under the bus, too? The only question I have is whether you, or any man for that matter, could accomplish the job for a ten-percenter like me, a Mount Everest kind of a girl. I highly doubt it. But, damn, I sure do wish someone, someday, somewhere, would prove me wrong—especially someone with exactly your sad eyes and luscious lips and chiseled abs. At any rate, even if you could do it, Mr. Faraday, on the following point I think we can both agree: It would most certainly take you a helluva lot longer than four minutes—two hundred and forty measly little seconds—as you so confidently claim, to do it. Puh-lease.

"Truthfully yours,

"Your Beautiful Intake Agent."

"Yo," Josh says, picking up my call on the first ring.

"Is it possible to trace an email to identify the sender?"

"What?"

"How the fuck do I find someone who sent me an anonymous email?"

"Whoa, no need to yell. Someone's a little high strung today."

"Josh, I don't have time for bullshit. Can it be done or not?"

"Calm down. It depends."

"On what?"

"On what server she's using."

"How do you know I'm looking for a 'she'?"

He laughs. "A wild guess."

"Fuck you."

He laughs again. "If I can get her IP address off the email header, then we're in business. If we're lucky, that'll cross-reference with her name on the server's account records. But I'll have to get a hacker involved to check the server's records on the down low—"

"Do whatever you have to do. Just keep it confidential."

"How much are you willing to spend?"

"Whatever it takes."

"Wow. What's—"

"Don't ask."

He sighs. "Okay. Don't get your hopes up on getting the name, bro. It's unlikely. We might get a physical address, but more likely it'll be a defined area—you know, like a one-mile radius. Maybe just a city. It depends."

"Can you do it right now?"

"What's going on?"

"It's personal."

"Sounds fun."

"Josh, seriously, I can't—"

"I'm just fucking with you, bro. Forward me the email. I'll take care of it."

"I'll forward you the email *header*—not the message itself."

"Damn. Sounds like it would have been some interesting reading."

"Oh man, you have no fucking idea."

I gather up my laptop and burst out of my office.

31

"I'll be gone the rest of the day," I murmur to my assistant as I whiz past her.

"What about your appointments this afternoon?" she calls after me.

I don't answer her. I've got to get out of here. I reach the reception area and punch the call button for the elevator. My head is spinning.

My Beautiful Intake Agent has never had a fucking orgasm! Not even once! Oh, what I would do to this woman. How I would lick this woman. How I would fuck this woman. Just the thought of her feeling so warm and wet and convulsing around my cock for the first time in her life makes me so hard I have to hold my laptop in front of my pants as I wait for the elevator. I'm going to be the first man ever to witness pure ecstasy on her face, to watch her eyes roll back into her head and her cheeks flush as she comes for the first time in her life—with me—because of me—*thanks to me.* The thought makes me moan involuntarily, just standing here waiting for the goddamned elevator.

Thankfully, the elevator arrives before I have a heart attack. I step inside and pound on the button for the parking garage over and over as the doors close.

Fuck. I don't even know what she looks like. I can't even imagine her face experiencing rapture because I don't know what her face looks like! Fuck, fuck, fuck. No woman has ever turned me on like this. Especially not a woman I've never even seen.

The elevator stops after a couple floors, before I've reached my destination, and a woman from the bank two floors down gets on. She's hot, but I don't give a shit.

"Oh, Mr. Faraday." She smiles and bites her lower lip. "Hi."

I can't even speak, I'm so distracted. So hard. So utterly disinterested right now in anyone or anything other than My Beautiful Intake Agent. All I want to do is get home so I can close my eyes and let her words wash over me and think about fucking this woman and licking her and making her come. I've never wanted to make a woman come so bad.

I nod at the woman and pretend to look at my phone. She gets off at the next floor, her nose out of joint.

I press the button for the parking garage again, even though it's already lit up.

I've got to get home. I want to read that email again and again and again and jerk myself off. Through her written words alone, My Beautiful Intake Agent's managed to turn me on like nobody ever has. That woman just kicked my ass. Hard. And I liked it. *My Beautiful Intake Agent.* My smart, sexy, hilarious, pulls-no-punches, kicks-my-ass intake agent. She called herself a "Mount Everest kind of a girl." Now that's a girl who knows how to dangle a fucking carrot. Damn.

When the elevator doors open, I sprint toward my car on the far end of the garage—not an easy thing to do with a raging hard-on, mind you. *A raging hard-on to rival the size of my raging God complex.* I can't help but smile. Holy shit, I've got to find this woman.

Who is she? *Where* is she? She could be anywhere in the world right now, working remotely from some intake center in Malaysia or India for all I know. But, wait, no—she mentioned Chicago, the Ritz Carlton, two-buck chuck. And, hey, she easily adopted my references to Lifetime and Hallmark, too. Yeah, she's definitely American.

I reach my car and jump inside, fumbling with the key.

She's here in the States. Somewhere. And I'm going to find her.

I pull out of my parking spot and peel out toward the exit.

Yes, I'm going to find her. And when I do, I'm going to lick her and then fuck her like she deserves—so well, so expertly, in fact, with such care and attentiveness and precision and unflinching devotion, she's finally going to discover the incredible power that's lain dormant inside her for so long. Yes, I'm going to make that woman come so hard, and with such velocity, she'll see God for the first time in her life. And when she does, she'll be surprised to find out he's a cocky-bastard-asshole-son-of-a-bitch motherfucker with so-called "sad eyes" and "luscious lips" who doesn't have an ounce of humility or charity in his body. Oh my God, I've got to find this woman before I have a fucking stroke.

Chapter 4
Sarah

By all outward appearances, I'm doing my job right now, exactly the way I've been trained to do it. I'm sitting in my nondescript Honda hatchback, scoping out my assigned applicant's place of business from an unobtrusive vantage point (in this instance, from across the street), for the purpose of visually confirming the man works where he says he does, looks roughly the way he claims to look in his photos, and, generally speaking, appears to be the man he claims to be.

I am emphatically *not* staking him out to get my rocks off. I am emphatically *not* feeling all gooey inside at the possibility that I'm going to lay eyes on the most gorgeous creature on the face of the earth. Nope. Hellz no. Not me. I'm all business, people. This is precisely the way I've been taught to do the surveillance portion of my application processing procedure. So, really, I'm just following protocol. So why do I feel like a stalker, then?

Because I'm a stalker. A sick, perverted, obsessed, panties-on-fire, spent-all-night-scoping-him-out-on-the-Internet stalker. Last night, I researched and researched online and read every bit of information I could find on the guy. Which wasn't much, really, unless you're super interested in acquisitions and real estate investment trusts.

Here's what I know so far: Jonas Faraday is a "well-respected" business up-and-comer with a "shrewd" mind for crunching numbers, who has "unconventional" but almost always "uncanny" investment instincts. He's a Seattle native, though it seems he travels frequently, often with his twin brother, Josh. He attended Gonzaga undergrad and went on to get an MBA from Berkeley (which makes me think he must be pretty liberal, but I couldn't find anything about his political affiliations).

Jonas Faraday runs Faraday & Sons with his twin brother, Josh (who lives in Los Angeles but apparently travels the world for business and pleasure even more than Jonas does) and also their uncle, William Faraday (who lives in New York). The company website says his father, Joseph Faraday, the founder of Faraday & Sons, died thirteen years ago (when Jonas and Josh were seventeen). Looks like the uncle stepped in to run Faraday & Sons after Joseph's death, seeing as how Jonas and Josh were still teens at the time. Countless business and investment-related articles and blogs recount the rise and rise of Faraday & Sons, detailing and analyzing the key acquisitions and investments that have put them on the map in the global investment community.

I devoured everything I could find—all the while feeling like I'd found absolutely nothing of any interest. What I really wanted to read about wasn't Jonas Faraday the businessman—I wanted to know about Jonas Faraday the man. But I kept coming up with zippo. He's not engaged in any kind of social media whatsoever—no Facebook or Instagram or Twitter or Pinterest. No pictures of his eggs benedict. No snapshots of him partying with his buddies in Vegas. No "likes" to tell me his favorite books and movies and places to eat. He doesn't write a blog or otherwise post information about himself, and he doesn't seem to attend fundraising galas or sit on any boards or date socialites or models or otherwise seek attention of any kind.

Now, if I were researching his brother, Josh, I'd have an endless supply of reading material, since Josh, unlike Jonas, has a penchant for attending parties all over the world with his high-profile-celebrity-athlete friends and girlfriends and tweeting out pictures of his adventures. Seriously, Josh was at Justin Timberlake's birthday party? What the hell? But not Jonas. Jonas is nowhere to be found on the party scene.

Unpredictably, the most detailed personal information I uncovered about Jonas Faraday, by far, came from a short transcription of an interview for a local middle school's career day. How the heck that interview came about, I cannot even begin to imagine—Jonas Faraday doesn't strike me as a charter member of the Big Brothers of America program—but Jonas seemed surprisingly forthcoming in the short interview.

When the boy asked Jonas' advice about picking a career, he

was quoted as saying, "Find what you're good at, whatever it is, and become excellent at it. Excellence isn't magic—it's habit, the by-product of doing something over and over and striving to be the best at it. Simply figure out what your passion is, and resolve to make excellence your habit."

When asked about his hobbies and interests, Jonas responded, rather curtly, "Climbing," and I could almost imagine him squirming uncomfortably in his seat as he realized the interview was verging away from career advice and into personal information. But the kid pressed for more information, bless his little heart, and Jonas obliged him. "Rock climbing, mountain climbing. My goal is to climb all ten of the world's highest peaks during my lifetime."

"What else do you like to do besides climbing?" the kid asked, apparently uninformed of his subject's innate distaste for human interaction outside the walls of his bedroom.

"Well," Jonas was quoted as saying, "I also enjoy reading, particularly books about psychology, philosophy, fitness, and, especially, the mysteries of the human body." I liked that last topic the best—*"books about the mysteries of the human body."* A clever euphemism, I'm sure, for books about the puzzle of the female orgasm. Just the thought of him studying up on female sexuality turned me on more than I care to admit.

"Anything else?" the kid asked, and I laughed out loud, wishing I could have seen Jonas' body language at that point.

"I love music," Jonas answered. "And, of course, going to football and baseball games, as you know."

"As you know?" That part of his answer intrigued me. Why did the kid know Jonas likes going to football and baseball games? Is Jonas Faraday's interest in sports a well-known fact in the world at large—like, does his family own a sports team or something?—or was this information known specifically by this kid? And if so, how? Did the pair have a casual chat over juice and cookies before the interview started? Or do the two share some other relationship that led to this interview in the first place? The latter seemed more plausible to me, or else why on earth was Jonas there, but my research uncovered nothing to answer that question or any other. I couldn't figure out who the kid interviewer was, other than his first name (Trey), and I couldn't find anything in particular to explain Jonas' "as you know" comment.

The kid wrapped up his interview with a real humdinger of a question: "Do you have a favorite inspirational quote?" he asked.

"I have many," Jonas replied, and I could almost feel his intensity leaping off the page. "But one of my all-time favorites is from Plato: 'For a man to conquer himself is the first and noblest of all victories.'"

And that was the entire interview. Not much, really, and yet that little two-hundred-word interview by a middle-schooler revealed more about Jonas Faraday, and inspired more curiosity and interest in me, than every other business article about him combined. I must have read that little transcript twenty times, parsing and analyzing every word obsessively, feeling more and more attracted to him each time.

And now, here I am, sitting in my car, staring across the street at his building like a lovesick puppy, waiting to catch a glimpse of the hottest physical specimen I've ever seen—who also happens to quote Plato and read books about psychology, philosophy, and "the mysteries of the human anatomy." Be still my beating heart. And other pulsating parts, too.

If I were dealing with any applicant besides the scrumptiously delicious Jonas Faraday, I'd probably just walk into his office lobby and ask the receptionist if Mr. Faraday might answer some questions for my law school newspaper (since, hey, it seems like the guy is open to school-related interviews), and regardless of whether the receptionist were to say yes or no, I'd at least be able to minimally confirm his identity for purposes of my surveillance checklist by snooping around his office lobby and looking at the plaques and pictures on the walls.

And yet, for some reason, when it comes to conducting surveillance on Jonas Faraday, I'm instead sitting in my car, staring across the street at his building, freaking out about whether or not he's read my email from last night, worrying he's going to report me to headquarters, and just generally losing control of my mind, impulses, and body in general. For some reason I can't fully understand, I don't want to go in there and let him catch a glimpse of me.

Damn! Last night, I was so cocky and sure of myself when I sent that crazy-ass email, drunk on three glasses of cheap wine, listening to loud music, my head swimming from his sexy note to me and those intriguing answers in his career day interview. But today is a different story. Today, I can't stop worrying that maybe I made an epically huge mistake.

Why was I so damned sure I could trust him not to tattle on me? And what was so important to say to him that it was worth risking my job in order to say it? And why on earth did I tell him the embarrassing truth that I've never had an orgasm before? I've never told anyone about that. Ever. Not even Kat. Why on earth did I tell *him*? Ugh. He must have been, like, "Thanks for the over-share, dearest intake agent, now please get back to processing my application."

Gah.

What if he feels like I've compromised his privacy so egregiously, he withdraws his application and demands his money back? Oh my God, The Club sure as hell won't take kindly to an applicant demanding a quarter-million-dollar refund because their horny pony of an intake agent couldn't keep her hands in her pants and hormones in check. Oh man. I screwed up. I never should have sent him that email. I never should have had that third glass of wine. I never should have given in to temptation and touched myself like that—

Oh my God! There he is, racing like a bat out of hell from his parking garage in a sporty BMW. I cover my face with my hands as he flies past my Honda, but a split second is all I need to confirm he's even more gorgeous in person than in his pictures. Holy crappola, what a beautiful-looking man. Damn.

My heart is racing.

I start my car and try to wedge immediately into traffic, but a fast-moving stream of cars prevents me from pulling out from the curb. Damn.

I wait. And wait.

When traffic clears after half a minute, he's long gone from my sight.

Shoot! He could be headed anywhere right now. It'd be a wild goose chase to try to find him. I'm certainly not going to park my car outside his house and stare at him with binoculars like some kind of creeper. It's one thing to camp out on a busy commercial street and another thing entirely to stalk the man at his house. Wow, that probably would be actual "stalking," come to think of it, like, technical, legal "stalking" according to statutory definition. I'll have to research that. But I digress. I'm sure he lives in some fancy mansion behind a gate, anyway, even if I did want to legally stalk him. Which I don't. Of course not. Because that would be desperate and pathetic. And out of control. And bordering on obsessive behavior.

Gah.

My breathing is shallow. I groan. Good God, I'm desperate and pathetic. And out of control. And completely obsessed. Damn. I didn't expect him to fly out of his parking garage like that. I wasn't ready. I'm so bad at this.

I turn off my ignition and sit in my parked car, staring out my windshield at the leafy trees lining the street.

Holy moly, the man is gorgeous. Like, insanely, utterly, undeniably, breathtakingly gorgeous. Like, holy shit on a stick I've never seen such a good- looking man in all my life kind of gorgeous. Like please, please, please, for the love of God, please let me have sex with a man as good looking as him once in my entire life kind of gorgeous. Like, God have mercy on my soul I cannot be held accountable for my actions kind of gorgeous. Like, maybe sending him that email wasn't such a bad idea after all kind of gorgeous. Like, yes, maybe having a one-night stand with a man like that, with no tomorrow, and letting the door hit my ass on the way out, would be just fine with me kind of gorgeous.

I groan and rub my eyes in frustration. Aw, who am I kidding? It's time to stop the insanity and get real for a second here. I'm exactly the kind of girl he loathes—a hopeless romantic who naively mistakes physical chemistry for emotional connection. I'm his kryptonite.

Even after that drunken one-night stand six months ago, the following morning, I was idiotically hoping the guy would call me and say, "Hey, can we start again? How about I take you to dinner tonight?" Right then, I promised myself I'd never, ever do a "one and done" again. I'm just not cut out for it. I sigh. Or maybe promises to myself are meant to be broken when unforeseen and irresistibly compelling and good-looking circumstances present themselves.

Lauren Rowe

Rain begins to dot my windshield and quickly turns to a steady downpour. Hello, Seattle.

I stare at the rain for a moment.

My first solo review and I've already hopelessly messed everything up, and then some. When I conducted surveillance during my training period with supervision, it seemed so easy: Observe the applicant in a public place, note the time and details on my intake log, and file report confirming the guy is who he says he is. Done-zo.

I recline my seat, gazing out my windshield, watching the rain batter my car.

I guess, technically, I've already fulfilled my surveillance if I think about it. Jonas Faraday, the same guy in the pictures, just came out of Faraday & Sons, looking the way he claims to look—only way better. So I should be done-zo, right? Not just with the surveillance, but with the application review process in total. I've got everything I need to mark him "recommend approve," don't I? I could go back home right now, note my successful Jonas Faraday sighting on my intake report, package my findings and research and recommendations together with the "all clear" that just came back from his psychological and medical testing (great news—he's definitely not a psychopath!), and when I get the go-ahead from headquarters, send out the automated "congratulations!" email to him and overnight his welcome package and instructions.

But goddammit! I don't want to do that. I don't want him to become a member of The Club just yet. The mere thought of him going on an epic cunnilingus spree with a long line of nameless women—all of them as depraved and devoid of humanity as he is— just makes me sick. Approving him would be like giving a toddler cotton candy for dinner, when what he needs is a big bowl of grilled fish and kale. He's a crack addict stumbling desperately into a crack house, when what he needs is a month of rehab. I could scream right now.

For such a smart man, he's so dumb. He may think he wants *less* human connection in his life, but what he needs, desperately, even if he doesn't realize it, is *more* human connection. Idiot. Sex-crazed, egotistical idiot. If only I had a little bit more time to ... To what? What the hell am I thinking? My Lifetime/Hallmark brainwashing is rearing its ugly head again. Man, he sure has me pegged.

40

What do I really expect to happen here? He didn't apply for membership so he could diddle the lowly intake agent. And he didn't apply for Club membership so he could find true love, either. And he certainly didn't join The Club to learn something new and beautiful about the depths of his fragile heart. Ha! The man explicitly wants unfettered access to women who are just like him, women who are as emotionally disconnected and damaged as he is, women who allegedly want pleasure and nothing else—women so motivated by this elusive pleasure he allegedly provides that they're willing to pursue it without even *hoping* for something more, without even leaving the door open the teensiest bit for the mere *possibility* of something more, of something beautiful. Something real.

Who are these hopeless, cynical, untethered women he hopes to find? What woman could possibly be happy being so hopeless and shutdown and hedonistic and out of touch with her own heart? Even if you know you're just having a booty call with a hot guy (and I've had *two* of those, mind you, including one I remember, so I'm pretty effing qualified to give my opinion on this subject), isn't part of the fun the slim *possibility* that it *could* lead to an unlikely romance? Or, at least, a fleeting but unforgettable romance in a "We'll always have Paris" kind of way? (Or, in the case of two of my booty calls, a "We'll always have the Wild Onion" kind of way?) No matter how cynical we think we are, isn't the whole point of being alive and interacting with other humans—and especially having sex with other humans—about believing love is possible for even the lowliest and loneliest of fools?

If Jonas Faraday doesn't understand that, okay. He's a man. But who the hell are these women in The Club, who don't understand it, either? And why would any man, including Jonas Faraday, ever want those kinds of women, anyway, if indeed they exist? If that's what he wants, if that's what he really wants, then why not just date other men, for Pete's sake?

And the worst part is I know for a fact that each and every woman in The Club is going to lie like a rug when they see My Brutally Honest (and extremely hot) Mr. Faraday and tell him every ridiculous thing he wants to hear, no matter how far from the truth, because they won't be able resist the fantasy of taming this unbreakable stallion any more than I can.

41

Wow, I'm really going off on an internal rant here. Kat would laugh her ass off at me right now. I'm so predictable.

I sigh.

I just wish I had access to female membership profiles, so I could see exactly what I'm up against here. But all I've ever seen are male applicants—and only those in the greater Seattle area, at that. Why the hell am I so goddamned upset at the thought of all these other women sleeping with My Brutally Honest Jonas Faraday, all the while telling him what he wants to hear? Just the thought hurts my heart, even as my body aches for him.

I'm being an idiot.

I'm imagining something between us that doesn't exist. He sent that note to me on a lark, sight unseen—and it wasn't even a message to *me*. It was a message to some fantasy girl who bears no resemblance to me—a nameless Intake Agent without a romantic bone in her anonymous body. He was just having a bit of pre-approval fun with the idea of me—but not with me, personally.

Certainly, once he reads my response email and realizes the kind of hopeless romantic I am (not to mention the kind of smart-ass I am, too), all the fun of it will be gone for him. Even if by some small chance he likes my reply (which, I know, is a ridiculous thought), where could it lead? Nowhere. He sleeps with swimwear models and glamazons and socialites I'm sure—women who look like Kat—and probably not women who look and talk and act and think like me.

Now don't get me wrong; my self-esteem is just fine. In any crowd, I can usually count on at least a couple guys being drawn pretty enthusiastically to my vaguely exotic Latina looks like moths to a spicy little flame. But it's never a sure thing, not like how it is with Kat. What if "vaguely exotic Latina" just isn't Jonas Faraday's thing? That'd be a cruel pill for me to swallow.

Of course, in my fantasy, I'm the woman who gives him an indefatigable hard-on like no other (which is probably saying a lot, considering how indefatigable his hard-on already seems to be), and he wants me like no man has ever wanted a woman, anywhere, anytime, ever in the history of the world. Mark Antony and Cleopatra? Pffft. They'd have nothing on Jonas and Sarah.

But even if that were the case, what would be the point? He's a one-night stand kind of guy and will never, ever change—he even says so himself—so, at best, even in this fantasy, I'm talking about having mind-blowing, orgasmic sex with the most gorgeous man in the world, just once, and that's it, nothing more. Is my job worth that? *Well, damn, when I say it like that, hellz yeah, it is! Hellz yeah!*

I feel like slapping myself. No, it's not worth it.

Maybe if the job weren't part of the equation. But, no, I can't risk it. If The Club ever found out, I'd be fired on the spot. And I need this job. I'm the one putting myself through law school, after all, and it was frickin' hard to get here in the first place. I'm not going to risk everything to have one heart-stopping orgasm that can't lead to anything else, ever. No matter how gorgeous he is. Or how cunning a linguist. Or how gorgeous. But I already said that.

And, anyway, the odds of me being this godlike man's cup of tea are slim. After all this build-up and dirty talk and masturbation and confession and "honesty," if he were to finally see me, there's a very real possibility he'd exhale and say, "oh." And I don't mean, "*Oh!*" with naughty raised eyebrows, I mean, like, "oh," with a droopy frowny-face. And that would be kind of soul crushing, I have to admit.

I look at my watch. Crap. I've got Constitutional Law in an hour. I bring my seat to an upright sitting position and start my engine.

Yeah, I've made a decision—a mature, responsible decision.

The minute I get back from class tonight, I'll delete that intake-agent Gmail account I made for him and forget this ever happened. I'll get approval to trigger the automated "congratulations!" email and overnight him his welcome package. And then I'll just try to erase the allegedly Brutally Honest Jonas Faraday from my memory. I won't even think of his mournful eyes and luscious lips and ridiculous abs and tattooed arms and round little nipples and intriguing interest in philosophy and "human anatomy" ever again.

I sigh. Yep, I'll just erase all of that from my memory. Boom.

I turn on my windshield wipers and pull my car into traffic.

But even so, there can't be any harm in keeping his photos on my laptop for occasional future viewing, right? Or, perhaps making his face the background image on my desktop? I mean, for Pete's sake, I might be mature and responsible, but I'm not freakin' dead.

Chapter 5
Jonas

I've read and re-read her email to me twenty times, jerked off and showered, and now I'm sitting at my computer, staring at a blank screen, trying to figure out how to reply to her.

I've got to be honest with her—this woman can spot bullshit a mile away—but I have to be careful not to spook her, too. She's already nervous about risking her job. Whatever I say to her better not make her wig out and delete her email account. That account is my only means of reaching her.

"My Beautiful Intake Agent," I write.

I stare at the screen, my fingers resting on my keyboard.

What do I want to say? Do I really want to say I want to fuck her, sight unseen? What if it turns out she's not at all physically attractive to me? What if she's a great-grandmother or something?

Fuck it. I can't think like that. She's hot. I know she is. I've got a sixth sense about these things. And I can't worry about scaring her off. I just have to tell her the truth. It worked the first time. I have to believe it'll work again.

I lay my fingers on my keyboard again.

"The only thing bigger than my raging God complex right now is my raging hard-on for you," I type, making myself smirk. "Your email made me hard from the minute it hit my inbox to the moment I stopped reading it for the twentieth time and jacking off to it fifteen minutes ago. Thank you for your brutal honesty. And, of course, for telling me your delicious secret, too. Yes, indeed, you're Mount Everest, my dear—and you must know what kind of allure you therefore present to a passionate climber like me.

"You're driving me fucking crazy, you know. (Of course, you do—and you like it.) I'm a man who needs to be in control, a fact that probably hasn't escaped your notice, and in this bizarre but delectable situation, you're the one holding all the cards right now. This is an upside-down distribution of power for a man saddled with a raging God complex, as I'm sure you can appreciate. But for some reason, I'm enjoying the torture.

"You know everything about me, and I know nothing about you—well, wait, that's not completely true. I know what I need to know. You're smart. And sexy as hell. And not afraid to kick my ass with some seriously brutal honesty of your own. And, of course, I know you've never experienced the most fundamental and ultimate pleasure known to human experience, a fact that pains me as much as it excites me. It's a fucking travesty, My Beautiful Intake Agent, it really is.

"I want to know everything about you. But let's start with your name. And where I can find you. At the very least, you owe me three photos, my beautiful one. One in clothes, one full bodied, and one headshot, of course. It's only fair. Take out your phone right now and send them to me. Show me your tit. (For my tat, of course. What did you think I meant? You have such a dirty mind.)

"And, by the way, of course, I won't tell a soul about your email, rest assured. I would never do anything to harm you in any way. I promise.

"Undeniably, faithfully, and truthfully yours (and also going crazy and losing my mind and thoroughly *not* enjoying the imbalance of power, though I have a hunch you *are*), Jonas."

What is it about this woman that gets me off like this?

I quickly press send, without even reading what I've written. I know if I don't just send it, as is, I'll start obsessing over whether the wording is exactly right, and whether I'm going to scare her off, and trying to make it perfect. Because I like perfect. But I've already left her hanging far too long without a reply, and I'm sure she's starting to wonder. And worry. And regret. Oh shit, what if she's already deleted her email account? That would be very, very bad for my mental health. I can't lose my only means of contacting her.

My cell phone rings and my heart instantly leaps in my throat.

"Josh," I say, my chest constricting. "Please tell me you've got good news."

"She's in Seattle."

I can barely breathe.

"Are you there?"

"Yeah, yeah. I just can't believe it. You sure?"

"Oh yeah, I'm positive. She's on U Dub's server."

"She's a student at Washington?"

"Or a professor, I guess. One or the other."

I've read her email so many times it's part of my gray matter now. *"Hellz yeah,"* she said. *"Helluva lot longer."* *"Puh-lease."* She said this job is the "best paying job" she's ever had.

"She's a student," I say slowly, putting the pieces together. Yeah, I'm sure of it. She said she was drinking "two-buck chuck." Yes, definitely a student. She said she's got rent to pay—and that she's got a laundry room downstairs. Okay, so she lives in an apartment. Student housing? My mind is clicking and whirring, gathering the pieces of the puzzle. Something is niggling at my brain. Something important. She used the word *allegedly,* didn't she? Yes, more than once. I smirk. Who uses that pretentious word but lawyers ... *and law students?*

"She's a law student," I whisper, smirking. And, suddenly, I'm sure of it—because, holy fuck, can that woman argue a point.

Josh laughs. "You always did like 'em smart. You're so predictable, man. Okay, let me see if my guy can get onto the university's server and take a peek around. There's probably some sort of distinction in their records between law students versus the entire student population. That would at least narrow the field. Do you know anything else about her?"

"Not yet. But I will."

"All right. When you get more information, get it to me."

"I will. Keep your phone handy. Thanks, Josh."

"No problemo. You know how much I love the chase—even if it's chasing a law student for you."

I'm about to hang up.

"Jonas."

"What?"

"Does this have something to do with The Club I was telling you about?"

I don't say anything.

"I knew it!"

"No."

"You joined."

"No."

"Bro, you're acting like a sexual deviant right now. That's

46

exactly what The Club does to a man. Oh man, you're about to have the best month of your life." He laughs again.

Wait, what? Josh only signed up for a *month*? Wow, I really *am* a sexual deviant. "It's none of your business," I mutter.

"Really? You've got me hacking the server of the fucking University of Washington, just to get you laid by some mystery law student with a fake email address—and it's none of my business?"

I exhale. "I submitted my application a few days ago. I'm not a member yet. And now, it doesn't even matter. I've gotten myself distracted. Hopelessly distracted." I grunt. "I don't give a shit about The Club. All I care about is finding her."

Josh laughs again. "Wow. Distracted from The Club? That's pretty intense. Sounds like this girl is a real stand-out." He exhales. "Okay, bro. Sit tight. I'll see what I can find out."

"Thanks again, Josh."

"Aw, you know I'm a sucker for true love."

"Fuck you."

I've been pacing around my house for the past hour.

She hasn't replied to my email.

And Josh hasn't called back, either.

I'm going crazy.

Why hasn't she replied? What's going on in her beautiful head? And, shit, what if her head's not quite as beautiful as I imagine it to be? No, that's impossible. I've got a sixth sense for hotness. I'm never wrong.

I change into my workout clothes and head into my home gym, music from Kid Ink blaring in my ears. Maybe lifting some weights will burn off some of my manic energy. I don't like feeling out of control.

I let the hot water beat down my back. How old is she? If she's in law school, she's probably anywhere from twenty-two to maybe twenty-five? Twenty-six at most? Right? Unless law school for her is a later-in-life, change-of-direction type thing. But that's probably not the case. God, I hope it's not.

Just as I'm wrapping a towel around my waist, I hear my computer beep with an incoming message. I sprint out of my bathroom to my laptop on my bed. I click open my private email account. I'm panting.

It's from her.

"Here you go," her message says. There's a photo attachment. I inhale sharply as I click on the photo and open it. Oh my God. It's a picture of a breast. One breast, singular. The smart-ass showed me her "tit"—for my tat, of course, just like I requested. I don't know why I'm even surprised.

I sit down on the bed, my erection poking up from beneath my towel. I can't stop staring at the picture. Her skin is smooth with an olive undertone, or is that barely-there mocha? I can't tell. Is she Italian? Greek? Latina? Light-skinned black? I can't tell from this tiny swatch of skin. All I know for sure is she's definitely not a platinum blonde Swede or a redheaded Irish Catholic. No, that skin is definitely tinged with some flavor. And the breast itself is round and plump, the perfect size for my hand plus a little extra. Definitely real. Her nipple is dark and round and standing fiercely at attention for me. Oh God, this woman. I wonder what she did to herself to make her nipple stand up like that? I wish I could have been there to see her do it, whatever it was. No, I wish I could have been there to do it to her myself.

"Thank you," I type. "You're beautiful. I can't stop looking at the photo. I'm totally obsessed."

"I know the feeling," her reply comes back immediately.

I practically growl with excitement upon getting her reply. "Tell me your name," I quickly write.

"No," she replies—again, immediately.

I can barely contain myself. This woman is somewhere in this city right now, staring at me through her computer screen. My heart is racing. "Not fair. You know my name," I type.

"Life isn't fair."

I half-smile at my screen. "Ain't that the truth," I type. Truer words were never spoken. I sigh. "If not your name, tell me something else. How about your age?"

"I just turned 24."

I'm thrilled. She finally threw me a bone. And I'm relieved, too—twenty-four is good. Very good. "See? That wasn't so hard. Happy Birthday," I type, smiling.

"Thank you."

"Pisces, then?"

"Oh my God. You did not just ask me, 'What's your sign?'"

I laugh out loud. "Yeah, I guess I did. I'm dumb like that sometimes."

"With cheesy pickup lines like that, it's clearly thanks to your supernatural good looks and *not* your sparkling personality that you've managed to be worshipped as a supreme sex-god by so many. Gosh, I expected a little more panache from you, Mr. Faraday. Aren't you supposed to be some kind of woman wizard? Oh, wait, that's only inside the four walls of your bedroom—never on the outside."

I can't help but smile from ear to ear. She's kicking my ass again. I love it. "You're right. I'm not very good at this." And it's true. I mean, I can *talk* to women, of course. I can even flirt. Sort of. But I've never been great at doing it. And especially not in a situation like this—when I can't look into her eyes and get a read on her. "I'm hopeless at small talk," I type.

"There's no such thing."

"No such thing as small talk?"

"No such thing as *hopelessness*. There's always hope. 'We must accept infinite disappointment, but never lose infinite hope.'"

Oh God. My cock has been leaping and lurching throughout our entire exchange, but my brain just joined the fray, too. "Who said that?"

"Martin Luther King Jr.," she types.

She's a whole new breed of woman I've never encountered before. I exhale loudly. "Here's one," I type. "'Hope is the dream of a waking man.'"

"Oh, I like that. Who's that?"

"Aristotle."

"That'd be an awesome episode of Epic Rap Battles of History—Martin Luther King Jr. vs. Aristotle. Hard to say who'd win."

I grunt. How did we get from her erect nipple to Martin Luther King Jr. and Aristotle waging an epic rap battle? "Stop trying to distract me, My Beautiful Intake Agent. I know exactly what you're trying to do, but I demand to know more about you. Come on."

"Okay, okay. You've worn me down, especially when you 'demand' like that. You're so manly when you do that, by the way—I like it. Okay, here's everything: I am a woman. I am 24. I have a Maltese named Kiki. I buy her little outfits with rhinestones on them. She is my world. The End."

She's killing me right now, even as I'm laughing out loud. "Come on. Please. Tell me something real," I type.

"Why?"

I sigh. Jesus, she's frustrating. "Because you know everything and I know nothing. It's not fair. Where's your sense of fair play and justice?"

"Just so you know, I'm sighing right now. Oh, and rolling my eyes, too."

"Please."

"Okay, okay. You wore me down *again*. You're so persuasive, Mr. Faraday. Irresistible! Okay, here you go: Blah, blah, blah. Prelude, prelude, prelude."

I burst out laughing. That's fucked up. I never under any other circumstance would have disclosed my thoughts about "prelude" to a woman—especially a woman I'm trying to get into bed. "Come on. Anything. How about this: What was the song you listened to when you touched yourself and thought about me?"

"How do you know I listened to music when I touched myself and thought about you?"

"You told me so."

"Did I?"

I've read her email so many times I can recite it word for word. "Yes, you did. You said you were spread out on your bed next to an almost empty bottle of wine, music blaring, and that you touched yourself and wished my warm, wet tongue were doing the touching instead of your fingers. Best line ever in the history of the world. Gave me a gigantic woody."

"Gee, thanks. But I'm sure you get a gigantic woody reading a grocery list."

"Only if it's yours."

"Oh, smooth, you woman wizard, you. See? You're not as bad at this as you think."

"Stop trying to change the subject. What was the song? Did you turn on Pandora and roll the dice, or did you choose a specific song?"

"I chose the song. The perfect song. Of course."

My kind of woman. "What was it?" My heart's pounding in my ears.

"'Pony.' The cover by Far, not the original."

Okay, this girl officially just blew my mind. That cover's not a mainstream tune—I'm shocked she knows it. The original song by Ginuwine is an old R&B cheesefest from the nineties about a guy looking for a horny pony to ride his saddle. The original was unintentionally hilarious, but Far's rendition of the song rocks—heavy guitars, crashing drums, crunchy bass. And the vocals are tongue in cheek and sardonic, while still managing to be raw and gritty and dirty.

If she picked *that* song for a session of self-love, that tells me I'm not dealing with the usual kind of girl—a fact I already knew.

"Excellent choice," I type. My entire body's coursing with electricity. I've got to find this woman.

"I agree," she types. "Hence, the reason I chose it."

I inhale and exhale deeply. I don't like being out of control like this. I don't like her holding all the cards. My knee is jiggling wildly.

"I want to meet you more than I want to breathe," I type. And it's the truth. "Please," I add. I've never begged a woman for anything in my entire life, but I'd get down on my hands and knees if I thought it would make her tell me where to find her.

She doesn't reply.

Up 'til now, her replies have been instantaneous. I wait.

My heart is pounding in my chest. Why isn't she replying?

As long as there's a break in the action with her, I reach for my phone to text Josh. *"She's 24."*

He texts back right away. *"Good. If we don't get a name, we can narrow the field by age. But get a name if you can, obviously."*

Why isn't she answering me? Did she get up to pour herself a glass of wine? Did she get up to turn on "Pony" again? Or is she just sitting there, staring at the screen, second-guessing herself and freaking out?

Still no reply.

I click onto the picture of her breast again and stare at her hard nipple. Oh man. You'd think I'd never seen a nipple before the way my body's reacting to the sight of hers.

Why isn't she responding?

I place my hands over my keyboard again. I've got to reel her back in. She's obviously starting to second-guess herself here.

"I interpret your silence to mean you're not ready to meet me. (As you can see, I'm super smart at interpreting a woman's nonverbal cues—just one more stunning example of my woman wizardry.) That's okay. We don't have to meet. Just send me another picture, then, to tide me over. It's only fair—you've got three of mine, after all. You owe me two, but I'll settle for one. How about a headshot?" My breathing is shallow. I want to type the word "please" fifty times, but I restrain myself.

"I'm thinking," she says immediately.

I exhale in relief. She's still there. Thank God.

"Don't think. Thinking is the enemy. Just do it. Right now. One picture. I won't breathe 'til I get it. I've officially stopped breathing. Please, please, don't let me suffocate over here. Hurry! I'm not breathing! Hurry! Aaaah!" I press send and sit and stare at the screen. Oh God, this woman is making me crazy.

After a moment, there's another email. Thank God.

"Please don't suffocate, for Pete's sake. That'd be a dumb thing to do. Here you go." It's another photo file.

I open the image. It's her thigh? Her hip? It's hard to make out. But there's that skin again. Smooth and even. And olive-toned. Definitely olive. Oh man, I want to touch that gorgeous olive skin. I want to touch every square inch of it, inside and out.

"Thank you," I reply, but that doesn't even come close to expressing what I'm feeling. "You're so beautiful. I want to touch you." I'm hard as a rock.

An immediate reply. "I want to be touched by you, My Brutally Honest Mr. Faraday."

My heart leaps. And so does my cock.

"Call me Jonas."

Again, an instant reply. "I want to be touched by you. *Jonas.*"

I am losing my fucking mind. "Tell me where to find you."

"I shouldn't."

"You should."

"Bad idea."

"How can I touch you if I can't find you?"

No reply again.

"I just want to touch you," I type again, not waiting for her reply. Thank God we're conversing over email. If I were speaking these words to her, I'm sure I'd be shouting them, I'm so amped up. "I won't tell anyone about our communications. I promise."

"I know you won't tell. I trust you. That's not why it's a bad idea."

I grunt in frustration. If she's not worried about her job, then why is it a bad idea? I don't understand. As far as I'm concerned, this is a fucking fantastic idea. Okay, new tactic. "How about you touch yourself and pretend it's me?"

"I already did that. That's what got me here in the first place."

"So do it again. Maybe second time's the charm. You never know."

There's a long pause. I'm just about to email her again, when her reply comes.

"Okay," she says.

I inhale sharply. "Good. Do it now."

"Yes, sir."

"Right now."

"Jeez, I said okay. You're so effing demanding."

I can't hold back anymore. I'm losing control. I shouldn't say what I'm about to say—it might scare her off. But I can't stop myself. "Go lie on your bed and touch yourself." My fingers are moving quickly on the keyboard. "Imagine my hands all over you, my lips on your neck, your nipples, your belly, inside your thighs and all around your pussy. Imagine my tongue caressing every inch of you 'til you're writhing and moaning and begging me to kiss your throbbing tip. Finally, imagine my warm tongue finding it, swirling it around and around, lapping at you, kissing you, licking you. Imagine yourself letting go in that moment, giving in completely to the pleasure—so completely your mind flashes into a blinding light and ceases to exist. And right then, right at the moment you imagine your mind disappearing into oblivion, I want you to say my name again, out loud. Go do that for me right now. I'll wait." I press send.

"Yes, lord-god-master," the answer comes back immediately. "Stay tuned. And keep breathing, for Pete's sake. This may take a while."

I wait. I'm shaking. I put my laptop next to me on the bed and yank my towel off. I lie there, naked on my bed, my hard-on straining up toward my stomach. I raise my hands above my head and grab at my hair for a moment, the muscles on my naked body tensing. I feel like I'm losing my mind. If only she were sitting on top of me right now. I moan, imagining her there, riding me. Oh God, how I wish she were on top of me right now, throwing her head back and coming.

I can't believe she's never had an orgasm, not even once.

I need to find this woman.

I need to fuck this woman.

I need to make this woman surrender to me.

I can almost feel her on top of me right now.

I'm going out of my fucking mind.

After what seems like forever, my computer finally beeps with a new email and I click on it.

"Jonas," the message says. "Jonas, Jonas, Jonas, Jonas, Jonas, Jonas, Jonas, Jonas, Jonas, Jonas, Jonas, Jonas."

I stare at my screen, losing my shit. Moments ago, somewhere in this very city, not too far from where I've been lying here naked on my bed and imagining her, she put her beautiful olive-skinned hand between her legs and touched herself at my command, all the while imagining my warm tongue on her sweet spot—and she said my name over and over and over again when she did it.

Fuck.

I'm trembling with the physical need to touch her, to put my hands on her body, to whisper her name in her ear—if only I knew her goddamned name, that is.

"Tell me your name." I type quickly, pounding on the keyboard. If I were saying these words out loud, she'd be shocked at the forcefulness of my tone.

"No," she replies.

I grunt. Why is she being so difficult? "Please," I type. If she understood my desperation, she'd give in and do what I tell her to do.

"Bad idea."

"Good idea. Please."

"Why?"

I grunt again. *Why?* What does she mean *why*? Why does she think? Because she's driving me out of my fucking mind, that's why, and I've never even laid eyes on her. Because she's somehow managed to hook me like a marlin on a line, that's why. I sigh. My fingers hover over my keyboard. "I want to know what name I'll be whispering into your ear as you experience pure ecstasy for the very first time." I swallow hard and press send.

I wait. No reply. Four minutes pass. Nothing.

My heart is in my ears. Oh man. She's not answering. Fuck. That wasn't the right message. She's scared to meet me, for whatever reason, and so what did I do? I told her I want to fuck her, sight unseen. Have I gone totally insane? If she's at all sane, unlike me, then I'm sure she's freaking out right now. Damn. I need to reel her back in, show her I'm not crazy, that I just sound that way.

"Just tell me your first name," I type quickly, even more frantically than before. "Have mercy on me. If you won't meet me, then I'll have no choice but to jack off again, thinking of you—and when I do, what name should I whisper into the dark, sad, lonely void of my bedroom? You're not really going to make me moan 'My Beautiful Intake Agent' over and over, are you? That doesn't exactly trip off the tongue. Come on, I'm begging you—and, believe me, I never beg."

I press send.

Almost immediately, my inbox beeps with a reply. It's a one-word message. But it's all I need.

"Sarah."

I exhale in relief and elation. I grab my phone and tap out a quick text to Josh. *"Sarah."*

"I'm on it," he immediately texts back.

Sarah.

I can only hope a first name is enough to find her. Because a first name is all I've got. That, and hope. Infinite hope. My fingers find my keyboard again. "Thank you, my beautiful Sarah. Sarah, Sarah, Sarah, Sarah, Sarah, Sarah." I grin. I feel like a little kid. I might even be blushing right now. "Please, Sarah, just let me meet you. Please, please, please, please, please. Tell me where you are."

I press send and wait. My stomach is flip-flopping. My heart is racing. She's close to giving in; I know she is. I can feel it—taste it. I stare at my screen. *Come on, Sarah. Don't think about it. Just take a leap of faith.*

Five minutes later, an email finally lands in my inbox. But it's not from her. It's an automated email from The Club. My breath catches and my heart sinks at the same time.

"Congratulations!" the automated email says. "Your application for membership to The Club has been approved. Once your membership funds have successfully transferred to us from escrow in approximately two business days, you will receive a welcome package containing detailed instructions about how to use and maximize your membership. Welcome to The Club. Where your every fantasy becomes a reality."

I'm frantic. "Sarah," I type out. "Did I scare you? I won't tell anyone about you, I promise. I just want to meet you. I just want to touch you. We could even just talk. I just want to see you. Please. Please reply right away." I'm typing like a maniac. I press send and wait.

Two minutes later, I receive a bounce back notification that makes me scream out in frustration. "Delivery failed. Server unable to locate email address. Please check your records and, if you feel this message is in error, try sending your email again."

Chapter 6
Jonas

"Hold your horses, bro. He's going as fast as he can," Josh says.

"It's been three days."

"Jonas, hacking into a major university's server is kind of a big deal. You have to be patient."

I grunt.

"I know patience isn't your strong suit. Just, please, try to relax."

"There's no way in hell I can relax."

"Well, try. I'll get back to you soon. He said he's close."

"Thanks. Sorry I'm such an asshole. I appreciate your help."

"No worries. You can't have the looks *and* the personality—you gotta leave me a little something."

"Call me the minute you hear—"

"I will. Bye."

Relax? I'm supposed to relax? There are only two things in this world that ever help me relax, and for the past three days since Sarah cut me off, I've only been doing one of them—working out like a madman. But I'm still relentlessly amped up. I can't get her off my mind. I don't understand what I did to make her run scared—other than show her what an asshole I really am. Yeah, come to think of it, maybe that was it. But she knew the truth about me when she first answered my email. So what changed? What did I do? Just the thought of her freaking out and wanting nothing to do with me is killing me right now. One minute she was touching herself and saying my name, and the next minute she was cutting off all ties. I have to find her and make her feel safe again, make her understand I'd never harm her.

I sit at my kitchen table in a pair of jeans and nothing else, my head in my hands. I should be working right now. We're planning another big acquisition and there's plenty to do. Josh has been picking up my slack, but there's only so much he can do from L.A. on this particular deal. Really, I should be in the office right now, managing my team. But I can't concentrate. I just keep staring at my phone, waiting for Josh to call me to say he's found her.

A couple times, I've tried her email address again, hoping maybe she'd calmed down and reactivated it. But no luck. Same bounce-back message both times.

I open my laptop and click into my email again, just in case.

There's a message from The Club, dated yesterday afternoon.

"Dear Mr. Faraday,

"Welcome to The Club! This is to notify you that your membership funds have successfully cleared from the escrow account. You are now a full-fledged member of The Club. Tomorrow, you will receive a welcome package at the address provided on your application, which will give you everything you need to maximize your membership. If you have any questions or concerns or suggestions, you may contact us at Member_Support@TheClub.com. Of course, all communications will be held in the strictest confidence. Please do not reply to this email, as your reply will not direct to anyone. Welcome to The Club. Where your every fantasy becomes a reality."

I feel sick. I just spent two hundred fifty thousand dollars on something I don't even want anymore. It kills me to waste money. Especially a quarter of a million dollars.

Two nights ago, I lay in bed all night, trying to figure out how I could withdraw my membership application and not cause a problem for Sarah. I went over it and over it in my head, lying in the dark, but I couldn't imagine a scenario where canceling that payment wouldn't end with Sarah losing her job—which, in turn, would mean breaking my promise to her. For a while, I considered withdrawing my membership application and agreeing to pay her a year's salary instead (which most certainly is a mere fraction of two hundred fifty thousand dollars). But it always came back to me breaking a promise to her and losing her trust forever—something I'm not willing to do. And, anyway, what if the big wigs at The Club are vindictive fuckers? They could sue her ass for intentional interference with contract and demand payment of my entire membership fee from her. The more I turned it over and over in my head, the more I knew I had to let that damned payment go through—even though joining The Club is the last thing I care about right now. I promised her I wouldn't harm her in any way. And I'd rather pay money—any amount of money—than harm her. Or break a promise to her. I'm a lot of things, but a liar I am not. Hopefully, when she finds out I didn't stop the wire transfer she'll realize she can trust me completely. She'll understand I'm a man of my word. Maybe then she'll contact me again. I can only hope. Because right now, I'm out of my head.

The doorbell rings. After a minute, I drag myself up from the table and shuffle to the door like a dead man walking. It's a guy from FedEx with a box.

"Jonas Faraday?"

"Yeah."

"Sign here, please."

Getting this box should feel like my birthday and Christmas all rolled into one. I should be chomping at the bit to open it. So why do I feel like throwing it, unopened, against the wall? I leave it on my kitchen table and head into my gym. I need to clear my head—and that means listening to music and working out 'til I'm dripping with sweat.

Two hours later, after a long workout powered by The Sound of Animals Fighting, a hot shower, and answering some work emails, I sit at my kitchen table and stare at the box. Fuck it. I can't resist.

When I open the box, there's a handwritten note sitting along with whatever else. My heart races as I pull out the note.

"My Dearest Jonas,

"You want brutal honesty? Well, here it is. When it comes to you, there's just too much downside and not enough upside. I lost my mind momentarily, but I've regained control of myself. If I were willing to lie to you, like everyone else apparently does—like you *want* everyone to do, despite what you delude yourself into thinking you want—things might have been different. Enjoy your membership. I'm sure you'll get exactly what you want out of it. My wish for you, however, is that, someday, you'll realize what you *want* and what you *need* are two very different things.

"Truthfully yours, Sarah."

I sit and stare at the note in my hand for a good long time.

Her swirling handwriting is distinctive and smooth and beautiful, just like her skin. And it's confident. Feminine. Bold. I run my finger over the indentions made by her ballpoint pen and an unexpected tidal wave of melancholy slams into me. Shit, I feel like crying for the first time since I was a kid. I feel alone. No, that's not it. I feel *abandoned.*

The scent of her dresses hanging against my face fills my nostrils for a fleeting moment—the image of her vacant face on the pillow. I shake my head, but her eyes—her beautiful blue eyes—are still staring lifelessly at me. I push it all back down. I wipe at my eyes and shake my head.

Why do I feel like she just ripped my heart out of my chest? My heart was never involved here. My attraction to her is purely sexual—out of this world, off the charts, insane, inexplicable, unconventional, maybe even bordering on obsessive, yes—but still, purely sexual. Well, no, maybe not *purely* sexual. Because I know she's smart as hell. And funny. And witty. When she cuts me down to size, I actually enjoy it. But all of that is just prelude, right? Just the lead-in to the main event, the sexy little things that make me want to fuck her, right? And that's all. Right?

I wipe my eyes again.

I've never even *seen* her and I was willing to take a giant leap of faith—to meet her and taste her and fuck her and make her come. And on the flipside, she knows everything about me—she's seen my photos, heard my secrets—and won't even agree to sit in the same room with me. What did she mean there was no upside to me? That I'm not the IKEA-shopping-on-weekends kind of guy? That I tell the truth about what I want, and what I don't? Is she saying she's not interested in what I'm willing to offer her? No, she's interested—or else she wouldn't have emailed me in the first place. Is she saying she would have wanted *more* than what I can give her, so why even bother with me? Yes, I think that's exactly what she's saying. But she knew that up front, so why'd she even reply to my note in the first place? I guess she realized she wouldn't give up all the Valentine's Day bullshit to howl like a monkey for the first time in her life, after all. Well, good to know, then. She saved us both a lot of hassle. Good to fucking know.

She thinks everyone lies to me—and that I want it that way? What does she mean? Is she calling me a liar—or, at least, a self-deluding prick? Fine. Maybe she's right.

I sit at the table, rubbing my face.

I remember how she looked over at me from the bed, her blue eyes frantic. *Don't move,* her eyes commanded me. *Stay hidden.* And I did. I stayed hidden. I didn't move. I didn't do a damned thing. And she paid the price for my worthlessness.

No upside, huh? Is that what she thinks about me? Well, guess what? She's right. I'm all downside, baby—I'm a fucked-up pile of shit without a single redeeming quality. You want to play with Jonas Faraday? Be prepared to get hurt, then. Boom. Because that's all I've got for you. A big, steaming pile of hurt.

Fuck it.

I pull the box toward me. Let's see what "all my fantasies becoming reality" looks like when delivered to my doorstep by FedEx. Hopefully, the rest of the box will be kinder to me than Sarah's brutal note.

There's an iPhone pre-loaded with an app, a welcome booklet, and a rubber bracelet. According to my brief skim of the booklet, if I'm in the mood to meet up with a female Club member, any time of day or night, anywhere in the world, I check-in on the app and register my current or future location with an anonymous pin number. "You have been meticulously matched with other members within The Club, and only compatible members will have access to your posts and check-ins," the instructions say. When I show up at the meeting spot, I'm required to wear my color-coded bracelet—I've been assigned purple, whatever that means ("self-deluding prick," maybe?)—and then wait for all the purple-coded women in The Club to flock to my registered spot and descend upon me like purple moths to a purple flame.

The instructions go on to explain, "Male members are required to wear their assigned color-coded bracelets at all check-ins. Women may choose to wear their bracelets or not—at their sole discretion—ensuring them the opportunity to assess the situation before identifying themselves. After much experimentation, we have determined this system maximizes satisfaction and safety for all involved."

Apparently, I can also send requests and invitations to specific members, soliciting their attendance at my check-in spot, or, I can just roll the dice and see who shows up. "No matter how you decide to check in, however, rest assured that only compatible persons, pre-selected for your preferences specifically, will respond. Persons outside of your color-code cannot access your posts and check-ins."

She sees no upside to me, huh? Fine. She's sure I'll get everything I want out of my membership? Damn straight I will. I spent two hundred fifty thousand dollars on this goddamned membership, might as well fucking use it. Why not? Why fucking not? Apparently, that's what she expects me to do. Apparently, that's what she *wants* me to do.

I unlock my Club-issued iPhone and open the pre-loaded app. I look at my watch. 3:06 p.m. Using the pin number assigned to me, I check myself into one of my favorite bars, a nearby place called The Pine Box, at 5:00 p.m. Fuck it. Let's see if someone besides My Beautiful Intake Agent—*Sarah*—can see an upside to me. Maybe some woman besides Sarah—whoever the hell she is—will be able to see an upside to a guy who can give her the best fuck of her life.

Chapter 7
Jonas

The Pine Box is packed, as usual. I take a seat at the bar.

"A Heineken."

The bartender nods.

I touch the purple band on my wrist. It feels like a neon sign flashing "pervert." I look at my watch. I'm a few minutes early. How long does it usually take for the purple moths to descend, I wonder? I scan the bar. I don't see any purple bracelets out there in the crowd. But, apparently, under the rules, I might never see one. Any one of these women could be a member, I suppose—and many of them are attractive. Highly attractive, actually.

Two women tucked into a booth in the far corner catch my attention. One of them is exactly the kind of woman I'd usually make a beeline for—tall and honey blonde with an athletic frame. Vintage Christy Brinkley. She's what anyone would go for—anyone who watches Hollywood movies or football or porn. But for some reason, it's the woman sitting across from her who's peaked my interest the most. And that's weird because I can't even see her face. She's intently studying a menu, and her face is completely hidden. All I can see is the top of her forehead poking out from behind the menu, and her long dark hair cascading down her shoulders. Her hands are particularly striking—long, slender fingers, natural fingernails and a simple silver band on her right thumb. Sexy.

But the thing that pulls my attention to her the most is her skin— what little I can see of it, anyway, on her hands and forearms and that tiny sliver of forehead peeking out from the top of the menu. Her skin is the exact same olive tone I imagine Sarah's would be, and it looks smooth and soft, too, just like Sarah's looked in the two photos she sent me. I can't peel my eyes away from the woman behind the menu. I just want to see her face. If I could just see her face, just once, maybe it'd give me something—anything—to imagine when I'm in the shower, lathering myself after a workout and fantasizing about making Sarah come.

The bartender puts my beer on the counter in front of me. I nod at him and throw down a ten.

But what am I thinking? I'm not going to think about Sarah anymore. That's the whole point of me coming here tonight wearing my pervert-purple bracelet, isn't it? I'm here to rid myself of her. She doesn't want to have anything to do with me? Fine. I'm done with her, too. Tonight, I'm going to give my undivided attention to my new purple fuck buddies, whoever they may be.

I glance at my watch. Five minutes past five o'clock. Come out, come out, wherever you are.

Once things get rolling with The Club, I surely won't have time to think about Sarah ever again. I'll be too busy making all my new purple partners lose their minds and then serenely saying goodbye to them without the tiniest need to feel remorse. And they'll be content and satisfied, too—because that's exactly what they'll have signed up for. Nothing more. There'll be no thoughts of soul mates and some sort of "deeper connection." We'll both be sexually satisfied, and that will be enough for us. No hurt feelings. I'll be like a kid in a candy store. Why did she say everyone lies to me and that's what I want? That's exactly the opposite of what I want. What did she mean?

I suddenly find myself wishing the woman behind the menu would turn out to be one of my new purple playmates. It seems quite possible, because it sure feels like she's been secretly staring at me every time I look away. Or maybe it's the blonde that's making me feel that way— the blonde's not even hiding her repeated glances and smiles over at me. Hey, maybe they're both up for grabs. But, no, that can't be. I didn't write anything about wanting a threesome in my application. Been there, done that. It's not my thing. Both times I tried it, I wound up focusing on one woman to the exclusion of the other, and the "extra" woman started getting all pissy and insistent and overcompensating, until finally she became a downright hindrance to me accomplishing my mission with the woman I wanted to focus on. I realized pretty quickly that I strongly prefer to give one woman my undivided attention.

To be honest, even if the blonde were wearing a purple bracelet right now, I'm not sure I'd be all that interested, even though she's exactly what I usually go for. For some reason, I just don't want my usual tonight. Tonight, I want to witness an olive-hued beauty writhing around on my white sheets. Hell, even if the woman behind the menu isn't a member, maybe I'll take her home anyway and give her the night of her life.

But that's just stupid. If I came here to pick up a random woman in the bar, why the hell did I just pay two hundred fifty thousand dollars for The Club to set me up with "uncannily compatible" women? I need to just cool my jets and focus on the task at hand.

I take a large gulp of my beer and look around the bar. There are a lot of good-looking women here. I still don't see anyone wearing a purple bracelet, though. I feel like the hunted, rather than the hunter, and I'm not used to it. I'm not sure I like it. In fact, I'm sure I don't. I like being in control at all times.

Maybe I'm supposed to check the app to see if someone else has checked in? And then go on some sort of wild goose chase, looking for her in the bar? Yeah, I bet I'm supposed to do that. I couldn't concentrate on all the instructions and materials The Club sent me—I was so fucking out of my mind about Sarah—I figured I'd just wing it.

Sarah.

Why'd she give up on me like that—without giving me a say in the matter? I thought things were going so well between us. I've never wanted a woman so much in all my life—and I've never even *seen* her! What the hell did she expect from me? What kind of *upside* did she expect me to promise her just to meet her in person? Talk about demanding. Unreasonable. I probably dodged a bullet there.

No, even in my anger, I know that's not true. The only one who dodged a bullet here was Sarah. She ran like hell because she's so damned smart. Even though I'm pissed, I can't help smiling, thinking about our email exchange. *"You did not just ask me, 'What's your sign?'"* she said. *"Smooth, you woman wizard, you,"* she said. Even when she kicked my ass, I loved it. If only she would have let me see her, things would have been different. I know they would have. The kind of chemistry we have—via fucking *email*—doesn't happen every day. It pains me to wonder how off the charts our chemistry would have been in person. It sure would have been nice if she'd have let *me* decide what I was or wasn't willing to give her, rather than her deciding that, whatever it was, it wasn't enough. Shit, I can't even think straight just thinking about her.

I look over at that corner booth again. Menu Girl's still hidden behind that damned menu. How long does it take to decide what to order? The skin on her arm is luscious. Yeah, I don't know if I can resist going after that woman behind the menu tonight, a quarter-mill spent on membership fees or not. I've got a whole year to dabble in The Club's offerings, after all. Why rush? Tonight, maybe I'll partake in Sarah's olive-skinned double. Yeah, Menu Girl can be my Sarah stand-in. What better way to help me lose interest in Sarah? I'll imagine that woman in the corner is Sarah, take her home, taste her, make her come, fuck her brains out, and then let the usual wave of complete disinterest wash over me. If Menu Girl gets her feelings hurt, that's her problem. It'll be classic aversion therapy—*A Clockwork Sarah*—and I'll be cured of Sarah forever.

I stand up from my stool. That's exactly what I'm going to do. Whoever she is, her feelings be damned tonight. If I can't get Sarah off my mind, then I'll fuck someone else's brains out until I can.

"Hi there."

It's a fair-skinned brunette with startling blue eyes. She's stunningly attractive—a real head-turner. She grins at me and pushes a lock of dark hair behind her ear, plainly showcasing the purple bracelet on her wrist as she does it. She smiles broadly when my eyes lock onto her bracelet. Her teeth are white and straight.

"Hi," I reply, glancing over at the corner, but a lingering group of people has moved between us and I can't see Menu Girl. Shit.

"I'm Stacy," my new friend says, putting out her hand. "You're a brand new member, right?"

"Yeah." As I take Stacy's hand, I glance back to the corner again. I'm startled to see Menu Girl's big brown eyes glaring at me over the top of her menu. The minute our eyes meet, she abruptly looks away and raises the menu again. What the hell? She was *glaring* at me just now.

Every hair on my body suddenly stands on end. Oh my God.

I look back at my would-be purple companion. "Would you excuse me for just a minute?"

Her face falls. "You're not going to buy me a drink?"

"I'm sorry, yes, of course, I am. What would you like?"

She stops to think about it for a moment and I feel like I'm going to explode with nervous anxiety. Come on. Please. Make up your mind. It's not a life-changing decision. It's a drink order.

"A glass of chardonnay would be great," she finally says, flashing me her most alluring smile, and I quickly place her order.

A growing urgency is swelling inside me. I'm having a crazy thought right now.

Stacy puts her hand on my arm. "You never told me your name."

"Jonas."

"It's nice to meet you, *Jonas.*" She licks her lips. Her features are ridiculously well put together. "What a pleasant surprise you are, I've got to say."

I try to smile back, but I'm too distracted to focus on her. I'm having an insane thought, a maniacal and self-deluding-prick thought. I'm thinking that Sarah came here tonight. I'm thinking Sarah, my beautiful Sarah, is sitting in this room right now, forty yards away, watching me from behind a fucking menu. I'm thinking that, despite her handwritten note, she can't stop thinking of me any more than I can stop thinking of her.

"You, too, Stacy. I'll be right back. Just enjoy your wine for a minute." I turn away from Stacy, without waiting for her reply, and instantly lurch toward the corner booth, my heart clanging in my chest all the while.

"Excuse me," I say, making my way through the lingering crowd, my pulse pounding in my ears.

No.

No, no, no.

She's not at the booth anymore.

I look around frantically, but she's nowhere to be seen. The woman behind the menu and her supermodel friend are both long gone.

Chapter 8
Sarah

"This is a bad idea," I say, looking at my watch. It's twenty minutes before five o'clock. My stomach is flip-flopping. He could walk through the door any minute.

"Why?" Kat sniffs. "You said yourself he has no idea what you look like—well, other than your boob." She laughs. "That was so badass of you, Sarah. I can't believe you did that."

I roll my eyes. "I know. It was so unlike me—I don't know what got into me."

"Oh, I know exactly what got into you."

I blush.

"Just relax, okay? He won't even know you're here. And the bar's plenty crowded, too. You'll have plenty of time to watch him and gather your courage."

"Courage to do what?"

"To say hi to him."

"There's no way I'm saying hi to him."

"Then why the heck are we here?"

"I just want to look at him." I sigh. "I can't resist. When you see him, you'll understand."

"You dragged me to The Pine Box on a moment's notice just to *spy* on him?" She looks at me dubiously.

I nod. "I've only seen him in photos—well, and for a split-second when he was speeding past me in his car. I just want to get one good, long, lingering look at him in the flesh." And, truth be told, I can't resist seeing what kind of woman The Club deems his perfect match.

"Sarah, I still don't understand—why not just sleep with the guy,

67

even if it's just once? If he's as hot as you say he is, why not have one amazing night you'll always remember?"

"I don't know if I'm capable of enjoying 'one amazing night' with him," I say. I don't know how to explain my unexpected feelings toward this guy. He's awakened a yearning inside of me like nothing I've felt before. Somehow, I know, deep in my bones, if I play with this fire, I'll surely get burned to a blackened crisp. Or at least my heart will. I'm exactly the kind of girl he joined The Club to avoid. I know I am. And I can't change any more than he can. So what's the point? There isn't one.

Kat shrugs. "Well, then, why are we here? You just want to torture yourself? I mean, come on, you know what he's looking for, and it ain't a relationship. This is a guy who joined 'The Club,' after all."

"Shh," I say. "Please." I've told Kat a thousand times that the very existence of The Club is über confidential. But she loves the whole idea of a secret underground club for rich freaks and always wants to know every juicy detail. "I just have to see him in action. Maybe it'll help me get him out of my system." I shrug. "What time is it?"

"Quarter to five."

My stomach flip-flops. I've imagined this man licking me and smiling up at me from between my legs countless times, for goodness sakes, and even imaginary sex with him has been the best sex of my life. I can only imagine how my nerve endings will react to seeing the genuine article in person. I'm not sure I'll be able to keep myself from screaming his name like a groupie at a rock concert.

"Oh my God. Is that *him?*" Kat whispers, cricking her neck toward the front door. I follow her glance and immediately throw a menu in front of my face.

I feel my cheeks flush. "Yes," I whisper.

I peek at Kat around the side of my menu. She's openly gawking at him.

"Holy shitballs," she says. "Wow. He's ... wow. I thought you were exaggerating. But, no, not at all. He must have made a deal with the devil or something."

"Don't look at him," I hiss. "Act natural."

"I *am* acting natural—"

"No, you're not."

"Yes, I am. If I *weren't* looking at him, now *that* would be totally unnatural."

"What's he doing?" I'm shoving my nose so far into my menu I can't see a thing—not even the items on the menu.

"He's sitting at the bar." She pauses. "He's ordering a drink." A long pause. "A beer." Another pause. "He's looking around." A long pause. "Drinking his beer." Another pause. "More looking around."

My heart is in my throat. My pulse is in my ears. My stomach is in knots. "Is it safe for me to look?"

"Yeah, he's not looking over here."

I peek over the top of my menu. "Oh." It's all I can manage—and it's a "maybe I made a huge mistake by blowing him off" kind of "oh." A "maybe I shouldn't have said there's no upside to him" kind of "oh." An "oh hell maybe it's worth getting my heart smashed into a thousand pieces to get a piece of that" kind of "oh." He's gorgeous.

His head starts to swivel in our direction, and I cover my face again.

"Sarah," Kat chastises me. "He doesn't know what you look like. Why are you covering your face?"

My hands are shaking as they hold the menu. Just that one glimpse of him was enough to send me into some kind of hormone-induced seizure.

"He's looking over here," Kat announces flatly.

I peek at her on the far side of my menu again. Her face is turned toward the bar. She's smirking at him.

"Don't look over at him!" I command. "Please. At the very least, don't *smile* at him. When you smile at a man, he comes over to talk to you. Every time. Kat, please," I whisper with urgency.

"And remind me why don't we want him to come over here again?" she asks between her smiling teeth.

"Because I'd have a nervous breakdown," I say, my voice cracking with anxiety. I think it's an accurate statement. I'd surely have a nervous breakdown or some other life-altering medical crisis, if Jonas Faraday waltzed over here at all, but especially if he came to flirt with *Kat*.

"Okay, okay, I'll stop," Kat says, apparently sensing my sincere anxiety. "Oh, hey, he's looking the other away again."

I peek at him over the edge of my menu. He's looking around the bar again, obviously waiting for a parade of purples to show up. The whole situation makes my flesh crawl. But what did I expect? For him to cancel his club membership and declare, "I don't care about The Club! I just want *My Beautiful Intake Agent!*"—for a woman he's never met or even spoken to on the phone? Talk about Lifetime-Hallmark-Valentine's Day brainwashing. What was I hoping for—some kind of meaningful human connection thanks to a little email-sex? Ha! I really am exactly the kind of woman who made him want to join The Club in the first place.

"What's he doing now?" I whisper, afraid to look.

"I don't know. A group of people just stood in my line of sight."

"Damn." A minute passes. "View still obstructed?"

"No. Would you just put that down already? Anyone looking at you would think you're deranged or something. Who takes this long to decide on a simple food order?"

I sigh. I'm being ridiculous. Life is short. I'm in the same air space as the scrumptious, if arrogant, Jonas Faraday. When will I ever get this chance again? I'm acting like a scared child—something I thought I'd given up for good a long time ago. "You know what? You're right. I should just go over there and talk to him like an adult."

"There you go—put your big girl panties on." Kat's beaming at me.

I put the menu down on the table. "I mean, even if I crash and burn, at least I'll never wonder 'what if.'"

"Exactly."

I gaze over at Jonas, resolving myself to just go talk to him.

I gasp. Oh crap. He's talking to a stunning brunette—and even from here, I can see the purple bracelet around her wrist. I grab the menu again and hurriedly raise it up, just below my eyes. Miss Purple smiles at him and licks her lips. Oh wow, she's really coming on strong—and she's smokin' hot, too. Even though Jonas' head is turned away from me, there's no doubt in my mind his eyes are bugging out with unfettered lust right now. She's frickin' spectacular—and clearly ready to jump his bones.

I want to scream. Or throw up. Actually, more than anything, I just want to cry. And, honestly, I'm confused. Why on earth did this gorgeous woman join The Club? What is she hoping to gain? Is she a gold digger? Is she looking for a husband? What? Because I don't believe for a second she's here to find serial sex partners with no strings attached. A woman like that could have any man she'd ever want. So why on earth was she matched to Jonas, a guy who wants to give her nothing but an orgasm and a polite farewell?

What's going on here? And why isn't Jonas wondering the same thing?

Out of nowhere, while I'm still peeking over my menu at Jonas and that woman at the bar, Jonas turns almost completely around and looks directly at me. My eyes are hard slits. *Bastard.* His eyes go wide. So do mine. Shit.

I quickly glance away and raise my menu to cover my entire face. I feel like I've just been caught in the act—the act of what, I'm not entirely sure. I'm seized with a sudden panic. Does he know who I am? No, that's a silly thought. And yet, for a split second there, I swear I thought I saw *recognition* in his eyes. But that's impossible. He can't *recognize* me—he's never seen me before. The man couldn't pick me out of a line-up (other than a line-up of left boobs).

I quickly peek again, but he's turned back to her, buying her a drink. Of course, he is. I could puke. Sure, Sarah, there was *recognition* in his eyes—so much so, he immediately decided to buy his new purple friend a drink. I'm such an idiot. Anger and embarrassment and humiliation flood into me all at once. And jealousy, too. Let's not forget jealousy.

"Let's go," I bark at Kat, leaping up from my seat. Without waiting for Kat's reply, I bolt to the front door like the place is on fire. In a flash, I'm flying up the sidewalk, away from the bar, as fast as my legs will carry me, the sound of Kat's high heels clacking on the cement behind me.

I can't believe I almost said hello to him in there. That would have been an awkward moment at best and a mortifying catastrophe at worst. I can't believe I got so wrapped up in the ridiculous fantasy of our little forbidden whatever-it-was (I was about to call it a romance, but obviously, that's the last thing it was). I can't believe I touched myself and said his name, that I wanted to have sex with him so much it physically pained me, that I researched him online for seven hours straight, a good six hours more than necessary for my intake report—when I should have been reading the next three cases for my contracts homework. Oh good God, I can't believe I sent him a picture of my boob! I've never done anything like that in my life. What the hell is wrong with me? And most of all, I can't believe I let my heart ache for the sadness in his eyes—a sadness I stupidly thought I could fix. A sadness I *wanted* to fix.

I was a fool.

I reach my car, panting. I bend over, catching my breath. After half a minute, Kat reaches me, equally out of breath.

"Wooh!" she breathes.

"Sorry," I choke out.

"I understand." She grimaces. "Ouch." I'm pretty sure she's referring to what we just witnessed in the bar, not her sprint up the sidewalk in heels.

My chest is heaving. "Ouch," I agree.

A minute passes. "I knew he was a man-whore," I say, "but seeing him in action like that . . ." I let out a shaky breath. "If that's the kind of woman I'm up against, I never stood a chance, anyway."

Kat shoots me a commiserating frowny face.

My shoulders slump. "I don't know why he has this hold on me." Tears are threatening my eyes, but I suppress them. "I keep pushing him away from me, telling him to leave me alone—and then I'm crushed when it works." I roll my eyes at myself. "I'm a mess."

Kat wraps me into a hug, and I put my cheek on her shoulder. "If he wants to chase tail for the rest of his life rather than have the most incredible girl in the entire world, then he just doesn't deserve you, anyway," she whispers.

Chapter 9
Jonas

I'm grateful to be showering alone right now. I usually like showering with a woman right after I've fucked her. But not tonight. Sex with Stacy was ... unfulfilling. No, actually, it was bordering on repulsive, if I'm being totally honest. I can't believe I just used the word repulsive to describe sex with a woman who looks like Stacy. But there you go.

The woman has an incredible body—tight and lean with curves in all the right places—and soft skin and thick hair and the bluest eyes I've ever seen. And yet, I wasn't into it from minute one. I definitely wasn't enthused to go down on her, so I don't for the life of me know why I did it anyway. Force of habit I guess. Convincing myself I was "back," maybe. Perhaps I thought I could fool myself into enjoying it, if I just gave it the ol' college try. But it was a huge miscalculation on my part. The minute my tongue hit her cunt, my stomach jerked, if you can believe it, like I was tasting rancid milk or something.

But Stacy didn't seem to notice me practically gagging down there. Nope, the minute my tongue hit her bull's-eye, she moaned and groaned and did all the right things—writhing and pleading and howling and begging—like I'd flipped some magic switch on her. She ramped up so fast and so hard, in fact, I actually rolled my eyes and pulled away from her, staring. It was all I could do not to yell up to her face, "Really, Stacy?"

I didn't say that, of course—I am a gentleman, after all—but I did stop licking her right then and gape at her in total disbelief. And the minute I stopped, do you know what she did? She whimpered and begged me to slam her with my cock like she'd never been so turned on in her life. It was almost funny. Even I knew I hadn't done a goddamned thing yet, and there she was, following the blueprint I'd given in my application, to the letter. Un-fucking-believable. But it's hard to resist a hot woman begging you to fuck her, even if she *is* a fucking liar. So, I did. I fucked her, though I'm not proud of myself for doing it.

When I entered her, which I did kind of roughly, to be honest, my only thought was getting myself off, as opposed to bringing her any form of pleasure. And guess what? Shocker! I was no sooner inside her than she came like a Mack truck—or so it seemed. (Or, as Sarah would say, she *allegedly* came like a Mack truck). And you know what I was thinking during her *alleged* orgasm? I was thinking, "Give me a fucking break." That's not the greatest thing in the world to be thinking while a woman squirms under you in apparent rapture. In fact, it's pretty fucking gross.

And that's when I thought, rather distinctly, "I want Sarah." And the minute I started thinking "I want Sarah" while my dick was pounding into Stacy, I felt so disgusted with myself, so physically repelled, so depressed, so fucking *lonely*, I wanted to pull out and not even bother coming at all. But that's not what I did. No, being the high caliber individual that I am, I did quite the opposite. I closed my eyes and forged ahead, imagining my cock was inside Sarah—Sarah with the olive skin and perfect breast and the hard nipple I'd give anything to twirl around in my tongue. Sarah with the bullshit-o-meter like no one I've ever met before. Sarah who's never come before, and who decided to trust me with that delicate pearl of truth. Sarah who knows I'm an asshole but touched herself and said my name, anyway. Yep. I closed me eyes and let my mind construct a blurry image of Sarah—a kind of amalgam of Sarah and Menu Girl fused together, and I fucked the shit out of Stacy.

Thinking about Sarah made me pump into Stacy even harder. As I slammed into Stacy—as she groaned and writhed under me—I told myself Sarah couldn't stay away from me, even though she deleted her email account, even though she wrote me that fucking handwritten note. With each thrust, I told myself Sarah had looked me up on the check-in app, that she'd figured out I'd be at that bar, that she couldn't stop thinking about me, aching for me—that she wanted me as much as I wanted her. I imagined everything went differently at The Pine Box— that Sarah was Menu Girl, and that I went straight over to the corner instead of buying Stacy a drink, that I went right over to her and took the menu out of her hands and said, "You're coming home with me right now." As my naked skin moved against Stacy's soft, fair skin, over and over, I imagined the rapture of feeling Menu Girl's smooth, olive skin rubbing against mine. I imagined Menu Girl's sweat was mingling with mine, that her long, dark hair was unfurled on my white pillowcase, that her slender hands were clutching my back, her fingernails digging into me, the silver band on her thumb scraping against my skin.

All of that pretending worked for me, and I was right the verge of coming, right on the verge of shouting Sarah's name—but then Stacy moaned and whispered in my ear. "You're amazing," she said, and I was instantly jolted back to reality. I opened my eyes and saw Stacy's blue eyes staring back at me, not Menu Girl's big brown eyes.

That's when I remembered Sarah didn't want me.

That's when I remembered Sarah didn't think I was worthy of her.

That's when I remembered Sarah didn't see an upside to me.

And that's when I got pissed.

I started fucking Stacy without mercy. I'm not proud of it—in fact, I'm so disgusted with myself, I feel almost physically ill about it—but I fucked Stacy so hard after her "you're amazing" bullshit comment, and with such animosity, I can't imagine she experienced anything but unadulterated humiliation, maybe even pain.

Though, of course, she pretended to like it.

Because she's a fucking liar.

"That was incredible," Stacy said after I finally came and collapsed on top of her in an angry, sweaty heap. I pulled back and looked into her face, ready to apologize—to beg her forgiveness—and she smiled at me. It was a smile that didn't reach her eyes—her very, very blue eyes—and it felt like a punch in the gut. I pulled out of her and yanked off my condom. I couldn't muster a return smile or any kind of reply to her hollow compliment. I certainly didn't feel like apologizing to her for fucking her so hard anymore. I knew I'd just sold my soul to the devil—for two hundred-fifty thousand dollars, to be exact—and I hated myself for it.

"I'm gonna hop in the shower," I mumbled, hoping Stacy would get the hint.

And guess what? She did. Without batting an eyelash. Of course, she did. Good ol' Stacy. I shouldn't have been surprised, since she's an android programmed to make my every fucking fantasy a reality. Well, an android programmed to make what I *thought* was my every fucking fantasy into a reality. As it turns out, what I wanted—what I *thought* I wanted—doesn't exist.

"Yeah, you go ahead," she said cheerfully, gathering up her clothes. "I've got to get going, anyway." Wow, big surprise. Right on cue. "Thanks for everything, though. You're amazing. Maybe I'll see you around." Without another word, she threw on her clothes and waltzed out the door, just like that. No request for my phone number. No hints about Radiohead coming to town the following week and, hey, they just happen to be her favorite band. No hopeful expression in her eyes. Not even a request for my Club identification number so we could check-in with each other again. Just in and out. Fuck and duck. Hit it and quit it. Exactly what I said I wanted in my application. But, ah, wasn't the second half of my "sexual preferences" that I didn't want to feel like an asshole afterwards? So why do I feel like the biggest asshole who ever lived right now? Actually, I feel like more of an asshole right now in this very moment than I've felt in my entire adult life.

I lather my body with shower gel, practically scrubbing my skin to get Stacy off me. I close my eyes and let the hot water pelt me in the face for a moment, and then I open my mouth and let the searing water flood my mouth, trying desperately to cleanse my tongue. Before getting into the shower, I brushed my teeth and tongue for, like, seven minutes, but I still can't get the sour taste of Stacy's cunt out of my mouth. Just the thought of my tongue touching her makes me shudder. What the fuck was I thinking?

I don't want Stacy.

Or Marissa. Or Caitlyn. Or Julie. Or Samantha or Emily or Maddie or Kristin or Lauren or Rachel or Bethanney or Natalie or Darcy or Michelle or Charlotte or Grace or Katie or Shannon or Juliana or Tiffany or Andrea or Melanie or Hannah.

My chest constricts. The truth is dawning on me as the hot water pelts me.

I want Sarah.

But Sarah doesn't want me.

I lost my mind momentarily, she said, *but I've regained control of myself.*

I'm what happened when she had an aberrant lapse in good judgment? I'm what happened when she let her guard down for once in her repressed life? I'm the bad guy who forced her to acknowledge and claim her deepest, most honest desires, instead of chasing bullshit rainbows like everyone else tells her to do? She's regained her control

76

now, huh? Well, lucky for her. Who knows what could have happened if she'd deigned to meet me—if she had lowered herself to giving me a fucking chance rather than unilaterally deciding I wasn't worth her time.

Fuck.

I lean my hands against the marble in the shower and let the hot water slide down my naked back. My head is spinning. She thinks I'm unworthy of her.

When it comes to you, she said, *there's just too much downside, and not enough upside.*

I grab the shampoo and massage a drop into my hair.

Thanks to that application, she knows better than anyone— literally, *anyone*—just what a cocky-bastard-asshole-son-of-a-bitch motherfucker I really am.

If I were willing to lie to you, like everyone else apparently does—like you want everyone to do, despite what you delude yourself into thinking you want—things might have been different. Her words sting like razors slicing my chest. Before Sarah, I fooled everyone else. Even myself. But not her. She knows the truth. *Enjoy your membership,* she said. *I'm sure you'll get exactly what you want out of it. My wish for you, however, is that, someday, you'll realize what you want and what you need are two very different things.* Shit. I don't know what the hell I need. But I sure as hell know what I want.

My cell phone rings in my bedroom, pulling me out of my thoughts. I leap out of the shower and run to my phone on my bed, dripping water across my wood floor as I go. I missed the call— fuck!—it was Josh. I call right back, my heart in my throat.

He picks up right away. "We found her."

I'm sitting on my bed in a pair of jeans, staring at Josh's follow-up email, trying to gain control of my breathing. Of the three Sarahs currently enrolled at the University of Washington's law school—Sarah McHutchinson, Sarah Jones, and Sarah Cruz—two of them are twenty-four years old: Sarah McHutchinson and Sarah Cruz. With Sarah's olive skin, my money's on Sarah Cruz. I suddenly remember she said *gracias* in her first email to me. I smirk. Yeah, she's Sarah Cruz. It doesn't matter if I'm right or wrong about my guess, though, because Josh styled me with all three women's cell phone numbers and email addresses, plus their physical addresses, too. But I know in my gut I'm right. *Sarah Cruz.*

"We can get their social security numbers and transcripts, too, if you want 'em," Josh said during our call, about ten minutes ago.

"I don't want to run a credit report on her," I said, "or interview her for a job. I just want to find her."

Josh laughed. "Lemme know what happens. At this point, I'm probably as invested in this romance as you are, bro."

I bristle. "It's not a romance."

"Jonas, you're such an idiot."

I Google the name "Sarah Cruz," but so many cluttered results and links and images come up there's no way I can possibly make heads or tails of all the information. I try "Sarah Cruz Seattle" to narrow things down, but it barely makes a dent in the white noise of information, and nothing that comes up looks even remotely promising, anyway. I try "Sarah Cruz University Washington" and a link to a pdf document pops up on some student forum—a list of first semester standings for the University of Washington Law School, Class of 2016. I open the document and scan the names, beginning at the top of the list. I don't have to go very far down the list—Sarah Cruz is ranked fourth in her entire class right now. Yeah, my clever Sarah is Sarah Cruz, I'm sure of it. And she's kicking everyone's ass, not just mine. Of course she is.

I pick up the phone and Josh answers immediately.

"Can your guy see if there are photos in the Sarah files—like for student IDs or something? I only need a photo for whichever one's got olive-ish skin. I know my Sarah's definitely not fair-skinned."

"Wait, you don't know what she looks like?"

I don't say anything.

"You've never seen her?"

I'm silent. Shit.

Josh makes a "mind officially blown" kind of sound. "I assumed you started this quest after she sent you some anonymous, sexy photo that rocked your world. But you've never even *seen* this girl? This is all because of something she *wrote* to you in an email?"

Well, shit, the whole thing sounds fucking insane when he says it like that. I sigh, unwilling to answer the question—but my sigh tells Josh everything he needs to know. Even I can hear how ragged and desperate it sounds when I exhale.

"Wow. This really *is* a romance of epic proportions." He laughs.

I can't even muster a "fuck you." I'm a wreck.
"Don't worry, I'll see what my guy can find. Sit tight."
"Hey, Josh, one more thing."
"Yeah?"
"Get me the transcripts, too."

I don't know what's taking so long. I thought Josh would get back to me right away with those pictures. But he hasn't called or emailed and I'm on pins and needles. So close, and yet so far. I can't concentrate on anything. I certainly can't do any work. Or even work out. I don't want to do anything that pulls me away from my phone and makes me miss a call from Josh.

I pace around my kitchen, staring at my laptop on the counter. I pull my phone out of my jeans pocket. Nothing.

Sarah Cruz. I can't stop thinking about her breast. Her nipple. Her thigh. Her skin. And about how she said she wished I'd realize what I *want* and what I *need* are two very different things.

Fuck it. I don't need to see her photo to call her. Whatever she looks like, I still want to talk to her, at least. I still want to meet her. If it turns out she's not classically beautiful, so what? Or even if it turns out I'm not physically attracted to her in the slightest ... But, no, I can't even imagine not being physically attracted her. She's hot; I'm sure of it. Her skin is heavenly. Her breast is perfect. Her nipple standing at attention gave me a raging hard-on. What more do I need to know? If her face isn't what I'd normally go for, all I'd have to do is look down at that nipple of hers, and I'd be all good.

I pull up Josh's email with the contact information for all three Sarahs and squint at my computer screen for the phone number listed under Sarah Cruz's name. I suppose she could be the other twenty-four-year-old Sarah—Sarah McHutchinson?—but I doubt it.

With shaky hands, I slowly dial the digits for little miss bullshit-detector, I-lost-my-mind-momentarily-but-now-I've-regained-control-of-myself, doesn't-see-the-upside-in-me, number-four-in-her-law-school-class, never-howled-like-a-monkey-once-in-her-well-ordered-little-life, makes-me-fucking-crazy, I-want-her-but-she-doesn't-want-me, Sarah Cruz.

Chapter 10
Sarah

Watching Jonas move in on that ridiculously hot woman in the purple bracelet was a sobering slap in my face—a wake-up call that Jonas Faraday is and always will be exactly the horndog he claimed to be from day one, and nothing more, and that all the depth and gravitas and yearning and loneliness and innate goodness I thought I saw in his eyes was a figment of my imagination. A mere projection. As much as it ripped my heart out to realize all that, the silver lining has been that I've decided to vigorously focus all my time and attention on my studies and crazy-ass job, just as I should be doing. Jonas Faraday was a distraction, an unwise and time-consuming distraction, that's all, and now I'm done with him.

I pulled a marathon study session after coming home from the bar last night, and now I'm all caught up on my reading for every one of my classes (and I've even read ahead in contracts, too). This morning, I started making myself a detailed study outline for torts that covers the issue, rule, analysis and conclusion of every case we've read since week one, and next week, I'll start my outline for contracts, and right after that, I'll dig into constitutional law. If I keep up this pace, I'll be completely prepared when finals roll around with plenty of time to spare. The top ten ranked students at the end of the first year are granted a full-ride scholarship for the remaining two years of the law program, and I'm hell bent on getting one of those coveted slots.

The Club has kept me busy, too. A new application from a guy in Seattle landed in my inbox this morning, and I've just now gotten back from conducting my confirming surveillance. I've only been back home for ten minutes and I've already logged into my intake report and recommended approval (contingent on an "all clear" from

80

pending medical and psychological testing, of course). The guy signed up for a one-month membership (always a good sign), and his sexual preferences section was the biggest vanilla-snoozefest I've seen yet. He's refreshingly normal. Sweet as can be, in fact—but, whoa boring as hell. I'm guessing he hasn't had a heck of a lot of luck with the ladies up to this point. Hopefully, membership in The Club will give him a shot at finding love—and, if not, then I hope it will bring him the most thrilling month of his life. Either way, I'm rooting for him.

When I clicked on the pictures he sent with is application, they were bursting with his normalcy and utter loneliness, and it was very obvious to me he was exactly who he said he was—I mean, who would pretend to look like that guy in a catfish attempt? All I had to do was stand in the lobby of his office building (he's a software engineer) at lunchtime and I quickly spotted him leaving his building to grab a sandwich, looking every bit the thirty-seven-year-old, five-foot-seven, introverted computer nerd he claimed to be in his application. Done-zo.

Maybe I'm just feeling emotional lately, thanks to seeing Jonas on the prowl flashing his purple bracelet, but when Mr. Normal walked past me, all alone and looking sad among his departing co-workers (all of whom were rushing off to lunch around him in animated, chatty groups), I felt like crying for him. Or maybe I just felt like crying for myself. Everyone deserves love, whether that simply means being invited to lunch with co-workers once in a while, or finding that one person with whom you can share all the sides of yourself, no matter how normal or boring, or maybe even a little bit freaky—or, as the case may be, no matter how cocky or arrogant or emotionally disconnected or, possibly, just a little bit sad. But, anyway, if a person can't find love on his own, who can blame him for plunking down his hard-earned savings for a shot at finding it through any means possible—or, at least, for a shot at experiencing a little excitement for once?

After appropriately logging the details of my surveillance onto my intake report, I pull out my phone. I've got a text from Kat asking if I feel better about the whole Jonas situation today. I was upset yesterday, but I'm fine now. It's time to move on. I text her that I'm good, followed by a string of winking emojis to emphasize the point.

Just as I'm about to put my phone down, it rings with an incoming call. I don't recognize the number. I usually let unknown calls go into my voicemail, but what the heck, I'm sitting here with a few minutes to burn before I jump back into my torts outline.

"Hello?" I answer.

There's an audible exhale of breath on the other end of the line. "Sarah?"

I'm suddenly uneasy. "Who's calling, please?" Why is my stomach doing cartwheels?

"It's Jonas."

I inhale a sharp breath, but I can't speak.

"Jonas Faraday," he clarifies.

I still can't speak. His voice is masculine. Sexy. It sends tingles up my spine and back down again.

"Are you there?"

"How did you get my number?" I'm suddenly panicked. Did he get my contact information from The Club? Did he tell them about me?

"I figured out you're a law student at U Dub." He clears his throat. "So I hacked into the university's server to find you."

I'm speechless. Did he just say he hacked into U Dub's server to find me?

"I had to find you, Sarah. I had to talk to you. I'm going crazy." His voice is low, intense.

There's a long pause. He's waiting for me to say something.

"You didn't get my number from The Club?"

"No, of course not." He sounds offended. "I would never contact The Club about you." Yeah, definitely offended. "I told you I wouldn't."

I can't believe what I'm hearing. I can't believe he called me. I can't believe he found me. And he hacked into a major university's computer system to do it? I'm silent for a minute, trying to process the fact that I'm talking to Jonas Faraday right now—that he *tracked me down*. I'm ashamed to admit it, but my body's beginning to react to his voice exactly the way it did to his application.

"Sarah, I have to see you—"

"How'd you figure out I'm a law student at U Dub? I didn't tell you anything except my first name." My mind is racing. What did I tell him? My first name and age, and that's it. How did he find me? I can't for the life of me understand how he's calling me right now.

He explains the deductions and conclusions and clues in my email that led him to this very moment. I'm impressed. Electrified, really. He loves my sense of humor, he says. He calls me "smart" like four times. And, wow, he's pretty fixated on my olive skin tone. Hearing him go bananas about my skin makes it zip and zap like a live wire. If he likes my skin, then maybe he'll like the rest of me, too. But, wait, hold on. It's suddenly occurring to me he hasn't complimented my looks, other than my skin. So, overall, he must have been disappointed by whatever photo he saw. I mean, isn't a guy saying, "You've got gorgeous skin" sort of like saying, "You've got a great personality?"

"So you find my *skin* attractive, huh?" I ask.

"Yeah," he says. "And now I can add your voice to the list, too. It's so sexy. I love that little edge in it. I was already dying to know what you look like, but now I'm losing my mind."

Hold up. He's never seen me? No, surely, he just means he hasn't seen me in person. "You mean you want to know if I look like my picture?" I wish I knew what photo he has of me.

He pauses and my stomach drops. Why is he pausing?

"Did you see the photo on my student ID?" I ask. "Because when that photo was taken, I'd just gotten back from the gym and I wasn't wearing any makeup—"

"No, no. I've never seen your photo."

My face flushes. He's never seen my photo? He hunted me down and called me—and has been going on and on about how attractive he finds me—and he has no idea at all what I look like? "Oh." I don't even know what to say. "Why did you pause before answering?"

He sighs. "Because I want to see you more than I want to breathe. And I had to get control of myself before speaking. I'm feeling pretty intense right now. I don't want to scare you off."

The floor drops out from under me. A throbbing in my panties announces itself. "Are you telling me the truth, Jonas?" I whisper.

"Say that again," he whispers back.

I know exactly what he wants. "Jonas," I say. And when I do, the pulsing between my legs becomes more insistent.

He lets out a shaky breath. There's another long pause. I can feel the electricity of his arousal on his end of the line. "Yes, I'm telling you the truth. I'll always tell you the truth, Sarah."

Well, that breaks the spell. I laugh. "Seeing as how your 'relationships' last two to seven hours max, depending on Your Holiness's mood on a particular day, your promise to 'always' tell me the truth isn't all that impressive a commitment."

He huffs. "Wow." By the tone of his voice, I know I've broken the spell for him, too.

"Yeah, well," I huff right back. What did he expect from me? I just saw him drooling over Miss Purple last night.

"You don't like me very much."

"I don't even know you."

"Yeah, you do." He pauses. His voice is surprisingly wounded. "You know you do."

My heart leaps.

Damn. I know I'm supposed to be all "righteous indignation" in response, maybe laugh at him or read him the riot act, maybe make him chase me and try to convince me, and all that other stuff I've been conditioned to think is the normal reaction of a sane, rule abiding, self-respecting woman—but suddenly, I don't feel like a sane, rule abiding, self-respecting woman. And I certainly don't feel like saying anything that's not one hundred percent honest.

"Yeah, I know you," I concede. I don't know why I understand this man, but I do. I just get him. And I want him, despite myself. "I'm sorry," I say. "I'm being a bitch."

He lets out a huge burst of air, like he'd been holding his breath.

"I'm coming to pick you up right now. I can't wait another minute to see you."

That pisses me off. "Yeah, okay, let's see, we can 'fuck' for— what?—about an hour?—does that work with your schedule?— because after that I've got to study, and you've probably got to go screw yet another hot brunette wearing a purple bracelet."

"Oh my God!" he shouts with glee. "I knew it!" He's effusive.

Did he not just hear a word I said? I just ripped him a new one— did he not hear that?

He chuckles. "That *was* you behind that menu yesterday! I knew it." He's thrilled. "Oh my God."

Oops. Oh, damn.

"You couldn't stay away." His voice is pure elation.

I can't speak. Shoot.

"You just couldn't stay away," he says again. He's utterly thrilled.

I'm silent. Pissed.

"I knew that was you. Just from the little patches of skin I saw on the photos you sent me." He sighs with delight. "I'm just that good."

"Fine, yes, it was me. Curiosity got the best of me. But then I saw you drooling over Miss Purple at the bar and I felt physically ill. No, actually, I felt like a piece of trash. Believe me, I think I'll be able to 'stay away' from now on."

His tone shifts to panic. "Oh man, we are so not on the same page here. You've got to let me explain something to you—"

"There's nothing to explain. You've paid two hundred fifty thousand dollars to have sex with a different woman wearing a purple bracelet every night of your life for the next year, and by God, that's what you're gonna do. I get it. Please, feel free—enjoy yourself—but leave me the hell off the roster—"

"Sarah, could you please let me get a word in edgewise here?"

I huff into the phone.

"Please? I know you're angry and confused right now—"

"I'm not angry or confused." The minute the words come out, I know they're not entirely accurate. "Okay, wait, yes, I'm angry. In fact, I'm really, really angry. But I'm not confused. At all. I'm pretty clear on everything—"

"No, wait, listen, you have no fucking idea what's going on—"

"I have no fucking idea?"

He sighs. "Correct. You have no fucking idea."

"I've read your application. And I saw you in action last night with Miss Purple. What more is there to understand?"

"If I gave a shit about The Club, then why the hell did I track you down? Why the hell am I calling you right now?"

"Because I'm Mount Everest, plain and simple—and you, Mr. Faraday, are an avid climber."

He lets out an exasperated noise. "I don't even know what you look like and all I've been able to think about is finding you, touching you, hearing your voice. I've been going out of my mind for you, Sarah. And then I finally find you and—"

"You sure didn't look like you were going out of your mind for me last night."

"I was going out of my mind for you *especially* last night."

"Really?" I chuckle. "Was that before, during, or after you fucked Miss Purple?"

He pauses. "Yes. All of the above. But especially during." His voice is soft but impassioned.

I laugh heartily. Spitefully. He wants me to believe he was losing his mind over me while having sex with another woman? Is that supposed to make me feel all mushy inside? Or turn me on? Even if it turns out I like things a bit naughtier than I realized (as I'm recently learning, thanks to His Supreme Holiness), I'm not effing deranged.

"Listen, it's not easy to explain." He sighs. "And not over the phone. But, goddammit, please, please, please, just let me see you. Just let me talk to you in person."

"Why? Talking is just 'prelude,' right? Right along with eating or laughing or going to a concert or doing just about anything that isn't 'fucking.' It's all one long, drawn-out 'prelude' to you becoming 'God.'"

He makes that exasperated noise again. "This is so fucked up. There is no other circumstance where you'd know all of that. This is . . ." He grunts with frustration. "This is so fucked up."

I don't say anything. He's right. There's no other circumstance where I'd know every single one of Jonas Faraday's twisted thoughts before he's had a chance to dazzle me with his smile and perfect abs. I smirk. It must be killing him that I know what I know. And thank God I do. Otherwise, I'd be in for a heart-shattering ride, I'm sure.

"Would you please just let me take you to coffee? Or dinner? I just want to talk to you."

"Why go through the motions of Valentine's Day bullshit, when I know you'd hate every minute of it?"

He grunts. I don't know what that sound means. "This is so fucked up," he mumbles again.

"And anyway, it'd be hard to have a normal conversation with you, knowing all the while you just want to 'fuck me in the bathroom,' anyway."

There's a long pause. He's not talking.

"Hello?" I say. "Are you still there?"

He lets out a shaky breath. "God, you're everything I thought you'd be." He swallows hard. "I want you so bad," he finally says.

That's not what I expected him to say. His words hit me right between the legs. "So," I huff, but there's no conviction in my tone—only sudden arousal. What just happened? "So I'm right—about the bathroom thing?" I can barely get the words out. I'm not sure if I want him to admit it or deny it.

"Halfway right. Yes, I absolutely want to fuck you. More than I've ever wanted to fuck any woman in my entire life. But not in a bathroom. In my bed. Nice and slow."

He lets that hang in the air for a second.

The throbbing between my legs is becoming insistent.

"When I finally get to fuck you, it's going to be in my bed where I can take my time, where I can see your gorgeous skin against my crisp white sheets." He lets out a ragged sigh. Oh, wow, he's really turned on. "But that's not why I called. I just want to see you," he continues. "And talk to you. I have so much to tell you, but I can't say it all in a telephone call. I mean, yes, of course, I want to do more than talk to you, much more, but if you let me see you tonight, I'll be happy to get to touch any part of your skin—any part at all—your hand, your arm, your face. Whatever you'll let me touch. Your ear. Your toe." I can hear him smiling. "Your elbow."

I'm on fire. He's ignited something inside me I didn't know existed. These are not the words I expected to come out of Jonas Faraday. Especially not directed at me.

"Sarah?"

"Did you fuck Miss Purple last night?" My tone is even.

"Yeah," he says gruffly, without hesitation.

"That was an odd thing to do if you supposedly wanted me, don't you think?"

My question is rhetorical—meant as a cynical, mocking barb. But he surprises me by answering in earnest.

"Not odd at all. You deleted your email account and wrote me that handwritten note, basically telling me to fuck off. So I decided to make myself stop wanting you the only way I knew how. I paid for that stupid membership; might as well use it, right? And then, it serves me right, the whole thing with Miss Purple turned into the biggest cluster fuck—the worst sex of my life. Totally backfired. Being with her just made me want you more." He exhales again. "So much more."

I'm breathless. I didn't expect any of that.

I know I'm supposed to be appalled and offended and skeptical, and I'm probably supposed to hurl some angry or snarky comment at him, cutting him down to size and lashing out at him for being sick and twisted. Maybe I'm supposed to say something simple and sarcastic like, "Oh, how sweet." But the truth is, I *do* think what he's said is sweet. He's never even laid eyes on me, and he spent last night screwing an incredibly hot woman and wishing she were *me*? Maybe someone else wouldn't understand—maybe someone else would judge me harshly for what I'm about to say—but I don't care what anyone else thinks. I know I just got the equivalent of a Hallmark card from Jonas Faraday—and it makes me want him. It makes me want him bad.

I unzip my jeans and let my hand wander in.

"Did you make her come?" I ask, arousal seeping into my tone.

He pauses a long time, considering. I'm sure he's wondering if this is a trap.

"Did you make her come?" I ask again. This time, there's no doubt I'm totally turned on.

He inhales sharply, obviously realizing I'm blazing hot. "No." His answer hangs in the air for a long time. "She faked it," he finally adds. "Just like you said."

After what he said in his application, I know how much her faking it must have upset him, but I'm selfishly glad she did. My fingers continue their exploration. "I'm touching myself, Jonas," I say.

I can hear him trembling across the phone line. "Sarah," he whispers.

"Did you go down on her?" I ask. I should be disgusted. Outraged. Hurt. But I'm not. Far from it. My fingers find their target. I moan. "Touch yourself, Jonas, touch yourself and tell me if you licked her," I say.

His breathing hitches sharply. "I started to, but the second my tongue touched her, I couldn't do it." He groans. "I was repulsed."

I should express utter indignation. I should call him a man-slut and hang up on him. I should say something about him being a pig. But instead, I fondle myself with even more enthusiasm. He was *repulsed* going down on that incredibly hot woman? "Tell me, Jonas."

As if reading my mind, he instantly adds, "Because she wasn't you." His voice is hoarse. I know he's handling himself roughly.

"More," I say. I can't for the life of me understand why I'm so turned on right now, but hearing him say he went down on that ridiculously good looking woman and wished she were me is the hottest thing I've ever heard. My hand is becoming insistent inside my jeans. "Touch yourself and tell me more," I insist. Oh God, my head is spinning. "Touch yourself, Jonas."

He tries to catch his breath. "I started in on her with my tongue ... and she started moaning and groaning and thrashing around right away." His voice has taken on a tone I haven't heard from him. It's guttural. "She said I was 'amazing.'"

A deep-throated chuckle escapes my throat. I can hear him smiling on the other end of the line in reply.

"Your laugh is sexy," he whispers.

"What was her name?" I ask.

"Stacy," he spits out.

"Stacy the Faker."

"Stacy the Faker," he repeats quietly. "I wanted her name to be Sarah."

My hand is getting pretty good at this. I moan. "What happened next, Jonas?" My heart is racing.

"I was down there for twenty seconds, practically gagging the whole time, and she acted like I was the second coming of Christ."

I lick my lips. "So what'd you do?" I begin sliding my fingers in and out of my wetness with surprising skill. I'm getting better and better at this.

"Oh, Sarah," He groans. "I love your voice."

"Tell me," I say. "Tell me, Jonas."

"You're driving me crazy. Let me come see you right now. I didn't call you to—"

"Tell me," I say, and my tone leaves little room for argument. My fingers are finding ways to give myself pleasure I've never discovered before. I'm frantic.

"I fucked her."

The words send a shiver down my spine. My breathing hitches.

"I closed my eyes and imagined she was you, and I fucked her. Hard. I didn't care if she came—I didn't want her to come. All I cared about was fucking her and imagining she was you." He lets out an animalistic sound that makes me want to leap through the phone and straddle him.

"Tell me how you imagined she was me."

"I imagined she was the woman behind the menu—I imagined you were the woman behind the menu."

I'm flabbergasted. How the hell did he make that connection? I was tucked away in the corner of a crowded bar, my face hidden. Why did he even notice me in that bar, let alone make the connection? "Why?"

He doesn't answer. I can tell he's busy on the other end of the call.

"Jonas," I whisper. "Tell me."

"Your skin, Sarah." His voice halts, like his pleasure just escalated on his end. "Your hair. Your hands. That ring on your thumb." He lets out a low groan. "Oh my God, that ring."

"You like that?"

"Oh, yeah," he moans. "I like that. And your big brown eyes over the top of the menu, glaring at me. You were so pissed at me. I liked it."

My hand is frantic now. I touch my thumb ring with my index finger and imagine he's the one touching it. If he were here right now, I'd take him into me and ride him as deeply as my body could manage. "What else did you imagine?"

"Your breasts. I imagined licking your nipples and making them hard." He moans again.

"What about my face?" The hair on my neck is standing up.

"I don't know," he mumbles. "It doesn't matter. Whatever you look like, I want you."

I am so aroused I'm almost in pain. "I'm so wet," I whisper. The nerve endings between my legs are frantic for him. I throw my head back and moan into the phone.

I hear him come on the other end of the call. It's an unmistakable sound. Wow, it's a total turn-on. Oh God, he makes me feel wild, like

I can say or do anything, no matter how depraved. I feel like such a bad, bad girl with him. And I like it.

My fingers continue their assault on myself. I want to join him in his climax so badly, and I've never been so hot in all my life. Maybe this is finally the moment, right here, right now, with him. Maybe discovering this bad girl inside me is what I've needed all along to finally let go, to finally let it happen . . .

I keep trying, insistently.

But after a moment, I realize it's not going to happen, no matter how crazy-aroused I am. It's just not going to happen. As usual.

And if not now, then probably never.

I pull my hand out of my pants.

He's quiet on the other end of the line.

There's a long pause.

That was the hottest thing I've ever experienced in my entire life, and I still didn't come. I'm hopeless. If I couldn't let go and let my deepest desires overtake me when I was having dirty phone sex with an outrageously sexy man who hacked into U Dub's server to find me, when I was feeling tingles and waves of pleasure I've never felt before, when his husky voice described fucking another woman and imagining she was me, sight unseen, then I'm obviously never going to get off.

I just have to face it.

And that's not good. In fact, when it comes to Jonas Faraday, it's a frickin' disaster. Getting women off is all this man cares about. If I can't get off, then what can I offer him? Frustration and disappointment. For both of us. Plus, quite possibly, a little heartbreak, too, at least on my end.

This is a no-win situation for me, I suddenly realize. If I never come with him (most likely outcome), he'll move along quickly to someone who will. And if I *do* eventually come—glory be!—he'll move along quickly then, too, just like he said he would on his application. Either way, this story ends with him moving along quickly—whether I want him to or not.

He's been honest about his disdain for messy female emotions—but I'm not sure my heart is capable of distinguishing the feelings he invokes in me from my perhaps naïve but sincere belief in love and hope and meaningful human connection. I don't need weekend trips to IKEA, mind you—I've got a whole lot of living to do before I start picking out end tables with anyone—but I certainly don't want to knowingly enter into some kind of meaningless fuckfest with a man who tells me right from the start he's going to toss me into the trash right after he gets what he wants. (Or doesn't, as the case may be.)

My high has crashed down around my ears. My brain has elbowed its way to the front of this parade, past my heart, way past my crotch, and taken over.

Jonas Faraday is a climber. And, yes, right now, he's climbing me—which of course feels pretty damned good. Intoxicating, like a drug. But I've got to get off the drug. For my own sanity. Once he's had me and gone on to tomorrow's purple-bracelet-wearing hottie, I'll be left in a state of pathetic withdrawal, like a junkie in a back alley hankering for my next fix—and wishing to God I'd never taken that first hit of Jonas Faraday in the first place. I might think I'm ready to give free reign to the bad girl I've recently discovered inside of me, but the good girl who's been in charge a helluva lot longer knows that even one hit of this addictive man will probably lead to irreversible, regrettable, heartbreaking pain. If not brain damage. And it's just not worth it. Look at what he's already done to me! For the love of God, I just masturbated to him telling me how he licked and screwed another woman last night. What's happening to me? I'm becoming just as sick and twisted as he is. Why, oh why does he make me so crazy?

I sigh. I'm resigned. "Did you come?" I ask him. My tone is matter-of-fact, though my intention is cruel.

I hear him smile. He sighs. "Mmm. I couldn't help myself. I've wanted to hear your voice for so long. You've got that little bit of gravel in your voice—"

"Well, I didn't."

There's a long pause as he figures out what to say. "Shit," he finally says, reality dawning on him. "I'm so sorry." His distress is palpable. "Sarah—"

"No need to be sorry. That's just the way it is with me, like I've been telling you."

"I'm sorry. I didn't call you with the intention of—"

"Don't apologize. You've been clear about what you want, and I can't give it to you. The reality of me just doesn't live up to the fantasy, as it turns out."

"You're better than any fantasy." His voice breaks with sudden emotion.

"No."

"Why are you doing this? Tell me what's going on inside that beautiful head of yours right now."

"Beautiful head? You've never even seen my 'beautiful head.'"

"I'll come over right now and fix that."

"What's the point?"

"Why are you doing this?"

"I'm not doing anything."

He doesn't say anything.

"I've got a lot of studying to do," I finally say.

He remains quiet.

"So, I'm gonna go."

"Why are you withdrawing all of a sudden? You don't have to do that. Just let me come see you. If you'd just talk to me in person, I know—"

"What's the point? Don't you see? What just happened is a gigantic metaphor—a metaphor for how it would be for you and me. Neither of us satisfied in the end."

"What do you mean?"

I don't answer him. I can't figure out how to explain what I'm feeling.

His voice suddenly flashes acute anger. "Oh, I get it. Not enough upside for you, huh?" He lets out an angry blast of air.

I pause, giving the matter due consideration. Well, that's one way to put it.

"Correct," I say evenly. "Honestly, when it comes to you, I don't see any upside at all."

Chapter 11
Jonas

I blew it. I fucking blew it. I'm such an idiot. She already thinks I'm chasing her with my dick and nothing else, and I just proved her point in spades. Fuck! I didn't call her intending to have phone sex with her! I actually wanted to *talk* to her—to tell her I can't stop thinking about her, that I've been going fucking crazy over her, to tell her she kicks my ass and I love it, that I moved mountains to find her, sight unseen, because she's worth it. I even wanted to tell her she's made me start to rethink a few things, that I might even have been wrong about a thing or two, and that's a hard thing for me to admit to anyone. I wanted to tell her I want to make her come more than words can say—*and I haven't even seen her yet*. So what does that say? It says she's driven me goddamned crazy, that's what. And then, despite all my good intentions, I just went right ahead and jacked the fuck off on our phone call—exactly what she would have expected me to do—and left her hanging out to dry with her hand in her own ice-cold pants, feeling like a cheap phone operator at 1-877-SEXTALK.

Why didn't I stop and *think* before I reached down and started jerking off like a jackass? This is a girl who's never, ever had an orgasm in her entire life. Why can't I get that through my thick head? I can't assume anything. I have to handle her with kid gloves so she doesn't freak out and get all up inside her own overthinking head and start getting some kind of complex about not being able to "give me what I need." If she would just trust me, learn to let go and trust me, I know I could deliver her to Nirvana. I know I could. But she doesn't know that—and that's the point. I can't even begin to understand how it must screw with her mind to have sex, time after time, without coming even once—to not even believe there's a *possibility* of

94

coming. I can't even fathom it. I mean, I've never had sex and *not* gotten off. Ever. Literally. Not even with fucking Stacy the Faker.

So what is sex all about for a woman like that? It's all about getting the guy off, right? Getting him off gets her off, I'm sure—but that can only take her so far for so long when there's no payoff for her at the end of it all, time after time. I mean, yes, I love making a woman come, but isn't that because, ultimately, it makes me come so hard I almost pass out? Huh. What if making a woman come was all there ever was for me, and it never led to my own satisfaction, ever? Huh. Something to think about. That puts things in a whole new perspective.

Who are these guys she's been with in the past, for Chrissakes? Do they not even *notice* she's not getting off—or do they just not care? Or does she fake it so well they don't know the difference? And didn't I used to be just like them, not too long ago? I have a pit in my stomach. Yeah, I was. I most definitely was. Hell, maybe I still am. Shit. It's suddenly hitting me like a ton of bricks. I'm no different than any of the guys she's been with. I just proved that in spades on the phone. Damn. I never should have jerked myself off—I should have kept my hand out of my pants and just *talked* to her.

But, hang on a second, she *told* me to touch myself, she *wanted* me to do it—oh God—her gravelly voice when she said, "Touch yourself and tell me how you licked her" was so hot, *so fucking hot,* how was I supposed to resist? No mortal man could have resisted. It was the most incredible thing a woman's ever said to me, hands down. Oh God, it brought me to my knees.

But I should have resisted, no matter how impossible. I should have had the presence of mind to say, "What's the rush? Let's just talk. Let me take you out for coffee." But when she ordered me to touch myself in that gravelly voice of hers—when she was *turned on* by the idea of me licking another woman's pussy and wishing it was hers—when she asked me for details about it and started moaning and saying my name as I told her—it was so hot, I almost came right then and there. I just couldn't believe what I was hearing, couldn't believe how hot she made me, couldn't believe she *understood* what I was trying to explain to her. She didn't pull the predictable "shocked and indignant" bullshit reaction on me. Nope. She understood what I was trying to tell her; it turned her on, and she admitted it.

Epic.

No one would even believe me if I told them what just happened (which, of course, I'd never do). I can barely believe it myself. When she told me to touch myself and tell her everything, that was when I knew this woman gets me like nobody ever has.

And now I've blown it. Was that one orgasm *during a fucking phone call* worth it, Jonas? Fuck! I never would have guessed I could lose control of myself so completely. I don't understand why she affects me like this. She thinks there's no upside to me, and I just proved it. Never mind I let a wire transfer for a quarter-million dollars go through just so she wouldn't lose her part-time desk job. *When it comes to you, I don't see any upside at all,* she said. None at all?

Well, what the fuck does she expect from me? I've never even laid eyes on this woman. What am I supposed to do—profess my undying love to her? Ride in on a white horse and swoop her up into my saddle and ride off into the sunset? Send her roses and candy and Hallmark cards? Hey, how about a teddy bear, too? That's such total and complete bullshit, all of it. Even if I were "normal," even if I were brainwashed into believing in happily ever afters like the rest of world, I wouldn't be able to make her any promises. Even normal people go out on a date or two or three before they run off to elope in Las Vegas, don't they? For Christ's sake, am I supposed to swear she's my soul mate—wear a vial of her blood around my neck—before she'll grab a cup of coffee with me?

I mean, yes, of course, I don't want to just grab coffee with her—I'm not saying that—yes, of course, I want to take her to my bed and lay her down on my white sheets and lick every inch of her olive skin and suck her hard nipples and kiss her everywhere and bury my face between her legs and look up and see her big brown eyes looking back at me and fuck her 'til she's screaming my name. Yes, of course, I want to do all that. But to get to do all that, I'm supposed to sign some contract that I'll never make one wrong move? That I'll never be an asshole? That I'll never hurt her feelings? Well, I can't guarantee that. Who can? Can normal people guarantee that? I don't think so.

What the fuck does she want from me? I've already hacked into a major university's server to find her, and it wasn't cheap. I called her sight unseen and poured my heart out to her. I knew full well a normal woman would bolt when I told her about fucking Stacy, and I told her anyway—because I promised to tell her the truth, no matter what. Fuck, I've already told her more than I've ever told any other woman, ever—which, by the way, she's using against me in the most fucked up way, considering how she acquired the information. And, worst of all, thanks to her, I've already gagged and quite sloppily banged my way through fucking a very hot woman, all the while thinking of her. What more does she want?

I'm done.

She doesn't want me? There's no upside when it comes to me?

Fine.

Guess what? There's no upside to *her*. That woman has been all downside from day one. I was happy before she replied to my note. I was looking forward to my membership in The Club. I was ready to have the best year of my life in that stupid club. She doesn't want me? Fine. I can have any woman I want—other than *her*, apparently—so I guess it's time for me to get out there and fuck them all. I've spent two hundred fifty thousand dollars on my Club membership, this supposedly mind-blowing, best-money-I-ever-spent-in-my-life-hands-down membership, so I'm going to start getting the most out of it. Or, hell, I could just go down to Whole Foods right now, crook my finger at that cashier with the piercings, and she'd come running to my bed like I was pulling her on a fucking string.

Fuck!

I get up and pace around my room like a leopard.

No upside.

Fuck.

I want her. Not whoever's next in the purple parade. Not the girl with the piercings at Whole Foods. I want *Sarah*.

Fuck.

I don't give two shits about The Club right now.

How am I supposed to know if I'd want to spend more than two to seven hours with her, anyway? I've never even *seen* her. Can she honestly expect me to know how much time I'm willing to give her, sight unseen? Yes, she turns me on now, of course, but *seeing* her might make a difference. A huge difference. All I've seen of her are pieces of a jigsaw puzzle—a breast, a nipple, a thigh. Some hair over

97

the top of a menu. Smooth olive skin. Big brown eyes. Beautiful, soul-stirring, brown eyes. A ring on her thumb. That voice.

I close my eyes. Shit. I just gave myself a woody.

I'm losing control of myself. No, I've already lost it. It's long gone. Joining The Club in the first place—for a fucking year, no less!— proved it. What was I thinking? I can't act on every single urge and whim. I need to reel it back in, take control.

From now on, I'll focus on two things: climbing and work. Yeah, Josh and I will climb Mount Everest next year when they reopen it. I know we said we'd do a bunch of other mountains first, but why wait? We can use this coming year to train like madmen. I'll put my head down and train and get in the best shape of my life. And I'll refocus on work, too. There's plenty of it. Business is through the roof.

When I need the kind of relaxation only a beautiful woman can bring, I'll check in on my Club app and meet some lonely, all-too willing Purple. No feelings involved. Especially not mine. But I won't do it every day. It won't be an addiction. I'll just do it occasionally, when I need to blow off steam. And by the time the year has passed, I'll be standing on top of the world, at the pinnacle of Mount Everest, as close to God as a human can get while still standing on planet earth—and, by then, I will have forgotten all about her.

Yes. That's the plan. And it's a good one.

I sit down at my desk and open my laptop. I've got a mountain of acquisition prospect reports to analyze and emails to send out. It's time to get back to work and get over myself. And get over her. I've never even seen her, for fuck's sake, it shouldn't be hard to forget her.

I've barreled through two acquisition reports in ninety minutes and sent out at least fifteen emails to my uncle in New York and Josh in L.A. and various members of my team here in Seattle regarding some due diligence action items. Being productive is calming me down. With each passing minute, I like my plan of action for the next year more and more. Train for Mount Everest, fuck purples in The Club, as needed (no feelings involved), climb to the tippy-top of the world, forget she ever existed. Everything back to normal.

It's foolproof.

I'm about to start on a third acquisition prospect report when my cell rings with a call from Josh.

"Hey," I answer, and launch right in as if we've already been talking for ten minutes. "I'm thinking we climb Everest next year. I know we projected ten years, but I don't want to wait." It's pretty much how phone calls with Josh always go—we don't have individualized conversations so much as one continuous conversation that's sporadically interrupted by life.

"Whoa, slow down, high-speed. What happened to us climbing Kilimanjaro next year? And K2 after that?"

"Scratch all that. Everest is the highest. Why bother with anything else?"

"Um, because we both agreed we need more experience before we tackle Everest. What's going on?"

I grunt, but I don't answer him.

"Jonas, you're freaking me out. *I'm* the reckless one. You're the look-before-you-leap twin. Stop trying to steal my thing."

There's another brief silence.

"You do realize *I* called *you*, right?" Josh finally says. "You don't even want to know why?"

"The EBITDA on the Jackson deal? I just emailed you about it."

"No, dummy, why would I call you about that? I don't give a shit about the EBITDA on the Jackson deal. No, bro, I got the photos." I can hear his shit-eating grin across the phone line. "I wanted to make sure you check your email."

My breath stops short. "I've been working."

"Do you know for sure which of the Sarahs is yours yet?"

I pause. I don't want to talk about her. "Cruz," I finally mutter.

Josh hoots like I just gave the right answer on *Jeopardy*.

"But she's not *my* Sarah, as it turns out."

"What?"

"I just talked to her."

"You *talked* to her? What the fuck! When were you planning to tell me this little nugget—"

"She's not interested in me. Doesn't even want to meet me for coffee."

He pauses. "You hacked into U Dub's server to find her, without

99

knowing what she looks like, and she's *not interested*? How the hell did you fuck that up? Is she married or something?"

"No, she's just not interested."

"I can't ... She knows you hacked into U Dub's server to find her, right?"

"Yeah."

"And she didn't go all weak in the knees over that?"

I'm silent.

"Well, has she *seen* you, at least? I mean, does she know what you look like?"

"Yeah."

"Really? Wow." He pauses, considering. "I'm shocked." He sighs. "Oh man, that sucks. Wow." He exhales loudly, totally deflated. "I was kind of excited for you—especially after seeing her picture. I was really hoping your Sarah was gonna be Cruz."

"You saw her photo?" My heart's suddenly racing, despite myself.

"Yeah, and she's—"

"No, don't tell me. Please. If she looks good, I'll just be even more bummed. And if she's the Bride of Frankenstein, I don't want to know that, either. I'd rather hold onto the fantasy I've created in my head."

"Bro."

There's a long pause. With just that word, he's chastising me—telling me I'm an idiot. I don't reply.

"Check your email," he says slowly, condescendingly.

I grunt.

"Bro."

I'm dying of curiosity, I must admit.

"Trust me."

My stomach is lurching. "Really?"

"Really."

"Really good or really bad?"

"Really, really, really good."

Holy shit, she's a knockout. I can't stop staring at her. It's just a snapshot for her school I.D. and she looks like a fucking model. Her dark hair is swept back into a ponytail and she's not wearing a stitch of makeup (the way I prefer most women, actually), and she's still an absolute head turner—distinctive, not a cookie-cutter beauty, by any means, faintly exotic—but fucking gorgeous. She'd definitely stand out in any crowd. There's something about her face—the way her features all come together—she slays me. Her eyes are the best part. They're big and brown and brimming with intelligence and humor and warmth and take-no-bullshit confidence. There's depth in those eyes. But, wow, her lips are a close second. Good God, I keep thinking of those lips moaning and saying my name and asking me about how I fucked Stacy—and all with that gravelly voice of hers, too.

Damn, what a fantastic surprise this is. It's Christmas morning right now. And to think I'd been bracing myself for disappointment—priming myself not to be overly critical when I saw her, telling myself I'd have to find one particularly attractive feature and focus on that to the exclusion of the not-so-great parts. But there's not a single not-so-great part. Especially when I look at her features all put together. If I didn't even know her, I'd beeline right to her in a bar. She's gorgeous.

Now that I know what she looks like, what just happened on the phone is even more catastrophic. If I'd only known she looked like this, I wouldn't have called. I would have gone straight over to her apartment and beaten down her door and made her talk to me. And then what might have happened? She wouldn't have been able to turn me down then.

But I couldn't wait to call her, could I? I just *had* to pick up the phone and call her, sight unseen. I thought calling her without seeing her first was some kind of proof of my good faith—some kind of romantic gesture of my unconditional attraction to her. I figured she'd get all swoony about it. Man, I calculated all wrong.

If I'd just waited 'til seeing this picture, I would have handled things differently. I wouldn't have let her take control of the situation like I did. I would have been in charge. She wouldn't have rejected me if I'd showed up on her doorstep, that's for sure. No woman has ever been able to resist me when I bring my A game. Damn, I should have brought my A game—but, instead, I brought my dick. I didn't even call her to talk dirty to her, I really didn't. And what did I do? I had phone sex with her. Why couldn't I control myself and talk to her like a lady and keep my pecker in my pants?

Lauren Rowe

I blew it.

And now I'm drowning in regret.

She's stunning.

I should have known my gut is always right when it comes to women. I could sniff out a hot woman blindfolded—and, actually, that's exactly what I did, come to think about it—I sniffed her out blindfolded.

Yeah, this is a game changer.

She doesn't get to dictate what happens between us anymore. I'm taking charge now. She's not interested in rolling the dice with me? She doesn't think there's enough *upside* to me?

Fuck that shit.

I'm done being a pussy-ass, sentimental whiner. I'm done begging her to pretty-please give me the time of day. I want her and I'm going to have her and that's all there is to it. Sarah Cruz is about to learn one of the immutable laws of nature, a principle as immovable and unavoidable as the theory of relativity or Boyle's law of gases or motherfucking gravity. It's called Faraday's law of attraction and it goes a little something like this: When Jonas Faraday wants a particular woman, Jonas Faraday shall have her. And in this particular instance, Jonas Faraday wants the magnificent Sarah Cruz. End of fucking story.

Chapter 12
Sarah

"But *why*?" Kat asks. "I mean, jeez, he went to all that trouble to find you, and you won't even go out to dinner with the guy?"

We're sitting at my little kitchen table eating Pasta Roni and Caesar salad for lunch after coming back from a yoga class.

I sigh. "It's complicated," I say.

"Even if he turns out to be a douchebag, worst case scenario you could just sit there and look at him and still have a spectacularly good time. Oh, and a free meal."

"We're fundamentally incompatible," I say evenly.

"But how do you know that if you won't even meet him?"

"Because I know," I say.

"So you say. I wish you'd tell me what he said in his damned application that's got you all aflutter." She turns her head and glances at me sideways. "Is he some kind of freak?" She winks.

I roll my eyes. "You know all that stuff is confidential." I lower my voice. "But no."

"He's into S and M, isn't he?"

"I can't talk about it—but no. We're just not compatible on a basic level, personality-wise, goal-wise, so it's pointless to subject myself to disappointment and maybe even heartbreak."

"But what if you're the *one* girl in the *whole* world who can change him?" She smirks.

I know she's kidding—mocking that clichéd impulse that attracts every girl to an irredeemable bad boy at least once in her life—but she's hit the nail on the head. That's exactly what I keep hoping I am—the one girl in the whole world who can change him. It's ludicrous. "Yeah. If he could just find The One, he'd be a changed man," I say, trying to keep my voice light and bright. But I don't feel light and bright. I feel miserable.

Kat laughs. "You're obviously obsessed with him. And he wouldn't have tracked you down like a big game hunter if he weren't at least slightly obsessed with you. So why not take him for a spin and at least *see* if you're more compatible than you think?"

"It's not as simple as test-driving a car—"

"Yes, it is. It's precisely as simple as test-driving a car. I say this with love, girl, but you make everything more complicated than it has to be. No offense."

"None taken." She's absolutely right. I hate that about myself. I sigh. "Maybe you're right. Maybe I should—"

There's a loud knock at my door.

Kat's eyes go wide. "Oh my God," she whispers. "I knew he wouldn't take no for an answer!"

My heart's in my throat. I'm wearing sweats and a T-shirt and no makeup right now. Oh my God, please, Lord, no. He wouldn't just show up at my house, unannounced, would he? Yes, he would. I know he would. That's exactly the kind of thing he'd do.

"I guess he's not letting you off the hook that easily, little Miss Over-thinker," Kat says, marching with glee to the front door.

I bolt to my bedroom like a mental patient escaping from a psych ward, trying frantically to think what clean clothes I have in my drawer that don't make me look like I'm dressed for a marathon study session. My heart's beating out of my chest and my pulse is raging in my ears. I can hear Kat opening the front door and greeting whoever's on the other side of it. I hold my breath, listening.

A male voice says, "Sarah Cruz?"

Oh God. This is disastrous. Worst case scenario. If he sees Kat first, he'll only be massively disappointed when I show my face and say, "Sorry. Sarah's me."

"No," Kat says, squealing. "But you've got the right place. I'll take those for her."

"There's more stuff in the truck, too. I'll be right back."

What the hell is going on? I march out of my bedroom back into the living area to find Kat standing before me with the most exquisite arrangement of roses I've ever seen—at least three dozen roses of every imaginable hue bursting out of an elegant crystal vase.

Kat laughs. "Looks like someone's not accustomed to being turned down."

Kat and I take stock of the various goodies littering my kitchen table. In addition to the six arrangements of outrageously beautiful flowers, there's a gigantic box of chocolates in a heart-shaped box tied up in a huge red bow (which Kat has already untied and dug into), a gigantic white teddy bear holding a red, heart-shaped pillow embroidered with the phrase "Be Mine," and, to top it all off, a sealed, pink envelope with my handwritten name across the front.

I stare at my treasure trove, unable to speak.

"Aren't you gonna open the envelope?" Kat asks, picking it up and handing it to me.

"Yeah, I'm"—I gesture toward my bedroom and begin walking quickly toward it—"just gonna read it in private."

Kat looks mildly disappointed, but she says, "Okeedoke."

In my room, I perch on the edge of my bed and stare at the sealed pink envelope in my shaking hands. I want to open it more than I want to breathe. But I'm nervous. If I know Jonas Faraday, the card will surely include words like "lick" and "come" and "fuck" and maybe even "clit," and I don't want to read those words right now, to be honest. I've got romantic visions of flowers and candy and teddy bears dancing in my head, and I don't want his unique form of "brutal honesty" to burst my bubble. Even if I know he's just making some sort of sardonic point with all this clichéd stuff, I can't help but enjoy the over-the-top romanticism of it all, even if he's only mocking traditional romance. Frankly, if all he's got to say to me at this point is "I want to make you come," I'm not in the mood to hear it.

I stare at the envelope in my hand. I feel so excited right now, so genuinely hopeful, I almost don't want to open the card and get let down. The odds are high that whatever's inside this card is going to ruin this moment—and the silly hopes that are rising up involuntarily inside me against my better judgment. I mean, no matter how cute that teddy bear is out there, we're still talking about Jonas Faraday, after all—and he's not a teddy bear kind of guy.

Well, there's only one way to find out what it says.

I take a deep breath and tear open the envelope.

It's a Hallmark card. I can't believe my eyes. It's a frickin'

Hallmark card, covered in pink and red hearts. The cover of the card says, "Happy Valentine's Day" in swirling gold letters. Where did he find this card in March?

The inside of the card is imprinted with a stock message that makes me gasp: *You are everything I never knew I always wanted.* The message is followed by a handwritten letter "J."

This is the last thing I expected him to say. My mind is reeling. I don't even know what to think.

"Sarah!" Kat calls from the kitchen. "There's a note in the flowers!"

I rush out of my room into the kitchen, and she hands me a tiny envelope. I open it to find a handwritten notecard.

"My Magnificent Sarah,

"I hereby decree today to be Jonas and Sarah's Valentine's Day—and since I am God, thus it is so. A car will pick you up for our traditional Valentine's dinner at 8:00, and we will dine at a candlelit restaurant, out in public, like normal people do. At the end of our dinner, I will kiss you goodnight, if you'll let me, and nothing more— like normal people do—and then the car will take you directly home, without me in it. (Come on, Sarah, it's just dinner. You need to eat, right?)

"Truthfully yours, Jonas

"P.S. After we spoke yesterday, I saw your photo for the first time—hence the upgrade in your name from 'My Beautiful Sarah' to 'My Magnificent Sarah.' Damn, Sarah, you're absolutely gorgeous."

Holy frickin' moly. My cheeks are burning. My head is spinning. My knees are weak. What the hell is going on here? I can't make heads or tails of it. I know in my head that this entire charade is a big fat satire to him—some kind of nod to an alternate, surrealistic reality he's poking fun at somehow—and yet it's making me swoon nonetheless.

"What does it say?" Kat asks.

I wordlessly hand her the card, my mouth hanging open.

"Oh my," she says as her eyes scan the note. When she's done, she looks up at me, smiling from ear to ear. "Oh my," she says again. "My, my, my, my, my."

Chapter 13
Jonas

It took an outrageous chunk of change to rent out every table at Canlis for the entire night on such short notice. I had to agree to buy out their highest projected nightly revenue, times *five*, before they finally agreed to shut down the entire restaurant and cancel all dinner reservations (on the pretense of a possible gas leak). But what the hell—I've already thrown a quarter-million dollars down the toilet plus twenty thousand on hacking into the University of Washington's server—what's another thirty thousand for a dinner date? Tonight, I'll pay and do and say whatever I have to if it will make her understand I'm more than just a gigantic, throbbing hard-on.

I look at my watch. It's just past eight. Soon. Very soon. I'm jittery.

What if she refused to get into the limo when it pulled up in front of her apartment? What if she got my gifts and threw them into a dumpster, or smashed each and every crystal vase to the ground?

"Is everything as you wish, Mr. Faraday?" the owner of the restaurant asks me, gesturing to the twinkling white lights strung around the place at my request.

"It's perfect," I reply. "It looks very Valentine's Day-ish. Thank you." I look out the floor-to-ceiling window overlooking the city. "And the view is incredible."

"Seattle never disappoints."

I exhale. I'm way more nervous than I thought I'd be. There's no guarantee she's even heading here right now.

I sit down at the table the restaurant has prepared for us and stare out at the twinkling skyline. My knee is jiggling. I force it to stop.

My cell phone buzzes with an incoming text. I look at the display and smile. *"ETA 5 min,"* the text reads. I'd told the limo driver to text me when he was five minutes away. Looks like she got into the car. That's a start—an excellent start.

As I stand in the cold night air in front of the restaurant waiting for her limo to pull up, my senses are heightened, like I'm a jungle cat stalking my prey. It's going to take all my restraint not to pounce on her when she arrives.

The limo finally pulls up and I open her door, adrenaline flooding my entire body.

And there she is.

Damn.

Wow, her photo didn't even begin to do her justice.

Some sort of primal hunting instinct is threatening to overtake me. I want to tackle her and ravage her right here and now. But, of course, that's not an option. I've got to make her understand I'm not all about fucking her. If that were all I wanted, I could get that in The Club. Somehow, I hold it together well enough to pretend to be a civilized human being, capable of normal conversation.

"Sarah," I breathe, holding my hand out to her. "Happy Valentine's Day."

She smiles up at me. Oh, those lips. They slayed me in her photo, but in person, they make me want to get down on my knees.

"Happy Valentine's Day, Jonas," she replies. Oh, that hint of gravel in her voice. Maintaining control over myself tonight is going to be a tall order.

She takes my extended hand.

Her skin is soft and warm. I look down at her hand in mine and see that damned thumb ring of hers, and that just about does me in. For a split second, I contemplate pushing her back into the limo, crawling on top of her, and running my hands over every inch of her. Instead, I bring her hand up to my mouth and gently kiss the top of it—and then, slowly, pointedly, I lay a gentle kiss right onto her thumb ring.

Her eyes blaze—she knows I'm already a goner. She smiles and slowly pulls her hand away from my mouth—but the expression on her face tells me she likes the feel of my lips as much as I like the feel of her skin. Just that simple exchange, and the air is sexually charged. Not good. I mean, it's *fucking awesome*, don't get me wrong—but tonight is supposed to be about everything *except* my insatiable hard-on for her. In fact, tonight is emphatically *not* about that. Tonight is about showing her she's not some phone sex operator to me. Tonight is about showing her I'm quite functional in ways that don't involve my tongue or dick. I've got to make her understand that what she knows about me, she's learned only thanks to a uniquely exposing circumstance—a situation unlike any other that, by its nature, compelled me to reveal the darkest, most primal parts of myself, parts I've never shown or talked about with anyone else. In real life, I swear, I'm really quite charming.

She needs to understand that, if you only look at my sexual appetites, out of context from other stuff about me that's actually kind of normal, you'd get a pretty warped view of me—which she undoubtedly has. Wouldn't that be true of anyone? I'm sure of it. I've got to show her that, despite my insatiable and seemingly uncontrollable desire for her, I really do possess some attributes that aren't even the least bit sociopathic. So, yeah, the more I think about it, tonight is all about showing her the parts of me that aren't the least bit sociopathic.

I exhale, trying to get ahold of myself. I can't allow myself to have a raging hard-on all night long. I'd never be able to concentrate on anything she's saying—and that would blow my show-her-I'm-not-a-sociopath strategy to bits.

"So nice to finally meet you," she says, smirking.

"No, Sarah, believe me, the pleasure's all mine."

The view is spectacular, all right. And I'm not talking about the skyline. She's wearing a green dress that hugs her curves in all the right places, and the view of her backside as we follow the maître d' to our table is something else. Now *that's* an ass I could really sink my teeth into.

"We're alone?" she asks, scanning the empty restaurant.

"I didn't want there to be any distractions."

"You rented out the entire restaurant?" Here eyes are wide.

I love the look on her face right now.

We reach our table and take our seats.

"Wow. This is amazing." Her face is awash in childlike giddiness. "You rented out Canlis," she mutters, seemingly to herself. "Wow. Thank you. That's ... wow."

A man could get addicted to trying to make her face look like that.

I take my seat across from her and smile. Or, at least, I try to smile. I'm finding it hard to relax my face into any kind of normal facial expression. It feels unreasonably warm in the restaurant.

I flag the maître d' back to the table as he's leaving.

"Yes, sir?"

"Can you turn down the heat just a tad?"

"Of course, sir."

Sarah smiles at me, her eyes flickering with some sort of amusement.

Oh, that mouth. Oh God, if I let myself focus too long on those lips, this dinner date will take a sharp detour. And I'm not going to let that happen. Not tonight. I already made that mistake on the phone, and I'm not going to do it again. Tonight, I'm going to show her the upside of Jonas Faraday—yeah, tonight, I'm all upside, baby.

A waiter comes to the table with wine and an appetizer.

"You're gorgeous," I say after the waiter leaves. And she is. "That dress is incredible."

She looks down as if to remember what she's wearing. "Thank you. Unfortunately, I couldn't wear my favorite dress for you. Such a pity." She smiles mischievously and takes a sip of her wine.

"Why not?"

"It's *purple*." She laughs her gravelly laugh.

Somehow, that laugh of hers puts me at ease. I can feel my shoulders relaxing a bit. I lean forward onto my elbows. "If I could order a woman out of a catalogue to my precise specifications, I'd order you."

There's a brief silence.

Shit. I need to reign it back in. I'm coming on too strong. I can't blurt out every damned thought that flitters across my mind. I take a long swig of my wine.

She moves her mouth to speak—to make some sort of snarky comeback, I'd guess—but then she closes her mouth without speaking.

"What are you thinking right now?" I ask.

She purses her beautiful lips. "A thousand things. Mostly, I can't believe I'm here right now. At Canlis. With you." Her mouth twists for a moment. "And, well, that you're probably the most outrageously good-looking man I've ever laid eyes on, let alone been on a date with. And, yeah, that I can't believe I'm here. With you."

Damn, I want to take that dress off her. "I'm so glad you're here. You're absolutely beautiful."

She looks at me like she's trying to figure out the last piece of a jigsaw puzzle that doesn't fit. "What are *you* thinking right now?" she asks. She leans forward onto her elbows in mimicry of my position and the tops of her breasts push out of her neckline.

My cock springs to attention. "If I answer that question, my entire strategy for the night will be blown to bits."

"You have a strategy for the night?"

"Absolutely."

"What is it?"

"If I answer that question, my entire strategy for the night will be blown to bits."

"So you won't tell me what you're thinking, then?"

I exhale, thinking about her olive skin writhing around on my crisp, white sheets. "You know exactly what I'm thinking."

She licks her lips. "Oh, well, good luck with your strategy, then." The candlelight flickers across her face. She leans back and so do I. I'm not sure who just dominated and who submitted in that exchange. Maybe it was a draw.

There's a brief silence as we assess each other and sip our wine. We each sample the appetizer. It's delicious.

"Thank you for the Valentine's Day gifts," she says. "You shocked the hell out of me."

"Did you like them?"

She pauses. "If I answer that question, my entire strategy for the night will be blown to bits."

"You have a strategy for tonight?"

"Absolutely."

"So you won't tell me if you liked my gifts?"

She smiles. "No, I'll tell you. Strategies are over-rated." She leans forward again. "I felt light-headed and weak at the knees when your gifts arrived. The scent of the flowers wafting through my little apartment made me swoon. As I got ready for our date this evening, I danced around my apartment just for the heck of it—out of sheer joy. Oh, and I must have hugged that teddy bear fifty times, imagining he was you."

My heart is suddenly pounding a mile a minute. I'm smiling from ear to ear. "Yeah, okay, but did you *like* them?"

She laughs.

"How could that answer ruin your strategy for tonight? It's the best answer ever."

"Well, considering how you feel about Valentine's Day 'bullshit'— and the women who are brainwashed into wanting it—it's fifty-fifty you might run for the hills now that you know for sure I'm one of the droning, brainwashed female masses. Honestly, I wasn't sure if you *wanted* me to like everything or if you sent it as some sort of test—like, if I swooned, then I failed the test and proved I'm brainwashed."

"You thought I sent you all that so I could say, 'gotcha'?"

"I'm not sure why you sent that stuff." She shrugs. She takes a sip of her wine.

I look at her, incredulous. Wow, I've really got my work cut out for me tonight. I have to keep remembering that, thanks to that application, I'm starting out in a deep hole, trying to dig my way out. "I'm sorry you even had to wonder. That sucks."

"Come on. You're the one who insists a woman has to choose between 'Valentine's Day bullshit' and monkey-sex that makes her see God. I didn't want to be an idiot and think you were serious if you weren't."

I sigh. "Oh, Sarah, just forget that stupid application, okay? I sent you those gifts because you deserve to have *both* Valentine's Day bullshit *and* monkey-sex." I lean forward again. "And because I want to be the man who gives you both."

She blushes. There's a long beat. "I think you missed your calling as a greeting card writer," she finally says. "'My darling, you deserve Valentine's Day bullshit *and* monkey-sex. Happy Valentine's Day.'" She throws her head back and laughs a full-throated, gravelly laugh. It makes me want to kiss her neck. She beams at me. "Did you come up with the message inside the card you sent me? 'You are everything I never knew I always wanted.' I loved it." She sighs.

"Well, I selected the quote to be printed onto the card, but I didn't write it. It's from a movie."

"What movie?" she asks.

"*Fools Rush In.*" I take a bite of food.

"That one with Matthew Perry?"

"I like to think of it as that one with Salma Hayek."

"Oh, yeah, of course you do." Her eyes blaze. "I can't imagine how you wound up sitting through that movie."

"I didn't mind it at all. I've had a thing for Salma Hayek ever since. Good soundtrack, too."

"But it's a romantic comedy. Like, hopelessly, unabashedly romantic."

"I didn't say it was great cinema. I just said I didn't mind it."

"But that movie was all about two mismatched people finding

true love against all reason and logic. A movie like that represents everything you abhor."

I'm quiet for a moment. She thinks I "abhor" true love? I don't abhor true love. Do I? Is that the gist of what I said in my application? Have I become that big an asshole? Maybe I'm a sociopath, after all.

She shifts in her seat and studies me. "Did a former girlfriend force you to watch that movie? I mean, I guess what I'm really asking is have you ever had a committed relationship, or have you always been like this?"

"Have I always been like what?"

"Emotionally damaged—seemingly incapable of forging any kind of intimate human connection."

I feel like she just punched me in the gut. My sociopathic, asshole-y gut.

I consider. What's the honest answer here? "Yes," I answer, "I've always been like this—or, at least since I was seven years old. And yes, despite the way I am, I've had several girlfriends—all of whom complained of my 'emotional unavailability.' And, yes, it was a former girlfriend—a live-in girlfriend, briefly—who forced me to watch *Fools Rush In.* But I didn't mind it."

"What happened to you when you were seven?"

Shit. Why did I mention that?

She waits. When I don't respond, she continues. "Okay," she says softly. "Not a casual dinner topic." She pauses. "I'm sorry."

I want to tell her, "Oh, no problem," and make the tension in my jaw go away, but I can't. The muscles in my jaw are pulsing.

She barrels right ahead. "So when was your last relationship?" She takes a long sip of her wine.

I sigh. At least it's better than talking about what happened when I was seven. "It ended a couple years ago. That was the live-in relationship."

"Why'd it end?"

"Because she said I 'wouldn't let her in'—and it was true. Because I never told her even one of the things I've already told you. Because I knew if I told her the truth about me, how I really think, how I really talk, how I really am, she wouldn't sit across the dinner table from me, looking at me the way you are right now. And at least some part of me knew I wanted a woman who'd know everything you know and still sit across the table and look at me the way you're looking at me right now."

113

She opens her mouth but doesn't speak. She blinks slowly at me. Her cheeks are flushed.

"But enough about that. The Internet is very clear we're not supposed to talk about past relationships on a first date."

"You read up on what's appropriate first date conversation?"

"I didn't want to fuck up dinner like I fucked up our phone call."

She looks at me sympathetically. "You didn't fuck up our phone call. That was all me. And, anyway," she says, "this isn't a first date. We're way, *way* past that, and you know it."

I can't hold off anymore. I reach out and touch her hand and then her arm. Her skin is so smooth. Our eyes lock. An electricity courses between us.

"You drive me fucking crazy," I whisper.

Her eyelids lower to half-mast. Oh, she wants me, too. "How's that strategy of yours going?" she says. She parts her lips.

"It's about to be blown to bits."

She leans forward and whispers to me. "You drive me fucking crazy, too."

And that does it. She just hurled my strategy right off a cliff. I want to swipe the dishes and cutlery to the floor and take her right here on this table.

Thank God, the waiter comes with a refill on the wine and another appetizer. His presence gives us both a chance to collect ourselves.

"You like seafood?" I ask, suddenly anxious that everything I've ordered won't be to her liking.

"I grew up in Seattle," she says.

I take that to mean she loves it.

She takes a sip of wine. "This is really good wine, by the way. I'm not really knowledgeable about wine, to be honest, but it seems like a good one."

"Well, yeah, anything's better than 'two-buck-chuck.'"

She laughs. "I like two-buck chuck."

I shake my head.

"What can I say? I'm a cheap date."

I resist the urge to roll my eyes. If she only knew everything I've shelled out to be sitting here with her right now, she wouldn't say that. "I'm no wine expert, either," I assure her, and it's true. "I just know what I like." Again, there's that heat between us. "I ordered seven courses for us. I hope that's okay. They'll just keep bringing us food all night long."

"Wow, thank you. That's amazing."

"So you grew up in Seattle?"

She nods. "With my mom. You?"

"Haven't you researched me?"

Her mouth twists. "For hours and hours."

"Well, then, you already know the basics. Which means you've got a distinct advantage over me. It's only fair we talk about you for a while." I take a bite of the new appetizer. Again, the food is delicious.

"You want to know about my 'passions and hobbies and my beloved Maltese Kiki'?" She takes a long sip of her wine.

"Exactly."

"Ah, but you see, I happen to know—unlike any other girl who'd otherwise be sitting here right now under any other circumstance—that you don't give a crap about my precious Kiki—not even about her new rhinestone jacket and tutu—because the only thing you're thinking about is getting down and dirty in the bathroom."

I sigh. "You're misquoting me. I never said I don't give a crap about your precious Kiki."

"Well, okay—you didn't say you don't give a *crap* about her, which is good, because she's the apple of my eye—what you said is that when you ask a woman about herself you're *actually* thinking the whole time that you just want to get down and dirty in the bathroom. Of course, you didn't use the words 'get down and dirty'—you used your all-time favorite word—but this is the nicest restaurant I've ever been to in my whole life and I'm trying to act like a fancy lady."

I rub my eyes. "Oh my God, this is so fucked up," I mutter.

She nods and picks up her wine goblet. "Hey, your words, not mine." She takes a dainty sip.

To my surprise, I laugh. Not too many people can make me laugh—especially not at myself. I lean back in my chair. "Actually, I *want* to know all about you—even about your Maltese Kiki, if you happen to have one. Surprising, but true."

"Let's not go overboard. No one wants to hear about anyone's Maltese named Kiki."

I laugh again. God, I want to take that green dress off her and touch every square inch of her.

"So let me see if I understand this situation correctly. You want to know about my hopes and dreams and passions (and my imaginary Maltese Kiki), and you emphatically *don't* want to get down and dirty with me in the bathroom?" Her eyes are suddenly on fire as she picks up her wine glass again.

Oh, wow, my dick is at full attention. I can't formulate a verbal response. My heart's clanging in my chest. I bite my lip. Oh shit, suddenly, that's all I want to do right now—fuck her in the bathroom. But that's exactly what I absolutely cannot do if we're going to get off on the right foot here.

When I don't speak, she grins. "Oh, yes. Your brilliant *strategy*." She leans forward. "Well guess what? I don't want *strategic* Jonas. I want *honest* Jonas." She licks her lips. "I like My Brutally Honest Mr. Faraday." She smiles slyly. "A lot."

I'm so turned on right now, I can't think straight. I lean forward, too. I whisper, "Yes, I want to fuck you—more than anything. But not tonight. And not in the fucking bathroom. Because fucking you in the bathroom would be no different than what we did on the phone yesterday—and I promised myself I'm not going to do that to you again no matter what. When I finally do fuck you, Sarah—and, believe me, fucking you is the highest priority in my entire life right now—I'm going to do it right so that we *both* experience something we've never felt before." My erection strains inside my pants. "We're going to wait and do it nice and slow and right—and it'll be worth the wait, I promise." My brain is quite certain of this entire speech, even if my hard-on begs to differ.

Her eyes are flickering, and I can't tell if that's because of the candlelight, or because of something heating up inside her. "So that's your strategy? A slow burn? Making me wait? Making it worth the wait?"

My nostrils are flaring. "In a nutshell." I can't read her expression. "What are you thinking right now?" I ask.

She takes a bite of food, and then a long sip of wine, making me wait. "Two things. First, that I really, really like it when you're honest." She grins.

I smile.

"And second, that your precious strategy is about to get blown to bits."

Chapter 14
Sarah

Oh, he's yummy, all right. Just yummalicous. Of course, he's gorgeous—but I already knew that. What I didn't know is that he'd smell so good, too. Or that he'd rent out a fancy restaurant just for me and send a limo to pick me up, too. I don't consider myself a materialistic girl, but come on—who wouldn't swoon just a little bit at all this *Pretty Woman* treatment?

But the thing that's getting to me right now above everything else is the way he's looking at me like he's going to devour me in one bite like a great white shark snacking on a sea lion. I don't think a man has ever looked at me quite like this before—and, if so, certainly not a man I find this irresistibly attractive. His eyes are mesmerizing to me—full of exactly the kind of soul and depth and even sadness I thought I glimpsed in his photos. Now that I see him in person, I know there's something behind those eyes—and I can't wait to find out what it is. When he said that thing about him being incapable of human connection ever since he was seven—oh my God—the look on his face, it was like he was seven years old right then. He looked so small in that moment, so lost, I wanted to reach over the table and take his face in my hands.

Coming here tonight, I was nervous. Nervous I wouldn't live up to all the hype. Nervous he'd regret all the effort he's taken to find me. Nervous the chemistry I'd felt in emails and on the phone somehow wouldn't translate in person. Well, damn, I was nervous for nothing. Our chemistry is through the roof. It's taking all my effort to sit in my chair like a civilized person, rather than leaping onto him like a cheetah on an impala. It's all I can do not to pull the tablecloth off the table and jump his bones right here, right now. I don't know

117

what it is about him, but I feel like someone else around him—but in a good way. Not so inhibited. Not so worried about what anyone else might think. Like I want to take a risk—something I usually avoid at all costs.

What if I got up from my seat and sat myself down on his lap right now and helped myself to those incredible lips of his? Would he be able to stick with his strategy then? I'm dying to find out. In fact, the minute he revealed his stupid strategy, the only thing I wanted to do was force him off it. I guess he's not the only one who loves a good challenge. What if I went over to him, lifted up my dress, pushed my G-string aside and slammed his hardness into me, deep inside me, right here at the table? I can't stop imagining myself doing just that as I sit here sipping my wine and staring across the table at him.

I think it's distinctly possible I'm going insane. These thoughts are not the things a normal woman imagines while sitting in a nice restaurant, overlooking the Seattle skyline. I'm not some kind of sex addict. I'm not some kind of pervert. I'm a "good girl" kind of girl. Dependable. Responsible. A rule follower. So why does he make me want to be so, so, so, so bad? If only he knew what I was thinking. I wonder how he'd feel about his stupid strategy then?

The waiter comes to the table and places salads in front of us.

Jonas looks across the table at me mournfully, as if he knew exactly what I was thinking right before the waiter showed up.

"So, how do you like working for The Club?" Jonas asks. He takes a bite of his salad.

I shift in my seat. "I like it a lot. More than I ever thought I would."

There it is again—that look. It's like he's going to swallow me whole.

I clear my throat. "I've only been working there three months," I say. "Your application was the first one I processed all alone, without supervision."

He meets my direct gaze with a smoldering stare of his own. "I'm your first." He grins broadly. "I like that."

My mouth twists into an amused smile. I like that, too.

"How did you start working for The Club?"

Why are we going through the charade of carrying on a normal conversation? We both know what we'd rather be doing right now. And it starts with the letter "f."

"I answered an ad in a law school forum seeking a student for a work-from-home, part-time research position. It was really vague and kind of mysterious sounding, but the pay was ridiculous, so I applied. I had to undergo all this testing and psychological assessment and jump through weird hoops and sign a non-disclosure agreement before I ever found out the details on the job. But the pay was too good to pass up. After all that, when I finally found out what the job really was, I was floored, but intrigued. Kind of compulsively curious, you might say. And the work turned out to be so fascinating and the paychecks started depositing like clockwork, so . . ."

"Do the applications ever freak you out?" He takes another bite of his food.

"All the time. Including yours." I smile. "But as it turns out," I say, leaning forward, "I like getting freaked out."

The smile that unfurls across his face is wicked.

"I like knowing people's secrets," I say.

His eyes are twinkling.

"Well, mostly. Some of it's totally disgusting, I have to admit. Some of it, you can't un-see. But it's like a car crash, you know? You can't look away. Even the disgusting stuff is fascinating."

"Tell me some of the disgusting stuff."

I tell him the worst of the worst and he laughs heartily. Midway through my storytelling, he has to put down his fork and wipe his eyes, he's laughing so hard.

I love his laugh. Something tells me it's hard to elicit.

"And that's all in the first three months?" he asks, bringing his napkin to his eyes.

I nod. "I'm only planning to keep the job 'til the end of the school year. Hopefully, my grades will cooperate with my big plans—the top ten students at the end of the first year get a full-ride scholarship for the rest of the program, so I'm crossing my fingers." I bite my lip. "I've got an unpaid internship this summer, so I'm really gambling on that scholarship."

"Is your internship at a law firm? I bet you had your pick of jobs—fourth in your class." He smiles.

"You looked that up?"

"I told you, I'm obsessed with you."

My nerve endings sizzle and pop for just a moment. I shift in my seat again.

"No, my internship's with a nonprofit—it's where I'm gonna work when I graduate."

"Really? What nonprofit?" He looks genuinely interested.

I'm a bit caught off guard. Why is he interested in this? Isn't this the part where he yawns and wishes we were having monkey-sex in the bathroom right now? This isn't how I pictured this night going. I never expected Jonas Faraday to ask me about my hopes and dreams. I thought, maybe even hoped, he'd make it easy to resist him by being self-involved and going on and on about what he planned to do to me.

"It's an organization that provides aid and free legal services for battered women." I feel my cheeks involuntarily flush with the fierce emotion I feel about the topic.

He pauses, considering me. "A cause close to your heart, I take it?" he asks softly.

My heart is beating fast. I can't speak, so I simply nod.

There's a long pause. Clearly, he expects me to elaborate. But I'm not here to regale Jonas Faraday with the sob story of my childhood. I don't want to talk about what my dad did to my mom all those years ago that made her run away—to escape, really—and raise me all by herself. I'm not going to talk about how she worked two jobs my whole life, dreaming of a better life for me. No, I'm not here to talk about how brutally he used to beat her while I cowered in the corner, or about how much she's sacrificed for me, or how strong she is, or how much I admire her, or how important it is for me to make all her sacrifices worth it. I'm not here to tell him all that just so he can file me away in a folder with all the other "girls with daddy issues" he's banged. I might not know what I'm here to do, but it's certainly not to talk about any of that.

I shrug.

"So, no interest in corporate law, then? There are plenty of top law firms in Seattle offering ridiculous salaries to starting lawyers. Trust me, I know—I've probably funded a sizeable number of their salaries myself over the years."

I don't like this topic. I want to know more about *him,* not tell him about *me.* "I didn't go to law school for the money," I say simply.

His eyes flash and I feel his desire for me in no uncertain terms. The way he's looking at me, I know he's hard right now. Yet again, I imagine myself sitting on his lap and taking his hardness into me. I wonder if his "strategy" could withstand *that.* By the expression on his face right now, I'd swear this man can read my exact thoughts.

"What are you thinking right now?" I breathe.

"Why do you ask?"

"Because you're looking at me like you want to swallow me whole."

"I'm thinking I want to swallow you whole."

I can't help but smirk.

"I'm thinking you're everything I fantasized you'd be. And more. And I'm thinking I want you so bad, it's causing me physical pain. And, most of all, I'm thinking you're so fucking beautiful."

Boom. Just like that, I'm throbbing. And wet. I want him.

We stare at each other for a moment.

He leans back and sighs. "Tell me more about what you do for The Club, My Beautiful Intake Agent."

I sigh, exasperated. "Why?" I whisper. I hope my voice doesn't sound as impatient as I feel. I don't understand why he's so chatty tonight. Isn't this the man who thinks about fucking a woman in a bathroom while chatting over a nice glass of pinot noir? I check the label on our wine bottle. Yep. Pinot noir. So what gives?

"What do you mean, *why*?"

"Why do you want to know more about me? I thought you didn't care about any of that kind of thing."

He rolls his eyes. "I'm not a monster." He leans forward. "Talking to you is turning me on. And I like getting turned on."

There's that throbbing again. I lean forward onto my forearms. "I review applications assigned to my geographic territory—Seattle— and read all about people's deepest secrets and fantasies. I research to find out if they are who they say they are, and then I do surveillance on each applicant—"

"Did you do surveillance on me?"

"Of course." I tell him every detail about how I saw him fly past me in his BMW.

He exhales sharply, his mind blown. "To think I drove right past you when I was desperate to find you." He shakes his head.

I grin. "Normally, I would have just waltzed into your office to ask about you. But I didn't want you to see me. When it came to you, I didn't do anything the 'usual' way."

"Why didn't you want me to see you?"

I purse my lips. "I guess I wanted you to see me for the first time ... on a night just like this."

He arches his eyebrows and smiles. "Good call."

I grin.

"So, usually, you just walk right into a guy's office when you're doing surveillance?"

"Yeah, I just go wherever they are and waltz right in. Who cares, since they'll never see me again?" As an example, I tell him about my recent trip downtown to watch that software engineer leave his building for lunch.

"What did that guy write in his application?"

"Actually, he didn't care about the sex all that much. I think he's genuinely looking for love."

Jonas scoffs. "In The Club? Yeah, right."

I'm offended. "Anything's possible. And he only signed up for a month. So that says a lot."

"Why does that say a lot? A fucked-up deviant can't sign up for a month?"

"No, the fucked-up deviants are the ones who sign up for a full year."

His eyes flash at me. Was that anger? Humiliation? I can't tell.

"I don't understand," he mutters, his cheeks blazing.

"The ones who sign up for a year have zero faith they'll ever find love—or else they wouldn't commit to a year up front. For them, it's all about the sex. Nothing more."

His eyes are hard.

Shit. Clearly, I'm pissing him off right now. I forge ahead anyway. Screw it. He wants "brutal honesty," right? "The ones who sign up for a month are the romantics," I explain. "They're hoping to find love right off the bat and never need The Club's services again. I think they're sweet."

"Ah," he says. Yeah, he's pissed.

"Not everyone is scared of love, you know." I sniff. "Some people actually think love is the most important thing in the world.

And why shouldn't that software engineer find someone to love—in The Club or however he can find it? He deserves love as much as anyone." I'm becoming angry and I don't understand why. "Even if *you* don't believe in falling in love, Jonas, that doesn't mean the rest of the world doesn't believe in it. When I saw that software engineer leaving his lobby for lunch, he looked so alone, so lonely, so *sad,* I actually cried a little bit." And, what the hell, I feel like I could cry all over again, just talking about that guy. Why am I taking up the software engineer's cause so passionately? Why am I blasting Jonas right now? I knew what he was before I agreed to dinner. So why hold it against him now?

Jonas looks at a total loss.

"I'm sorry," I say quickly, but my pulse is racing. "I don't know why I got so riled up there. I've known all about you from the start. It's not fair to hold it against you now."

He runs his hand through his hair.

I exhale. "I'm sure you're plotting your swift escape right about now," I mutter.

"Correct," he says.

My stomach drops. I've blown it. I've totally and completely blown it.

"But only to take you away from this table to a place where I can touch and kiss every inch of you."

I exhale sharply.

His eyes are on fire. He's like a caged lion.

"Why me, Jonas?" I ask. I can't help myself. This man can have any woman he wants. I wish I could let it go, go with the flow and not ask, but I don't understand why he's moved heaven and earth to find me, and rented out this restaurant for me, and is now looking at me like I'm a bottle of whiskey and he's an alcoholic, especially now that I just ripped him a new one. "Please. I don't care about your strategy, whatever it is," I whisper. "I just have to understand why you've gone to such extremes to pursue me."

His eyes darken with intensity. "You want to know?"

I nod. "Please."

His eyes are blazing. "The minute I read your email—the minute I saw the *sender name* on your email—even before I'd read the goddamned message—I knew you'd change everything."

I can't breathe. My heart's thumping in my ears.

"And, Sarah, I *wanted* you to"—his jaw muscles pulse—"change everything." He puts his fork down and stares at me.

My heart is beating like I just ran a hundred-yard dash. That throbbing between my legs has returned with a vengeance. I'm a whirl of unbridled emotion right now.

His chest is heaving.

I stand up from my chair. I'm his for the taking. *Take me.*

He leaps out of his chair and grabs me, pressing his body fervently into mine, his hardness nudging against my hip. He swoops down to my mouth for a kiss, and electricity floods my every nerve ending. Oh my God, his lips are warm and soft and delectable. When his tongue parts my lips and enters my mouth, I smash my body against his, and we're both instantly impassioned. In a flash, we're moaning and clawing and grasping at each other, both of us savage animals.

"Now," I whisper. "Right now."

"Sarah—" he begins, and it's clear he's going to protest.

I reach down and touch the bulging package between us. I want to wrap my legs around him and take him into me right here. "Jonas," I moan. I'm so turned on I'm in danger of losing my legs out from under me. If he doesn't take me into the bathroom this very second, I just might unzip his pants right here in front of the waiter.

"It's either on the table or in the bathroom," I breathe. "Take your pick."

He looks around for a brief second and back at me.

My stare is unwavering.

He grips my hand and pulls me toward the back of the restaurant. Everything is a blur around me. I'm in sensory overload. I'm having trouble walking—my legs are rubber under me. I'm enraptured by the scent of him, the rawness of him—by the all-encompassing throbbing between my legs. Oh God, I want him.

We're in the bathroom. The women's bathroom. There's an anteroom with a feminine-looking couch. He brings me to the couch, his lips assaulting mine, and lays me down on my back. He's frantically unzipping the back of my dress and pulling it down, roughly, while at the same time pulling up the hem. He's groaning. His hands are all over me. Now there are soft, warm lips on my shoulder, my neck. Oh God, a finger slips inside my underpants, inside of me, eagerly working me, rhythmically caressing me, making me wet. I cry out. Lips on my nipples. I fumble for his zipper. I'm clawing at him. I can't breathe.

His fingers work themselves to my clit. I cry out again and reach for his hard shaft. He yanks my underwear off. My dress is pulled down from the top and hiked up from the bottom, bunched around my waist. I'm soaking wet between my legs, aching, yearning for him. My thighs are covered in my wetness.

"I'm on the pill," I whisper. "Now, Jonas."

"No," he says, bending down toward my crotch, clearly intending to lick me.

I pull at his head, forcing his face back toward mine. I glare at him, desperate. "There's no time for that," I hiss back. "Now, Jonas."

I grab feverishly at his penis and pump his shaft up and down as his fingers work their way to the exact spot that drives me wild. I groan and lean back onto the couch, pulling his hardness toward me, positioning him right at my wet entrance.

"Now," I plead. "Please, now."

"No," he says, but I feel the tip of his penis resting at my entrance. He moans.

I thrust my hips toward him, urging him to enter me, teasing him. "Do it now," I say, gritting my teeth.

"We're at cross-purposes here," he says, trembling, but a second later, he plunges into me, making me cry out.

He slams into me, in and out of me, over and over. He lets out a choked noise that tells me he's already close.

I reach my hands under his shirt to find warm, taut muscles. He pulls down my bra and pinches my nipple—and when he does, something deep inside me faintly ripples at his touch. I make a sound I don't recognize—a sound I've never heard myself make before— and he shudders visibly with his arousal.

He pulls out of me and bends down toward my crotch, yet again intending to lick me, but I get up and push him onto the couch, onto his back. In one swift motion, I straddle him and take him into me again, riding him roughly. I gyrate on top of him, moaning. His fingers quickly move to massage my clit.

I'm on fire. I'm feeling so much pleasure it's beginning to feel like pain. My nerve endings are zapping me like live wires. Glimmering waves of pleasure begin nipping at me from a distance. Again, that foreign noise escapes my throat.

He cries out and I feel his ejaculation inside me, spilling into me.

I'm shaking. Panting. Wanting more. I'm not done yet. I've never been this aroused in all my life. I want more.

I open my eyes to look at him.

He's looking right at me. He looks like a Greek god reclined beneath me. I've never even kissed a man this good looking—and now I've just had the best sex of my life with him. Holy crap, this was amazing. I'm panting like a rabid dog, aching for more. Needing more.

He's still.

He touches my clit again, but I jerk away.

Now that he's done, I don't want to be touched. The moment has passed for me. When he was fucking me and touching me at the same time, my body belonged to him. But now—now that he's climaxed—my body has closed up shop. I don't want all attention on me—I know exactly how that ends. Not well.

But, oh God, I was close. I know I was. I was closer than I've ever been before. I felt like I was about to lose myself—like I was losing control. And I liked it. I really, really, really, really, really liked where this was heading.

I want to do it again.

I feel his hands on my breasts again. And then on my stomach, my hips, my butt.

He moans underneath me. I tilt my head back and sigh, remembering how I felt a moment ago—how everything started warping inside me. I want to feel that way again—I think I could feel that way again.

His hand moves between my legs and I gently guide him away again. No. The moment has passed.

He looks defeated.

Oh, I've disappointed him. My stomach drops into my feet. Of course I have. Good sex means only one thing to him. How could I forget that? I get off him quickly and angrily and start pulling my dress back down and up, trying to put myself back together.

"What's the matter?" he says, shocked.

"Sorry to disappoint you," I hiss.

"Oh my God!" he shouts, throwing up his hands. "And here I thought I was supposed to be the fucked up one. Sarah, do you even know how fucked up you are?" Wow, he's angry.

I wheel around to look at him, incredulous. "*I'm* fucked up? Why? Because I won't pretend to have an orgasm for the sake of feeding your ego?"

"No, because you're hell bent on sabotaging yourself. Look at you. It's text book defense mechanism." He grabs my shoulders. "Well, guess what? I'm not going to let you do this. Do you understand me?"

"Do what?"

"Sabotage this."

"There's nothing to sabotage," I say.

He looks wounded. "You don't mean that."

He's right. I don't mean that. Not at all.

And he's also right that I'm so fucked up. I've been fucked up for a really long time, now that I think about it, despite how much it might appear I've got it all together. No matter how hard I try to be perfect, and rule-following, and smart, and keep it together, no matter how great my grades are and how well I convince the world I'm Sarah the Straight Arrow, Sarah the Studious One, Sarah the Snarky One, I'm always one hair away from falling apart, pushing people away, quickly rejecting before I can be rejected. Holy shit, he's right. I'm so fucked up. I've always been so fucked up, despite appearances. And he figured it out this fast? No one ever figures me out this quickly, because I don't let them.

I finish putting my dress back together, slowly, and then I sit on the edge of the couch and put my head in my hands.

"I'm sorry," I say. "You're right."

"About which part?"

"All of it." I bury my face into my hands. Tears are threatening. "I'm trying to screw this up." I turn to look at him, cringing.

"Why?"

I sigh. "Come on, Jonas. I've read your application." I search for the right words. "I know you're just going to move on. I'm damned if I do and I'm damned if I don't. Either way, you're gonna reject me. Sooner rather than later, too."

He exhales. "So you're gonna do it first, then. Is that it?"

I nod slowly. "I guess so."

He sighs. "Understandable. Given what you know about me. And who you are."

I shrug. I am what I am. So is he.

He puts his finger under my chin and guides my face to look at him. The moment my eyes meet his, my eyes moisten.

"I'm glad you're fucked up," he whispers. "If you weren't, you wouldn't want me. No one's more fucked up than me. You have no idea."

I can't help but smile through my impending tears. I trace his lips with the tip of my finger. "Why are you so fucked up?" I ask him.

His eyes are soulful, earnest. Sad. He leans his forehead against mine. "It's a long story."

I understand. I don't know why I understand, but I do.

"Why are *you* so fucked up?" he asks, his nose touching mine.

"It's a long story," I say quietly.

He leans back, exhaling. "Oh, Sarah."

I look up at him and a lone tear escapes down my cheek.

He wipes it away and kisses me. It's a gentle kiss—a kiss of sheer kindness.

He reaches into his pocket and pulls out his cell phone. "Bring the car to the front now," he says, never taking his eyes off me. "Thank you." He stands and grabs my hand. "Come on. I'm taking you home."

I bristle. He banged me, and now it's time to send me packing—is that it?

He shakes his head, obviously bewildered by my facial expression. "To *my* home, you big dummy. I'm taking you home *with me*."

The streetlights flash on his face as we sit together in the backseat of the limo, our bodies close and our hands clasped. He holds my hand with supreme confidence, like I'm his. I like it. I want to be his. Even if I wanted to freak out again (which I don't) I couldn't possibly muster the effort—not with him holding my hand like this.

I hate the way I reacted in the bathroom. I shouldn't have done that. I ruined what should have been an incredible moment. I need to just turn off my brain and go with the flow and see where this leads. No more self-sabotaging. He was right.

I don't know what's going to happen next, it's true—but I don't need to know. We're going to his house, and that's exactly where I want to go. I want to see him naked. I want to touch every inch of him. I want to find out everything there is to know about him. I want to see his family pictures. I want to see how his house is decorated. I want to see if he's neat and tidy or a slob. I want to see what's in his fridge. I want to make love to him in a bed. And I want to turn the tables on him and lick every inch of him 'til he begs me for mercy. Yes, for some reason, I want to bring him to his knees and thwart his every strategy.

I shudder at my inner monologue. Where are these thoughts coming from? I never think this way, about anyone. I don't understand what he ignites in me. It's something primal—not controlled by conscious thought. I want him. I want to know what makes him tick and deliver it to him, whatever it is. That's just not like me. Usually, if I'm being perfectly honest, when it comes to sex, I could take it or leave it. So why am I so sexed up around him?

He turns and sees me staring at him. He squeezes my hand. "That wasn't how I wanted tonight to go."

"I thought it went pretty frickin' well."

He glances up at the driver. "Put the partition up, please," he says, and immediately a dark barrier rises up. Jonas squints at me. "Of course you did. Sex for you is all about one thing—getting the guy off. And as fast and hard as possible because, without the possibility of an orgasm for yourself, that's how you get validation. Totally unacceptable." His tone is matter-of-fact.

My mouth is hanging open. "Do you always say whatever the heck you think, no matter how rude?"

"I'm not being rude. I'm being honest."

I stare at him.

"But no, I don't. Only to you—and also to my brother Josh."

"Because that was pretty damned rude."

"Maybe. But true."

I consider for a moment. "Making you want me, forcing you into me, even though you wanted to hold out, even though that wasn't your plan—yes, that turned me on, I admit it." I sigh, remembering that glimmer I felt as Jonas slammed into me. "God, that was hot. I liked feeling like you were powerless to resist me."

"Aha." He smirks. "I'm not the only one with a raging God complex."

I laugh. "Apparently not." We smile at each other.

"Well, there's only room for one god in this limo," he says. "And it's me." He pauses. "And, yes, I *am* powerless to resist you, by the way."

"Good," I say. There's a beat. "Sex for you is all about getting the girl off," I challenge. "What's the difference?"

"There's a big difference. I want to get you off, true—but only because it gets *me* off. I mean, it *physically* gets me off. I'm quite selfish—as I'm innately wired to be. But you? Your only pleasure is derivative."

I look at him, not sure I understand his meaning.

"You're sexually co-dependent," he clarifies.

I glare at him. "No I'm not. I get off, too—just not culminating in an orgasm. What we did back at the restaurant was incredible."

"You don't even know what you're talking about. You've come to expect nothing for yourself sexually, so you don't even try anymore. You get the guy off as fast and hard as possible to prove your sexual worth, end of story."

"You really are rude, you know that?"

He shrugs. "Honest."

"I really don't like how you've turned everything around and made it all about *me* being the weirdo here. Maybe you've forgotten—I've read your application, Jonas. You're the one who's fucked up, not me."

"Absolutely, I'm fucked up. No argument there. You don't even know the half of it." He looks out the window, thinking. "I know I am," he says softly. He turns back to me. "But you're totally fucked up, too, and you don't even know it."

"So you're some sort of expert in psychology, huh?"

"Yeah, you could say that."

Oh. That's not the answer I expected. "Really?"

"Well, not technically. But I went through years of forced therapy as a kid—most of it total bullshit, of course—and I picked up a thing or two." He looks out the window again and the flickering lights illuminate his perfect features.

My stomach drops. Why was he forced into therapy as a kid? What the hell happened to him when he was seven?

He doesn't give me the chance to broach the topic. "And, in recent years, I've acquired what you might call a healthy interest in female psychology." He turns back to stare right into my eyes. "And sexuality."

I'm turned on and I'm sure my face shows it.

"I've read everything I could get my hands on about the female brain, female psychology, the female sexual experience. Female sexuality is definitely my favorite topic." His eyes blaze. "Fascinating stuff."

I don't know why this revelation titillates me, but it does. "Well, then, surely you know that for a woman, sex is about so much more than the big 'O.' It's the whole fantasy of it—more mental than physical."

"Yeah, yeah, yeah. But with all due respect, My Beautiful Intake Agent, you're not qualified to give me this speech, whether it's true or not." He unclasps his hand from mine and places his hand confidently on my thigh, under the hem of my dress, as if he's been touching me for years. "It's like you're trying to tell me green beans taste better than chocolate—but you've never had a single bite of chocolate in your whole, deprived life."

I can't help but laugh. He's got a point.

He smirks. "You're one of the shackled men in Plato's cave."

I raise my eyebrows. *Please explain.*

He smiles and begins lifting the hem of my dress to reveal my bare thighs. He exhales a loud breath at the sight of me. "Oh God, your skin," he whispers. "I can't resist it." He reaches out and gently caresses the tender skin on the inside of my thigh, causing every hair on my body to stand at attention. When he sees my eyelids go heavy with desire, he smiles at me.

I bite my lip.

"Plato wrote an allegory about some men sitting in a dark cave, all of them shackled together in a line, facing the cave wall."

I nod. *Go on.* With the story. And the touching, too.

His hand travels back down my thigh and begins caressing the sensitive skin on the inside of my knee. "There's a line of men sitting shackled in a dark cave, facing a cave wall. A bonfire rages behind them, but they've never seen it, since they've been shackled and forced to sit facing the wall their whole lives." Now his hand works its way back up my leg, up my inner thigh.

I let out a shaky breath, anticipating where his hand might travel next.

"The only thing the shackled men have ever seen is the cave wall—their own shadows dancing in the reflected firelight. Of course, since they don't know any better, they think the reflected light and dancing shadows are the ultimate in beauty."

I can instantly see where this is heading. But a man explaining Plato to me while touching the inside of my thigh is by far the sexiest thing I've ever experienced, so I'm not about to interrupt him. Now his hand moves farther up my leg, toward my G-string.

He's staring at me, his eyes like laser beams.

I'm trembling.

"One of the men in the cave, a guy at the end of the line, breaks free of his shackles." His voice is low and measured. His hand caresses the crotch of my panties, making me jump.

I close my eyes and exhale, trying to control my breathing.

He brings his lips right to my ear as his hand continues caressing the fabric of my panties, right over the exact spot that's throbbing for him. "The one who's broken free of his shackles turns around for the first time and sees the bonfire behind him," he whispers. "And he cries at the sight of it. He didn't know anything could be so bright and beautiful."

He kisses my neck as his hand forcefully yanks at the waistband of my panties. I lift my hips so he can get them off. He quickly succeeds in guiding my panties all the way down and I kick them off. My heart is racing. He licks my neck and his hand returns to the inside of my thigh, slowly working its way back up again. Oh my God, I'm on fire. My hips are writhing beneath me, straining toward him, yearning for him to penetrate me.

"I've unshackled you, My Magnificent Sarah," he whispers in my ear, "but you've only seen the bonfire." His hand reaches my wetness. His finger gently enters me.

My body jerks involuntarily toward him, aching for him.

He leans into my mouth and kisses me as his fingers work in and out of me. I moan loudly. He pulls his mouth an inch away from mine, but his fingers continue their exploration.

"The man sees a distant light at the mouth of the cave and he runs toward it." His fingers expertly plunge in and out of me, owning me, making me slick and wet and hungry for him. "And when he finally bursts out of the cave, he's blinded by the light, by the beauty he beholds."

His fingers find the most sensitive spot on my entire body, and I cry out.

He moans. "He sees sunlight and blue sky outside the cave." His voice has become ragged. He presses his body against mine. His erection bulges into my leg from underneath his pants.

"Fuck me, Jonas," I say, shocking myself. I've never uttered these words to anyone in my life.

He nips at my ear as his fingers move expertly back and forth from my tip to my wetness and back again. Oh my God, I've never been so turned on in all my life.

"The man sobs at the sight of the beauty outside the cave." His fingers are making me delirious. "He didn't know such beauty even existed. Oh, Sarah." His voice is hoarse.

His fingers are massaging me like no one ever has. My entire body ignites into sudden flames.

"Fuck me," I whisper urgently. "Please." Oh God, he's so good at this. I've never been touched like this, ever. Not by anyone, not even myself. My body is writhing and gyrating in syncopation with his magical fingers. "Now, Jonas."

"You want me to fuck you?" he asks, his voice suddenly edged with aggression.

"Yes," I say hoarsely. "Right now."

"No," he says, his voice steely. "We're gonna do things my way. No more hard and fast for you."

"Please, Jonas," I moan. "Now." I lift my hips toward him, begging him to enter me.

"No." His fingers slide back into my wetness and then to my clit again with fervor, and back and forth again, back and forth. "I'm gonna take you to the mouth of the cave, baby. No more bonfire bullshit. No more fucking around."

133

He kisses my mouth, and I respond with voracious enthusiasm.

"Now," I beg again. I'm whimpering. "We'll do it your way next time." I feel like I'm going to scream if he doesn't give me what I want. I can't contain this rising tide of hunger inside me. "Now, Jonas."

"No," he says. "You want the bonfire, but I'm gonna give you the true light. You're gonna surrender to me whether you want to or not."

"Please," I beg. I'm desperate. Pathetic. What if my body can't come, no matter how golden his tongue? Right now, I'm not ready to find out. I just want to enjoy this delicious moment with this amazing man. Suddenly, I'm pissed. He's not in charge here. He doesn't get to tell me how we're going to do this. He doesn't get to call the shots. I grab at his crotch and his hardness makes me moan. "If you won't fuck me, then I'm gonna fuck you," I whisper.

He grunts and I feel his body shudder. I know he can't resist me, despite his big talk. I know it.

I frantically unzip his pants and his shaft springs toward me.

He tilts his head back and groans as I grip his full length. Quickly, before he can change his mind, I lean down and take him into my mouth. His entire body jerks and shudders with pleasure. He lets out a long, strangled groan. He touches the back of my head and grabs at my hair, moaning. "Sarah," he mutters. "Not fair."

My crotch is throbbing. I reach down and touch myself as I take his hardness into my mouth, all the way to the back of my throat. My nipples are so hard they hurt. He moans again, and suddenly, there's that faraway glimmer again, deep inside me, just like the last time— like a butterfly fluttering inside me far, far away. I can't stand it. I can't wait anymore. I pull away from him and swing my leg over his lap, briefly positioning his tip at my wetness, and then I slam myself down on top of him, as hard as I can, plunging him into me.

We both cry out at the same time. He shudders and immediately begins thrusting into me and grabbing my ass like it's his lifeline. I rest my palms on the limo ceiling and ride him like he's a bucking bronco, craning my neck so my head won't bang into the ceiling. My body's never felt this much pleasure, ever.

"Sarah," he mutters again, his thrusting becoming savage.

"Harder," I gasp. "Harder."

He complies, making me gasp. His hand reaches down to my clit as his shaft burrows into me and I throw my head back, yelping. I'm not myself right now. I'm a wild animal—a wild animal trapped in the back of a limo—trying to break free. Sweat is beading down my back. My head is spinning. I grab the back of his neck as I ride him and pull him to my mouth for a voracious kiss. I'm riding him as hard as my body will tolerate, gyrating, my nerve endings exploding as he so expertly touches and fucks me.

He pulls at my hips, forcing himself into my body even farther. Oh God, he's deeper inside me than anyone's ever been. I look down at him, and his eyes are closed, his face enraptured. Those butterfly wings are fluttering inside me, rising and gaining strength. I lean down and lick the entire length of his beautiful face, groaning and slamming my body down onto him as I do.

"Oh God," he moans. He gasps as his body finds its release.

My heart is racing.

I'm trembling.

Sweat is dripping down my back.

But my ache hasn't released. I'm still throbbing. Yearning. Desiring.

The faraway fluttering begins to recede.

It's gone.

After a moment, we unravel from each other. I look out the window and realize we're parked in front of my student apartment complex. What the hell? How long have we been sitting here? Thank God the windows are tinted. Thank God the driver didn't open the door to announce our arrival—or maybe he did. Who the hell knows? I wince at the thought. And why are we here, anyway? I thought Jonas was taking me to his house?

"That was the last time we do it your way," Jonas says evenly. His voice is surprisingly stern. "You keep hijacking me against my will—and against your higher interest."

I shrug. It sure seems like he's enjoying getting hijacked. And I'm sure enjoying doing the hijacking—turning the tables on him and making him abandon his strategy. Fuck his strategy. What if an orgasm just isn't something my body's designed to do? Why must he be so damned focused on that one small thing? Why can't we just keep doing things this way—my way—and not worry about it one way or another? If it's meant to be, it's meant to be. But we don't have to *try* for an orgasm, do we? Why set me up for failure—and set him up for frustration and disappointment?

"From here on out, we do things my way," he says.

I'm noncommittal. "I think my way has worked out pretty damned well."

"Of course you think that—but you're clueless, remember? You're too fucked up to know that what you *want* is different than what you *need*."

"That's my line," I mutter.

He smiles. "I know."

"Are you always this rude?" I ask.

"Only with you." He touches my face and sweeps my hair away from my eyes. His eyes have that mournful look in them again. "Sarah." He kisses my neck. "You make me crazy." His lips graze my neck. "I can't resist you."

"I don't want you to resist me."

"I know. But you *should* want me to. If you'd just let me do things my way, your body will thank me."

"I think maybe you're too focused on the whole orgasm thing."

He takes my hand and kisses it. "You don't even know what you're missing. Just wait 'til your eyes behold the sunlight outside the cave, My Magnificent Sarah."

What if I can't deliver what he wants? How long will he keep trying? Certainly not indefinitely. But how long? A night? Two? What if he does his damned best—what if I let him lick me with his allegedly masterful tongue—and absolutely nothing happens? What then? Then I'll know for sure I'm a lost cause. Men have tried before him and they've failed. Could he possibly be so much better at it than anyone else?

"We do things my way next time," he commands. "And after that, we can do it again any way you please." He kisses the ring on my thumb.

I close my eyes, enjoying the feel of his lips on my fingers. "I'm just saying women don't always need to have—"

"No," he cuts me off. "Stop. When you finally know what the fuck you're talking about, then I'll sit and listen to you talk all day long about how sex isn't about coming, and that men and women are wired differently, and that women are more about the mental and emotional blah, blah, blah. Okay? But until then, I'm in charge. No more hijacking. No more going for the jugular. No more fucking around."

I don't know whether to pout or smile. I'm nervous and excited and anxious and exhilarated at the same time. "I think I was close," I whisper.

He pulls back sharply from me, his eyebrows arched. "When?"

I'm surprised at his sudden excitement. "Both times. I felt something new. Like I was just about to tip over the edge of something." I close my eyes, trying to recall the faraway glimmering I felt, especially just now in the limo.

"Oh man, we're close," he breathes. "If I'd only stuck with my strategy." He runs his hand through his hair, thoroughly energized. "You're wired so fucking hot and you don't even know it, Sarah. When I finally light your fuse, it's going to be the Fourth of fucking July."

I guess there's only one way to find out. "Okay," I say. I want nothing more than for him to be right about that.

His smile spreads across the entire expanse of his beautiful face.

I look out the window at my building. There are students lingering out front, chatting.

"I thought we were going to your house? Why are we here?"

"We're just stopping here so you can pack a bag. You're spending all night with me." He rubs his hands together like a villain in a James Bond movie. "I'm finally gonna get to see your beautiful skin on my crisp white sheets."

Chapter 15
Jonas

I'm sitting on my couch, waiting for her to come out of my bathroom, and, if my rambling thoughts are any indication, possibly spiraling into madness, too. I think I'm addicted to her. I can't get enough. Everything she does, everything she says, everything she *is*—she's perfect. She's better than any fantasy. I can't resist her. One command from her, and my plans are shot to hell. I never, ever planned to fuck her in the bathroom at the restaurant. Or in the limo. Jesus. But I'm not complaining, believe me. Missing out on either one of those delicious fucks would have been a goddamned travesty. And, anyway, it's clear to me now she has to get the crazy out of her system before she'll be anywhere near ready to start her long, slow, sweet surrender. She's like breaking a wild horse. I've just got to let her jump and buck and jerk a little before I try to throw a saddle on her. And that's fine with me—every second with her has been sheer perfection. Except for when she cried. Damn, I never want to see her cry again as long as I live. Just that one tear and I was wrecked.

So it turns out she's got daddy issues after all. I've always been drawn to the girls with daddy issues. I'm so predictable. She didn't say that, of course, but I knew her whole story the minute she talked about helping battered women—could see it playing in my head like a movie. I guess her daddy did quite a number on her and her mom. Bastard.

I sigh. I've really screwed things up so far. I had it all worked out in my head exactly how the night was going to go—she was going to be Meg Ryan in *Sleepless in Seattle* or some other fairytale like that—but damn, I didn't count on her being so damned bossy and taking control. Orgasm or no, that woman fucked my goddamned brains out. It turns out she's got a little crazy inside of her—and, damn, I love me a little crazy. Damn. Damn. Damn. When she turned all bossy on me, when she turned into a fucking she-devil on me, it was so hot. Sure, I came into the night with my big strategy—and I'm gonna get back to it, I swear I am—but who could resist her? Who'd *want* to resist her? Her ass, oh my God—her ass. It's the best ass I've ever laid hands on. And her eyes. When she looked at me like she was going to pounce on me ... "Fuck me," she said, right in my ear, and my head just about exploded. When she said that, that's when I knew for sure: she's perfect.

But I've got to take control now, as pleasant as it's been having her boss me around. From now on, I have one purpose in life. I am on this earth to make this woman experience pure ecstasy, no matter what. And to do that, I've got to show some goddamned restraint around her for once. She needs a slow burn. She needs to feel safe. She needs to feel an emotional connection—because, of course, she was right, women are all about the emotional connection. But the weird part is, I honestly *do* feel an emotional connection with her. When I asked her about herself at dinner, I genuinely wanted to know the answers to my questions. If she'd had a fucking Maltese named Kiki, I actually would have listened to her talk about it all night long—and I would have *cared.* (Though, I was relieved as hell to find out she didn't have a Maltese named Kiki.) If I'm being honest, I already feel more emotionally connected to Sarah than I ever felt toward any of my girlfriends, even Amanda—and I lived with Amanda for almost a year. I've never felt so open, so comfortable as I do with her. It's like I can do no wrong with her. No matter how big an asshole I am, no matter how disgusting the truth is, no matter how honest I am, no matter how twisted I am, she's turned on by it. She actually likes the real me. Go figure. It's addicting.

And, holy fuck, the real Sarah turns me on like nobody ever has. When she said she didn't go to law school for the money, oh man, that was too much. I wanted to take her right there on top of the table. And when she got all pissy about me joining The Club for a full year, I *liked* feeling ashamed about it, because she was right. I *liked* feeling like I should be a better man for her. Hearing her talk about the one-month membership guys like they're all John Cusack holding up a boom box in *Say Anything* was pretty adorable, even though the whole idea is ridiculously naïve. Of course, a guy joining for a month is a diehard romantic, looking for love, *of course* he is. He couldn't possibly have signed up for a month simply because he didn't have enough cash for a longer term. But, hey, if she wants to see romance in the one-month guys, so be it. I think her optimism is cute.

And, hell, maybe she's right. What do I know? Josh certainly has all the money in the world, and he only signed up for a month—and that guy's as big a romantic as there ever was. At any rate, when she told me about that software engineer guy, when she defended his honor like he was a knight in Camelot, she was so sweet—so idealistic. So *kind*. Damn, that woman just gets me off.

My mind is racing. I think I'm losing my mind. I exhale. I have to calm the hell down. I just have to show some restraint and slow things down and stop letting her bring me to my knees every two seconds. Because, right now, I want to make her come more than I want to breathe—and to do that, I've got to take control of this situation.

The door to the bathroom finally opens and Sarah comes out.

"Do you want to finish the tour?" she asks.

"Sure," I say. "There's not much to see."

She laughs and rolls her eyes. "Ah, rich people. So funny."

I look around. By my standards, my house is modest. I mean, don't get me wrong, it's got all the important amenities—a home theatre, a gym, a killer view, a pool, a gourmet kitchen, a wine cellar. But, seriously, it's not outrageous. It's understated. Normal. No bowling alley or basketball court. Pretty modest square footage. Clean lines. Well, yes, the artwork on the walls is spectacular—but I like art. Always have. And, yes, all the floors and finishings are premium, some of the marble is even imported from Italy, but that's only because a person should surround himself with beauty whenever he can. Beauty feeds the soul. I look around, seeing my place through her eyes.

"You know what? Fuck the tour. Are you hungry?"

"I am," she says. "I've worked up an appetite tonight." She blushes.

"Yeah, and it doesn't help that I deprived you of the last five courses at dinner."

"*I* deprived *you*," she says. "I think that's a more accurate summary of tonight's events." She smiles. "You're not the only one with a God complex, remember?" She shoots me a smart-ass wink.

Oh man, she's delicious. "Let's see what we've got in the kitchen," I say.

"Do you have an apple? Or maybe PB&J?" she asks. "I'm easy to please."

She catches my eye and suddenly we both start laughing. Oh yeah, she's easy to please, all right—sure she is. The girl who's never climaxed once in her entire life is as easy to please as falling off a log.

"Well, with food, anyway." She laughs again, reading my thoughts. For a minute, conversation is impossible because we're both laughing so hard.

When her laughter dies down, she wipes her eyes and throws her arms around my neck. "Thank you for the best night ever." She lays an enthusiastic kiss on my cheek.

I nuzzle into her ear. "I still can't believe I found you."

"Pretty crazy, huh?" She disengages from me. "I never thought in a million years I'd be standing here with you—the woman wizard himself."

I pull out the peanut butter and jelly and bread and place them on the counter, and she immediately gets to work. "You want one?" she asks.

"No," I say. "Gross."

"Then why do you have this stuff in the house?"

"Josh. He could live on PB&J and be happy forever. He's gross like you."

She smiles. "Does he come visit you a lot?"

"About once or twice a month, usually. We hike and climb. He comes to Seattle on business, ostensibly, but then we always wind up playing hooky for a few days to climb. We're planning to climb Kilimanjaro next year."

Her sandwich is made and she takes a big bite. She's adorable.

"You want milk with that? Oreos?"

"Oh, yes, please, Oreos with milk. Mmm."

"I was kidding. You know, making fun of the whole little-kid-food thing?"

Her face falls. "Oh."

"That crap will kill you, you know."

She shrugs. "I love Oreos."

I make a mental note to buy Oreos as soon as humanly possible. I don't want to see that look of disappointment on her face ever again if I can help it.

"Kilimanjaro, huh?" She looks wistful for a minute. "Africa."

"Yeah. Should be pretty epic. Water?"

She nods. "Thank you."

I grab two glasses from the cabinet and fill them with ice water. She's already sitting at my kitchen table and I join her. When I place the water in front of her, she thanks me politely and smiles.

"Have you been to Africa before?" she asks.

"Several times," I say. "You?"

"I've never been out of the country."

"No?"

She shakes her head.

"No passport?"

She shakes her head again.

"Well, jeez, you've got to have a passport. I'll have my assistant send you the paperwork. We'll get it expedited."

"Why on earth do I need a passport—and expedited no less?" Her cheeks are suddenly flushed.

"So you can take off on a moment's notice. You never know."

"Well, shoot. That's what's been keeping me from jetting off to Africa on a moment's notice?" She laughs. "Damn." She's playing it cool, but the sudden rosiness in her cheeks is unmistakable.

I laugh.

"I like it when you laugh," she says.

I tilt my head and look at her. I don't normally laugh this much.

She sighs and leans forward onto her elbow. "I bet being so damned good looking can be hard on you sometimes." She takes a big bite of her sandwich.

I raise my eyebrows at her. I can't tell if she's teasing me or not.

"Nobody around you can ever concentrate. Everyone around you turns into a swooning zombie, lost in a daze of idolatry." She pauses. Her voice shifts to something unmistakably serious. "Nobody tells you anything but what you want to hear."

Yeah, she's definitely serious—at least about that last part.

"I'm totally serious," she says, reading my mind. "*Attractive* people have it easiest—the ones smack in the middle on the good-looks spectrum. People are drawn to them and like them because they're not threatening. On the other hand, people who are supernaturally gorgeous like you, the ones on the very edge of the looks spectrum, they're on the wrong side of the tipping point."

142

"What tipping point?"

"That point when people start resenting and projecting and feeling threatened. They start thinking you're a jerk when you're not. Or that you're self-absorbed when you're not. Just because you're so ridiculously gorgeous. They judge you differently."

"Yeah, but what if I *am* a jerk and self-absorbed?"

"Oh, well, then, in that case, you're just plain screwed."

We smile at each other.

"But seriously, you probably have to bend over backwards to make people think you're not a total and complete jerk. It's got to be exhausting."

"So you feel sorry for me for being attractive?"

"No, I told you—you're not *attractive*. *I'm* attractive. You're jaw-droppingly gorgeous." She purses her lips.

I lean forward. "You're jaw-droppingly gorgeous, Sarah." Is it possible she really doesn't know that?

"Gah, I'm not fishing for a compliment here." She sighs and squints her eyes at me. "I'm just trying to figure you out." She takes another bite of her sandwich and shrugs. "You're perfect—except for the fact that you're out screwing a different woman every night, that's a little bit imperfect. But, yeah, other than that, I can't find a fault."

I don't know what to say. She's complimented me and punched me in the gut at the same time. I'm sure my face conveys my confusion.

"I'm not trying to beat you up. It's just ... I'm having a hard time reconciling the Jonas who wanted a lifetime supply of coochie with the Jonas sitting here watching me eat a PB&J after renting out an entire restaurant for me."

Goddamn that fucking application. "Well, I think the answer is that the Jonas who wanted a lifetime supply of coochie didn't actually want a lifetime supply of coochie—he was just too stupid to realize it."

She stops chewing her sandwich mid-bite.

I sigh. "Do you think it would be possible for you to forget about my application and take me as I am, right here, right now, sitting here with you? Because right here, with you, is where I want to be. So whatever phantoms of fuckery you see floating all around me, do you think you could, maybe, possibly, just willfully ignore them, and choose to believe the man you see before you is the real Jonas? It would save us a whole lot of time."

She swallows and nods. She places her hand on her heart, as if to steady it.

"Excellent." My heart is leaping, too. "That'd be really great." I clear my throat. "Really great."

She leans back in her chair.

I stare at her, my jaw muscles pulsing.

"I'm sorry," she says.

I shrug.

"You've been nothing but incredible to me. And I keep testing you, waiting for the other shoe to drop. That's not fair."

"It's an understandable reaction, given who I am and what you know about me—and, of course, all you've been through."

She bristles.

Oh shit.

"All I've been through?"

"I mean, no, I don't know what you've been through. I'm just saying, it's understandable, considering . . ." I trail off. I'm about to come up with some bullshit backpedal to get me out of this mess, but then I remember I promised never to lie to her. "I'm just making some assumptions about you. I probably shouldn't do that."

"What assumptions?"

I clear my throat. Oh shit. Here we go. "I assume you had a real motherfucker for a father. You probably saw him hurt your mom, which had to be pretty traumatizing. I don't know if he hurt you too, physically, but, at the very least, he most certainly abandoned you—emotionally or physically or both. And if I'm right, that's scarred you and fucked you up—maybe more than you even realize—and, in particular, made it really hard for you to trust men. Probably a big reason for your ... sexual ... issues." Oh shit. I'm screwed.

She blinks her eyes several times quickly, like I just gave her mental whiplash. She's quiet for a long time.

My stomach drops. I'm an idiot. Why did I say all that? To show off? I'm such an asshole. It's too sensitive a topic. She doesn't trust me enough yet for me to play armchair psychologist with her. If the girl's got trust issues—raging daddy issues—what better way to push her away than to call her on them? Fuck.

"It's spot on," she finally says. "All of it."

My shoulders relax.

She looks down at the half-eaten sandwich on her plate. "He never laid a finger on me—but, otherwise, yeah." Her eyes lock onto mine.

I nod. My heart is racing.

She sighs. "I'm that transparent?"

"No, not at all." I shrug. She's not. For some reason, I just get her.

She bites on the tip of her finger, lost in thought for a minute. "Yeah, I definitely have trust issues," she says.

I exhale. I'm so glad she's not pissed at me. "I know. It's okay."

"I *can* trust, really I can. Just not quickly. It takes me a while. Longer than it should."

"Okay."

"And maybe you're on to something about how this all ties into my ... sexual ... issues." She tilts her head to the side. "I never put two and two together like that. But you're probably right."

I inhale deeply, trying to regulate my breathing.

"So, Jonas."

"Yes."

"Can I ask you a favor?"

"Anything."

"If, occasionally, I wig out, or kind of ... push you away, could you just not hold it against me?"

"Only as long as you keep your promise not to hold the endless parade of coochie against me."

She half-smiles. "Deal."

"And, anyway, you've already wigged out and pushed me away. Repeatedly. And I didn't hold it against you."

"That's true." Her eyes search mine for a moment. "Thank you for finding me."

"Thank you for being findable."

She laughs that gravelly laugh of hers. "That's not a word."

"It is now. I'm God, remember? It shall be."

She laughs again.

"Can I get you anything else?" I ask. She hasn't touched her sandwich in a while.

"Yeah. Maybe can I see a picture of your family?" she asks.

That's not what I meant. I was talking about an apple or a

cracker. I pause, considering. "Sure," I finally say. I look around. "Um, yeah." I go into the living room, and she follows me. "Um. Here. This is Josh and me." I hand her a business magazine from a couple years ago with Josh and me on the cover. They did a big list of the top thirty business executives in the U.S. under age thirty. Josh and I cohabitated number twenty-five on the list.

"Oh yeah, I saw this picture on your website."

"Yeah. That's Josh. We're twins. Fraternal."

"He's awfully good looking too," she says. "But you're the one who knocks my socks off, by a mile." She makes a sound like she's licking barbeque sauce off her fingers. "You've got that ... darkness. A kind of melancholy in your eyes. I can't resist that."

I'm floored. "You see that in me?"

"Of course I do. In your eyes."

My voice goes quiet. "And you *like* that about me?"

"Are you kidding? It's the best part."

Where did this woman come from? She's everything I was looking for when I joined The Club in the first place—what I was looking for and didn't even realize.

"Any other pictures?" she asks. "Anyone else in your family?"

I'm about to say, "Just my uncle," but instead, I shake my head. For some reason, there's a lump in my throat. "Can I show you another time?" I manage to say. I clear my throat.

"Of course," she says gently. She lays her hand on my forearm.

I nod. That lump hasn't gone away.

"You know what I want to do right now? I want to hold your face in my hands and pepper your beautiful cheeks and eyes and nose and lips with soft kisses."

I exhale. I can't imagine anything better than that right now.

"But seeing as how you hate peanut butter and jelly, I think that would be most unkind of me to do without first brushing my teeth."

Somehow, she's managed to make me smile, just like that. "Good thinking."

She taps her temple with her finger. "I'm always thinking, Jonas," she says. She winks.

I smirk. "That's the understatement of the year."

Chapter 16
Sarah

I'm standing in Jonas Faraday's bathroom, brushing my teeth in Jonas Faraday's sink, staring at myself in Jonas Faraday's mirror. How did I get here? Life is full of surprises; that's for sure.

I close my eyes as I scrub my teeth.

The look on his face when I asked him about his family—that deep sadness that crept into his eyes—just about broke my heart. What happened to this poor man when he was a kid? Clearly, he's not ready to talk about it with me.

From my research, I know Jonas' father, Joseph, died when Jonas was seventeen. But I didn't see anything in particular about how his father died. And, come to think about it, I didn't see any mention whatsoever of his mother. I guess I just assumed she was alive and sitting on the board of some children's hospital or planning tea parties for her local chapter of the Daughters of the American Revolution. But based on what I saw in Jonas' face just now, it's clear she's not alive and well—and whatever happened, he's deeply pained by it.

I place my toothbrush on the counter next to the sink and rinse my mouth out.

There's a soft knock on the door.

"Sarah?" he asks.

"Come in."

He does. "Will you shower with me?" he asks.

"I'd love to."

He steps right up to me like a panther, his muscles taut and overwhelming.

"But first." I reach out and take his face in my hands. "I've been

147

wanting to do this all night long." I kiss his lips gently. It's not a passionate kiss—it's a nurturing one. A kiss that says, *No matter how fucked up you happen to be, Jonas Faraday, I still want you.*

He closes his eyes and sighs deeply as my lips skim past his lips to his eyelids, across his eyebrows, and to the tip of his perfectly sculpted nose. I bring my fingers up to his face and trace his brow line, marveling yet again at the perfect symmetry of his features.

He sighs again, melting into my touch. When he finally opens his eyes, he looks at me with such need—such earnest, raw, vulnerable need—I reach out and hug him to me like he's the lost child I've finally recovered at a busy mall.

He returns my fervent embrace and exhales into my hair.

We stand, embracing for a moment in silence. When he pulls away and looks at my face again, he looks instantly concerned.

"What's wrong?" he asks.

I shake my head. There's nothing wrong, as far as I know. I'm just finding it hard to ignore the fierce emotions swirling inside me. "Nothing's wrong," I whisper. I attempt a smile.

He disengages from me briefly to turn on the hot water in the shower.

When he turns back to me, he brushes my hair out of my eyes.

"How are you feeling?" he asks.

I shrug. "If I answer that question, my strategy for the night will be blown to bits."

He half-smiles. "I mean physically. Down there."

Down there? This from the man who spews words like "pussy" and "cunt" as easily as "hello" and "goodbye?"

"Wow, a kinder, gentler Jonas," I mumble.

He looks sheepish.

"I like it," I assure him. "I'm pretty sore," I say. "You nailed me pretty good tonight, big boy."

"Yeah." His eyes light up. "Twice."

I smirk.

"Let's recharge our batteries a little," he suggests. "Even *I* need to get my second wind. You're killing me."

"Old man," I tease.

He flashes a crooked grin. "We're not in any rush. We've got all the time in the world."

"More than two to seven hours?" I smile so he knows I'm trying to be funny. But, honestly, I'm nervous. If I'm reading this situation wrong, if this is just a one-night, Cinderella-at-the-ball kind of thing for him, I'll be crushed. Am I feeling the way every woman feels after experiencing the divine Jonas Faraday? Is what I'm feeling right now the precise "problem" he described in his application—the female inability to distinguish physical rapture from some kind of romantic fairytale? Are the feelings I'm having exactly what pushed him into The Club in the first place?

"Yeah, longer than two to seven hours," he says softly.

It's vague, yes, but, hey, it's something. I'll take it.

"All I wanna do is touch your skin. Okay? That's all for now."

I nod. Thank God. I really, really don't want to disappoint him—and, of course, faking it is out of the question—but I just don't think I've got enough gas left in the tank to attempt those butterfly flutters for the third time in one night. I'm only human, after all.

Steam is beginning to fill the bathroom and cloud the mirrors.

He reaches behind my back and unzips my dress. Unlike in the bathroom at the restaurant, he gently pulls it up, over my head, prompting me to instinctively hold my arms up over my head. When my dress is off, he surveys my body with fire in his eyes. With one swift motion, he reaches behind my back and unclasps my bra, freeing my breasts. His breath halts as he takes in the sight of them.

He bites his lip.

Without being asked, I take off my G-string and stand before him in nothing but my smile. He looks me up and down, blinking slowly, like he's trying to control himself from tackling me.

"You're incredible," he says, his voice brimming with desire.

I reach out with a trembling hand and unbutton his shirt, slowly pulling it down, off his shoulders. Holy crap, his torso is a work of art. I can't imagine how many hours he's spent in the gym to sculpt his body into such a breathtaking display of the human form. He's glorious.

I run my fingertip over the long, tattooed inscription running down the length of his left forearm. Now that I see it in person, I can tell it's written in the Greek alphabet. But now's not the time to ask him about it—now's not the time for words. And I'm pretty sure I know what it says, anyway. I run my finger down his other tattoo,

too, on his right forearm—also in Greek. I don't have a guess as to what this one says, but, again, I don't need to know right now.

He reaches down, pulls off his pants and briefs, and throws them across the bathroom with gusto.

I laugh. But when he turns back to me and stands squarely in front of me, his muscles tensing and his erection at full attention, I stop laughing. Holy hell. I've never seen a more spectacular looking man. And he's looking at *me* like I'm beauty incarnate.

With a loud exhale, he grabs my hand and leads me into the steaming shower. The hot water pelts me in the face and runs down my chest as he stands behind me, gliding his hands over my wet hips, my butt, my back, nudging me with his hardness. I spread my legs slightly and brace myself for him to enter me, but he doesn't, so I turn back around to face him, the hot water cascading around us. His lips are instantly on mine, his hands on my breasts.

I wouldn't have believed it possible after the rigorous sex we've already had tonight, but I'm yearning for him again. But just when I'm about to grab his penis and guide him into me, Jonas pulls away and grabs a washcloth. He pumps some shower gel onto it and glides it across my back and down to my butt.

"Best ass ever," he whispers in my ear.

An all-consuming ache has consumed me. I want him again. I don't care if I'm sore. And I certainly don't care about coming. I just want to feel him inside me again—to be as close to him as humanly possible. I reach for his erection, but he gently guides my hand away.

I glare at him and he smiles.

He pumps some more shower gel onto his hand, and reaches down between my legs. I gasp at his gentle touch, bracing myself for more—wanting more—but he merely cleans me, ever so gently, and then pulls his hand away. He grabs the showerhead off its attachment and carefully washes the suds off every inch of my skin. When he holds the showerhead between my legs, he leaves it there for a moment, letting the warm, strong stream caress me. His kiss is becoming more and more impassioned. I lift my leg, aching for him to enter me again—and he takes the showerhead away. He turns the water off, smirking at me.

What the hell?

He exits the shower, leaving me standing there, dripping and panting. He grabs a thick, white towel off the rack.

Not at all what I expected.

With great care, he wraps the towel around me and grabs one for himself. Without a word, he takes my hand and leads me out of the shower.

What the effing hell? He actually wanted to take a *shower* in the shower?

"Slow burn, baby," he whispers, reading my thoughts. He winks. He dries us both off and leads me out of the bathroom to his bed. "Please." He motions to his bed.

I'm happy to comply. With great fanfare, I crawl onto his bed like a minx—arching my back and sticking out my butt like I'm a wildcat stalking my prey. After a moment, I swing my face back to look at him, smiling broadly.

But he's not smiling. No, he's staring at me, his eyes smoldering, his erection straining. His eyes could cut glass.

Oh man, just that look from him, and I'm on fire. I flip over onto my back and spread myself out, inviting him to join me.

But he doesn't join me in the bed.

I glance up at him.

His eyes are fixed on me.

I raise my arms above my head and spread my legs out wide. "I'm all yours," I say.

His erection twitches, but he stands stock still, not taking his eyes off me.

What's he waiting for?

He takes a deep breath and strides purposefully to his laptop across the room. "I Melt With You" by Modern English—one of my all-time favorite songs—begins playing. My heart soars. This is the last song in the world I'd expect him to play for me. I would have figured him to be a Nine Inch Nails kind of guy.

Jonas is a jungle cat. I'm his prey. He crawls slowly over to me on the bed as the singer from Modern English croons about us melting together. In a flash, Jonas' commanding body hovers over mine, his muscles bulging and tensing as he rests on his forearms on either side of my head.

The song is seducing me, swirling around me, captivating me.

"I love this song," I murmur as his lips press into mine.

"Best song ever," he says, kissing me slowly.

Here I thought he was going to fuck me like a beast again, and he wants to stop this perfect moment and melt with me? My heart is bursting.

He kisses me deeply. His hands are touching me, every inch of me.

He groans with pleasure. "Sarah," he mumbles into my lips. "Oh my God."

I close my eyes. The song lyrics, his strong body pressing into mine, his hands on my skin, his soft lips tenderly kissing me—it's all swirling around me and over me and through me, transporting me to another dimension. This might be the most sublime moment of my entire life.

"You're perfect," he says.

I can't respond. I'm floating, reeling, flying.

His hand finds the wetness between my legs and gently caresses me with the softest, barely-there touch. A soft moan escapes my mouth.

I follow his lead and touch him slowly, gently.

He lets out a long, shaky breath.

I'm suddenly anxious. This is it. He's going to try to make me come, and I know in my heart it's not going to happen right now. I'm sore and exhausted. I've never had this much sex in my life. Even if having an orgasm were possible for me, which is not a sure thing *at all,* what if my body's just not up to it right now? I'll never know if I failed because of my body's current state of exhaustion or if I'm just not capable of it, period.

"Just relax," he coos. "We're not trying to accomplish anything. We're just touching each other, that's all."

He kisses me and I wrap my legs around him, pressing my body into his.

"No pressure," he whispers, pressing against me, nipping at my ear. "We'll just make out."

I don't want this magical night to end in disappointment for him—or for me. I want to be the live wire he thinks I am. But I've never had sex three times in one night in my life, and I'm losing steam. If he finally goes down on me now—the thing he loves to do more than anything—and absolutely nothing happens for me, then what? Other guys have tried, and other guys have failed. What if I just *can't*? I want to give it the ol' college try when I can give it my best.

His hand strokes my cheek. "We'll just pretend we're teenagers tonight. We'll just make out."

It's like he can read my mind. I nod and close my eyes.

The song enraptures me.

I feel his lips on my neck and then on my breasts. He licks my nipples and I can't help but arch my back with pleasure. His tongue is warm, confident. His hands rub my thighs, my belly, and my butt (which he squeezes with enthusiasm). His fingers return to lightly caress the increasing wetness between my legs.

Another soft moan escapes me. I'm suddenly aching for him, longing for him to slip his fingers inside me—I don't care if I'm raw and sore from our previous escapades. I gyrate with pleasure, straining toward him. I reach down and gently fondle him.

He moans.

My head is spinning. I like the feel of his erection in my hand. I like the feel of his warm, taut muscles against my body. I like the feel of his lips on my body, his fingers. Oh God, his fingers have just found the exact spot that drives me wild. I moan. Lord have mercy, he is so effing good at this.

His tongue flickers onto my breasts, my nipples, and then moves south, down to my belly. His tongue visits my belly button and heads to the inside of my thigh. I strain toward the warmth of his tongue, willing him to move to the left and find my epicenter, but his tongue remains on my inner thigh, teasing me. My body is throbbing, yearning for him, apparently oblivious to the self-doubt wracking my brain.

Jonas exhales audibly. His face is perched between my legs. I can feel his warm breath on me. I spread my legs wider, yearning for him. He pauses, his mouth hovering right next to me. Oh my God, I'm throbbing for him. Forget what I said about holding off. I shift, positioning myself, making it easy for him. I tilt my hips up to him.

I'm trembling.

He sighs audibly.

I open my eyes and look up at him.

His face is hovering between my legs. His eyes are on fire. He exhales again and a puff of air teases me.

He licks his lips. He looks like a big cat right now. "There's no rush." Clearly, he's saying that more to himself than to me. He brings his hand to my clit and brushes it ever so gently again.

I shudder. But I don't want his fingers anymore. I want his tongue.

He licks his lips. "I've got to taste you, just once. I have to know what you taste like or else I'm gonna have a fucking stroke."

I nod and close my eyes. Since I first read his words describing his allegedly mind-boggling lingual talents, I've fantasized repeatedly about him using his nimble tongue on me, his somber eyes gazing up at me from between my legs.

"Just one taste."

I nod again. I can't breathe. I'm panting.

Nothing.

Why isn't he doing it? I open my eyes and look down. He's staring at me, clearly waging some kind of internal battle. "I want to lick you so bad," he says.

"So do it already. Jeez."

He exhales like a boxer about to go into the ring. He makes a big show of loosening his jaw. "This isn't it, okay? I'm gonna do this for real later when you're not sore and tired. This is just for me—because I'm an idiot and I can't resist you. Don't get a complex about it, okay? You're not gonna come right now, so don't get all fucked-up in the head about it, okay? This isn't it."

I nod. No pressure. Just a little taste. Got it.

"Don't think."

I nod again and lean back, closing my eyes. "Hit me."

Without warning, his tongue licks me in one clean swoop like I'm a melting, dripping ice cream cone on a hot summer day.

I cry out. Holy fuck, that feels good. My entire body jerks violently at the shock of it.

He makes a low, guttural sound, and then his warm tongue is penetrating me, his lips devouring me. And, just like that, I'm losing my fucking mind. Forget butterfly wings fluttering at a distance—a fighter jet just revved its engines somewhere deep inside me. Holy motherfucking shit.

His mouth abruptly stops its assault and his face is suddenly an inch away from mine.

"Taste yourself," he whispers, pressing his lips to mine. "So good." He plunges his tongue into my mouth, and my entire body bursts into flames. I've never tasted myself before. I'm barely there on his tongue, but I'm there. And I'm undeniably delicious.

The song tells me again how much he wants to stop everything and melt his body into mine.

"I want you inside me," I breathe.

I don't have to ask him twice. I wince at first—I'm pretty raw—but as he burrows deeper and deeper into me, my body relaxes and receives him. His tongue explores my mouth as his shaft begins moving in and out of me, slowly, gently.

"Is this okay?" he asks softly, his voice halting.

"So good," I breathe back. I want to melt with him—to fuse my body into his.

His skin is warm and firm and rippling in all the right places. He's kissing me, touching me, moving in and out of me. I'm lost in the moment. I'm lost in him.

The song restarts from the beginning. He must have set it to play on a loop. I bring my legs up around him, drawing him into me. His hand reaches down and touches the backs of my thighs, my butt.

He groans and thrusts into me even more deeply. "You feel so good," he says. I open my eyes to find his blues eyes an inch away from mine, gazing at me as he moves inside me, the music washing over us. He brings his hand up to my cheek as he gyrates inside of me.

Oh God, the singer keeps telling me Jonas wants to melt with me.

Electricity is coursing through my veins. My heart is leaping out of my chest, overflowing with joy and relief and sheer awe that I'm here, with him, in his house, in his bed. I hug him to me, wanting to absorb him into me. I tilt my hips forward and back in synchronicity with his thrusts, willing our bodies to become one.

"Sarah," he whispers.

I don't know what's happening between us, but I never want it to end.

He yelps and devours my mouth with fervor, his tongue mimicking the gyrating motion happening between our bodies.

That faraway fluttering announces itself again faintly. I hitch my legs up even higher around him, as I high as I can manage, trying yet another means of allowing him entry into the deepest recesses of my body. But it's not deep enough. I need to be on top.

He pulls away from our kiss and looks at me intensely. "I want to taste you again," he says, his voice hoarse.

I shake my head emphatically. "Not this time."

He touches my hair. "I want to taste you."

I shake my head. If it turns out I really am a ten-percenter, I don't want to prove it unequivocally right now—that's not how I want this magical night to end. "Next time," I breathe. "I promise." I push at his chest. "Me on top," I whisper.

His strong arms reach behind my back and cradle me. In one deft maneuver, he's suddenly on his back and I'm on top of him, straddling him, riding him, losing my mind. He's thrusting into me, grabbing at me, groping me, kissing me, groaning, and I'm gyrating my hips to take him into me as deeply as possible. He touches my clit—damn, he's good at that—and that's it. I'm a goner. I can't think, can't form words. I'm losing my mind. The pleasure's incredible.

Something is welling up inside me. I feel like an animal. I throw my head back and groan loudly. I'm losing control. I feel outside myself. I scream his name. I scream it again. Oh my God, I can't control myself. Sounds are emerging from my throat I've never made before. I'm panting. My heart is racing. My head is spinning.

"Sarah," he chokes out.

My body convulses and shudders around him, like a giant internal slap. It happens only once, but it's forceful and undeniable.

"Oh God," he groans. His body shudders and shakes from deep inside me with his release.

There's a long pause. His breathing is ragged. His muscles are glistening underneath me.

The song reaches its chorus again, telling me yet again how Jonas feels about me.

I bite my lip. There's a dull ache in my lower abdomen. I'm still throbbing. Aching. Yearning. I'm not finished.

He reaches up to my shoulders and pulls me down to his face. He kisses my eyelids, my nose, my cheeks. "So much for a slow burn," he murmurs.

I laugh.

"Oh, fuck," he says, and sighs. "You're killing me." Something flickers in his eyes I don't recognize.

"What are you thinking?" I ask.

He sighs. "That I keep fucking this up."

"Oh my God, no, this has been the best night—"

"No, trust me. I'm fucking this up. But, soon, very soon, I'm gonna taste you, and learn you, and lead you to the light."

"This is the light. Right now."

He sighs. "No, you're still stuck in the cave. I told you, I'm gonna give you *both* Valentine's Day bullshit *and* howling-monkey-sex. I haven't delivered on the second half yet."

How can that be? This was the most romantic night of my life and also the best sex I've ever had. Okay, granted, I didn't technically come—I mean, I don't think I did—I'd know it if I did, right? But I was closer than I've ever been, for sure. And, really, it doesn't matter anyway. I've decided I don't care about coming. What we just did was more than enough for me.

"As far as I'm concerned," I say, "we just had howling monkey-sex. It can't get any better than that."

His mouth hitches up on one side. "Oh, Sarah. My poor little bonfire-admiring-green-bean-eater."

I laugh out loud.

He shakes his head and sighs in frustration.

Oh, I don't like that sigh. I smile at him, but I'm uneasy. Obviously, I'm already starting to disappoint him. "I can't imagine anything better than what we just did, Jonas," I say, but even as I say it, I know my words won't convince him. The man wants what he wants. Why, oh why is he so focused on me having an orgasm? Wasn't tonight incredible? Wasn't it enough? It was for me. If I had to choose between having this day over and over, and trading it in for some mythical orgasm that "untethers" me in some vague way I can't begin to understand, I'd pick this night every single time. No orgasm could beat the way I feel right now.

We've stopped everything and melted together.

He kisses me gently. "Just you wait 'til you finally see the light outside the mouth of the cave, baby." He laughs like a villain in a cartoon. "Bwahahahaha!"

I can't help but smile. I like it when he's playful. But I'm anxious. What exactly is he promising? I wonder how long he'll keep trying before he throws up his hands and says, "Forget it."

"But right now, I gotta pee," he says.

He tilts suddenly to the side, throwing me off his lap onto the bed in a crumpled heap. He rolls off the bed and heads into the bathroom, practically whistling a happy tune as he goes, stopping first to turn off the music.

I lie in the bed, looking up at the ceiling. I've never felt so compulsively attracted to another human being like this. I don't want this to end—but what if I can't deliver his "holy grail"?

He returns and scoots next to me in the bed. He's got his laptop with him. He grins at me mischievously.

"I thought we could take a look at my very first note to you— My Beautiful Intake Agent—seeing as how it's what made you throw yourself at me and beg me to find you."

I swat him on the shoulder. "I thought you were a narcissistic jerk."

"Well, I was. *Am.* But you wanted me anyway, right?"

I nod profusely. "Yep."

"Well, then, let's enjoy my narcissistic ramblings together, shall we?" He clicks into his email account to retrieve the document. "Oh, wow," he says, his attention diverted from the task at hand. "I've got an email from The Club. Lovely."

Every hair on my body instantly stands on end.

"'Dear Mr. Faraday,'" he says, reading from the email on his screen. "'Our records indicate you have not been using your membership. Do you have any questions or concerns? Please let us know if we can assist you in any way.'"

I have a pit in my stomach.

"Fuck you," he mutters to his computer screen and looks at me, smirking. His grin instantly vanishes. "Why do you look like that?"

"Why would a sane person spend two hundred fifty thousand dollars on something and not use it?" I feel sick.

"Maybe I'm not sane."

"But they've got to be wondering *why*."

"They got their money; that's all they care about."

I keep having this unshakeable feeling—or is it a

premonition?—that violations of The Club's rules don't go unpunished.

"Sarah," Jonas says, "what's wrong?"

I sigh. "I don't know. Never mind. I'm probably just being melodramatic."

"What?"

"I just keep feeling like there's got to be some sort of consequence for what I've done."

"What you've *done*? Sarah, I know you're fucked-up, but are you batshit crazy?"

I don't return his smile.

His face registers acute concern again. "You didn't defy *The Church*. You defied *The Club*. Big difference."

I'm unconvinced. I keep feeling like the shit's going to hit the fan at some point—and sooner rather than later.

"Is there something you're not telling me?"

I shake my head.

He looks wary.

"I'm sure I'm just being paranoid. Forget it." I shake it off. "Why don't you read your cocky-motherfucker-asshole message to me? I could use a good laugh."

He closes his laptop and puts it on his nightstand. "Come here," he says, pulling my naked body to his. I love the feel of his warm skin on mine. I lay my head on his chest.

He strokes my hair. "What you did was a good thing. A very, very good thing." He kisses the top of my head.

I close my eyes, enjoying his embrace, his touch.

He continues stroking my hair. "The best thing."

The anxiety I was feeling vanishes. My entire body relaxes.

"You're safe."

I can't believe his first cocky note to me—well, not to *me*, but to some nameless, faceless "intake agent" who turned out to be me—has led to this exquisite moment.

His hand moves to the curve of my lower back and stays there. "You're safe," he whispers.

"Mmm," I say. I'm drifting.

Jonas' breathing has become rhythmic under my head.

I'm floating between consciousness and dreamland, the words of that first note scrolling through my head like a news ticker: *Nice and slow ... only ever dreamed ... like no man before ... surrender, totally and completely.* I never thought in a million years I'd be lying here now with the author of those words, our naked bodies pressed together, my heart beating against his.

Jonas is asleep underneath me. His chest is rising and falling slowly.

My breathing is beginning to match his.

My mind is blissfully deserting me.

I'm falling, falling, falling. Darkness is overtaking me. But just before I fall completely, just before I slip into serene unconsciousness, one last thought—an admission, really—the exact admission he predicted I'd make in that first arrogant note—flitters across my mind: *"In addition to you being one cocky-bastard-asshole-motherfucker, you're also the man of my dreams."*

Chapter 17
Jonas

"Mmm," she moans.

It's morning. Rain is beating against my bedroom window. We're lying in my bed together, naked, tangled up in my sheets. I don't know when we fell asleep last night, but we must have. The last thing I remember was stroking her hair as she laid her head on my shoulder.

I've been awake for a few minutes, listening to the sound of the rain, enjoying the sensation of her bare skin against mine. I've had a boner from the minute I opened my eyes, but I've let her sleep. Unfortunately, my time is limited this morning—I've got something really important scheduled at the office in about an hour—and since I've decided that Jonas-gets-off-but-Sarah-doesn't is no longer acceptable from this moment forward, sex simply isn't going to happen this morning. No more quickies—no more fucking around. I'm going to do it right from now on. As I've been lying here, feeling her soft skin against mine, listening to her breathing, I've decided not to have sex with her again until I'm sure the situation's perfectly ripe for her to come. No matter what. She doesn't know what she's been missing, but I do. And I hate myself for continually leaving her standing on the proverbial curb while I peel away in a Ferrari. It's not fair to her.

I thought I'd be calling all the shots, but that's not the way things have worked out. Damn, she's bossy. I didn't fully grasp that aspect of her personality until last night. If she'd have let me be in charge like I wanted to be, I'd be lying here right now replaying her first orgasm over and over again in my mind. And giving her an encore this morning. But no. She had to take control, and I had to be a

161

pussy-ass and let her, and now everything's all built up in her mind and she's probably got performance anxiety like a motherfucker. Now, thanks to my inability to resist her, I've got to be especially mindful about next steps. We're at a tipping point here, and I don't want to screw it up.

She's so close. Oh my God. Last night, I felt her body constrict and collapse and shudder around my cock, I'm sure of it. It was brief, just once—but it was *ferocious*. If she'd just listened to me and done things my way, she'd have come by now, I'm sure of it—but no, my crazy little bucking bronco has to go for the jugular every time. And I keep bending to her will because, truth be told, she owns me. Damn. She really does. And the worst part is that, intellectually, I know exactly what buttons she's pushing—exactly what defense mechanism is coming into play—and I *still* can't resist her. It's like I'm playing chess with a girl who tells me, flat-out, "I'm moving *here* so you'll move *there*, so I can take your king"—and yet I'm still dumb enough to move exactly where she tells me to, anyway. Am I stupid or just going crazy? I think it's the latter. I think I'm devolving into a certain kind of madness, thanks to her—an all-consuming madness. And it's fucking amazing.

She moans again and stretches her hands above her head.

Damn. If I'd only known she was that close, I'd probably have done things differently last night. I would have licked her nice and slow, just like I'd planned from the get-go. I just overthought everything, that's all. I was so worried she was too tired, and I didn't want to give her some kind of complex when it didn't work out. But I was wrong. If I'd only done it right, if I'd have let her simmer, anticipate, *yearn* like her life depended on it, it would have worked last night. She's ready to go off like dynamite. But, no, I barreled right in and fucked her exactly like she wanted. Why can't I control myself with her?

She props herself onto her elbow and looks down at me, her dark hair falling around her bare shoulders. "Good morning, Jonas," she says with mock politeness, as if we're just meeting for the first time.

"Why, good morning, Sarah," I reply, mimicking her tone. "So lovely to see you this fine morning." She looks beautiful.

She sighs audibly. "Lovely, indeed." She grins.

I glance over at the clock and grunt. Damn. I've got to get to the office. If all goes according to plan, today's meeting just might change my entire life.

She follows my gaze to the clock. She purses her lips. "I've got a class in an hour," she coos. She touches my face with the back of her hand. "But I suppose I could miss it just this once, if a tragically good lookin' guy with sad eyes and bulging biceps were in the mood to show me the 'culmination of human possibility.'" She flashes me a mischievous smile and leans in for a kiss.

I grimace. Oh my God. This is the worst timing in the history of the world. "I've got an important meeting," I say—and the minute the words leave my mouth, I know they sound like a kiss-off.

She tries to mask her face in nonchalance, but she can't hide the fire in her cheeks. She pulls away, smiling. "Oh, yeah, I should get to class, anyway." Her cheeks are blazing. She quickly begins untangling herself from me, obviously planning to exit the bed as quickly as possible and hightail it out of here.

I grab her arm. "Sarah, no."

She turns to me and feigns a lighthearted smile. "It's fine."

"Listen to me. It's this huge thing with Josh and these guys coming in from Colorado. Life changing, maybe. If it were anything else, anything at all, believe me, I swear, I'd clear my calendar for the whole day—for the whole *week*—and spend every single second with you, right here in my bed, exploring every inch of you, day and night. There's nothing I want more than to be with you."

I've never said anything even remotely close to these words to a woman before, ever—never even felt remotely *tempted* to utter words like these—but as I say them, I know they're one hundred percent true.

Her shoulders relax. "Oh," she says softly.

Jesus, did she really think I was kicking her out? Like, literally, kicking her out of my bed? After the incredible night we just had? I sigh. Of course she did, thanks to that stupid application. I wish she'd never read it.

The smile that spreads across her face this time is genuine. Unguarded.

"Yeah, oh." I push her hair behind her shoulder. "I keep telling you—I can't get enough of you. Please, please, please believe me. I'm telling you the truth—I'll always tell you the truth. Good, bad, ugly. The truth."

Lauren Rowe

She bites her lip. "I can't get enough of you, either." She rolls her eyes. "Obviously."

My cock is tingling with anticipation. Well, maybe there's time, after all?

I look at the clock again. Damn. No. There's no time. I'm going to be late as it is. Sure, Josh can start the meeting without me—but I've definitely got to get over there. Josh is Mr. Personality, Mr. Close-the-Deal—but I'm the one who understands the numbers. He needs me. And this deal is the biggest deal of my life.

I sigh at my predicament. She's as ripe as a summer peach. If I licked her now, nice and slow on her sweet button, she'd go off like dynamite. But I don't have time to do it right, so I shouldn't do it at all.

"I wanna do it when we've got time. No pressure on us."

She nods. "I know."

I grin. "I've got a proposition for you."

"Oh yeah?"

"Well, it's more of a decision."

"Oh? You've made a *decision*, have you?"

"Yes."

"Enlighten me, oh, Lord-God-Master. What have *you* decided?"

"From now on, *I* don't come if *you* don't come."

She pulls back sharply. "What?"

"I don't come 'til you do. I'm all about you from now on. Period."

"Jonas, no. You can't do that. Who knows how long it will take me? No, that's just plain stupid."

"It's not gonna take long, believe me. Next time, if I do it right—when you're relaxed and we've got all the time in the world—you're gonna be dancing in the beautiful sunlight outside the cave. I guarantee it."

"But what if I don't? What if it never happens?"

"Ridiculous. You're this close." I just need to get her out of her head. I just need to take it slow—with lots and lots of prelude. "We're a team. You don't get yours, I don't get mine. I'm all-in, baby."

She twists her mouth up. "Well, damn, that's a lot of pressure."

I sigh, exasperated. "No, the whole idea is there's *no* pressure." I grunt. "How does me being all-in possibly make you feel like there's *more* pressure?"

164

She shrugs. "Now I've got your satisfaction to worry about, not just mine."

"Jesus, woman. You're impossible. Will you just trust me? If you'd just let me do my thing, you'd realize I'm *excellent* at sex, okay? Like, a fucking master. Aristotle said, 'We are what we repeatedly do. Excellence, then, is not an act, but a habit.' I've acquired a habit of excellence in this particular discipline—just let me do what I'm excellent at."

She laughs. "I wonder how Aristotle would feel about you quoting him for this particular purpose."

I shrug. "Excellence at doing something, whatever it is, is still excellence. I am what I repeatedly do. And so are you." I look at her pointedly, letting that sink in. "What you've repeatedly done has led you to the same frustrating result over and over. And I've let myself perpetuate your habit because I'm a weak-willed, pussy-ass who can't resist you any more than a junkie can resist smack. But I've made a decision. I'm gettin' off the dope. I'm gonna change your sexual *habit* to give you a different result." I wave my hand in flourish. "You're gonna get nothing but sexual excellence from me from now on, baby—*sexcellence.*"

She can't help but laugh.

"So here's what we're going to do and there shall be no arguments—I've had it with your bossy bullshit."

She bites her lip, trying to hold back a smile.

"I hereby grant you, Sarah Cruz, membership in The Jonas Faraday Club—and you're this club's only member, if you're wondering—the mission of which is quite simply the ultimate sexual satisfaction of one Miss Sarah Cruz, the goddess and the muse."

Giddiness instantly washes over her. Wow. It's an instant transformation. She really likes this idea.

I'm only just now formulating my plan on the fly, even as I speak, but it's got me excited, especially seeing the look on her face. Oh man, that look on her face could launch a thousand ships. Yeah, my mind is really clicking now. "You'll fill out an application—revealing all your sexual preferences—and I'll make them come true."

"Wow," she says, her cheeks blazing. "How long does this membership last?" Her eyes flicker with anxiety the second the question pops out of her mouth. She looks like she wishes she could stuff it back in.

Oh shit. My chest is suddenly banging. I didn't think about that. How long am I willing to commit to this little idea?

With each second I pause to consider my answer, her expression devolves further into anxiety. Shit. I've really stepped in it. What am I willing to commit to, right here and now? Shit. Shit. I don't know. Fuck. Why did I barrel right in without thinking this through? There's a lot riding on what I say here. I've got to get this right. I need a minute to think about this.

Her chest is heaving up and down. So is mine.

Wow, her breasts are incredible. I want to lick them. No, back to the task at hand. I glance at the clock again. Shit. I'm late for the most important meeting of my life. My entire body is tingling, not just my hard-on. I'm onto something here, and I don't want to screw it up. I offered her membership in my "club" as a total whim—an off the cuff remark. But holy shit, the look on her face—I had no idea she'd react quite this way. And now I want to deliver on whatever it is she's hoping for.

"Let's talk about it in the shower," I say.

She nods, biting her lip again. Damn, she's adorable.

The hot water is beating down on us. Clearly, she thinks I've moved this party into the shower for some good old-fashioned fuckery, but that's not the plan. No more fast and hard for My Magnificent Sarah—no more letting her go for the jugular to distract me from her insecurities. I brought her in here for three reasons. One, I'm late for my meeting—and I sincerely need to shower and get out of here. Two, I just needed a change of scenery, a minute to think things through. And, three, and most importantly, I just wanted to touch her again. I can't be expected to stare at her breasts during an entire conversation without getting to touch the merchandise.

Her skin is slick under the water. I lather her, sliding my hands down to her ass, nip at her neck, kiss her lips, nudge her with my erection. It's torture not taking things further, but it's a delicious kind of torture. Slowing things down, weaning her from what she's used to doing, might not be what she wants—but it's what she needs. I'm sure of it. So says Aristotle, and so says Jonas Faraday. And, maybe, just maybe, slowing things down is exactly what I need, too. I kiss her, the hot water pelting us, but I can tell she's on pins and needles, waiting to hear what I'm going to say about how long her membership in my club's going to last.

"A month," I whisper into her ear, and instantly regret it. Too short. Offensive. She's gonna freak out and do her self-sabotaging "push me away" thing.

But, no, not at all. In fact, her face is beaming with joy. Holy fuck, she's thrilled. What did she think I was gonna say?

She squeals. She actually *squeals.* She nods profusely and lunges at me. Her kiss is on fire. Her body is grinding into me. Oh my God, she's attacking me. "A month," she mutters.

"A month," I mumble into her lips. "And we do everything my way," I say.

She laughs in my ear. "Right," she says. "But how 'bout you have one last hurrah before my month officially starts—while you're processing my application." She grips my shaft and kneels down in front of me, grinning like a Cheshire cat.

She doesn't ask for permission. Doesn't hesitate. She takes me into her mouth and instantly begins devouring me.

My knees buckle. Holy shit.

I know I said we were gonna do things my way. But ... oh, yeah, wow ... so good. Just like that, good. Oh, she's good. She's ... oh ... she's good at this. I know I said ... She's really, really good at this. I throw my head back. Hot water's pelting me, cascading down my chest, making my skin red and hot. Her lips are slick and wet, her tongue is voracious. The water's so warm and wet, and so is her mouth.

I can't keep letting her . . .

She's talented. She's so fucking talented. And relentless. Oh fuck.

She moans.

My knees buckle.

I look down. She's got one hand on me, and one hand between her legs.

My entire body shudders at the sight.

I reach down and grab her wet hair, pushing myself into her. She moans again.

Fuck. I'm out of my fucking mind. I'm on the verge. Yes. Yes. Yes.

No, wait, no, no, no. I don't want to come yet. No fucking way. There's no way I'm letting her walk out of here today like this. No way in hell.

I pull on the back of her hair, gently, pulling her off me. She looks up at me and licks her lips. She looks drunk. "I'm not finished yet," she says. "I like it." She licks her lips again. Her eyes are blazing. "I like it, Jonas." Her hand is between her legs, working herself.

"I wanna taste you for a minute."

Her chest heaves. I don't need to ask her twice. She stands upright and leans against the marble shower wall, her hands fondling her own breasts. She lifts one of her legs onto shower ledge as an invitation.

I bend down and begin lapping at her, letting the hot water hit the back of my head and stream down my back. Holy fuck, she's delicious.

She yelps and grinds into my tongue. "Oh, yes," she says, her voice muffled by the water. "Oh, God, Jonas, yes." Her fingers are in my wet hair. Her pelvis tilts into me. She shoves my face into her. My tongue finds her sweet button. She moans. "Oh my God," she says. I lick her with a bit more pressure. Her body jerks violently. She's moaning and writhing like crazy.

Fuck. I have a decision to make. If I keep going and she doesn't come, she's going to get all freaked out and become convinced she's hopeless. Better to stop now and leave her wanting more. As a parting shot, I suck on her clit. She screams and her entire body jerks.

I stand up and instantly plunge myself into her. She's all over me, grabbing me, lifting her leg to allow me entry into her. I grab her ass and thrust into her, deeply, the hot water cascading all over and around us.

She's licking my neck, slamming her body into mine. She bites my neck and I shudder.

I reach down and fondle her as I move in and out of her and she screams at the top of her lungs.

I'm shocked. What the fuck is happening right now?

She's frantic. Her movement is urgent, primal. She's totally uninhibited. Oh God, she feels so good. It's like we were born to fit together, the two of us.

"This is the last time," I breathe. "And then it's only about you."

"Don't fucking talk about it anymore," she says. "Just fuck me."

She hops up and straddles me and I hold the full weight of her body in my arms, thrusting into her as deeply as I've ever been inside a woman. Oh God, this is good. She's riding me, up and down, her breasts heaving up and down with her motion, the hot water making her skin slick. I pin her against the shower wall, fucking her like my life depends on it.

She screams my name.

Oh God, this is heaven.

She's unleashed. She throws her head back, and it bangs into the marble wall. She's jerking feverishly against me, sliding around against me, in my arms. She's in a trance.

"Yes," she grunts. "Don't stop."

I begin thrusting harder.

"Yes!" she screams. Her body is frantic.

I'm so turned on right now, I can't ... I can't ... Oh my God, I can't even ... I thrust and thrust, holding her entire body in my arms, and she thrashes around, her wet, slick skin sliding around against mine. I'm drowning—in the hot water, in delirium, in her. She's getting ready to howl, I can feel it. Oh my God, we're close. I've never seen her like this. She throws her head back and moans loudly. She screams my name again, at the top of her lungs.

I'm on the verge. I can't hold on anymore. I'm only human.

Her entire body shudders from the inside out—once—but then stops. I can't hang on. I've never been so turned on in all my life. Oh fuck, I can't stop myself from coming. I'm gone.

She screams my name, jerking violently.

But I'm done.

She moans, disappointed.

Her body isn't shuddering any more.

Fuck, fuck, fuck!

She was so close. She was on the verge. And I couldn't hang on. I just couldn't hang on. I move to touch her clit—she's so close, I want to push her over the edge—and she bats my hand away.

Her voice is raw, almost hoarse. "It won't work now."

I drop my hand. "Fuck!" I shake my head. "Fuck. I'm sorry."

"No, no." She slides her legs back down underneath her. "I saw the light in the distance, Jonas." Her eyes are on fire. "I could see it. I... I *visualized* it. I was running to it." She's rambling, panting, euphoric. "It's gonna happen, I know it is." She brusquely grabs the showerhead off the wall and urgently cleans herself between her legs as she chatters away. "I know what I'm doing now—I know exactly what I like. I know what to imagine, Jonas." She's beaming at me.

We step out of the shower and I begin to dry her off. She's still giddy, rambling, practically incoherent. "It's gonna happen," she says. She's effusive.

"Yeah, I know, that's what I've been telling you this whole time."

She's giggling. Did she just smoke crack or something? It's like she's high.

"Turn around," I command. She complies, and I dry off her backside with the towel. "Okay, that's it. Your membership just started. Your application has been processed and approved. Back around."

She faces me, her cheeks glowing.

"And the most fundamental rule of the club is that I'm in charge. No more bossy bullshit from you."

"What bossy bullshit? I'm never bossy."

I tilt my head and squint at her.

She laughs. She puts her arms around my neck and I place my hands on her waist.

"God, I've never had this much sex in all my life." She laughs again.

"I should hope not," I say. Even I haven't had this much sex before in such a short window of time. I'm a Sarah-addict on a binge.

She closes her eyes, remembering something. "My body was, like, out of control."

"You were on fire."

"I felt *free*—like I could just let go and ... I don't know. I felt so turned-on, and my body just . . . ." She squeals.

I chuckle. "You were right on the edge, as close as you could possibly be. I can't wait to push you over it next time."

"Kiss me," she says.

"Bossy."

She rolls her eyes.

I kiss her, of course. Wow, something's changed. She's like a caged animal set free.

"When can we do it again?" she asks. "I wanna do it again and again and again. As soon as possible. When is your meeting gonna be over?"

"My meeting could end right away or it could go on for days—it just depends how it's going. But you don't get to call the shots, anyway. I'm in charge from now on, remember?"

She nods.

"Say it."

"You're in charge."

"I'm serious. I'm on a mission now. I don't come 'til you do. So don't mess things up for me—I've got as much riding on this as you do."

She nods. She laughs her gravelly laugh.

"Tell me exactly what turned you on so much this last time? Was it the shower?"

She purses her lips, thinking. "No. I mean the shower was crazy-sexy, but that wasn't it. It was the *month*," she says. "Knowing it's gonna be me and you for a whole month, no matter what, made all the difference." She smiles. "The pressure's gone. Poof. No more two to seven hours hanging over my head."

Of course. *Of course.* How could I not understand how much she needed that kind of security right from the start? I put my hand under her chin and make her look at me. "We have all the time in the world."

She beams at me. "A month," she says. She nuzzles into my neck.

I want to speak, but I don't. There's something on the tip of my tongue, something that wants to blurt out of my mouth—but I'm not exactly sure what it is. Or if I'm truly ready to say it.

She doesn't seem to notice I've left something unsaid. She's still bubbling over with enthusiasm. "You're really gonna go a whole month without getting off?"

"It's not gonna take you a month."

"But, hypothetically, if it *did* take me a whole month ... you'd hold off?"

I think for a minute. There's no way I could live without getting off for an entire month. I don't know if I can make it two *days* in this woman's presence. When I made my grand proclamation, *I don't come 'til you do,* I was thinking it'd take two more tries, at most.

"Well, yeah," I say, unsure. It couldn't possibly take a month, could it? "I don't come if you don't." I swallow hard. I can't go a whole month, no way. "During sex," I clarify. "But, hypothetically, if it takes you a while, which it won't, yeah, I might have to jack myself off once or twice in the meantime."

She laughs a full-throated laugh. "There's the Jonas I know."

"But I tell you what. If I do have to jack off, I'll do it to the photo of your boob."

She laughs. "Aw, how sweet."

"So we're making a mutual promise? You're a member in my club and I'm in charge from now on?"

She nods.

"Say it. Say 'I promise you're in charge from now on, Jonas.'"

"For a whole month?"

"Yes."

She screws up her face.

"What?"

"A whole month's a long time to let you be *totally* in charge of me."

I sigh. Yet again, she's a pain in the ass. "Say it."

"Okay, okay. I promise you're in charge for a whole month."

"It's a solemn oath—you have to keep to your word. And I promise this to you: If you let me do what I'm excellent at, you'll leave the bonfire behind and dance in the sunlight outside the cave."

She giggles.

"What?"

"You and your metaphors. You're so cute."

I stare at her, annoyed.

"I'm sorry. Continue. Dancing, sunlight, outside the cave . . ."

"I'm not *cute*."

She looks at me sideways. "You really are. But please, go on. I'll be dancing in the bright sunlight outside the cave, twirling through fields of daffodils and lilies and daisies, with bees buzzing happily around me, in a state of post-orgasmic euphoria. You're so damned cute, Jonas Faraday, you know that?"

I relent and smile. Yeah, I guess my metaphors can get a little overblown at times. It's just the way my mind works—the way it's always worked. I can't help it.

She smirks. "So, how much is this membership gonna cost me, huh?" She squints at me.

"Hmm." I hadn't thought about that. Yet again, I need time to think this through.

"Let's talk about it over breakfast," I say.

"I thought you had to get to the office."

"I do. But I'm already so ridiculously late, what's another half-hour? And anyway, I can't send my baby off to school without a good breakfast, can I? It's the most important meal of the day." I wink at her and she blushes.

Chapter 18
Jonas

"An egg-white omelet good? Spinach, broccoli, sprouts, mushrooms?"

"Ah, so that's why you look the way you do."

"My body is my temple. Well, it used to be—your body is my temple now."

She flashes me a giddy smile.

I pull out the ingredients from the fridge and get to work.

We're both dressed in T-shirts and boxers, but she looks way better in my clothes than I do.

"Okay, so membership fees," I say. "Your membership can't be free, or else you won't value it—it's basic marketing psychology. You have to have some skin in the game."

"I'm definitely in favor of skin in the game." She shoots me a naughty grin.

"As long as it's yours." I glance at her thigh peeking out of my boxers under the table. "So, what I'm thinking is this." I'm doing my damnedest to keep my voice casual, playful, carefree. "How 'bout you quit your job at The Club and come stay here with me for a month."

Her mouth hangs open.

I turn back to the eggs on the stove, my heart racing. "You'll still go to your classes and study, of course, and I'll go to work and work out, of course, but, otherwise, we'll just relax and stop the world and melt with each other—in our little club."

She's silent.

I keep my attention on the food I'm making, but there are butterflies in my stomach. I can feel my cheeks blazing. "Our little club for two," I add lamely, shifting the eggs in the pan.

She's silent, so I steal a glance over at her.

She's not happy. This is not the expression I was hoping to see. I was hoping for another one of those giddy, elated expressions from her.

I try to salvage the situation. "You don't have to worry about a thing. I'll pay all your expenses—your rent, whatever you need—so you can stay here with me and just relax and . . ."

Her eyes are inscrutable.

"And be my sex slave," I add, hoping to make her laugh. Oh, that didn't make her laugh.

"I'm not gonna quit my job," she says evenly. "It's how I pay for stupid things like, you know, tuition, rent, food. I'm not with you because I'm looking for a handout."

Well, of course she's not. I didn't think that for a minute. That was a fucked-up thing to say. "Would you just listen to me? I understand all that, but I'm actually being selfish here."

She opens her mouth to protest.

"I want your undivided attention this whole month. I don't want to share you with anyone or anything. And you said you'd do whatever I tell you to do."

Her expression quite plainly says, *Not this.*

I leave the eggs cooking on the stove and sit at the table with her. "I want you here with me—not doing surveillance on every sexual deviant in Seattle who wants to fuck the Queen of England dressed up like a donkey."

She can't stifle her smile. "Hey, you read that application, too?"

I grin. "I want you here," I say softly. I grab at her thighs under the table. "With me, in my bed, at my beck and call."

Her smile widens.

I push her thighs apart. "Spread eagle."

She chuckles.

"Sarah, I just want you here with me," I say again, softly. "That's your membership fee."

She sighs. "I'm not gonna quit my job."

"You're gonna quit anyway after the school year's up, you said so yourself. So what if you quit a little earlier than you thought you would? I'll pay for everything so you can have sex with me around the clock."

175

She leans back. "I know you didn't mean to, but you just asked me to be Julia Roberts in *Pretty Woman*—and not the part at the end when Richard Gere comes for her in the white limo, the part at the beginning, when she's a streetwalker in thigh-high boots."

I exhale in frustration. "Sarah, I'm not treating you like a *prostitute*." I throw up my hands. "Don't you understand? I'm treating you like my *girlfriend.*"

Her eyes widen.

We stare at each other for a moment. I can't believe I just said that any more than she can. There's a long pause. Shit. What the fuck am I saying? Have I gone completely insane? A sudden panic washes over me.

She leaves her chair and sits on my lap. In a flash, she's peppering my face with soft kisses, just like she did last night in my bathroom. I close my eyes and let her lips transport me to another place. The panic that was threatening to engulf me vanishes.

"Jonas," she breathes, kissing my cheek, my ear, my eyebrows, my eyelids, my nose. I shiver under the gentle touch of her lips. "You're beautiful, you know that?" she says, still kissing me. "Inside and out."

My heart's thumping so hard, I worry it's going to knock her right off my lap.

"Stay with me," I whisper.

"I can't quit my job." Her tone makes it clear this is non-negotiable.

My heart sinks. For a minute there, I convinced myself I could stop the world and melt with her. For a month. In my house. Just the two of us. Without a care in the world. Fuck everything and everyone else. But that was just wishful thinking. Shit. I probably would have fucked it up, anyway. She probably did us both a big favor by refusing me.

"The eggs," I suddenly blurt. She leaps off my lap and I bound over to the stove.

They're okay—drier than I'd like, but still okay. Luckily, I'd left the heat on low.

I bring our plates to the table and she moans her approval.

"This looks incredible," she says. "Wow." She takes an enthusiastic bite. "Mmm. So good."

I stare at her, enjoying her unbridled enthusiasm. Even when she eats, she turns me on.

"What?" she says.

"You're so voracious."

"I've probably burned, like, eight thousands calories in the past twelve hours. And it's delicious. Wow, you can cook, boy."

"Of course."

"Not of course. I've never known a man who could cook."

"Neanderthals, all of them."

"Your mama taught you well, Jonas Faraday."

My eye twitches. I look away. I can feel color rising in my cheeks.

"Oh," she says. She exhales in frustration, like she's mad at herself.

I know her eyes are on me, but I can't look at her. I need to collect myself. I stand up. I should go in the other room for a minute. I can feel my cheeks blazing. She had me feeling so soft, so weak—I didn't have my guard up. I wouldn't normally have reacted to a throw away comment like that.

She stands up and wraps her arms around me. I start to pull away, but she insists. Her lips are on my cheek and then my lips. I return her kiss. I melt.

"Sweet, sweet Jonas," she murmurs into my lips. "Such a sad little boy."

I nod, kissing her.

"Will you tell me why?" She pulls away and looks into my face. "Will you tell me?"

I shake my head. I'm overwhelmed with emotion.

She puts her forehead on mine and sighs.

Why won't she stay with me? I just want her all to myself. I could make her feel so good, if she'd just let me. I could take the pain away.

She runs her hand through my hair. "Sweet Jonas," she says again. She takes my face in her hands.

I close my eyes.

She kisses every inch of my face again.

Jesus, I feel like crying. Why am I so weak around her? Where's the cocky bastard motherfucker I am night and day with everyone else? That cocky fucker executes high-risk-high-reward strategies on a daily basis and climbs mountains with his bare fucking hands. He's the fucker, not the fuckee. I like that guy. Why can't I be that guy around her? It's like she's discovered an unlatched window into me, and she keeps sneaking through it every time I look the other way.

Enough. I'm acting like a pussy-ass. I'm being soft. I need to pull myself together. I need to regain control.

I peel myself away from her embrace. I kiss her on the cheek and glide over to the fridge. "Orange juice?" I ask, clearing my throat.

She shakes her head slowly.

"Coffee? Cappuccino?"

"Um, yeah, a cappuccino would be great," she says softly. She sits back down in her chair. She looks anguished.

I grab a mug and press the cappuccino button on my machine. I pour a glass of juice for myself. I bring both drinks over to the table.

"Thanks," she says, her mouth tight.

There's a long pause.

Whatever weakness I was feeling a moment ago has receded. I'm back. "Okay, new idea. If you won't agree to my preferred payment plan," I say, "I've got an alternate one." I take my chair.

She purses her lips. She's looking at me like she can see right through me, like she's got x-ray vision—like my bullshit doesn't fool her for a minute. Oh yeah, I'd forgotten about her impeccable bullshit-o-meter.

"Okay," she says, wary. "What's your next brilliant idea, Lord-God-Master?" She crosses her arms in front of her. Clearly, she's ready to reject whatever I'm about to say. Well, then, I'll just have to make her an offer she can't refuse.

"I want you come away with me this weekend."

Instant elation washes over her. She tries to stifle it, but she can't. She uncrosses her arms and leans forward. Her eyes are blazing.

"We'll make it a long weekend—we'll leave Thursday." I'm putting my plan together on the fly.

Oh, wow, she's freaking out—in a good way. This is good.

"That should give us enough time to get you a passport, if we expedite it."

"We're going *out of the country?*" She's losing it. "Oh my God!" Oh yeah, she's definitely losing it. She's squealing. I like this.

I nod. "Hey, membership in this club doesn't come for free."

"Where are we going?"

"Does it matter?"

She laughs. "Not at all."

I think for a minute. I have no idea where we're going. Wait. I know exactly where we're going. *Exactly.* Yes. Oh my God, I'm a goddamned genius. "We're going to one of my favorite places in the whole world," I tell her. "And that's all you need to know." Damn, this is going to be perfect. Talk about a metaphor.

She squeals. "Wow, you drive a hard bargain, mister." She laughs—and there's that gravel in her voice I love so much. "I really hope you're better at negotiating your business deals, because from what I can see, you don't quite grasp the concept of *payment.*"

I laugh. Yeah, I feel good again. It's like my near meltdown a minute ago never even happened. I'm me again. I'm in control. "And one more thing. Before we leave for our trip, I want you to fill out a membership application for me—for the Jonas Faraday Club—describing each and every one of your sexual preferences in intricate detail."

She sighs.

"Tit for tat." I grin.

"It's not necessary," she says. She's stone-faced.

Why am I surprised she's being difficult? Nothing is easy with this woman. Why can't she ever do what I tell her to do?

"Yes, it is," I say. "I want to know everything about you, every single thing you—"

"No, no, I mean, I don't need to write it down." She shrugs. "I can just tell you my sexual preferences right now."

I'm about to protest, to tell her we don't have time for a detailed discussion right now and that, even if we did, I'd rather have it in writing so I can read and re-read her words later, alone in my bed. But she speaks before I can say anything.

"What I have to say on the topic of my 'sexual preferences' is pretty short and sweet."

I bite my lip. I have no idea what she's talking about. But she's definitely got my attention.

"My 'sexual preferences' can be summarized in two little words, as a matter of fact." She twists a lock of hair around her finger. Her eyes are twinkling. Damn, she's a good-looking woman.

179

She's got my full attention. I can't for the life of me predict what those two little words are going to be. *On top? Doggie style? Hard and fast?* But that's technically three words. *My way? Anything goes?*

She rolls her eyes like she can't believe I don't already know what she's about to say. "*Jonas Faraday,*" she says. "My sexual preference is you, Jonas, plain and simple. *You.*" She smiles at me wickedly. "You woman wizard, you."

Chapter 19
Sarah

I pack up my books and shove them into my backpack amid the bustle of students exiting the lecture hall. I've just sat through a particularly interesting constitutional law class about fundamental rights under the U.S. Constitution versus the states' constitutions. The Supreme Court cases we discussed during class were divisive and thought provoking, and I loved every minute of the discussion. And yet, when I looked down at my notebook at the end of class, I'd doodled "Jonas," surrounded by a heart, over and over again in the margin of my notes—and I didn't even remember writing it. What am I, fourteen years old?

"You coming to study group tonight?" a fellow student asks me as he's packing up his laptop.

I pause. I don't know if Jonas is going to be done with his big meeting by tonight—he seemed really unsure of how long it would last. But even if he is, I should study tonight, anyway. I'm going to miss several classes and lots of study time during our four days away—and I already ditched class this morning, too.

"Yeah, I'll be there," I say, even though it pains me to say it. I'd much rather roll around naked in bed (or in a bathroom, or a limo, or a shower) with Jonas than analyze case precedents with my study group. But I've got to stay focused. If I can finish this year in the top ten students, I'll have my entire tuition paid for the next two years. Not too shabby. Yeah, now that I think about it, I absolutely need to study like a lunatic every available minute before our trip, just to make sure I don't fall hopelessly behind while I'm gone.

I sling my heavy backpack over my back and head out of the lecture hall. If I go back to my apartment, I'll surely break down and

181

invite Jonas over, or, if he's still busy, lie on my bed listening to that Modern English song instead of studying. I sigh and take a sharp left toward the library.

He wants an exclusive relationship with me for a whole month? A month! Maybe I should be worried about what's going to happen in a month and a day, but I'm not. I don't care. I want him, and I'll take what I can get. When the limo picked me up for dinner last night, I thought for sure it was going to be a one-night stand—I never thought there'd be a second night with him, let alone a third or fourth—and instead the man brings me to his beautiful home and proposes an *exclusive* relationship with me for a whole frickin' month after only our first night together? And, oh my God, he wanted me to stay with him at his house. He used the word *girlfriend!* True, he was about to pass out or throw up when that word slipped out of his mouth—he's so out of his depths with all this—but he said it, and he didn't take it back. And he didn't run away. And he didn't shut down. Quite the opposite.

And on top of all that month-long-membership stuff, holy crap, I almost came. *I almost came!* Oh, I was *this* close. If he could have held out just a little bit longer inside me, if he could have stayed hard and strong and continued pumping into me and touching me like he was doing. I bite my lip, remembering. He's magnificently talented at touching me—way better at touching me than I am, that's for sure. How does he know exactly where to touch, and when, and how hard or soft? He's got magic fingers, that boy. I was a hair's breath away from total and complete rapture with him. I felt like a wild animal.

And I want to feel that way again. As soon as possible.

My heart's racing just thinking about him. Dang, I've got to calm down and get my mind in study mode.

I've reached the entrance to the library. Before I go in, I pull out my phone.

"Kat," I practically scream when she answers the phone.

"Oh my God, Sarah. You're going to burst my eardrum."

I laugh.

"What happened last night? I'm dying to hear about it."

"It was better than the best case scenario."

She squeals.

"I'm a goner, Kat. I'm so effing gone." I sigh.

"Can you meet for drinks after work?"

"Gah, not tonight. I've got study group tonight. Tomorrow?"

"Can't tomorrow. A work thing." Kat works at a PR firm.

"Wednesday night?"

"It's a date. I'm all yours," she says.

"That's what he said."

"What?"

"Yup."

"Wow. That good?" Kat's bursting.

"Better than good. Incredible. Hot. Amazing. Mind-blowing. *Romantic.*"

Kat lets out a giddy squeal.

"He's taking me away on Thursday for a long weekend—to some mystery locale *out of the frickin' country.*"

"What? Holy shitballs, girl. I'm dying to hear everything."

"Can't wait to tell you. I'll text you about Wednesday, okay? I gotta study for a bit."

I shift my backpack to find the front pocket so I can put my phone away, and it rings. I look at the display screen. It's Jonas. My heart leaps out of my chest.

"Hey," I say, my cheeks instantly hot.

"Hey," he says back. Oh, his voice. I remember his voice whispering in my ear as he made love to me.

"Whatcha doin'?" I ask.

"Thinking of you. Thinking about what I wish I was doing to you right now."

I hope he can hear my smile across the phone line.

"Where are you right now?"

"At school. I just got out of con law and now I'm going to the library to study. You?"

"Still in my meeting. It'll probably keep me busy the rest of the day—but maybe I can see you late tonight?"

What I'm about to say is going to make me sick to my stomach, I know, but it has to be done. "I've got to study all night. I really, really do."

"Maybe I could come over and help you study?" Oh, he's smirking; I can feel it.

I pause. "Here's the thing—and it kills me to say this, believe me—but I really, really have to get my work done before we go on our trip so I can run off and feel zero stress about it. I've got a lot riding on my grades." I want to slap myself for turning him down, but oh my God, I have to do it.

"I totally understand." He sighs. "You know what? It's for the best. I need you totally relaxed on our trip—and, hey, not seeing each other for a couple days will help build the delicious anticipation."

"'Build the delicious anticipation.' You're such a poet."

"Fuck, yeah, I am."

I laugh. Oh God, this man makes my pulse race like nobody else, even over the phone. But no, no, no, I have to keep my eye on the prize. Study now. Sexy time with Jonas later. I have to do everything in my power to get that scholarship at the end of the year or I'll never forgive myself.

"I really do want to see you, but I have so much studying to do."

"No, no, it's fine. No worries. You're right. I'll see you when I pick you up for the airport on Thursday morning. Our slow burn starts now, baby."

"Oh, you're cooking up another strategy?"

"Of course. And this time I'm sticking to it. I've made a solemn oath."

I smile broadly.

"I'll send a courier to your apartment with the paperwork for your passport this afternoon. Our flight leaves early Thursday morning, so we need to get your passport back by Wednesday night. Can you be home in the next couple hours to meet the courier?"

"Yeah, does four o'clock work?"

"Yep. Four o' clock sharp, okay?"

"Got it. Thank you for taking care of that. I'm excited."

"It's my pleasure." His voice lowers. "I'll be counting the minutes 'til Thursday morning."

"Me too."

"Well, I'd better get back in there. I'll send you the details about Thursday."

"Okay. Hey, Jonas?"

"Hmm?"

I'm not sure how to ask this. "Um, since we're not seeing each other for three whole days, can my month officially start Thursday?"

He pauses, not understanding my concern.

"I mean, I wanted to mark the end of my month on my calendar .
. ." I don't finish the sentence. Does my month with Jonas end a
month from today, or a month from Thursday? I want as much time
as I can get.

"Oh," he says, suddenly understanding my concern. "Well."
He's considering something. "Your membership is locked in now—
no changing your mind—but your membership *period* officially starts
on Thursday morning when I pick you up for the airport." His voice
is oozing with reassurance.

I exhale in relief. "Sounds good."

"And, hey, how about this—any days we're apart won't count
toward the month. Good?"

My cheeks hurt from smiling. "Good. But that'll make it kinda
hard to mark the month on my calendar."

"Well, I guess you just won't mark it, then."

We're both silent on the line, but I'm sure he's smiling as
broadly as I am. My heart is soaring. Jonas doesn't want to envision
the end of this any more than I do.

"We've got all the time in the world, baby," he whispers.

"Okay," I whisper. My eyes are suddenly moist.

"We've got plenty of time."

"Okay," I say again, lamely. "Talk to you later," I manage.

I can hear his humongous smile on his end of the line. "Bye,
baby. I'll call you later."

My doorbell rings at four o'clock on the button.

I open the door to find a delivery guy holding a medium-sized
box and a middle-aged woman in a post office uniform standing in
my doorway. Both of them are smiling broadly at me.

"Sarah Cruz?" the courier guy asks.

"Yes, that's me."

"Here you go." The guy hands me the box in his hands. "I'll go
get the rest," he says. He rushes off.

The rest?

The woman in the post office uniform is holding some forms.
She's got kind eyes and skin the color of a Hershey's kiss.

"Hi, Miss Cruz. I'm Georgia. I'm here to help you fill out your
passport application and get it processed as quickly as possible."

"Wow, thank you. Yes, come in." I show her to the kitchen table, where I put the box down.

I offer her something to drink, which she gratefully accepts.

"I didn't know the post office made house calls. Thank you so much."

"Oh no." She laughs. "We don't make house calls—but anything for Jonas." She smiles like we're sharing some sort of inside joke, even though I have no idea what she's talking about. Why "anything for Jonas"?

"He was so excited to make this happen." She smiles again. "I told him there's no way you're gonna get the passport back in time without a little nudge from me on the inside—and, honestly, I was thrilled to finally get to do a favor for *him* for a change."

"Oh, you and Jonas are friends?" This is already abundantly clear, but it's so unexpected, I can't help asking the question nonetheless.

A look of pure gratitude, or maybe even love, flashes in her eyes. "Jonas is a godsend." She smiles wistfully, but then quickly looks at her watch. "Okay, honey, we're really cutting this close." She spreads out the papers. "Let's do this."

I'm floored. Jonas is a godsend? I'm dying to know more. But she keeps looking at her watch anxiously, so I don't ask her to explain.

The courier returns with several vases of flowers—a ridiculously excessive gift considering the "Valentine's Day" roses already crowding every countertop and dresser and table of my apartment. The courier places one of the vases on the table next to me, and I smile from ear to ear when I see what flowers Jonas has selected this time—daffodils, lilies, and daisies—the exact ones I named when he painted his poetic picture of us basking in the post-orgasmic light outside Plato's cave. I can't help but giggle.

Despite how stressed she must be about getting my paperwork done in time, Georgia flashes a wide smile when she sees the flowers. "Jonas," she says, shaking her head, as if this is exactly the kind of thing she'd expect from him.

Why? Why would she expect such a romantic gesture from Jonas?

She draws my attention back to the forms. "I'm sorry to rush you, but we're really short on time."

"Oh, yes. Sorry." I blush.

The delivery guy returns with bunches of helium balloons emblazoned with messages like "Celebrate!" and "Welcome!" and "Congratulations!" which he releases like doves into my small apartment.

Georgia laughs with me about these latest gifts from Jonas, and then she proceeds to usher me through completing the forms and taking my headshot in front of my white wall pursuant to precise passport specifications.

"I'll head back to the post office and get this submitted for processing right away," she says, gathering everything up. "You should have it back just in the nick of time on Wednesday."

"Do you have far to go?"

"No, not too far. I work at the downtown branch. I'll get everything taken care of in time."

"Thank you so much."

"You're welcome," she says, running out the front door. "Have a great trip."

"Hey, Georgia?"

She turns around, clearly anxious to get going.

"Did Jonas happen to tell you where he's taking me?"

"Yes, he did." She beams at me. "But I'll never tell." She winks and leaves.

I look around. Wow. My bursting apartment looks like a flower shop. Or a Hallmark store. Or maybe the aftermath of a Valentine's Day-baby-shower-birthday-housewarming-graduation barf-o-rama. It's nuts.

I sit down in front of the box with a pair of scissors, my pulse racing, and open it. I pull out the bubble wrap on top and peek inside.

"Oh gosh," I say out loud. There's a package of Oreos. I pull it out, grinning. Oh, Jonas. I peek inside the box again. Two envelopes—a tiny one with something bulging inside it and a flat, letter-sized envelope. I open the flat envelope first. It contains a typed note:

"My Magnificent and Beautiful and Funny and Sweet and Classy and Dirty and Irresistible and A-Little-Bit-Crazy and Smart and Sexy-as-Hell and Ass-Kicking and Insightful and Oh-So-Talented and Fucked-Up (like me) and Tasty (holy fuck!) Sarah,

"Congratulations! Your membership in the Jonas Faraday Club has been approved! Your sexual preferences have been duly noted and meticulously vetted against our sprawling database of potential candidates and, lucky you, you've been assigned one, and only one, uncannily compatible match: Jonas Faraday. Yes, it's true! From here on out, Jonas Faraday will make it his mission (from God, of course) to deliver unto you sexual satisfaction and ecstasy beyond your wildest wet dreams. In other words, you'll be getting nothing but *sexcellence* from now on, baby.

"In order to receive the coveted bounty you so richly deserve, you need only follow the club's singular (but non-negotiable) rule: Member Sarah Cruz must do whatever Club Master Jonas Faraday demands. (That means no bossy bullshit, no hijacking, no hard and fast, and no going for the jugular. Got it?) Again, Miss Cruz, welcome to The Jonas Faraday Club!

"Sincerely,

"Your Hopelessly Devoted Intake Agent,

"Jonas

"P.S. I'll pick you up for the airport this Thursday at 4:30 a.m. Pack casual clothes for tropical weather, including a bathing suit, sturdy hiking boots with ankle support and the thickest tread possible, long pants with moisture-wicking technology, a hat for strong sun, and, of course, something pretty (and easily removable). Please use the enclosed card to purchase anything at all you might need or even remotely desire for the trip—and don't even think about refusing to use it because you absolutely must have the appropriate gear, and, anyway, you promised to do everything I say."

There's a pre-paid Visa card folded into the letter, loaded with $3,000.

This is too much. Too generous. Over the top. But how else can I possibly afford all the stuff he's telling me to pack? I guess I'm going shopping. My stomach is leaping and twisting with excitement. I can't believe this is my life right now.

I pick up the small envelope with the little bump inside of it. Handwriting on its face declares: *"Delicious Anticipation: The Soundtrack."* When I open the tiny envelope, there's a flash drive inside. I insert it into my laptop and music files pop up onto my screen. My heart leaps. That boy made me a mix tape.

The first song is a classic I know well—"Anticipation" by Carly Simon. I click on the song and listen to Carly sing about the torture of anticipation for a moment. You can say that again, Carly. The next song is called "Slow Burn" by David Bowie. I've never heard of it. I click on it. Sexy. I like it. And, yes, Jonas, I get the message loud and clear. We're going to do this your way, whatever that means—no more hijacking. I smile. The next song is "Lick It Before You Stick It" by Denise LaSalle. I roll my eyes. If the song title is any indication, it's clear what this one's going to be about. I press play on the song—and, yep, the saucy blues singer is singing explicit instructions on how to give a woman premium pleasure through oral sex. Oh, Jonas. Where on earth did he find that one? And, really, would a traditional love song be too much to ask? As if he can read my mind, the next song is utter perfection: "I Just Want to Make Love to You" by Muddy Waters. The title alone feels like a special kind of valentine from Jonas—I've never heard him use the phrase "make love" (except, of course, indirectly, when he selected the Modern English song last night—but in that song the phrase is tucked away in a verse, not front and center, as it is here). I click on the song, and I'm instantly blown away. This is old-school blues—pure and raw and effective. Oh yeah, this song is, most definitely, the musical embodiment of delicious anticipation—sensuous, pained, yearning anticipation. Delicious, indeed.

There's no topping the Muddy Waters song—no way—and yet, there's another song on the playlist. "I Want You" by Bob Dylan. I've heard of Bob Dylan, of course—one of the most influential singer-songwriters of all time—but I don't know this particular song. I click on it. The verse is poetic madness—a jumble of disconnected, almost nonsensical, ideas—and Dylan's delivery is slurring and hard to understand. I know Dylan's one of the greats and all—and he's obviously got a lot to say here—but, honestly, I'm not sure why Jonas picked this particular song. It's definitely not hitting me like the Muddy Waters song did, that's for sure.

But then, oh my gosh, the song arrives at its chorus, and, in the midst of rambling incoherence, there's sudden and succinct clarity. Bob Dylan confesses, quite simply, what he wants: *I want you.* The simplicity of the words combined with the authenticity of Dylan's yearning delivery hit me like a ton of bricks. This song makes me feel like Jonas wants me in a way that transcends our (off-the-charts) physical attraction—it makes me feel like he wants me outside of his bedroom. Or, hell, maybe I'm just hearing what I want to hear.

I grab my phone. "Jonas," I breathe when he picks up. "Can you talk?"

"Of course. Hi."

"I just got my welcome package." My voice is bursting with excitement. So many emotions are swirling around inside me, and hearing his voice is tipping me into near-euphoria. "Thank you."

Jonas chuckles, obviously amused by my exuberance. "Welcome to my club."

I let out a loud sigh. "The music, Jonas. Oh my God."

He pauses. "Sometimes, music says things better than words."

The hairs on the back of my neck stand up.

"I want you," he whispers.

I bite my lip. I wish I could leap through the phone line. "I want you, too."

"Talk about delicious anticipation—I'm already losing my mind." He sighs. "So, did you get your passport worked out?"

I take a deep breath. Okay, normal conversation. Yes, I can do that. "Yeah, Georgia said I'll have it on Wednesday."

"Good."

"I really liked Georgia."

"Yeah, she's great, isn't she?"

I wait a beat, but he doesn't say anything more about her.

Come on, Jonas, tell me why you're Georgia's godsend. "How do you know Georgia?" I finally ask.

"Oh, we met a few years ago." There's a beat. "It's a long story."

I'm quiet. I've got time for a long story.

"Her son interviewed me for this thing at his school." He audibly shrugs over the line.

Hold up. *Georgia's son* was the kid who interviewed him for that middle school career day thing? My brain is having a hard time connecting the dots.

"So are you slipping into an Oreo-induced coma right now?" he asks, clearly changing the subject.

How did Georgia's son wind up interviewing him at his school?

"Yeah," I answer, "I've already scarfed down a whole row of Oreos—I can't stop," I answer.

He laughs.

I guess he's not going to tell me anything more about Georgia and her son. I'm dying to know, but I'll let it be. For now. "And, Jonas, the flowers and balloons and the shopping spree—oh my God, the shopping spree. You're too generous. I'm sure I won't need more than a couple hundred dollars."

He scoffs. "No, I want you to get the best hiking shoes you can find—good ones with really deep tread—and those alone will run you a couple hundred bucks. Plus, get some moisture-wicking socks so you don't get blisters—just go to REI, they'll know exactly what you need. Oh, and make sure you get long hiking pants in a breathable fabric."

Why the heck do I need all that stuff? His note said we were going to a tropical place. Doesn't "tropical" mean drinking piña coladas on a beach by day and making hot, sticky, moonlit love by night? Where do hiking boots with deep tread and moisture-wicking socks fit into any of that?

"Where the hell are you taking me?" I ask.

He ignores my question. "And besides all that, get yourself anything else you want, too—maybe a pretty dress, oh, and a teeny-tiny string bikini would look so hot on you, and lingerie, definitely lingerie."

"Wow, you're my very own personal shopper."

He chuckles. "I want you to go crazy, get anything you like. And if it turns out it's not enough money, let me know and I'll—"

"Oh my gosh, no, you're insane. We're only going to be gone for four days, for Pete's sake. I'm sure I'll return the card to you with lots of money left over on it—"

"No, no, spend it all. I won't take the card back."

I'm trembling. I don't know why. "Jonas, you're overwhelming me."

"Good."

"You're sweeping me off my feet."

"That's exactly what Valentine's Day bullshit is meant to do."

I'm reeling.

He sighs. "Sarah, just let me . . ." He pauses. "Hang on." There's

191

an insistent male voice in the background. "Okay," he says to someone. "Just a sec."

Is he talking to Josh? Oh my gosh, he's still in the middle of his meeting. Why on earth did he even take my call?

His voice comes back on the line. "Sarah, just let me do this stuff, okay?" He lowers his voice. "It turns me on to do it—like, seriously, I've got a boner just hearing the excitement in your voice."

His words have an instant effect on me. "I want to kiss every inch of you right now," I whisper, emphasizing the phrase "every inch of you" with particular care.

He moans. "I'd be with you right now if I could, you know that, right?" He exhales. "But this meeting's gonna take for-fucking-ever. Josh and I still have a couple fires to put out to close the deal—and I *really* wanna close this deal."

I sigh. "I totally understand." I better let him get back to whatever he's doing. It sounds important. "Holy moly, when you finally pick me up on Thursday, we're both gonna be rarin' to go."

He sighs. "Seriously. This delicious anticipation thing is gonna be the death of me." He groans. "You better make sure your sweet ass is ready for me on Thursday—because I'll be bringing my A game, baby."

The balloons are making soft poofing noises all around me as they bump against the ceiling and each other. My apartment is bursting with bright colors and thick floral fragrances, thanks to the virtual garden of flowers surrounding me. The bear Jonas sent me before our dinner date is sitting at the table, smiling at me and shouting "Be Mine!" And to top it all off, I've still got the taste of Oreo cookies in my mouth. I'm so frickin' happy right now, I could pass out. *Poof ... poof . . .poof,* the balloons say softly around me. Clearly, they're happy, too.

"Oh yeah, my sweet ass will be ready for you, you can count on it," I say. "You just make damned sure *your* sweet ass is ready for *me,* Mr. Woman Wizard, because, come Thursday, it's gonna be on like Donkey Kong. Oh, and I should warn you: As a paying member of the Jonas Faraday Club, I'm gonna be expecting a helluva lot more than your A game, big boy. You better be ready to bring nothing short of *sexcellence.*"

Chapter 20
Sarah

Six hundred forty-three dollars and sixty-four cents. That's what I just spent in a matter of two hours during a whirlwind shopping spree. It's more money than I've spent in a single shopping session in my whole life, but I sure managed to spend it with ease. I got everything Jonas told me to get, and then some, and I still didn't come close to his budget for me. Where did he expect me to shop—Hiking by Prada? True, the high-tech gear I got from REI was on the expensive side, but still, I was never in danger of spending anything close to three thousand dollars—even including the brightly colored tank tops, shorts, string bikini, cover-up, and two sundresses I bought. I didn't bother buying lingerie, despite Jonas' oh so helpful suggestion, because it seemed like a colossal waste of money to me. If there's going to be a situation suitable for skimpy lingerie, I'd rather just wear nothing at all. And, to be perfectly honest, I had an ulterior motive in keeping my clothing expenditures as low as possible—a much better idea for any leftover funds than buying expensive lingerie that Jonas is just going to tear off me, anyway. I just hope Jonas isn't mad when I tell him how I've already dispensed with all the leftover money on his card.

It's only two o'clock and it's already been a long and exciting day—two classes in the morning followed by a giddy shopping spree in the early afternoon. Already, I want nothing more than to go home, pack for my trip (because if I wait for tomorrow to do it, I'm going to stress out), and then curl up for the rest of the night with my contracts textbook. But I've got one more important errand to run before heading back home to study—overnighting my little software engineer his welcome package, complete with a bright yellow bracelet and a pre-loaded iPhone. Normally, I'd go to the post office a half-mile from school to mail a welcome package. But today, I've gone way, way, way out of my way to the post office downtown to send it out.

The minute I walk through the front door of the post office, clutching my outgoing package, I see her. Georgia. She's one of four postal clerks standing behind the long counter, ministering to customers. I step into the line, holding my box, twitching with nervous energy. I steal a glance at her. She doesn't see me. She's laughing with a customer. Her eyes are dancing. She's kind, this woman, genuinely kind.

The line is slowly inching forward. When I get to the front of the line, Georgia is still detained with a customer. I let the person behind me go ahead to the available clerk. And the next person, too. Finally, Georgia looks up, her station available. "Next customer, please," she says, and her eyes lock onto me. She smiles with instant recognition.

"Hi, Georgia," I say when I get to her station.

"Why, hello, Miss Cruz, what a pleasant surprise." She looks around and lowers her voice. "Your passport will be hand-delivered to your place tomorrow evening—we won't have it back 'til then, probably by the skin of our teeth."

"Oh, yes, thank you." I place the box on the counter. "I didn't expect to get it today. I came to overnight this."

"Oh yeah? What brings you downtown?"

"A little shopping for my trip with Jonas."

She eyes me skeptically.

"Well, and visiting you."

She smiles. She knew it.

Georgia asks me all the necessary questions about whether I want tracking and insurance on my package, and we complete my postal transaction.

"Georgia," I begin, tentatively, looking behind me at the growing line, "I was wondering if you had a few minutes to chat."

She purses her lips. Is that amusement? "Actually, yes, right now would be a great time to take my break."

Georgia blows the steam off her hot cup of tea and takes a careful sip.

For some reason, I'm holding my breath. I know she's got something important to tell me, I just don't know what it is.

"A few years ago, my son Trey's little league team had an incredible season, like a once in a lifetime season. They wound up getting a lot of local press because they had this incredible pitcher, you know, a true natural—already blowing everyone away at age twelve with his fast ball."

"And what about your son? Is he really good, too?"

"Oh no, not at all." She laughs. "Every team he's ever been on, he's always the bottom of the order, by far." She laughs again, and I join her. Nothing like a mother's honest assessment of her kid. "But every coach he's ever had has kept him around because that boy's got so much heart. Oh Lord, does that boy shine with pure love of the game. He inspires everyone around him."

Her face glows with pride for a moment. "There's just no quit in him. But he's really small for his age—and not particularly fast, either. Not a great combination." She sighs. "And painfully shy. I've always encouraged him to be on a team because it helps him with his shyness."

I smile. Her face is awash in motherly love.

"So, anyway, when Trey's team had their golden season, the whole city really took notice of them—there was a little parade in the neighborhood when they got back from a big tournament in Vancouver, and the team was interviewed on the local news several times. Jonas' company apparently took notice and was kind enough to invite the boys and their families to watch a Mariners game in their fancy box seats. I'd taken Trey to a few Mariners games before—but always in the nosebleed seats. He was pretty impressed with those box seats, I tell ya. We felt like royalty."

I wonder if that invitation was Jonas' idea? Or was it Josh's? Or maybe a PR firm's?

"And that's when you met Jonas?" I ask.

"Yes. And right away, I knew he was special. All season long, everyone always crowded around that spectacular pitcher on Trey's team—and deservedly so, the kid is just amazing and also bursting with personality—and Trey always hung back, feeling shy and sort of insecure. Well, at that Mariners game, it was more of the same. Everyone was chatting up that pitcher boy—he was cracking everyone up, in fact—and Trey just sat quietly, watching the game, sitting by himself." During much of this story, Georgia has been glancing away, lost in her own thoughts, but now she looks right at me. "Do you like baseball?"

"I've never followed it. My dad wasn't around when I was growing up, and my mom isn't a baseball fan. I've never even been to a game."

Georgia nods knowingly. "Any siblings?" she asks.

"Nope. It's just my mom and me. The two musketeers."

"Yeah, it's just Trey and me, too. It's special that way, huh?"

I nod.

"I can't afford to take Trey to baseball games very often, believe me. But Trey loves it, so I do my best."

We share a smile.

"So, anyway, for the first half of the game, I noticed Jonas in the corner of the box, not talking to anybody, but he kept glancing over at Trey. Trey was totally absorbed in the game, keeping score on his clipboard, just totally fixated. Finally, midway through, Jonas came right over and sat down next to him." She sighs, remembering. "Trey lit up like a Christmas tree, and they wound up watching the whole rest of the game together, jabbering away the whole time." Georgia beams and leans into me. "Trey *never* jabbers away, with anyone."

I bite my lip. I can't imagine Jonas jabbers away with too many people, either.

"By the end of the game, Trey and Jonas were best friends, talking about everything—not just baseball. Jonas asked Trey what he wanted to do when he grew up, and Trey told him he wanted to do something with computers, maybe. Jonas asked, 'No baseball, huh?' and Trey said, 'Naw, I'm too small, too slow.'"

"Well, that really got Jonas going. 'If there's something you want, whatever it is, then you have to go after it relentlessly,' Jonas told him." Georgia looks wistful. "And before we knew it, Jonas was telling Trey how to run wind sprints to increase his speed and eat all the right proteins to increase his muscle mass and giving him a list of books he wanted Trey to read." She chuckles. "He was just really, really sweet. By the end of the game, Trey worshipped the ground Jonas walked on. I don't think Jonas realized what he was getting himself into. As we were leaving, Trey got up the nerve to ask him to come to career day at his school." Georgia rolls her eyes, but she's still smiling. "The kids could either do a written report on what they might want to do when they grew up, or they could bring in an interview subject with a fascinating career—sort of like a human show and tell—and conduct an interview in front of the whole school."

I blush vicariously for Jonas. I can only imagine how little he wanted to do that.

"Honestly, I was shocked Trey wanted to interview Jonas in front of the whole school—he's usually so shy." Georgia's eyes flicker at the memory. "It's like Jonas worked some kind of spell on him."

Based on personal experience, yes, I'm quite sure that's exactly what Jonas did.

"I could tell Jonas was about to refuse, but then Trey explained that a lot of the kids were inviting their dads to be interviewed, and that was that. Jonas said he'd do it. So, anyway," Georgia sighs, but trails off. "I'm sorry—this story is probably so much longer than you bargained for." She takes a sip of her tea.

"No, it's not. It's exactly what I was hoping to find out. So what happened next?"

"Well, Jonas went down to Trey's school and did the interview, and he seemed to enjoy it, too; and after that, he and Trey kept in touch. Jonas sent him a bunch of sports equipment for his birthday, he invited him to a couple more Mariners games, and he even gave him a jersey signed by the entire team. Jonas just spoiled him rotten. Trey was over the moon."

"And you?" I ask. "How did you feel about all this?"

She let's out a huge sigh. "I was thrilled. Grateful. Trey is just the sweetest, most wonderful kid. Just a giant, beating heart. And, you know, growing up without a father has been hard on him, so having a man like Jonas pick him out of the crowd and make him feel special meant a lot."

I nod. I'm swooning. I can relate.

"And then I got sick," Georgia says, her face darkening.

My swoon instantly vanishes. "Oh no, what happened?"

"Cancer."

I reach across the table and touch her hand. "Oh no, Georgia. Oh my God."

"No, I'm fine now. Perfectly fine. This was well over a year ago.

And we caught it early, thank God. I had surgery and radiation—no chemo, thank goodness—and I was as good as new, knock on wood." She knocks her knuckles against the wooden table. "But Trey called Jonas and told him, and ... " In a flash, she's totally choked up. She shakes her head. Words won't form in her throat. She looks up at the ceiling, trying to compose herself.

I squeeze her hand.

"I'm sorry," she squeaks out.

She holds my hand silently for a moment. "I'm sorry. I don't know why it still makes me so emotional." She takes a deep breath. "When you're sick, and scared, and all alone, and you've got a child to worry about ... To have someone swoop right in and just *take care of you*, and especially someone who has no reason whatsoever to do it . . ." She tears up again. She grabs a napkin and wipes her eyes. "It was just so unexpected. And so wonderful. He was just a godsend."

My heart is racing. "What did he do?"

"What didn't he do? He sent flowers after my surgery, arranged a car to take me to and from radiation treatments for a whole month. Meals were delivered to our house. My sister's here in town, thank goodness, so I wasn't alone—but she has work and her own kids." She wipes at her eyes. "Everything was so overwhelming. I had to take time off work, get help with Trey. And Jonas just swooped right in and made everything better."

I'm tearing up right along with her. If I didn't already want to tackle Jonas and make violent, savage, primal love to him, I sure as hell do now.

"When treatment was all finished, I got what looked like a bill from the hospital. I thought I was gonna throw up when I got that envelope in the mail; I was so scared to look inside. I knew, whatever the amount, it was going to ruin me."

She unclasps my hand so she can take a sip of her tea with a shaky hand. I follow her lead and take a swig of my cappuccino.

I'm on the edge of my seat, even though I know what she's about to say. There's only one possible ending to her story, after all— but I can hardly wait to see her face when she tells it.

"And when I opened the envelope, it was an invoice, all right— for even more than I'd feared. Trying to pay that bill would have been impossible. I would have had to file bankruptcy. But guess what?"

I shake my head, even though I know what. I'd never deprive her of telling me the fairytale ending to her wonderful story.

"The invoice was stamped 'paid in full,'" she says, her eyes wide. "Can you believe it? The balance owed on the invoice was *zero*. I just couldn't believe it. I cried like a baby." And with that, she's crying like a baby now, too.

I hand her a napkin and pick one up for myself. I'm a puddle right alongside her.

"A godsend," she says in a muffled voice. "He's just been a godsend."

I grab Georgia's hand again, and she grabs mine. Her hand is soft and warm. I have the sudden impulse to bring her hand to my mouth and kiss it—and so that's exactly what I do.

A smile bursts across her face at my sudden show of affection.

She pats my cheek with the palm of the hand. "He's a good one, honey," she says, composing herself. "Hang onto him."

I can't speak, so I just nod and smile.

I want nothing more than to "hang onto" Jonas, believe me. But can a girl, even a very, very determined girl, even a very sincerely smitten girl, hang onto a boy if that boy doesn't want to be hung onto? The answer, of course, is no. It's out of my hands. I'll just have to wait and see if Jonas wants to be hung onto.

I sigh and look up at the ceiling of the coffeehouse. Jonas has my beating heart in his hands. It's his to do with, or not do with, as he pleases. And for the life of me, I don't know where that's going to leave me at the end of all this.

Chapter 21
Sarah

Kat and I shouldn't be here right now. But when it came time to meet Kat for drinks, I couldn't resist killing two birds with one stone and spying on my little software engineer, too. I overnighted him his welcome package yesterday, complete with a bright yellow bracelet, and lo and behold, when I checked his account at lunchtime today, he'd already posted a check-in at a downtown sports bar for seven o'clock tonight. Talk about an eager beaver. And now, here we are at the sports bar, even though we shouldn't be, even though I'm breaking The Club's rules (yet again). But I have to see what kind of yellow-coded woman has been deemed a perfect match for a sweet, hopeful, lonely, normal, yellow-coded man like my sweet software engineer. I hope he finds true love tonight. I really do. I check my watch. 6:45.

Kat and I arrived plenty early. For the past hour, we've been drinking beer and talking nonstop about my night (and morning) with Jonas. Of course, I didn't tell her any graphic sexual details and I certainly didn't mention the whole "yippee, I almost had an orgasm" thing. Kat doesn't know I've never had an orgasm in the first place— I've never told anyone that, other than Jonas—so, obviously, I'm not going to brag to Kat about getting closer than ever with Jonas. Plus, I would never tell Kat, or anyone, about Jonas' particular fixation on getting women off—so that entire topic of conversation was off limits. And yet, even without revealing any sexual details or Jonas' private information, it appears The Story of Jonas and Sarah is still a damned good one, because, throughout the entire conversation, Kat has been "oohing" and "aahing" and gushing and swooning.

"He sounds amazing," Kat says, "which he'd better be to deserve you."

200

I smile at her.

"So, where do you think he's taking you tomorrow? Jamaica? Tahiti? Borneo?"

"Borneo?" I say, laughing. "Where is Borneo?"

I turn to glance around the bar. Is the software engineer here yet? I look at my watch. We're still a few minutes early yet, but he could come at any time. I look around again. I can't wait to see his Miss Yellow. I hope she's looking for love every bit as much as he is. You never know—maybe their happily ever after will begin tonight, right here, in this sports bar. Why not? I mean, jeez, he's off to a fantastic start—he's not a fucked-up Purple, after all. I smirk to myself. I'm quite fond of my sweet, fucked-up Purple.

I realize Kat's been talking.

"What?" I ask. "I'm sorry, I zoned out for a minute."

"I'm just trying to figure out where he's taking you."

"I have no idea," I say. "Where in the tropical world does a girl need hiking boots with extra-thick tread?"

She grimaces. "Maybe he's going to hurl you into a volcano."

"God, I hope not. Getting chucked into a gurgling pit of lava would not be my preferred ending to this story."

She giggles. "That would definitely be anti-climactic."

I grin. That was a funny choice of words right there.

We both pause to sip our beers.

"So, what did he say about your chat with Georgia?" she asks.

My stomach drops. "I haven't told him about it yet." I blush. "When I talked to him last night, it didn't feel like the right time to tell him about it."

Jonas and I had a heart-racing conversation last night about how much we missed each other and couldn't wait for our trip. He was effusive, and explicit, in telling me just how much he missed me and wanted to see me. Well, and touch me. And kiss me. And taste me. And make love to me. It just didn't feel like the right moment to tell him about my conversation with Georgia.

Kat looks at me skeptically.

"He seemed like he was under a lot of stress to get his deal done before leaving on our trip. I figured it'd be better to tell him about it tomorrow, in person."

Kat pointedly takes a long swig of her beer.

201

I sigh, exasperated. "*And,* yes, I'm a little bit worried maybe he's going to be upset with me for going to talk to her."

Kat rolls her eyes. "Why on earth would he be upset?"

I sigh, collecting my thoughts. No, that's not it, either. "I don't know. My conversation with Georgia just felt so *game changing.* It made me ... My attraction just went to a whole new level, that's all. And I'd rather talk to him about it in person." I blush.

Kat squeals. "Oh, girl, you're a goner."

I sigh. "Yeah, I'm freaking out just a wee bit."

"Oh, Sarah, don't overthink it. Just *enjoy* it. He's obviously—"

I gasp and grab Kat's forearm. She instantly stops talking.

The software engineer just bellied up to the bar on the other side of Kat.

I crick my neck toward him, but I'm not sure Kat understands what I'm trying to communicate.

The guy takes a seat on the stool next to Kat and acknowledges her with a friendly, "Hi." She replies in kind. Apparently, I'm invisible, but that's okay, seeing as how I'd like to crawl under a rock right about now, anyway.

Wow, he's got quite a spring in his step tonight. He looks nothing like the lonely fellow I saw leaving his building to grab a sandwich all by himself. The man's downright bursting with hopeful anticipation.

I bang my knee into Kat's knee. When she looks at me, I silently mouth the words, "That's him."

Her eyes go wide, and she inhales sharply.

"Are you rooting for Kentucky or Connecticut?" the software engineer asks Kat, motioning to a basketball game on one of the television screens above the bar. As he does, I can plainly see the yellow bracelet on his wrist.

"Uh. Neither. I don't follow basketball," Kat answers. She drinks down the last few drops of her beer.

"Can I buy you another one?" he asks.

Wait just a cotton-pickin' minute. Does he not understand the rules of The Club? Kat's not wearing a yellow bracelet. Why is he hitting on her? Even if she were in The Club, which she's not, it would be up to *her* to decide whether or not to approach *him.*

"Sure," Kat answers. "Thanks."

I practically slap my forehead in disbelief. Why did Kat say yes to him? I bang Kat's knee under the bar again, but what I really want to do is smack her upside the head. She turns to me and shrugs innocently. That's Kat for you. Ted Bundy could offer her a free mojito and she'd gladly accept.

"And for you, too, of course," the software engineer says, grinning at me. "Hi."

I guess I'm not invisible after all. I try to smile back and nod, but I'm freaking out. What the hell is going on here? He shouldn't be talking to us right now. A woman specifically matched to him—a woman who is uncannily compatible with him and his sexual preferences and fantasies and romantic hopes—is going to walk through the door any minute. And she's coming here just to meet *him*. Heck, she might already be here, watching him right this very second, trying to decide if she wants to slip her yellow bracelet onto her wrist and identify herself or turn on her heel and flee.

I make a big point of checking my watch so Mr. Yellow can see that I am *not*—emphatically *not*—wearing a yellow bracelet right now.

"Kat," I say. "I think my watch died. What time is it right now?" I stretch out my wrist, yet again, for the benefit of my software engineer. *See? No bracelet.* I'm hoping Kat will get a clue and display her bare wrist, too.

But before Kat can even process my question, the guy looks at his watch. "Seven-oh-five," he says.

The bartender puts two tall beers in front of us.

"Thank you so much," Kat says, raising her glass to Mr. Yellow. "Cheers."

"Cheers," he replies enthusiastically.

I try to squeak out a polite "thank you," but nothing comes out of my moving lips. I'm really anxious.

Everyone takes a sip but me.

I glance around. Is his Miss Yellow here? I look around the bar for a loner-ish, normal-ish, sweet-looking woman—perhaps a nurse or patent lawyer or dentist or computer programmer?—who's intently watching him from a corner of the bar. Nope. I don't see a single woman in this entire bar paying him any attention whatsoever.

He tilts his head toward Kat like he's about to tell her a secret.

"So, I'm crossing my fingers and toes right now that you're in The Club?" His face is awash in hope and excitement.

Oh God, did he really just ask her that? Did he not read a word of the instructions in his welcome package? How could he not understand the way this works? He's a goddamned software engineer! How hard can this be? Does he seriously think every knockout at this bar is here specifically for him? I'm not trying to be cruel here, but come on. The Club matches people up—that's the whole point—and Kat is a frickin' ten. A flaming, raging, unquestionable ten. Every man on planet earth wants a woman like Kat. There is no person alive, no standard of beauty in any culture, that wouldn't view Kat as an ideal manifestation of perfect beauty. And this guy is *sweet*. Unassuming. Normal. But you know, a four, if he's lucky. Well, maybe a five on a good day. And unless he runs a publishing empire or invented the Internet or runs a global organization dedicated to eradicating human trafficking or discovered Justin Timberlake or belongs to Doctors Without Borders, his chances with Kat are slim to none. The Club might boast the ability to make a guy's dreams a reality, but it can't turn water into wine, people. Wow, I'm getting kind of riled up here.

Kat shifts in her chair and turns her head to look at me. Her expression is one of utter befuddlement.

"No," she says softly. "Just here to grab a beer with my friend. Thank you again for supporting the cause." She raises her beer in salute to him. Her tone is gracious. This is not a cruel kiss-off. This is a kind kiss-off.

But he looks totally deflated nonetheless. "Oh."

Poor thing. But what did he expect? That he'd be Charlie and The Club would be his own personal Chocolate Factory come to life? Come on.

There's an awkward pause.

"Well," I say, trying to alleviate the discomfort. And I'm about to say something more—something lame and not helpful, I'm sure—when I'm interrupted.

"Hi there," says a voice from the other side of Mr. Yellow. He turns to look at the source of the greeting, and so do I. And much to my shock and horror and total dismay and confusion, the woman standing on the other side of my little software engineer, the woman who just said hello to him, the woman who's smiling at him and batting her eyelashes—and blatantly displaying a goddamned *yellow* bracelet on her wrist—is none other than Miss Purple from the other night. Stacy. *Stacy the Faker.* The totally hot woman Jonas fucked mere days ago, wishing she were me.

I quickly look down at my hands on the bar. Oh my God, Jonas' penis was inside that woman. I cringe. And his tongue touched her ... I can't finish the thought. I want to barf.

"Hi," my software engineer says, his voice spiking with excitement. "Please, have a seat."

"Well, I don't want to interrupt anything," Stacy says, glaring at Kat. She touches her hair and makes a big show of flashing her yellow bracelet again. "But I was hoping to talk to you for a bit." She shoots daggers at Kat again.

"No, please," Kat says, motioning for Stacy to take a seat. "He's all yours. I'm just here with my friend."

Stacy's eyes lock onto me and then dart back to Kat. And just that fast, her eyes flash with unmistakable recognition.

"Yes, please, have a seat," my little software engineer says. He holds up his yellow bracelet right next to hers. "I've been waiting for you." His head is turned away from me, looking at Stacy, but based on Stacy's wide smile, I'd guess he's smiling broadly at her, too. "I'm Rob," he says, putting out his hand. "Thank you for coming."

"Nice to meet you, Rob," Stacy says, her tone flirty. "I'm Cassandra."

Cassandra? What the hell?

"Do you like basketball?" my little software engineer—Rob—asks, motioning to the TVs.

"I love it." Stacy grins. "Especially college ball. I don't really follow the NBA—until play-offs, of course."

"Same here!" Rob says, elated. "Exactly what I always say."

"You wanna go sit?" Stacy asks, motioning to a corner booth. Her eyes wander ever so briefly to me and flash, just for a nanosecond, with undisguised contempt.

"Absolutely."

The two lovebirds get up and move toward the corner of the bar.

"Well, nice talking to you," Kat says sarcastically to Rob's back when he's out of earshot. She turns to me, her face awash in disgust. "Holy shitballs," Kat says. "What the hell is she doing here?"

205

I shake my head, thoroughly confused. I open my mouth to speak, but close it again. I have no idea what she's doing here.

"Sarah, she's wearing a *yellow* bracelet," Kat whispers urgently, as if I hadn't noticed. "I thought she was *purple?*"

Now my mouth is hanging open. I don't even know what to say. Even if Stacy were, theoretically, assigned two different compatibility colors (which, based on my understanding, is impossible), how on earth could she possibly be a match for both Jonas *and* the software engineer—two men who are polar opposites in every way? That'd be like saying, "I like incorrigible man-whores *and* virginal boy-next-door types. I like savage fuck machines and guys who love rainbows and baby chicks. I like men with raging God complexes and indefatigable hard-ons *and* mendicants sworn to a vow of poverty, chastity and obedience." You couldn't even say Jonas and Mr. Yellow are two sides to the same coin—they're a frickin' Euro and a nickel. Does not compute.

"I thought the colors don't mix. Purples get matched with purples, yellows with yellows."

"Right. A purple can't even see a yellow's check-ins. It's all separated by color-code."

"Well, then, how did that woman show up to meet *both* Jonas *and* Mr. Software Engineer, too?"

Exactly what I'm wondering.

A guy sits next to Kat at the bar. Wow, he's really cute.

"Hey," he says. "I'm Cameron." Oh boy, he's just her type. Dark, athletic. Gleaming white teeth.

"Hi," Kat replies, instantly distracted from the conundrum of why Stacy is here to meet Mr. Yellow. "Kat." She puts out her hand and he shakes it.

"Cat? Like meow?"

She laughs. Oh, she's already in full flirt mode. "Yeah, but with a 'K.' Katherine. But call me Kat."

"Nice to meet you, Kat. Can I call you Kitty Kat?"

Kat giggles. "Absolutely not—at least not yet. You've got to earn the privilege."

It takes all my restraint not to roll my eyes. Oh, Kat.

"I'm going to the ladies' room," I mumble, getting up from my stool.

Kat peels her eyes off her new admirer just long enough to nod her acknowledgment of my departure.

I steal a glance at my little software engineer—Rob. He's sitting at a table, smiling broadly, deep in conversation with Stacy. Or Cassandra. Or whatever her name is. His face is glowing with excitement. Oh, it's hard to watch—his heart is on his sleeve. I feel sick to my stomach. I can't figure this out. But whatever's going on, it can't be good for him. He came here for love tonight—I know he did—and something tells me he's going to be sorely disappointed. If not crushed.

In the bathroom, my head is spinning. I'm so confused.

Just as I'm drying my hands with a paper towel, the door opens and Stacy bursts in.

She beelines right to me. She's not even pretending she came in here to pee. She bends over to check for feet in the two stalls. Finding none, she whips back up and leans into me.

"I saw you and your friend at the check-in with the hottie, and now, gee, what a coincidence, here you are again, both of you, at this check-in with the nerd. What the fuck?"

I'm speechless. My mind isn't processing fast enough to come up with an explanation for our presence at both locations. But why is she on the offense? What the hell was *she* doing at both check-ins?

"Did the agency send you?" she barks at me. It feels like more of an accusation than a question.

I open my mouth to speak.

"They don't think I can handle this guy on my own, is that it? They think he needs some additional options, just in case I'm not acceptable to him? That's bullshit." She's seething. "I don't need backups. I've never once not closed a guy. Not once. And this one's already slobbering all over me, like they all do."

I shake my head. "No, I . . ."

"This is *my* territory," she fumes, taking a menacing step closer to me. "They think they've gotta send not one but *two* other girls to back me up?"

"Nobody sent us. It's just a coincidence," I finally manage.

"Ha! Fuck you," she seethes, her nostrils flaring. "You tell the agency—was it Oksana who sent you?—you tell Oksana this is *my* account, *my* territory, *my* score—and I don't need anybody checking up on me or making a play for my sloppy seconds." She leans right into my face, her eyes narrowed to slits. "Don't fuck with me, bitch." With that, she turns on her heel and marches out of the bathroom, leaving me standing with my mouth agape.

I steal a glance at my alarm clock. 3:20 a.m. My alarm is set to go off in ten minutes, so I lean over and turn it off with a groan. Jonas is going to be here to pick me up for the airport in just over an hour, and I haven't gotten a wink of sleep all night long. Ever since I laid my head down on my pillow at midnight, I've been tossing and turning, my mind racing, thinking about my horrific encounter with Stacy in the bathroom, and the horrific implications of what she said to me. Worst of all, the thing that's kept me awake above all else, is wondering how I'm going to tell Jonas about all of it. I've been such an idiot working for this disgusting organization. No wonder the women in The Club are so perfectly compatible with the men. They're *paid* to be. Stacy, or whatever her name is, is a frickin' prostitute, plain and simple. For the right fee, she'll be anybody's perfect match. For hours, I've lain here in my bed, staring at the ceiling, the full weight of the situation dawning on me.

I head into the bathroom and brush my teeth. I've got a headache.

I work for an online whorehouse. A global brothel. That's bad enough. But the men buying these women's services don't even know what they're buying. That poor software engineer joined The Club to find love—I'm sure of it. He thought this was a high-priced, exclusive dating service; he really, really did. And even someone like Jonas, who clearly didn't sign up to find his soul mate, at least craved honesty with his partners.

He's going to be furious. Probably humiliated. Most certainly disgusted. I just don't know him well enough to know how he'll react. It makes me physically sick to think about breaking this news to him. I didn't want to do it over the phone when I got home last night, so I waited—but I certainly don't want to ambush him with the news during our trip, either. Maybe I should have called him with the news the minute I got home? But, no, it just didn't feel right to tell him over the phone.

I hop in the shower, my mind reeling like it's been all night.

When I first got home from the sports bar, I was beside myself, trying to figure out what to do. After a while, I texted Jonas, just to see if he was still awake, perhaps hoping he'd call me and make my decision easy about whether or not to tell him over the phone. He texted back right away to say he couldn't wait to see me, that he was going crazy missing me, that it felt like a month since he'd laid his hands on me.

"Only a few more hours!" he texted. But he didn't call.

"See you soon!" I texted back.

"I've got something big to tell you!" he replied. *"Bwahahahahaa!"*

My stomach lurched with anxiety. *So do I,* I thought. But what I texted back was, *"Can't wait."*

Chapter 22
Jonas

I didn't think it was possible, but I've forgotten just how beautiful she is during the three days we've been apart. When she opens the door to her apartment, I feel like I'm being reunited with the girl who waited for me to come home from fighting a brutal war. I can't help taking her face into my hands and kissing her deeply. She tastes good. Minty.

"Welcome to your first day in The Jonas Faraday Club," I say, breaking away from our kiss.

She nods and smiles. But her smile isn't as beaming as I was expecting it to be. Something's off. I can feel it. Is she having second thoughts about going away with me? I thought we were past the whole "I don't trust you because you're incapable of forging intimate human connection" thing. Fuck. How much more upside can I possibly show her? I'm running out of ways to assure her.

"I'm so glad you're here," she breathes, throwing her arms around my neck. She hugs me close and plants a kiss on my lips that makes it abundantly clear she's most definitely not having second thoughts about our trip. But I know I didn't imagine the anxiety that flashed across her face a second ago.

"Jonas," she says, kissing me again and again. "I've missed you so much." I might be crazy, but I feel like she's about to burst into tears right here in my arms. Yeah, something's rattling around in her beautiful head right now—but what else is new.

"Are you okay?" I ask, making her look at me.

She nods. "Just so glad you're here." She kisses me again and my entire body sizzles with electricity.

"If you keep kissing me like this," I mumble into her lips, "we're not going to make our flight."

She pulls away from me, reluctantly. "Are you gonna tell me where we're headed?"

"Ah, ah, ah," I say, holding up my index finger. "All will be revealed soon enough." I motion to a suitcase by the front door. "This it?"

She nods. "Oh, and this." She grabs her laptop off the couch.

I take the computer out of her hands and return it to the couch. "Nope."

"I thought maybe I'd go over my study outlines if we have any free time."

I smirk. We won't have a minute of free time. Do I really need to spell that out to her?

She blushes.

Apparently not.

"No computer, then," she agrees. Her mouth twists into a what-was-I-thinking half-smile.

"Nice to see you're already taking instruction so well."

"A deal's a deal," she says. "I'm paying an arm and a leg to be in this club, might as well get my money's worth." She laughs, clearly still amused by the form of "payment" I've exacted from her.

"You got your passport?" I ask.

She pats her purse. "It came last night, just like Georgia promised."

"Then let's do it." I grab her suitcase and lead her out into the pre-dawn morning to the limo waiting at the curb. The driver comes out and stashes her suitcase in the trunk as I guide her into the backseat, memories of our last limo ride instantly rushing me when she bends over to climb in.

"Surprise," Josh says as she enters the car.

She visibly startles.

"I'm Josh," he says, extending his hand to her as we settle into our seats. "Jonas' brother."

"Oh, yes, of course," she says, turning back to look at me. She's totally confused. "I've seen your picture. So nice to meet you. I didn't know . . ."

"You mean Jonas didn't tell you I'm joining you two on the trip?" He looks at me, appalled. "Why didn't you tell her, bro? That wasn't very nice of you." He turns to Sarah. "That wasn't very nice of him."

211

I shrug. "It must have slipped my mind." I grab her hand. "I hope you don't mind. Josh is a lot of fun."

"Oh," she says. Damn, she's adorable. "No, I ... That's great."

"Good," Josh says. "Because Jonas and I have so much planned for us." He high-fives me. "Gonna be fucking awesome, bro."

Sarah's speechless.

Josh leans into her. "Jonas and I never travel without each other. Ever. It's a twin thing." He winks.

She's pale. Her hand stiffens in mine.

Josh gazes wistfully out the window as we pull away from her apartment building. "Yeah, it's gonna be amazing. We'll be three peas in a pod all weekend long."

If I blew on her right now, she'd tip over.

I can't do this to her anymore, as cute as she is right now. I laugh. "We're just fucking with you, baby," I say.

Her hand relaxes in mine as she exhales. She swats at my leg and laughs.

"Unless you *want* me to come?" Josh says. "I mean, if you *want* me there, I'll clear my calendar, no problem. Just say the word."

"Okay, enough, Josh. Don't scare her away." I turn to Sarah. Color has returned to her cheeks. She's breathing again. "Josh has been staying with me the last few days while we've been working on our deal—"

"—which we finally closed," Josh says, finishing my sentence and looking at his watch, "about two hours ago." He lets out a hoot of celebration and pulls out a bottle of champagne that's chilling in ice.

"We're just giving Josh a lift to the airport," I explain. "He's catching an early flight back to L.A."

Josh leans into Sarah like he's telling her a secret. "I could have taken a much later flight today, but I wanted to see the woman who's reduced my brother to a mushy pile of goo." Josh succeeds in opening the bottle and I wordlessly hand him three glasses.

Sarah looks at me, clearly wondering how I feel about being called a mushy pile of goo, and I beam at her. I don't mind it one bit. I know the truth when I hear it.

"And you do not disappoint, Sarah Cruz," Josh says politely, handing her a glass of champagne. "Sorry I messed with you. It won't happen again."

"Ha," I say. "Don't believe him."

"Strangely, I wasn't all that freaked out about you joining us on the trip," she says to Josh, "but I admit the whole we-never-travel-without-each-other twin thing got me all kinds of flustered." She takes a sip of her champagne and her eyes light up. "Yum. I've never had champagne this early—but, hey, I make it a policy never to turn down a glass of champagne."

"Duly noted," I say, grabbing my glass from Josh.

"All right, bro, are you gonna tell her the news or should I?" Josh asks.

We've got her undivided attention. She looks anxious. Why does she think big news must be bad news?

I squeeze her hand to reassure her. "Josh and I have been working around the clock these past few days," I begin, my excitement barely containable, "or else I would have been beating down your door like the Big Bad Wolf, believe me."

"Did we ever go to bed last night?" Josh asks.

"No, sir, we did not—though I'm slightly delirious from sleep deprivation so I can't be sure."

"No, we didn't; you're right," Josh says. He looks at Sarah, smiling. "We finished all the paperwork on the deal just a couple hours ago—by the hair on our chinny-chin-chins."

"Are you guys gonna tell me the news? I'm dying here."

"Why, yes, we are, My Magnificent Sarah. Patience." I lean into her ear and whisper, "Stop begging for everything hard and fast, baby."

She blushes. She's so fucking adorable.

I clear my throat. "Raise your glasses, please." They do, and so do I. "And, a drum roll would be awfully nice, if you would."

Simultaneously, Josh and Sarah begin trilling their tongues and slapping their thighs with whichever hand isn't holding a champagne glass. Josh beams at Sarah, laughing at her exuberance. He already likes her, I can tell.

"We are hereby celebrating a new beginning." I shoot Sarah a look that tells her my new beginning includes her. "Sarah, you're looking at the new owners of Climb and Conquer Indoor Rock Climbing Gyms." My smile hurts my cheeks.

"Oh my God," she says, beaming. She clinks my glass and then Josh's. "Congratulations, you guys." She leans over and kisses me.

"Twenty gyms in five states," I say, my skin coursing with electricity. "It's something we've wanted to do for a really long time."

"Something *you've* wanted to do," Josh corrects me. "You were always the one with the dream, bro, from day one. I'm just along for the ride."

"Here's to figuring out what you want in life and going after it," I say, my eyes fixed on Sarah. "Relentlessly."

She clinks my glass again and shoots me the sexiest smile she's ever bestowed upon me.

I wanna tear her limb from limb right now. What better way to celebrate the best day of my life? I turn to Josh. "You're fucking awesome, man, but you're such a cock blocker right now."

Josh laughs. "Sorry."

Sarah giggles. "It's probably good you're here to protect me, Josh. Jonas looks like he could turn into the Incredible Hulk right now."

I smirk. I am, in fact, feeling very Incredible-Hulkish right now, or actually, King-Kong-ish. Yeah, I definitely want to beat my chest, throw her over my shoulder, and climb to the top of the highest building.

"So, is this, like, an investment, or are you two going to personally manage the gyms?" she asks.

Josh and I look at each other. This is an unresolved subject. Josh wants to treat the venture as a passive investment—hire a couple regional managers, oversee things from afar. But I want to make the gyms my passion, the center of my universe. In fact, the minute the deal closed, I didn't give a fuck about doing anything else, ever again. Suddenly, I felt like I'd finally figured out my life's purpose. Fuck Faraday & Sons. I never asked to be a part of it—never *wanted* to be a part of it. Fuck global investments and real estate investment trusts and EBITDA and acquisitions and asset management and weighing tax consequences for every move and counter-move. Fuck it all. I just want to climb rocks and mountains and train to climb rocks and mountains and be with other people who are obsessed with climbing rocks and mountains. And then go home and climb Sarah, my own personal Mount Everest.

"We haven't worked out all the details yet," I say slowly, and

Josh smirks in reply. We both know how things are eventually going to shake out. I'm leaving Faraday & Sons. And soon.

"Jonas wants to spend every single minute of the rest of his life climbing mountains," Josh says.

I look at Sarah, my eyes undressing her. "Not every single minute of the rest of my life."

She returns my gaze without flinching. After a moment, she exhales and parts her lips. Oh, yeah, she wants me, too.

"Unless, of course, that mountain is Mount Everest. In which case, yes." I touch her cheek.

Her eyes are on fire.

And, shit, just like that, my cock springs to life. If Josh weren't here, all my careful planning for this weekend would go right out the window. Actually, it's probably good he's here.

There's an awkward silence for a moment as Sarah and I continue to stare at each other, our mutual desire sucking all available oxygen out of the limo. She touches my hand against her cheek.

I close my eyes.

"Oh, wow, you two are gonna burst into a giant ball of flames this weekend, huh?"

Sarah blushes and drops her hand.

I drop my hand, too, but I don't take my eyes off her. "Fuck, yeah, we are," I say. I exhale slowly. "Fuck, yeah."

Finally. We're all alone. Well, as all alone as any two people can be in the first class cabin of a 737, sitting on a runway and waiting for takeoff. But, hey, it's better than sitting in that limo with my fucking brother for another minute. He kept looking at me the way only he does, shaking his head like he's laughing at me with just his eyes. And when the limo pulled away from the curb, he hugged me and whispered in my ear, "Bro, she's totally worth it." And then he winked at me.

I didn't know what he was referring to. She's totally worth the effort it took to track her down? Duh. She's totally worth the expense of hacking into Washington's server? Of course. Or was he referring to something else—something bigger, more philosophical than any of that? Josh doesn't usually get bogged down with philosophy or deep thoughts the way I do, so I can only assume he was talking about the hack job. But I'm not sure. Regardless, after the hug, he just gave me that smart-ass wink of his, hugged Sarah goodbye, and marched off in the direction of his flight with the kind of swagger only a guy as fucking awesome as he is could ever pull off.

As our airplane lifts off the runway, I grab Sarah's hand and she rests her head on my shoulder. She's trembling.

"You afraid of flying?" I whisper into her hair.

She shrugs but doesn't say anything.

We're quiet for several minutes as the plane reaches its flying altitude.

I know it's inhumanely early in the morning, and she said she didn't sleep a wink last night, but still—she seems unusually quiet, like something's troubling her. Is it just being on an airplane? I doubt it, but I don't want to press her. She'll tell me what's going on when she's ready.

"Belize," she finally says when it's clear takeoff has been successful. She sighs and nuzzles into my shoulder. "I still can't believe it."

Unfortunately, I couldn't keep our destination a secret forever. The minute we checked in for our flight, the jig was up, and she squealed like she'd just won the Showcase Showdown on *The Price is Right*. It was exactly the reaction I was hoping for. I wish I could have dazzled her even more by flying her on our company jet instead of going commercial—first, so I could have kept our destination a secret 'til the minute we stepped off the plane, and, second, so we could have flown straight there without laying over in Houston—but my uncle is using the jet for a business trip to London this weekend.

"Wait 'til you see it. I think you'll find it profoundly *inspirational*."

She looks at me quizzically.

I just smile. I can't wait for everything I've got planned for her. I feel like rubbing my hands together and giving her a really hearty villain laugh, but her hand in mine feels so good, it's not worth pulling away from her to do it.

She leans into me again.

"I have a confession to make," she finally says.

My stomach drops. I knew she had something big on her mind all morning.

"I don't even know where in the world Belize is."

I chuckle. Has her anxiety been about not knowing where we were headed? This is her first trip out of the country, after all. I sigh, relieved. "Central America. Bordered by Mexico, Guatemala, and the Caribbean Sea. Fun fact: It's the only country in Central America where the official language is English—though, of course, they speak Spanish there, too."

Her head remains fixed on my shoulder. It feels nice.

"I'm so excited," she says. With her free hand, she runs her fingertips gently along the tattooed inscription on the inside of my right forearm. Just that simple touch alone makes my breathing halt.

"Do you speak Spanish?" I ask.

"Mmm hmm," she says, sounding drowsy. "My mother's half Colombian—American-born, but her mom was from Colombia. Her father was Irish. She spoke Spanish to me growing up, though of course she speaks perfect English, too."

"And your dad?

She pauses. "American. Spanish-Italian heritage. Cruz is from his Spanish side."

"So he speaks Spanish, too?"

"Nope, just English. But he's also fluent in motherfucking asshole, too."

I can't help but raise my eyebrows at that. But I remain quiet. I wish I could give that bastard a taste of his own medicine.

Her fingertips lightly trace the length of my tattoo again, up and down, up and down, caressing the entire length of my forearm. I keep expecting her to do it, but she never asks me what my tattoos mean. I like that doesn't ask me about them. Most women ask about them first thing, like they're grasping at straws for anything to talk about and can't think of anything else to say. But not Sarah. Somehow, she knows my tattoos aren't fodder for small talk. Somehow, she always just knows.

I exhale. She's driving me crazy with her soft caress.

She's still leaning against my shoulder, not looking at me. "My mom left him when I was ten. Or, more accurately, she *escaped* him. We haven't seen him since. He's never contacted me."

Her fingertips move above my forearm and find my bicep, and begin caressing the muscles of my upper arm, under the sleeve of my T-shirt.

"His loss," I say quietly.

"I don't want to see him, anyway," she mumbles. "Ever."

After a minute, she raises her head up from my shoulder and looks into my eyes. She's holding back tears. "I've got something I need to tell you," she says. "Well, actually, three things. And one of 'em's a doozy."

My stomach drops. "Okay," I manage. "Shoot."

She straightens up and sighs. "I don't even know where to start." She looks like she's going to be sick.

I'm instantly on high alert. "Just say it. I'm a big believer in ripping off the Band-Aid."

She exhales. "I'll go in order from bad to worse."

I nod. "Okay."

"First, hopefully not too bad: I went to see Georgia on Tuesday—at the post office. And I bought her a cup of tea."

I laugh. Oh fuck, I'm so relieved. This is what she was nervous about all morning? "Sarah, I know. She called me. I don't know what you said to her, but she fell, like, head over heels in love with you. She called to tell me to grab you and never let go."

Her eyes light up. "She said that?"

"Yeah." I suddenly wish I hadn't repeated that exact phrase. I mean, I'm smitten here, don't get me wrong, but I don't want to give Sarah the impression I'm anywhere near ready to grab her and 'never let go.' I mean, come on. That's something I don't know if I'll *ever* be able commit to doing with anyone—even someone as incredible as Sarah. "So, anyway," I say, trying to change the subject quickly, "I don't know what Georgia told you, but I don't want you to get the wrong idea about me."

"Wrong idea? No, she said amazing things—beautiful things." Her voice lowers. "Things that made me see you in a whole new light."

"That's what I mean. I'm not that guy." I exhale, trying to figure out how to explain myself without pushing her away. "I'm not myself when it comes to Trey and Georgia. The Jonas Faraday I am for them is the exception, not the rule. Those two just bring something out in me I can't control." I clear my throat. A lump is rising up there.

Her eyes are shining.

I roll my eyes. "Stop looking at me like that. Seriously, I can't

218

run around trying to be everybody's hero all the time—and I don't. I'm vastly under-qualified for the job of hero."

She pauses. "Well, I think you're vastly underestimating yourself." She squints at me. "And I think you're in the process of transforming into Georgia's Jonas Faraday as we speak, even if you don't realize it. And, if you must know, I think the rock climbing gym is happening right now for a reason—it's not a coincidence. In fact, I don't believe in coincidences at all."

She flashes me a know-it-all look that makes it clear she's the smart one here and I'm just along for the ride.

"Well, I think you're a pain in the ass," I say, but I'm smiling broadly.

Damn. I wish I had the courage to say what I'm thinking, but I don't. It's too much. If I did, though, I'd blurt, "You are everything I never knew I always wanted." But it's one thing to say that kind of thing in a Valentine's Day card, and a whole other thing to say it out loud—especially when I'm not even sure what the hell it means. So, instead of saying it and sounding like a total sap, I just kiss her. And I kiss her and kiss her and kiss her again. My heart's racing. If we were alone, I'd rip her clothes off and kiss every inch of her, including her glorious pussy and suck on her clit and make her come right now, to hell with everything I've meticulously planned in Belize. So it's a good thing we're not alone. Because, with God as my witness, I'm going to do everything according to plan from here on out. No fucking around this time.

Oh man, our kissing is turning passionate. Too passionate. If we continue this way, I'm going to be tempted to drag her into the airplane bathroom—and that absolutely cannot happen. I promised myself I'd lead her outside the cave in a way that's worthy of her. I've got it all planned in Belize. And, God knows, fucking this gorgeous creature in an airplane bathroom would most definitely not be part of the plan.

She pulls away, licking her lips. "I have more to tell you, Jonas."

"Okay, okay." I sigh. "What's the second horrible thing?"

She gathers herself. "I spent six hundred and change of the money you gave me for shopping. And, thank you so much, by the way. I had so much fun. I felt like a princess."

I grunt. "Aw man, I really wanted you to go crazy—"

"No, no, that's not the bad part. I'm not gonna apologize for *not* spending three thousand dollars. That was too big a budget—totally ridiculous. I mean, thank you so much, you made me swoon—but I'm not gonna spend money just to spend money."

I smile. I would have been thrilled if she'd spent every last cent of that money spoiling herself—but I've got to admit it turns me on that she didn't. "So what's the big confession, then?"

"I gave all the leftover money on the card to that nonprofit I was telling you about. They provide shelter for battered women, and they also donate suits and work clothes to women going on job interviews."

Before I can speak, she continues. Clearly, she's nervous.

"And there's something I didn't tell you before. It's my mom's charity." She clears her throat. "She started it ten years ago. She runs it. Oh my God, Jonas, it's her life, her passion." Her face is bursting with pride. "So, yeah, technically, I gave the money to my mom, but not to run off and get her nails done or whatever. She'll use it to help a lot of women in need."

There are no words to describe the way I'm feeling right now, so I kiss her again. And again.

She pulls away. "So you're not upset about any of that?"

"Upset? Of course not. In fact, when we get home, I'll make a proper donation to your mom's charity. I'm sorry I didn't think of doing it when you first told me about it. See? I told you, I'm vastly under-qualified to play hero."

"Thank you," she says.

"You thought I'd be *upset* about that?"

"No, not really *upset*, but I wasn't one hundred percent sure how you'd feel about me giving your money away without asking first." She sighs. "And, well, Jonas, I didn't buy a single item of lingerie, either—that's the most appalling part of the whole confession."

I feign indignation. "Don't speak to me ever again."

She laughs. "I just figured lingerie would be pretty useless. Why not just go buck naked and give you unimpeded access to every inch of me, instead?"

"I like the way you think," I say.

So far, her supposed mountain of bad news has turned out to be a whole lot of nothing. Damn, from the way she was looking so nervous a minute ago, you'd think she had something genuinely horrible to tell me.

"So what's the third horrible thing?" I ask. "It's the worst one, right? Should I brace myself?"

She furrows her brow. "Yeah, this one's really, really bad, Jonas. Really bad." She's shaking again.

My stomach instantly twists into a huge knot.

"Remember that software engineer I told you about?" she begins slowly. "The one who joined The Club, looking for love?"

"Yeah, the one who joined for a month," I say, nodding. Yeah, yeah, yeah, I know—he's a romantic and I'm a fucking sociopath looking for nothing but endless coochie. She already made that abundantly clear.

"He checked in for the first time last night at a sports bar. So Kat and I went to spy on him."

I don't know where this is heading. Something in her eyes is making me dread whatever's coming next. Jesus, did she go home with him or something? Please, God, no.

She sighs. She's trembling. She shakes her head, unable to go on.

"Sarah, just tell me." I'm officially about to fucking freak out.

She shakes her head again.

I pull back from her to look into her eyes. "What's going on? Whatever it is, it's okay, I promise." *Unless you fucked him. That would most definitely not be okay.* I'm about to lose my fucking mind here. "Sarah, tell me." There's an edge in my voice I can't suppress.

"Jonas, the guy couldn't have been more opposite you in every way—talk about being brainwashed by Lifetime and Disney. Seriously."

My cheeks blaze. Yes, I know. He's sweet, I'm an asshole. He signed up for a month, I signed up for a year. He applied to The Club to find love, and I applied to find a year's worth of no-strings-attached fuck buddies who wouldn't make me feel like an asshole when I sent them packing night after night. I got it. Is she still judging me based on my application? I thought we were all done with that. Did she have an epiphany that she wants a guy who wears his romantic heart on his sleeve—that she *needs* a guy like that? What is she trying to tell me?

"So, anyway, the guy came to the bar wearing a yellow bracelet—which, like I say, made perfect sense. If *you* were assigned purple, then I knew *that guy* had to be whatever color is the opposite of purple. Kat and I were just dying to see what kind of Miss Yellow was gonna be this normal, boring guy's one true love."

Okay, I'm oddly reassured by that last part. If I know anything about Sarah by now, it's that she doesn't want normal and boring. She wants fucked up and abnormal and sometimes pretty fucking dirty—she wants an asshole she can redeem. So, really, she's complimenting me in a twisted kind of way. My heart slows slightly. I wait.

She pauses a ridiculously long time, obviously getting up the nerve to blurt it out, whatever it is.

"Sarah, rip off the Band-Aid," I huff, verging on exasperation. "Come on."

She exhales. "When Miss Yellow showed up in her yellow bracelet ... " She sighs again. "Jonas, she was your Miss Purple. Stacy the Faker."

I'm floored. "What?" My head is reeling. What the fuck?

She proceeds to tell me every last detail about the night, including exactly what Stacy said when she ambushed Sarah in the bathroom.

I run my fingers through my hair, my mind reeling.

Tears have pooled in Sarah's eyes. "I'm sick about it," she chokes out. "I swear I didn't know." She puts her hands over her face. "I work for a frickin' whorehouse," she whispers.

My heart is beating a mile a minute. If I could punch a hole in the wall, I would—but that's a non-starter on an airplane. I run a hand over my face. I can't even process what I'm hearing.

Sarah puts her hands over her face and begins to cry.

I know I should comfort her right now, I know that's the right thing to do, but I want to kill someone. So much adrenaline is coursing through my body it's a good thing I'm strapped down by a seatbelt. I look out the airplane window, trying to corral my racing thoughts, but it's no use. My stomach is flip-flopping and my fists are clenched. Holy shit, I fucked a prostitute. I *licked* a fucking prostitute's cunt. It doesn't matter that it was for twenty seconds; I tongued a fucking pay-to-play pussy. I physically shudder at the disgusting thought. My tongue suddenly feels like it's covered in a thick grime. I can practically hear my father's ghost laughing in my ear.

I unbuckle my seatbelt. My head is spinning.

"I'll be right back," I mumble over my shoulder as I bolt to the bathroom. I know I shouldn't run away, shouldn't leave her crying and all alone. I know I should be reassuring and compassionate, tell her we'll figure this out. *I'm not mad at you,* I should say, *I just need a minute alone.* But I've got to get the hell out of here. I feel like I'm going to be sick.

I slam the bathroom door behind me.

I fucked a goddamned hooker. I've become my fucking father. Fuck me.

In the bathroom, I put cold water on my face. I rinse out my mouth. I stand over the toilet, ready to puke my guts out. But nothing comes up.

After a minute, I rinse my face again.

This is karma, really. Bad things happen to bad people. And, anyway, what did I think I was getting into when I signed up for The Club? Who did I think was out there in the universe, eager to fuck me with no expectation or even desire to feel anything, ever? What kind of woman did I think I'd find matching those criteria? Seriously, what kind of woman yearns for nothing but a good fuck followed by a swift push out the door? I knew there was no such woman—deep down, I knew it. And I just ignored what I knew to be true. Ha! I convinced myself I was looking for brutal honesty, but the whole time, I was looking for lies. And I got what I deserved. I got what I fucking deserved.

I look at myself in the mirror. Water's dripping off my brow.

I licked at Stacy for five seconds before she started howling like I'd blasted her to the moon. I'm good, but I'm not that good. And I knew it. And then I fucked her so hard I practically tore her in half, and she pretended to love every minute of it. So what fairytale did I tell myself to continue believing Stacy had signed up for The Club the way I did? Oh yeah, a woman who looks like that wants nothing more than to get fucked and tossed aside? I knew something was wrong when she left without a word. I knew I was deluding myself. But I didn't care. Josh told me his membership was the "best money he'd ever spent." What the fuck Club did *he* join? Because I knew all along I'd paid The Club to lie to me. Deep down, I knew. Well, now I'm getting exactly what I deserve.

An image floods me—a vision I've tried my whole life to forget. He's binding her arms and legs to the bedposts. Blood is trickling from her nose.

I grip the cold metal sink, trying to steady myself, trying to keep the rest of the images from leaping into my mind, but I can't stop them. They're slamming into me.

He's forcing himself on her, his pants around his ankles, his hairy ass hanging out. He's grunting like an animal. She's screaming. I'm burrowing myself deeper behind her dresses in the closet, but I can't look away. I cover my ears, but I can still hear her blood-curdling screams. He whacks her across the face and bends down to pull up his pants. As he leans over, she peeks over at me in my hiding spot. Her blue eyes are wild. She shakes her head frantically at me. *Don't come out,* she's commanding me. *Stay where you are.* But she doesn't have to command me to stay put—my legs have been frozen since he first dragged her into the room, kicking and screaming.

I run water through my hair and let it drip down my face. I stare at myself in the mirror. I can see my eyes staring back at me now. Those long-ago images are gone, at least for now.

Well, I guess I can't hide from the truth about myself forever. Yeah, I can wear the custom suits Josh always insists I should wear, even though I hate them. I can work out three hours a day and sculpt my body into a façade of perfection. I can read and read and aspire and reach for enlightenment all I like, but I'll never be able to change what I did.

Tears are threatening, but I won't let them come. Even if I were a fucking pussy-ass crier, which I'm not, even if I were "soft," like he always said I am, I'd never let myself cry in a fucking airplane bathroom. But, anyway, I'm not a fucking pussy-ass crier and I'm not soft, so it's a moot point.

If I'd known he had that knife, maybe I would have done something differently. Maybe I wouldn't have stayed in the closet, hiding behind her dresses, frozen with fear. Maybe I would have at least tried to pull him off her. Maybe then everything would have turned out differently.

I unzip my pants and take a whiz.

I'm getting exactly what I deserve. I wanted brutal honesty, huh? Something *real*? I scoff at myself. I was lying to myself. I wanted a quarter-million dollars' worth of pussy, plain and simple. I just wanted to numb the pain, just like my father always did. Where did I think all that pain-killing pussy was gonna come from? Pussy heaven? The Pussy Fairy? I didn't care. I didn't care about anybody or anything but numbing the pain. It serves me right. What kind of sick fuck joins a sex club for a fucking year, anyway? Josh joined The Club for a fun-filled month—just a little vacation—and I'm the sick fuck who joined for a fucking *year*? What the fuck is wrong with me? I'm not normal.

I zip my fly back up.

I wash my hands.

I wipe at my eyes.

I'm getting exactly what I deserve.

As I take my seat again, she looks at me expectantly, tears streaming down her face. She looks half her age—so small and vulnerable. Even before I buckle my seatbelt, even before she can speak, I take her face in my hands and kiss her deeply. She sobs into me, returning my kiss.

After a moment, she pulls away from me. "I should have told you everything before you were stuck on an airplane with me—so you could cancel the trip if you wanted to."

I exhale with exasperation. That's the last thing in the world I'm thinking right now. "Nothing in the world could make me want to cancel this trip with you. Not what you just told me, not the world crumbling down, not the fucking apocalypse. Nothing. I want to be here with you right now, headed to paradise, more than I want anything in the world—and now more than ever." I kiss her again, and her body melts into me.

"Just give me a little time, okay? I don't know how to explain everything I'm thinking right now—everything I'm feeling. It's complicated."

"Okay," she says meekly. She's hiccupping, trying to suppress her sobs.

"Sarah, I'm not upset at you. I promise." I smooth away a lock of her hair that's stuck to her wet cheek. "I'm disgusted, furious, ashamed. But none of it at you."

"I'm sorry," she says. "I didn't know. I never would have taken that stupid job if I'd known."

"I know that. Just give me a little time to think. I can't talk to you about everything right now. I just can't."

She clamps her mouth shut into a thin line and nods.

"It's not you. Sometimes, I have a hard time expressing my feelings out loud. I just need a little time to think everything through, that's all. Maybe listen to some music. Music is what I use to sort out my feelings."

"Okay," she says again. "I totally understand." Without saying another word, she plants a gentle kiss on my cheek, grabs my hand, and leans against my shoulder. Her fingertips begin lightly tracing the tattooed inscription on my forearm and then, slowly, working their way up to my bicep.

I grab my phone and ear buds and scroll into my music library. Arctic Monkeys. I put on my headphones and sit back.

Sarah's fingers are caressing my forearm.

The music is calming me.

Sarah's touch is calming me.

My breathing is returning to normal.

What did Sarah say in that handwritten note of hers, the one she put into the welcome package? "If I were willing to lie to you, like everyone else apparently does—like you actually *want* everyone to do, despite what you delude yourself into thinking you want—things might have been different." She sure saw right through me, right from the beginning, didn't she?

Her hand has stopped moving. It falls into her lap.

Yeah, she had me pegged right from the start.

"My wish for you," she wrote, "is that someday you'll realize what you *want* and what you *need* are two very different things."

Her head flops forward on my shoulder. I glance down at her beautiful face. She's out like a light. I turn off my music and gaze at her for a moment. I love the shape of her lips. Her eyelashes are long and lush. Her fingers are elegant. That silver band on her thumb slays me.

I sigh.

I bring her hand up to my lips and gently kiss her sexy little ring.

Well, if that's her wish for me—that I discover what I *want* and *need* are two very different things—then her wish is never gonna come true. Because sitting here with her, feeling her body rising and falling rhythmically against mine, a wisp of her hair brushing up against my jawline, I'm suddenly quite certain, for the first time in my life, that what I *want* and *need* are one and the same thing. And that thing is sitting next to me, fast asleep.

Chapter 23
Sarah

"Holy moly," I say. "Wow! Oh my gosh!" I can't stop the exclamations of excitement and glee from pouring out of my mouth. "Wooh! Did you see this? Wow!"

After almost twelve hours of travel—two planes, a layover in Houston, and a long, bumpy Jeep ride out to the middle of nowhere— we're finally here at our destination, a secluded resort in the heart of the Belizian jungle. I'm panting like a dog, thanks not only to my excitement, but also thanks to our trek up ten flights of rickety wooden steps in the ink-black night to reach our accommodations. Because Jonas and I are staying in an effing *tree house*—a luxurious, honeymoon-suite *tree house*!— surrounded on all sides by the lush jungle canopy. Holy crappola. Or, holy shitballs, as Kat would say. (*Juepucha,* as my mom would say.) Whatever—it's un-frickin'-believable.

I don't know where I'm getting this sudden burst of energy, but I'm running around the spacious suite, squealing and shouting about every fabulous detail. "Did you see this?" I shout, pointing at the flower petals strewn all over the white bed covers. "And look!" The towels in the bathroom have been twisted and sculpted into two perfect swans. "Woah!" The bathroom shower is even bigger than Jonas' spacious shower at his house. "Ooooh!" A bottle of champagne sits on ice, waiting for us. Holy frickin' moly.

After the steward opens the champagne bottle for us and tucks our luggage away, he explains how to light the mosquito lamps and close the mosquito netting over our bed while we sleep. Jonas hands him a large bill, and he ducks out with a big smile on his face.

"Alone at last," Jonas says, handing me yet another glass of champagne. I think this is my fourth glass over the course of this long day.

"This is the most amazing place, ever," I say, my eyes blazing. I take a sip. "Wow. The best champagne of the day."

Jonas is beaming at me.

"I never thought I'd get to see a place like this in my entire life." I gaze out the screened windows surrounding us. It's pitch black outside.

"Wait 'til you see it in the light," Jonas says. "The jungle's gonna blow your mind." He grabs my hand. "Come here." He pulls me out to the deck. I can't see a thing in the blackness surrounding us.

"What?" I ask, looking around. Light is wafting out of the suite behind us, but looking out toward the jungle, I can't make out a single thing.

He puts his finger to his mouth and tilts his head toward the edge of the balcony. "Listen."

I stand quietly, pricking my ears for any kind of noise in the darkness around me. I smash my body against his and he puts his arm around me. I listen. And I listen. Well, I definitely hear birds. All around me, in fact. Leaves are rustling as animals move around us. Jonas puts his finger to his mouth again, instructing me to keep listening quietly. Yep, birds. And movement everywhere. We stand stock still for what must be a full two minutes. Finally, a screeching howl cuts through the dark night.

I gasp. "What—?"

"A howler monkey," Jonas says quietly, grinning mischievously.

Oh, Jonas.

A moment later, there's another scream, even louder and more piercing than the first one. I burst out laughing.

"They're all around us in the trees." He pulls me close to him. "A little inspiration for you, baby." He kisses me. "Let the monkeys be your guide."

My heart is in danger of hurtling right out of my chest and flinging into the dark night like a Frisbee. "Oh, Jonas. Right here, right now, on this very spot on planet earth, with you"—I point to the ground I'm standing on—"is the most glorious five square inches in the entire world."

His smile lights up the dark night.

"When you said 'tropical,' I pictured us lying on a sandy beach drinking piña coladas," I say.

"Yeah, well, Belize is famous for its beaches. But we're not going to the coast this time. We'll do that next time. This time, we're all about the jungle."

Next time? He's already contemplating a *next* time? I try to suppress a squeal, but I don't succeed.

"But, hey, I can certainly get you that piña colada." He looks at his watch. "But not tonight. We've got a big day tomorrow. Gotta be up bright and early."

"What are we doing?"

"Wouldn't you like to know," he says.

"Yes, I would. But I'll be patient and wait to find out. On this trip, I'm doing whatever you say, Lord-God-Master-Woman-Wizard."

He nods. "Good girl."

In a fit of sudden glee, I twirl like a little girl. "This is like a dream."

He's smiling from ear to ear. It's a welcome change from the storm cloud that's been hanging over him since our horrific conversation on the plane.

I yawn. I don't mean to, but I do. I didn't sleep at all last night, and I caught maybe two hours of sleep today on the plane, if I was lucky. And all the champagne I've had today certainly isn't helping me keep my eyes open.

"What do you say we take a shower," Jonas says, "and then get into bed?"

He's wearing only boxers, glory be, and his taut muscles are on full display. I watch him light the mosquito lamps on either side of the bed, the muscles over his rib cage tightening as he bends over to position the lamp. I'm wearing a tank top and plaid pajama bottoms, my hair tied into a ponytail, and my skin feels squeaky clean and moisturized after our shower together, a welcome sensation after our long and grimy travel day. Showering with him was particularly enjoyable this time, maybe because I was so relaxed. Somehow, I knew he was going to wash me and lather me, and that sex wasn't in the cards. I just knew it.

And I was right. He lathered me so tenderly, so delicately, he wasn't so much *washing* me as *worshipping* me. Delicious.

And now, I can't believe I'm lying here in this four-poster mahogany bed in a tree house in the middle of a deep, dark, noisy jungle, basking in the warm night air, as the most beautiful man I've ever laid eyes on climbs into bed and secures mosquito netting around us.

"It's a little cocoon," he says, fastening the net and lying down right next to me. "A cocoon built for two."

"I like that," I say, nuzzling up to him as he scoots his body against mine. His skin is warm. "A cocoon built for two," I repeat.

A monkey screams just outside our window in the darkness and we both laugh.

"That was a good one," he says. "Are you taking notes?"

"Yes, sir." I mimic the sound the monkey just made.

He laughs. "Pretty good."

We lie on our sides, smiling at each other, staring at each other, lost in each other's eyes. After a moment, he rubs the tip of his nose against mine. "Thank you for coming here with me."

"You're welcome," I say. "But you owe me big."

He laughs. "I do, actually."

"You really don't understand the concept of payment, do you?" I ask.

He grins.

I want to kiss him. But tonight I'm going to honor my word and let him take the lead. He's my master tonight. His hands rest comfortably on my waist, not moving, not exploring, not pressing for more. So I rest my hand on his thigh.

"I'm happy," he says.

My heart leaps out of my chest. I can barely breathe. "So am I, Jonas."

He hugs me to him and squeezes me tight. I rest my head against his chest. I wait. Is he going to make love to me now?

After a moment, his fingers lightly skim the curve of my hip.

I follow his lead. My fingertip drifts to the tattoo inscribed on the inside of his left arm.

"Is this Greek?" I ask.

"Mmm hmm," he says. "Ancient Greek."

231

"Are you Greek?"

"No."

I wait. I've wanted to know the meaning of his tattoos since I first saw his heart-stopping, full-bodied selfie. I smile wistfully to myself. Back then, he was nothing more than an idea—a vision of unattainable perfection, a work of art. Not the flesh and blood man lying next to me now. When I saw that photo, I never would have thought I'd be lying here, touching his muscled arm, drifting off to sleep in his arms. In effing Belize.

I yawn again. Damn. I can't help it. My body is so relaxed and I'm so sleepy. My mind keeps slipping, floating, and then jolting back awake. I don't want to fall asleep. I don't want to miss a thing.

My fingertips track the inscription on his arm again. These words, whatever they are, are the key to unlocking him; I know it. But, somehow, I've known from the start to wait for him to hand me the key in his own time.

He pulls back slightly and displays the inside of his arm to me. "It's a quote from Plato," he says. He waits a beat.

I'm tingling with anticipation at his next words. "Yeah?" I say, breathless.

"'For a man to conquer himself is the first and noblest of all victories.'"

My pulse is suddenly pounding in my ears. "That's the quote you mentioned in your interview with Trey." And it's what I guessed the longer of his tattoos would say.

"Ah, you read that interview, huh?"

"Like twenty times. That interview told me more about you than anything else I could find. And believe me, I was thorough in my research."

He's quiet for a minute as my fingers migrate up to his biceps. Man, I love the feel of his biceps. He's got the kind of arms most girls could only dream about wrapping around them one day. And here I am, my dreams a reality.

"Why did you get that tattooed onto your arm?" I ask.

He's quiet for so long, I begin to wonder if he's ever going to answer me. "Because conquering myself is my life's greatest struggle," he finally says. "It's a constant reminder for me to keep working at it, to keep trying. Not to give up."

When it's clear he's not going to go on, I finally say, "What happened to you, Jonas?"

His body tenses and he shifts uncomfortably. He exhales. "Josh and I were seven." He pauses.

I'm holding my breath.

"My dad was taking the whole family to a Seahawks game—my mom, Josh, and me." He pauses again.

I wait. The light from the mosquito lamp is flickering in the room, casting shadows across his beautiful face. A bird screeches loudly in the jungle, just outside our bedroom window. There's a rustle in the trees.

His voice is low, barely audible. "I worshipped the ground she walked on, followed her around like a puppy. She used to pat me on the head and say, 'Good doggie' and I'd make puppy noises." He closes his eyes, remembering something. "She was so beautiful. And she was *kind*."

I'm afraid if I move or talk or breathe, I'll break the spell and he'll stop talking.

He opens his eyes again and pain flashes across his face. "It was time to go to the football game, but my mother had one of her headaches. She didn't want to go to the noisy stadium."

There's a rustling sound outside our window.

His eyes dart to mine for reassurance.

I nod, ever so slightly.

"Dad was mad. He was like, 'Take a fucking aspirin, you'll be fine.' But I said, 'No, she needs to rest. I'll stay with her and make her all better.' I used to rub her temples when she got her headaches. She always said my touch was the only thing that could take her pain away. She said I had magic in my fingers."

His eyes are moist. I touch his cheek, and he closes his eyes at my touch. He leans his cheek into the palm of my hand.

My heart breaks at this simple gesture.

He continues talking with his eyes closed, his cheek in my hand. "Dad was pissed. He stormed out with Josh. Didn't even say goodbye." I caress his cheek with my thumb and he opens his eyes. His expression is one of unadulterated anguish. "We were cuddling in her bed, snuggling, my favorite thing. I loved having her all to myself. I was rubbing her temples so she could fall asleep." His entire body tenses next to me in the bed. "There was a loud noise downstairs, a crashing noise. She jumped off the bed and I started to follow her, but she said, 'No, baby, stay here.' So I hid in the closet because I was scared. I was shaking." He swallows hard. "And before she got two steps out of her bedroom, there was a man. He dragged her back into the room. She fought against him and he punched her in the face with his fist. She was bleeding out her nose." His voice hitches. "I knew I should run out of the closet right then to help her, but I didn't."

Oh, his voice. I've never heard it sound like this—so small. My heart is aching for him.

"I just stood there, peeking through a crack in the closet door, hiding in her dresses." He inhales, like he's remembering the scent of her. "He tied her up. He ... he ... pulled down his pants. I remember what his ass looked like."

I inhale sharply, anticipating the horror to come. My stomach is twisting into knots.

"She was screaming, but I just let him do it to her. I didn't help her." His eyes are glistening.

I don't speak. I just wait. My heart is banging in my ears.

"I wanted to help her, to pull him off her—I wanted to make him stop. But he was so big and my legs wouldn't work. I imagined myself sneaking out of the closet and finding a golf club in the garage and running back up to the bedroom and bashing him over the head ... But I didn't move." Tears are pooling in his eyes. He looks up to keep them from falling down his cheeks. "Then I realized I could take her pain away after the man left—with my magic fingers. I decided to wait and untie her after he was gone and make it all better with my hands, like I always did." He's choking up. "I didn't know he had a knife." Jonas blinks and, despite his best efforts, big, soggy tears stream down his cheeks. "I didn't know what he was gonna do with that knife—it happened so fast—or else I wouldn't have waited. If I'd known, I would have saved her the minute he punched her. I would have done *something*." Tears are pouring out of his eyes, and out of mine, too.

"Jonas, you were seven," I say.

He lets out a soft groan. "I should have saved her."

"You were *seven*," I say again. "There was nothing you could have done."

"I should have at least *tried* to save her." His voice catches in his

234

throat. "I should have at least *tried* to pull him off her." His body twitches violently, straining to suppress the tidal wave of grief threatening to rise up out of him. "Or I should have died trying."

"Oh, Jonas, no." I take his face in my hands and he melts under my touch. "Oh, baby," I say, pulling him to me. "No."

He nods, unable to speak.

"No," I whisper. "No." My heart is breaking in two.

"If it wasn't for me, she would have gone to the football game like my father wanted her to—she wouldn't have been in the house when the man came. It was *me* who said she needed to rest. It was me who *wanted* her to stay behind so I could have her all to myself. I wanted to be alone with her—no Josh, no Dad. I wanted to touch her and take her pain away. I wanted to lie in bed with her. I wanted her to say I was the only one who knew how to make her feel better." He's on the verge of a total breakdown. "If it hadn't been for me . . ." He can't contain himself anymore. Grief and guilt and heartache and pain burst out of him in a singular, violent release.

There is nothing more heartbreaking than seeing a grown man sob—especially when that man has a hold on your heart like nobody ever has. I hold him to me—rocking him, nuzzling him, stroking his hair—as his anguish rises up and pours out of him like a tsunami.

"It wasn't your fault," I say again and again.

His body twists and shudders.

"Shh," I soothe him. "It wasn't your fault."

After a while, he quiets down. His chest is heaving. He leans his forehead into mine, but he doesn't speak. He's spent.

A howler monkey screams in the dark jungle right outside our window.

He pulls back from me and wipes his eyes with the back of his hand. He moves a wisp of hair out my eyes.

"Did they ever catch him?"

"He was our housekeeper's sister's boyfriend. Our housekeeper had mentioned getting the day off because the family was going out to the Seahawk's game—it wasn't her fault. She had nothing to do with it." He pauses. "He thought we'd be gone. He just came for her jewelry." He sighs deeply. "It was just bad luck we were there—bad luck he turned out to be a psychopath." He sighs again, slowly, trying to control his breathing.

"What about your father?" I ask. I know Jonas' father died about thirteen years ago, when Jonas was seventeen, but I couldn't find anything on-line detailing the cause of his death. "I can't imagine how devastated he must have been."

At my question, Jonas' eyes darken. He inhales deeply and exhales slowly. "My father never got over losing her. The grief—the guilt—it ate him alive. So he turned it into blame. He blamed himself, blamed me. Mostly blamed me."

I shake my head. That can't be true. "No," I say softly.

"Yes. My whole life, I knew it. He blamed me for what happened."

"No. He couldn't have blamed you. You were seven."

"Even Josh knows he blamed me. It wasn't a secret. It's just the way it was. It was my fault. We all knew it. I'm the one that made her stay behind."

A shiver runs down my spine. What kind of man could even think of blaming a child for a horror like that?

"I tried to make up for what I did. But it was never enough. How could it ever be enough?"

I shake my head. Horrible. No wonder Jonas needed years of therapy. "He died when you were seventeen?"

Jonas grunts.

Maybe I should let it be, change the subject. But now that this man has shown me the deepest parts of himself, I'm aching to know every last thing. I wait. But he doesn't say anything. I'm about to say, "It's okay—we don't have to talk about this," when he finally speaks.

"He killed himself."

I moan softly. How much tragedy can one family take?

"He just couldn't ... He never got over losing her. In the beginning, he tried to forget what happened by throwing himself into his company."

I'm surprised at the edge in his tone when he says "his company," especially since that company ultimately became Jonas'.

"And when all the money in the world didn't take the pain away, he turned to booze, and then to women—lots and lots of women—prostitutes, mainly." He scoffs angrily at this last part. "He had the famous Faraday libido, of course, so becoming a monk wasn't realistic, and yet he didn't want to foul her memory by *feeling* something with another human being ever again, God forbid." He clenches his jaw. "He never told the truth about any of it, acted like all those hot women were falling all over him thanks to his fucking personality, acted like his shit didn't stink 'til the bitter end—but Josh and I knew exactly what he was doing. It was disgusting." He sighs. "He fucked every hooker he could get his hands on for about a year—and then he finally put himself out of his misery."

I'm speechless. Does he not see the parallels between himself and his father? Or does he? I've suddenly got goose bumps.

"My uncle took over the company. Josh went off to college that fall, and I went off the following year, when I was all better." His eyes flicker. "But we both knew, when we graduated, we'd have to come back. We knew we had a duty to become the 'Sons' of Faraday & Sons." His jaw muscles are pulsing.

"Not what you wanted?"

"My dad started Faraday & Sons right after we were born. We were *babies* and he called it Faraday *& Sons*. There was never any question about who we were expected to become." He looks up at the ceiling, lost in thought.

I stroke his cheek with the back of my hand.

His eyes soften. "I like to imagine there's another version of me, the 'divine original' form of me, floating in another realm. A not-fucked-up version of me. In that realm, that one horrible day never happened and I became the man I was originally designed to be." He sighs. "The man I would have been if I didn't get hopelessly fucked up."

"Is that what your other tattoo is about?" I ask, but I already know it is.

He half-smiles at me. "You're so smart, Sarah—you'd give Plato a run for his money, you know that?" He shifts his body and holds his right arm up to display his tattoo. "'Visualize the divine originals.'"

I look down at the lettering. Greek again. "Plato?" I ask.

He nods.

"Why the devotion to Plato?" I ask.

He sighs. "After my dad died, I had a bit of a rough time." He smiles wanly, like this is the understatement of the year. "When all the doctors in the world couldn't fix me, I started reading philosophy—everything I could get my hands on, just reading,

reading, reading, trying to make sense of things, trying not to have a nervous breakdown again, honestly—trying not to go completely insane again. I'd had a total fucking meltdown after everything with my mother, and I'd been in therapy ever since—and doing pretty well, actually—but then I lost it again after my dad ... And I finally figured out talking about my fucking *feelings* just wasn't gonna be enough this time, especially after what my dad said to me in his fucking suicide note."

Oh my God. What did that bastard say to my sweet Jonas as an unanswerable parting shot? I'm afraid to ask, and he doesn't offer any specifics. A chill runs down my spine.

He shrugs. "I knew I needed something more, something wise. Timeless. I needed answers. I read everything I could get my hands on, and when I discovered Plato, I don't know, he just spoke to me, especially his Allegory of the Cave, the one I told you about in the limo." He grins, obviously remembering our eventful limo ride. "I don't know, people always talk about Aristotle—and he was great, of course, obviously—but Plato was Aristotle's *teacher*, you know? Plato was the fucking *forefather* of modern thought, you know? The divine original. His ideas gave me something to latch onto—something to focus on. He had ideas about everything—music, science, death, family, mortality ... love." He blushes.

I feel my cheeks flush. My heart is racing. I touch his cheek again.

He turns his head and kisses the palm of my hand.

"Plato was an idealist." He says the word 'idealist' like he's paying the man his highest compliment.

"But what does it mean—'visualize the divine originals'?"

He looks down at his tattoo. "Visualize the divine originals." He sighs reverently. "It's from Plato's Theory of Forms." Oh wow, his eyes are suddenly animated. Clearly, he's passionate about this, whatever it is. "Plato had the idea that truth, idealism, perfection, it's all an abstraction that exists separate and apart from the physical world we live in."

I shrug. I still don't understand.

He grins. "It's really esoteric stuff. Plato thought there were two realms—the imperfect physical world we live in—the one we experience through our senses, the one filled with pain and imperfection—and also an ideal realm, completely separate, a realm we can't experience, but which we nevertheless innately understand."

"Sorry, I'm still totally lost."

He grins. "So, let's say you see a tree in the physical realm. It's got a couple branches missing. And there's another tree burned in a fire. And another one with initials carved in the bark. How does your mind recognize all of these forms as trees? They're all imperfect, and differently so. And yet your mind recognizes them all as *trees*. Plato said it's because the *ideal* form of a tree—the abstraction of *tree-ness*—exists in the ideal realm. And our minds, our souls, innately understand and recognize the perfect tree-ness in those imperfect trees, even if we've never actually witnessed perfect tree-ness. Tree-ness is what the imperfect trees *aspire* to, and our souls are designed to *aspire.*" His face is flushed, glowing.

I smile at him. This man is stunningly beautiful in every way.

"What? Why are you looking at me like that?"

"You're such a poet," I say.

"No," he replies. "Not usually." He opens his mouth to say something else but thinks the better of it. He clamps his mouth shut.

"So if I understand this correctly, your tattoo means you aspire to the ideal form of Jonas Faraday-ness, like a broken tree aspires to tree-ness?"

He smiles broadly at me. "Exactly. My soul recognizes the divine original of Jonas Faraday-ness, even though that perfect abstraction doesn't exist in the physical world." He sighs. "Basically, I aspire to the un-fucked-up form of me. My soul can envision who he is, even though my physical senses can't. And I just keep visualizing and aspiring."

I cock my head to one side. God, he's beautiful, inside and out. If this man isn't perfection personified, I don't know what is. "You're already him, Jonas."

He shakes his head.

"Yes, you are. You're perfect, exactly as you are."

"No. I'm hopelessly fucked up."

"Yeah, you're fucked up. Of course you are. What you've been through would fuck anybody up. Horribly. But you're perfect—and definitely not hopeless. There's no such thing as hopelessness."

He doesn't understand me.

I sit up on my elbow and look down at his face. "You're scarred, that's for sure." I stroke his brow line. "You've been forced to experience the worst thing a human being could ever endure, and at such a tender age."

He looks away.

"Jonas." His eyes return to me. "You're not a tree. You were innately designed to *feel*—for better and for worse. Which means the perfect form of you was inherently designed to be scarred."

He clenches his jaw.

I sigh. I feel like I'm not expressing my thoughts very well. "If there's a divine original of Jonas Faraday floating around in some other realm, a perfectly unscathed and unscarred version of you, then I'd still choose you. Because if this allegedly ideal Jonas Faraday is perfectly unscathed by life, then he's never *felt* anything." I swallow hard and look him directly in the eyes. "If he's unscarred, then he's never loved," I whisper. "Or been loved."

His eyes flicker.

My heart is going to burst.

"It's *feelings* that leave scars on our hearts. It's *risking*." A lump is rising in my throat. "It's love," I whisper. "So if the divine original of Jonas Faraday has no scars, he's not perfect, after all." My eyes are pricking with tears. What this beautiful man has been through is unthinkable. "Jonas, we're here on this planet to do one thing: to *love* and be loved." My tears begin to flow. "And nothing else." I wipe my eyes. "Love leaves scars."

He exhales sharply. He's shaking. He opens his mouth to speak, but then apparently thinks better of it.

I lie back down and throw my arms around him, my tears flowing freely. The pain, the grief, the joy at being with him in his arms, the sorrow for all he's been through, the weight he's carried on his shoulders his entire life—it's all just too much for me. I'm suddenly overflowing with emotion. "You're not a tree, Jonas, you're not a tree," I mumble, burrowing into his chest. I can't even think straight anymore. I have to make him understand it wasn't his fault. I have to make him understand he's good—so very good. So very beautiful. He's worthy. He's kind. He's mine.

There's a rustling sound in the darkness surrounding our tree house.

He pulls me close. His body is warm against mine, his muscles taut. His arms feel so strong wrapped around me. He leans into me and kisses me oh so tenderly, even as tears inexplicably continue to pour out of me. His lips are slightly salty, maybe from his tears, maybe from mine. When his tongue gently parts my lips and enters my mouth, it's like he's touching my very soul.

When I first laid eyes on his photos, when I first bore witness to his breathtaking beauty, my body instantly yearned to fuse with his, to take him into me and let him fill me up as fully and deeply as my body would allow. But now, lying here, clothed in my pajamas, nestled next to him in our little mosquito-netted cocoon for two, I feel transported into another world—another realm, as Plato would say. An ideal realm. And in this realm, it's not my body that yearns to fuse with Jonas, it's my very soul. Yes, he's got broken branches and charred bark—of course—and so do I. But our imperfections don't matter. Because right now, on this particular spot on planet earth, in the middle of a jungle in frickin' Belize, we're perfect.

Chapter 24
Sarah

"Wake up, baby," he coos softly in my ear.

I moan.

"Good morning," he says. "Rise and shine." He kisses my cheek. "Up and at 'em."

I smile, remembering our beautiful, sexless night together. We kissed and cuddled and caressed softly until we couldn't keep our eyes open any longer, and then we fell deeply asleep in each other arms.

I rub my eyes and moan again. "It sounds like jungle sound effects for a movie."

Jonas laughs. "Your voice is so cute in the morning—so gravelly. I love it."

"Coffee," I mumble. I glance at him. He's already fully dressed, bright eyed and bushy tailed, raring to go. His eyes are blazing with excitement.

"Breakfast is out on the balcony waiting for us. Time to get up." He's practically jumping up and down. I've never seen him like this.

I raise my hands over my head and stretch myself from head to toe, purring like a cat. "Best sleep ever," I say dreamily.

He hops onto the bed and crouches next to me. His energy is through the roof. "Do you know what today is, My Magnificent Sarah?"

I smile at him. "What?"

"Today's the day I'm gonna make all your dreams come true."

"You already have."

"Says the girl who's lived in a cave her whole life, staring at shadows. Ha!" He abruptly rolls my entire body onto its side, yanks down my pajama bottoms to reveal my butt cheek, and bites my ass. I mean, really, really, like he literally *bites my ass.*

I yelp.

"Delicious!" he hoots. He snaps my pajama bottoms back into place. "Now go pee or shower or do whatever girly thing you've got to do and meet me on the balcony for some breakfast. Our guide's picking us up in forty-five minutes."

"Guide?"

Without warning, he leaps over me like a panther pouncing on its prey and holds himself in a plank position over my body, his muscles bulging and straining all around me.

I squeal yet again at his sudden movement.

"Yes, guide," he says flatly. He kisses the tip of my nose. "All will be revealed in due time, My Magnificent Sarah, all will be revealed." He leaps off the bed in one sleek motion, turns my body onto its side again, and slaps my ass.

I squeal again.

"Get moving, baby." He bounds across the room toward the balcony. "Time's a wastin'!"

I sit up and look around. Oh my God. Now that it's daylight, I can finally see the source of all the rustling and tweeting and screeching and howling we heard last night. "Holy frickin' moly," I say. Our tree house is surrounded on all sides by a lush, green, almost surreal jungle canopy, stretching as far as the eye can see. "Oh my God."

I leap out of bed, mesmerized by the jungle all around me. Oh man, I really, really, really have to pee, but seeing the jungle up close and personal is more important than any bodily function right now. I join Jonas out on the deck in the already-balmy morning sunshine.

"Incredible, right?" he says, grabbing my hand and leading me to the railing.

My jaw hangs open. "It's like I just leaped into an *Indiana Jones* movie—or, like, a real-life Disney ride."

He laughs. "Exactly. There's no other place quite like this on earth."

"Wow." I can't think of a better word than that.

Somewhere to the left of us, a monkey releases an urgent, plaintive howl.

"Are you taking notes on how to do that?" Jonas asks, laughing.

I dart toward the sound, trying to get a glimpse of the monkey who made it, wherever it is, but the foliage is just too thick to see anything. "I can't see him," I say, frowning.

"Don't worry, we'll see lots and lots of monkeys today. It's easier to see 'em from down below." He claps his hands in excited anticipation. "But, first, you've gotta get your *delectable ass* in gear."

He looks at me like a cat about to devour a mouse and it's suddenly, abundantly clear my butt's about to get chomped again. I squeal and run back inside, laughing, and he follows me, cackling wickedly and stomping loudly right behind me. When he catches me in the spacious bathroom, he wraps his arms around me and picks me up off the ground like I'm a rag doll. He gropes at my butt with exaggerated enthusiasm and nibbles voraciously on my neck.

Yet again, I squeal. I can't help myself.

"Delicious," he says in between bites. "Mmm mmm mmm. Tasty."

And, with that, his erection makes an enthusiastic appearance against my thigh. He gently places my feet back on the floor, but continues holding me tight, his hard-on grinding into me. "If your neck tastes this good, I can't wait to taste the rest of you tonight." He tilts his chin up toward the ceiling and he yells with glee at the top of his lungs. "I'm finally, *finally* gonna lick and kiss and suck my baby's sweet pussy tonight!" His eyes are on fire. "Mmm mmm mmm." He laughs and leans his forehead against mine. "Madness," he says simply, looking into my eyes. He smiles broadly. "Utter madness." Without warning, he slaps my ass again, this time with added gusto (making me yelp), and bounds out of the bathroom, hooting and hollering. "Meet me on the deck for breakfast, baby. You gotta fuel up!"

What have I gotten myself into? I'm slathered in a sticky combination of sunscreen and mosquito repellant—the most high-octane mosquito repellant known to man, so I'm told—slogging through a dense jungle rain forest along a narrow, uneven trail covered in thick mud, vines, tree roots and wet rocks. Miguel, our guide, is hiking through the mud in front of me, charting the least slippery path for us, and Jonas is behind me, variously reminding me to place my feet exactly in Miguel's footprints or watch out for a large root sticking out of the ground or to steer clear of an ant hill the size of a Volkswagen. Thank God Jonas told me to get extra thick-tread hiking boots, or I already would have slipped and broken my neck five different times—or, at the very least, sprained my ankle. It's not the rainy season this time of year, Miguel has told us, but even during this alleged "dry season," as he calls it, torrential downpours nonetheless rain down on this lush inland area at least three times a week. Hence, the sloshy mud I'm currently navigating.

At periodic intervals, Miguel points out a tree or root that he says has healing properties or a particularly nutritious tree nut a person could eat if they were lost in the jungle without provisions, or stops to single out a prehistoric-looking tree with poisonous spines covering its trunk. I feel like I've been dropped into *Jurassic Park*. I keep waiting for a T. rex to ramble into frame and swallow me whole like that guy who gets chomped while sitting on a toilet. Twice, Miguel's stopped to study the path in front of us with narrow eyes and sudden concentration, and when I asked him in a hushed voice what he was looking for, he whispered over his shoulder, "Snake." The phrase that keeps scrolling through my mind on an endless loop is, *This shit is real.*

I still don't know our destination in all this. Miguel has a huge pack on his back, filled to bursting with I don't know what. Jonas also wears a pack, but it seems to be filled with nothing more than sunscreen and jugs of water for the two of us.

"How you doing, baby?" Jonas asks. "You need a water break?"

"No, I'm good," I reply. "Great, actually. Freaking out a teeny bit. But great."

"You're hiking so well. And here I thought your ass was just for show, but it turns out it's functional, too."

I laugh.

"Must be all that dancing," he says.

"How do you know about my dancing?"

"I saw your undergrad transcripts."

I turn back and glare at him.

"Hey, if I'm gonna hack into a major university's server, I'm gonna damn well get my money's worth. You majored in communications, minored in dance. Graduated *magna cum laude*."

I don't know what to say. No man has ever researched me before. But, hey, tit for tat, as he always says—I've certainly researched him more than I care to admit.

"I bet every single guy in every one of your classes wanted to take a big bite out of that delectable ass, too."

I scoff. "I took a lot of *dance* classes, remember? Not every single guy." I smirk.

He laughs. "Touché." There's a beat as he traverses a slippery mud pit. "What kind of dance?"

"When I was young, anything I could find at the rec center. In college, lyrical contemporary, mostly." Under normal circumstances, I could probably talk for hours about dance, but it's hard to chat while concentrating on not falling on my face, getting eaten by a dinosaur, or being strangled by a boa constrictor.

"Do you still dance?"

I smile to myself. I still can't get over how chatty he is with me. "No. I realized it's not what I want to do with my life. Nowadays, I mostly run or do yoga with Kat. There's hardly time for much else between classes, studying, and work."

Oh crap. *Work.* I didn't mean to bring up The Club. He was in such a good mood, too. Damn. I glance behind me, dreading the look on his face, but he looks unfazed—or, at least, not about to hurl like on the plane yesterday.

He's about to say something, but Miguel holds up his hand—our agreed upon signal for silence—and we stop dead in our tracks. Miguel looks up into the jungle canopy for a moment. He silently points. I look up, trying to zero in on whatever he's focused on, and I gasp. No less than six monkeys are perched in the dense rain forest above—and one of them is leaping from one tree to the next, screeching as he does.

I turn back to Jonas, my face blazing with excitement. He's grinning from ear to ear. He nods and whispers, "Awesome, huh?"

I can't contain my excitement. Real monkeys in a real jungle? I never thought I'd see something like this in my entire life, ever.

Jonas grabs my hand and we watch the monkeys for a full twenty minutes, whispering to each other, laughing, gasping, cooing, our hands comfortably clasped, until, finally, Miguel whispers, "You ready to move on?"

"Let's do it," Jonas says, slapping my ass again.

We hike silently for a good ten minutes. I'm curious where we're headed, of course—and yet, it doesn't really matter. Wherever Jonas is leading, I'm following.

"You know, I was so caught up in my own bullshit yesterday," Jonas says out of nowhere, "I didn't stop to think about how this whole Club thing has affected you. I mean, damn, looks like you're unexpectedly out of a job."

I wasn't expecting him to bring up The Club, and certainly not to offer his condolences about me losing my pathetic job. "Oh, I'll figure something out," I say, stepping carefully over a gigantic vine. "I always do. I'm just pissed about the whole thing. It's gross. People joined to find other, consensual, compatible people—not to be lied to. It just boils my blood to think how they're taking people's money and not delivering on what they promise. It's just a scam, a gigantic fraud." My blood is boiling just thinking about it. "And some of these guys—granted, not lots, but *some* of them—join The Club looking for love—I know you don't believe it, but they really, really do—and they're being totally scammed. They have a dream—maybe it's naïve or stupid or whatever—but they do. And The Club exploits that."

Jonas is quiet behind me.

"So, yeah, big deal, I'm out of a job. I haven't been robbed of a dream." I think of Mr. Software Engineer's face when Stacy told him she only follows college basketball except during NBA play-offs. It was total and complete bullshit. I grunt. I'm pissed. "I mean, I'm not the one who had sex with a prostitute when I thought I'd met the woman of my dreams."

Jonas sighs audibly behind me on the trail.

Oh shit. How I wish I could stuff those last words back into my mouth. I was thinking of that poor software engineer who thought he'd found the woman of his dreams—but it sure sounded like I was talking about Jonas. I glance back over my shoulder. Yep, he's scowling. Damn, I'm an idiot.

We're quiet for a minute, listening to our hiking boots clomp and slosh in the mud.

Jonas doesn't say anything.

I shouldn't have said that. Was I subconsciously taking a jab at him? I don't think so. Dang it. "I'm just looking at the whole thing as a massive life lesson and leaving it at that," I say carefully, hoping positivity will help ease my foot out of my mouth.

"What's the life lesson for you?" he asks. I'm relieved to hear him speak again. His voice sounds calm.

I step over a large rock in the trail. "That I should *always* listen to my gut."

"Your gut was telling you something and you ignored it?"

"Absolutely. I knew deep down something wasn't right. I mean, I never saw a single application from a woman, not once—but I just convinced myself some other intake agent must have been in charge of processing female applicants. And I kept thinking there was no way in hell a woman would ever join a club like that—but I ignored my instinct the minute those fat paychecks started rolling in. It serves me right."

"Hmm," he says, considering what I've said.

We continue hiking in silence again for several minutes.

I glance behind me to get a read on him, but he's looking down, his features scrunched in deep concentration.

"You know what, Sarah?" he finally says.

I don't reply. My heart is racing.

"You're so smart," he says. "But even more than that, you're *wise.* You know that? I just ... wow, Sarah, I just genuinely *like* you."

I instantly stop walking and turn to look at him. My heart has leapt into my throat. I can't suppress the huge smile breaking out across my face. "Thank you."

"You're welcome," he says. He smiles at me. And then he *blushes.* Mr. I'm-Gonna-Lick-Your-Sweet-Pussy *blushes* like we're in fourth grade and he's just asked me to go steady.

"Hey, Miguel, can you give us a minute?" I call out over my shoulder.

"Sure," Miguel says. And because he's obviously a smart man, he traipses ahead into the jungle and out of sight, leaving Jonas and me alone.

I turn back to Jonas. "That's the best thing you could ever say to me. I like you, too. A lot. A lot, a lot, a lot."

"Well, I like you a lot, a lot, infinity," he says. His grin stretches from ear to ear. He looks like a kid right now. Like a glowing, happy, carefree kid.

I throw my arms around his neck. "Thank you for bringing me here."

I go in for the kiss, but he pulls back. "Well, actually, I should clarify one little thing. When I said I *like* you, I was talking about your ass. I really, really like your *ass*." I laugh and smash my lips into his.

His tongue enters my mouth and, holy hell, my entire body ignites like a matchbox lit with a blowtorch. He's instantly inflamed, too, quite obviously, because without hesitation, he grinds his hard-on into me as his hand claws at my T-shirt, untucking it indelicately from my pants and hiking it up. His hand burrows under my shirt and quickly reaches into my sport bra. His fingers are inside my bra, groping me, as his tongue explores my mouth.

That familiar throbbing has returned between my legs, with a vengeance. I'm practically gyrating in his arms like a fish on a line. How we went from feeling like grade school crushes a moment ago to ravenous nymphos, I'll never know. It happened in the blink of an eye.

He moans. "I'm going out of my fucking mind, Sarah." He claws at my pants, and I quickly unbutton them for him. He slips his hand down my waistband and his fingers plunge desperately into my wetness. I let out a loud, low groan and so does he. He's kissing me, touching me, making my knees weak. My body has gone from zero to sixty in a matter of seconds as his fingers slide in and out of me and his tongue explores my mouth. Every inch of my skin is vibrating with my sudden desire for him.

"I'm fluttering," I breathe. "Jonas, ooh, I'm fluttering."

I whip my head behind me to see if Miguel's still out of sight. "You wanna do it?" I whisper in his ear, pressing my palm against his hard-on. I nip at his lower lip and reach for his waistband, fumbling to unbutton his pants. "Jungle sex," I breathe, struggling with his fly.

He pushes my hand away as his finger continues to slick back and forth from my wetness to my tip. "I don't come 'til you do," he breathes, continuing his fingers' expert exploration.

"I think I'll come," I whisper into his ear. "I'm losing my mind."

With one final kiss, he pulls his hand out of my pants and embraces me. He's instantly in complete control. "I can't risk it." He pulls me to him and whispers in my ear. "This is just prelude, baby, sweet prelude." He smirks when he sees my glare. "I made a solemn vow, remember? I don't come 'til you do. It's my new religion." He kisses my forehead. "You're my religion." He suddenly grabs my butt with both hands. "I love this ass," he whispers. He whips his head over his shoulder. "Miguel!" he yells. "Let's go!" He releases me unceremoniously, leaving me dizzy and confused and raging between my legs.

Miguel appears out of nowhere within seconds.

"You see?" Jonas says in a low voice, scolding me. "If I'd let you have your bossy way, we'd have given Miguel quite a show." He laughs. "I told you—no more fucking around. I've finally got my head on straight."

I'm so aroused, I feel like rubbing my crotch against a goddamned tree—and I wouldn't even care if it's one of those prehistoric ones with the spikes. If he'd only give me the match to light my fuse, I'd go off like a rocket; I know I would.

"You ready?" Miguel says. He looks amused.

"Yup," Jonas says. "What do you think? Fifteen more minutes or so?"

"Yeah, 'bout that," Miguel says.

The minute Miguel turns his back to me to continue down the trail, I reach down and touch myself over the fabric of my pants. I just want to know if the outrageous throbbing I feel on the inside of my panties is palpable on the outside, too. It doesn't seem to be. I glance back at Jonas. He's looking at my hand between my legs, his face illuminated with arousal. I smile at him and wink. *Tonight's the night, big boy.*

We hike for a few more minutes, drenched in sweat, swatting at the occasional mosquito, quietly taking in the sights and sounds of the jungle around us. I still have no idea where we're going, and I'm really starting to wonder.

"I've been thinking," Jonas says out of nowhere, huffing and puffing with the exertion of our hike—or maybe thanks to his current state of sexual frustration. "This whole thing with The Club. It really threw me for a loop yesterday. But now that I've had a chance to think about it, I'm feeling kind of philosophical."

I remain quiet. I've learned not to break the spell when he's opening up—and especially when he's being Philosophical Jonas.

"The way I see it, I dodged a bullet. God only knows what would have happened if I'd gotten what I *thought* I wanted. I'm grateful."

I stop and look back at him. *Grateful?* For getting scammed? For unknowingly having sex with a prostitute?

"If it weren't for The Club," he says, smiling sheepishly at me, "I wouldn't have found you. So, when you look at it that way, it's the best money I ever spent."

Chapter 25
Sarah

"Wow," I say. That's the only thing my brain can come up with.

Miguel, Jonas and I are huddled inside the mouth of a gigantic, breathtaking cave, complete with rock formations and stalactites, as rain pours down mercilessly outside the cave, just a few feet from where we're sitting. The sheer volume of water pounding down from the sky is as if God is standing above, pouring out a humongous bucket of water onto the jungle beneath Him.

I'm shaking from nervousness. Now that we've trekked this long and far into the deep jungle, what the heck are we going to do in this cave? Or maybe I'm shaking because I'm soaking wet from head to toe. The torrential downpour started sheeting down from the sky about ten minutes before we reached the cave, and within seconds of the waterworks, I was as drenched as if I'd walked into a shower, fully clothed.

"There's nothing to be scared of," Jonas assures me, securing the strap on my helmet. "Tilt your chin up." I do. He bites his lip as he adjusts my helmet strap and I'm struck yet again by his sheer beauty. When he's finished with the strap, he places his hands on my shoulders and smiles at me. "There's another opening to the cave about four miles in. It won't take us more than three hours to get there."

"Three *hours?*" I say, shocked. "To hike four miles?"

"Yeah, the trek isn't exactly a straight shot." He smiles. "It's a bit of a hike." He turns to Miguel, and they both laugh, sharing some sort of inside joke.

The hair on the back of my neck stands up. What the hell is so funny?

"Hey, Miguel, why don't you tell Sarah about the cave?"

"Of course. The ancient Mayans, who lived all throughout what is now Belize and Guatemala, believed this cave to be the entrance to the Kingdom of Xibalba—the underworld. This cave, like others in Belize, too, is where the Mayans brought sacrifices to the gods to ensure their continued prosperity."

"Well said, Miguel," Jonas says.

"I've given that speech a time or two." Miguel laughs.

"But, Miguel, what *kind* of sacrifices did the Mayans make in this cave?" Jonas asks the question as if he and Miguel are doing a comedy routine for my benefit. Clearly, Jonas already knows the answer to his question; he just wants Miguel to say it out loud.

"Human sacrifices."

"But exactly what *kind* of humans, specifically, Miguel?"

"Virgins. Female virgins."

Jonas' eyes are dancing. Oh, brother, he's so proud of himself right now. I can't help but smile broadly. Oh, how Jonas Faraday loves his metaphors. Obviously, I'm his virgin—his orgasm-virgin—and I'm about to be sacrificed to the gods. Or, rather, to one almighty god—Jonas Faraday.

Jonas flashes me a wicked grin.

I laugh. "You proud of yourself, Jonas?"

"So proud."

"You really, really like your metaphors, don't you?"

He laughs like a kid on Christmas and pulls me into him. "Yeah, I really, really do."

"You truly are a poet at heart, you know that?" I say.

He leans into me and places his lips right on my ear. "'At the touch of love, everyone becomes a poet.'" He pulls back out and winks. "Plato."

My heart is instantly racing. Did Jonas just tell me he *loves* me? I bite my lip. He did, right?

He grins at me. "Did you get enough to eat?"

I nod. When we took cover in the cave, Miguel laid out a beautiful picnic for us. But I don't want to talk about food. I want to talk about what Jonas just said to me. Did I understand him correctly?

He slaps my ass. "Good." He turns to Miguel. "You got our headlamps?"

"Yes, sir," Miguel replies.

Yeah, I'm pretty sure Jonas just told me he loves me. I didn't imagine that, did I? I didn't just *wish* it, right? I said, *"You're a poet."* And he said, *"At the touch of love everyone becomes a poet."* How else could I interpret that comment, other than to conclude he's been touched by love? By his love for me? Or does he mean he's been touched by *my* presumed love for *him*? Do I love him? My mind is reeling. My heart is racing. Oh, if only Miguel weren't here. If only we were alone right now. There's only one thing I want right now—and it's not a three-mile hike into a blackened cave with Jonas and a guide (sweet as that guide seems to be).

Jonas pulls me to him, but not for a kiss—he's securing a headlamp onto my helmet with great care. "Once we get twenty yards into the cave, there'll be no natural light. It's as dark as ink in there—you can't even see your hand an inch from your face without a lamp."

My jaw is still hanging open. Yes, I'm almost positive Jonas Faraday, the man, the myth, the legend, the Adonis, the Woman Wizard himself, just told me he *loves* me. Unless, of course, he's telling me he feels *loved* by me—touched by *my* love—which wouldn't be a shabby thing for him to say, either. But do I *love* him?

He presses into me and his erection nudges against my leg. "Now come on, baby," he says quietly, grabbing my ass for the hundredth time today. "Let's go sacrifice your virgin ass to the gods."

This is insane. This is utterly, totally, and completely insane. He wants me to climb up *what*? For the past two hours, Jonas and I, with Miguel leading the way, have ventured deeper and deeper and deeper into the jet-black cave, hiking higher and higher along the bank of a winding, underground stream, past stalactites and swarms of bats and dripping cave walls that look like movie sets, wading deeper and deeper into the stream where the bank narrowed and narrowed and ultimately disappeared, climbing higher and higher over wet boulders and through jagged openings, sometimes having to drag ourselves through low rock hangings on our bellies. At one point, Jonas insisted we turn off our headlamps, just to experience absolute darkness, and it was unlike anything I'd ever experienced—truly, the eeriest and most disembodying thirty seconds of my entire life. The cave was so dark as to be disorienting. So dark as to invite panic. The minute I started shaking, though, Jonas sensed it and turned his lamp back on.

"I'm here," he said. "Sarah, I'm right here."

Just before we were forced by the narrowing cave walls to start trudging right up the middle of the deep stream, Jonas retrieved harnesses from Miguel's backpack and secured the thick canvass strappings around my thighs and waist.

"What the hell is this for?" I asked, my voice quavering.

"You'll see," he said, tightening a buckle on my harness.

"I'm scared, Jonas," I whispered.

"I'm in charge, remember?" he said, looking into my face, the light on his headlamp momentarily blinding me.

"In the *bedroom*," I corrected, shaking with cold and nerves.

He flipped up the trajectory of his headlamp so it wouldn't shine directly in my eyes and placed his hands on my cheeks. "My Magnificent Sarah," he said tenderly, looking deeply into my wide eyes. "I would never, ever let harm come to you. You're too precious to me. This is going to be one of the best experiences of your entire life—the perfect metaphor for the indescribable pleasure I'm going to give you tonight. If you'll trust me, completely, you'll thank me when it's over." He leaned in and kissed my wet lips, and my entire body melted into his.

Well, then. A harness it is.

And now, here I am, a harness secured around my body, a rope attached to the harness, standing in jet-black water up to my shoulders, at the base of a subterranean waterfall in a pitch-black cave—and Jonas is casually explaining the best strategy for my climb *up* the waterfall. Miguel already climbed up the rocks of the waterfall like a cat in a tree so he could secure the rope attached to my harness.

"Even if you slip, the rope will catch you," Jonas coaxes from behind me. "And I'll talk you through the whole thing."

I look up. The top of the waterfall is a good fifteen to twenty feet up, and the only way up is by grabbing rocks directly in the path of the cascading water.

Jonas is standing behind me in the deep water with his arms around my waist, speaking right into my ear. He points. "You see that crag right there?"

I nod.

"Just put your right hand *there* and your left hand slightly above, maybe *there,* and then just go slow and steady up, arm-leg-arm-leg, 'til you reach Miguel. He'll pull you up over the edge when you get there."

I nod again.

"You ready?"

I nod again. I'm shaking.

He pushes me forward and up, out of the water, onto a tiny footing at the base of the waterfall, just to the left of the cascading water. The cave is pitch black, other than the small orbs of light cast by our three headlamps. I look up. I can see Miguel's headlamp shining brightly down on us from the top of the waterfall, but I can't see Miguel.

I reach down and feel for the rope attached to my waist. Yep, it's still there. I'm clutching the rock wall, afraid to move. Water is sheeting down a few inches away from me to my right.

"You can do this," Jonas shouts from the deep water behind me. "Just do it, and don't think about it."

I look down at him and almost lose my footing on the slippery rock I'm teetering on.

"You got this," he shouts above the sound of the rushing water.

I look up at my destination at the top of the waterfall.

"I'm here," he shouts. "And I'm not going anywhere. I promise."

Sweeter words were never spoken. I'm still shaking, but I'm suddenly determined. I take a big breath and shimmy to my right, directly into the path of the pounding water. Holy hell, the water is pelting me, pounding the top of my helmet. I reach up and find the crags Jonas designated for my hands, and then I find places for my feet. And I climb. Midway up, I have trouble finding a spot for my right hand, and I'm frozen. The water's pelting me in the face. How did I get here?

"Move your hand up just a little," Jonas coaches. He's out of the water now, standing on the small footing at the base of the waterfall directly beneath me.

I do as he instructs.

"That's it, baby. Damn, you're doing great. Now reach your left hand up. That's it, good."

Before I know it, Miguel's hand is around my wrist, and he's pulling me up, over the lip of the waterfall. And not a minute after that, Jonas is already standing next to me, having ascended the waterfall like he was climbing a step stool.

Jonas clutches me. "You did it!"

I look at him and my headlamp illuminates his face. He's beaming at me. He's elated, triumphant. The waterfall below us is rushing noisily in our ears. But wait. That water-pounding sound isn't coming from *underneath* us, it's coming from *above* us. I tilt my headlamp up, and holy frickin' fuckity fuck fuck, there's yet another waterfall about twenty feet away on the far side of yet another deep pool of dark water yawning before me—only this waterfall is a good thirty feet high.

I swing my face back to Jonas, ready to read him the riot act, but the expression on his face makes me laugh instead. Oh, he's having the time of his life.

Climbing up the second waterfall proves much easier than the first, even though it's twice as high. This time, I just do it. I don't think about it. I don't worry about it. I just trust the rope. And Jonas. And myself. And Miguel. I just let go. It certainly helps knowing this is the last waterfall (which Jonas swore) *and* that our destination (the "back door" mouth of the cave) is only about two hundred yards from this second waterfall (which Jonas swore to be true).

When I arrive at the lip of the second waterfall, my legs wobbly beneath me, I'm aghast. The only thing at the top of the waterfall is yet another small, dark pool of water. This time, thankfully, there's no waterfall, just like Jonas promised—but the blackened pool is enclosed on all sides by low cave walls. There's no trail. There's no light. It's a dead end.

I don't understand. How do we get out of here? Is there some sort of underwater cave we have to dive down to in order to come up the other side and exit the cave?

"Wow," Jonas says, easily climbing over the lip of the second waterfall, "you kicked ass that time, baby. You're a natural. I can't wait to take you indoor climbing when we get home."

"Jonas, how do we get to the mouth of the cave from here?" I shine my headlamp on the nearby cave walls surrounding us. "Where's the opening?"

"Oh, yeah. Um." He looks at Miguel and they share another one of their oh-she's-gonna-shit-a-brick smiles.

"You said the mouth of the cave is only two hundred yards away from this waterfall." I can't keep the edge out of my voice.

"And it is. The mouth of the cave *is* only about two hundred yards away from where we're standing right now—but the *trail* to the mouth of the cave is right ... down there." He points back down to the base of the waterfall.

"What?"

"Yeah. There's a little trail off to right down there—we follow that, and—boom—we're out. Easy peasy."

"Down there? Then why did we climb up here?"

He smiles.

My stomach somersaults. "Oh no."

"There's no other way down."

"No."

"This is how we sacrifice you to the gods." His smile is from ear to ear.

"Jonas, no."

"There's no other way down, baby. No other option. Contrary to what your brain is telling you, contrary to instinct, you're just gonna have to let go and take a gigantic leap of faith into the dark abyss."

I shine my light into the blackness below me. "It's like thirty feet down!"

"Piece of cake."

I grunt with exasperation.

"You want me to go first?" he asks.

I cross my arms over my chest, thinking. There was a high dive at the rec center pool growing up. One summer, when I was eleven, I jumped off it, just to prove I could do it, and I never did it again. I don't like heights. I don't like the feeling of my stomach leaping into my throat. And I *really* don't like the idea of jumping thirty feet into a dark chasm below.

"There's no other way down," he says again.

I glare at him. I'm pissed.

He's anxious. "I wasn't trying to *trick* you, Sarah, I promise. I was trying to *surprise* you." His face contorts with worry. It's exactly the look he flashed at his house when he told me he wasn't treating me like a prostitute but, rather, like his girlfriend. This is the Jonas Faraday that melts my heart, right here, right now.

I grab his hand. "I know." My knees are knocking.

His eyes are pleading with me. His intentions are pure. He's put a lot of thought and effort into this entire trip—into helping me get out of my own way. He's right. I need to get out of my head and take a flying leap. With him.

I look down past the rushing water at my feet into the darkness below. Even with my headlamp pointed down past the ridge I'm standing on, I can't see the water below me—it's just opaque blackness down there. I look back up at Jonas and my headlamp shines in his eyes. He squints and shields his eyes at the sudden bright light. I point my light just to the side of his face and he drops his hand. His eyes are earnest.

"You okay?" he asks.

My heart is clanging in my chest. "Yeah." I exhale loudly. "Let's do it." I nod.

He smiles broadly and squeezes my hand. "I'll jump first. And you come after me." He smirks. "Ha! Of course, tonight we'll do things in the exact opposite order." He winks.

My cheeks flush. Oh yes, tonight. This crazy, beautiful madman has engineered this entire day as a prelude to tonight's main event. I've never wanted anything more in all my life than to make love to this gorgeous man tonight. But I have to survive this ridiculousness first.

"You sure you're okay?"

I nod.

He kisses me on the cheek. "Then I'll see you on the other side," he says. "Bye." He leaps, hooting as he disappears into the blackness. I hear a large splash, followed by a cheer from below. "Awesome!" he yells up from the darkness.

After a few seconds, a small pool of light shines on the black water below me. "Aim for right here!" Jonas yells up. "Don't think about it; just do it!"

I look at Miguel with my headlamp. His illuminated face smiles at me. He nods his encouragement. I look back down at the small pool of light below me. Jonas' hand flickers into the small orb of light, patting the water. "Right here!" he calls up.

"Fuck it," I mutter. I jump.

My entire body plunges into cold wetness. The water engulfs me completely, past my head. His strong arms embrace me. I'm clutching him, exhilarated, relieved, incredulous, shaking.

"So proud of you," he's muttering as he peppers my face with kisses. "So proud of you," he says again. His kisses are euphoric. "My little virgin sacrifice."

I'm clutching him like he's a lifeboat and I'm drowning. I'm not sure I could command my arms to let go of him, even if I wanted to— which I don't. I don't want to let go of him ever again.

"I'm so proud of you," he says again, in between kisses. "You did it."

He swims to the edge of the water with me on his back, my arms around his neck. When he reaches the shallow part of the pool, he trudges out of the water, cradling me in his strong arms. His legs are under him now, on solid ground. He heads through an opening in the rocks to the side of the waterfall—I can't believe I didn't notice it before I started that second climb. His powerful legs are pumping, his arms sheltering me. I feel weightless. I feel safe. The lights from our headlamps are converging and leading our way out of the blackness. I nuzzle my dripping face into his strong chest.

"Do you see it?" he says after a couple minutes, his breathing labored.

I open my eyes and look ahead of us along the trail—and sure enough, there's a faraway, glimmering light. The mouth of the cave.

"I see it," I say. "Let's run."

He puts me down gently and grabs my hand, and we begin running, hand in hand, toward the light outside the cave. As we run, the light gets closer and closer and brighter and brighter and bigger and bigger; the cave walls become higher and higher and more expansive and open—and our laughter spirals into uncontained delirium. I don't know why we're laughing so hard, but we are.

Finally, we burst out of the cave and into the light together, hand in hand, breathless and howling with our mutual euphoria. The rain from earlier in the day has stopped, leaving behind a glistening, lush wonderland.

"Oh," I say, finally collecting myself. "Oh, Jonas."

He's beaming at me. His face is flushed. "Beautiful," he mutters, and his lips find mine.

Holy moly, this is the best kiss of my life. It's electric. Who knew joining lips with someone could wreak this kind of havoc on an entire body, mind, and soul? His hands find my cheeks as his lips softly devour me. I'm floating, flying, reeling as his mouth continues its assault on mine. I reach for his hair—but my knuckles knock against the hard plastic of his helmet. He pulls away from me, his eyes heavy, and unlatches his helmet with an exasperated grunt. I follow suit. He tosses his helmet to the ground and so do I, and we continue our kiss to end all kisses. Ah, yes, my fingers revel in his wet hair. He pulls me into him, almost desperately, and I swear I can feel his heart beating against mine. After a moment, we pull apart, perhaps sensing Miguel's imminent approach from the cave.

"Tonight," Jonas says, his eyes blazing.

"Tonight," I reply. My heart is racing. Goosebumps cover every inch of my skin. "Hellz yeah."

He laughs. He cradles my back and pulls me close.

I've never felt so connected to another human being as I do in this moment.

I want to kiss him again, but Miguel appears out of the mouth of the cave, shuffling toward us, dripping wet, his large backpack weighing him down.

"Well?" Miguel asks when he reaches us, huffing and puffing. He looks right at me. "How'd you like the cave?"

I look at Jonas. His eyes are on fire.

"Incredible," I say. "But . . ." I motion to the awe-inspiring sights all around me—to the blue sky peeking out from the dense jungle canopy above, to the sun-dappled foliage that looks straight out of the Mesozoic era, to the bursts of color overloading my senses—and, finally, pointedly, to beautiful Jonas himself, standing next to me, his face aglow. "But this is pure beauty, right here." I shoot Jonas a look of unadulterated elation, and he returns it.

Jonas pulls me to him and whispers in my ear. "The culmination of human possibility."

Jonas and I are sitting in the backseat of a topless Jeep, being driven down the Belizian highway in the warm sunshine. My wet ponytail is whipping in the wind, variously bitch-slapping Jonas and me in our faces, making us laugh. Jonas hasn't said a word to me since our exchange outside the cave, but he hasn't let go of my hand, either. I suppose, though, even if he wanted to chat, it would be pretty hard to do, what with the wind blasting us like we're ants in a hand dryer.

Our driver turns on the radio. The song is "Locked Out of Heaven" by Bruno Mars. He turns it up and Bruno Mars sings about sex with a girl who makes him feel like he's discovering paradise for the first time. Jonas nudges me with his shoulder. I nudge him back and laugh. Yep, it's the perfect song. Surely, up 'til now, Jonas and I have both been locked outside the gates of heaven and didn't even know it. But we're inside the pearly gates now, baby—there's no doubt about it.

That kiss outside the cave was ... wow. It was like our souls grabbed onto each other. It was magical. That was heaven, right there. *Ecstasy*—in the way the ancient Greeks described it, as Jonas would say. But it wasn't just the kiss itself; it was everything that happened today that led up to that euphoric moment. I don't think it's an exaggeration to say today changed me. I feel lighter. Stronger. More sure of myself than ever before. Suddenly, I know exactly who I am, as opposed to who I'm *supposed* to be. I'm not a perfect little good girl—not all the time. And that's okay. And I know exactly what I *want*. I want to be my whole self and nothing less, without apology, from this day forward. I want to be true to myself, to the real me, to my deepest desires.

And you know what else I want? I want Jonas Faraday. Holy hell, do I ever. I want to show him every part of me, without holding back. And I want to discover every part of him, too, no matter how damaged he turns out to be. I've never felt like this with anyone. I want to take a flying leap into the black abyss. If my heart winds up getting broken on the rocky crags below, so be it. It was worth it. No matter what happens tonight—whether I have a physical orgasm or not—I've already experienced a spiritual climax of sorts today. And so did Jonas. I know he did.

"Can we stop there for just a minute?" Jonas suddenly shouts above the din of the wind and loud music, pointing to a quaint souvenir shop along the side of the highway. Even from the outside, I can see it's bursting with colorful beach towels and T-shirts, a real tourist-trap kind of place. I can't imagine what he wants to buy there.

Our driver nods and pulls over.

Jonas hops out of the Jeep and turns around to help me down.

"You're in need of a souvenir?" I ask.

He just smiles.

The interior of the tiny store is exactly as I expected—cluttered with mugs emblazoned with "Belize," bars of handmade soap, handcrafted jewelry, T-shirts, wood-carved plates, and colorful tapestries. What does he want to buy here?

"*Hola*," the old woman behind the counter says in greeting.

"*Hola*," Jonas and I reply in unison. I smile at Jonas. His accent is adorably Americano.

Jonas moves toward a rack filled with touristy-looking jewelry and key chains, but then he notices something in the back of the store.

"Sarah, you'd look so pretty in that," he says, pointing to the far corner of the store.

My gaze follows his sightline. He's referring to a white, flowing sundress hanging in the corner, brightly embroidered along the neckline and straps.

"It's beautiful," I say. And it is. It's stunning. But he's already been too generous.

"You like it?"

I nod sheepishly. "But you've already done too much. I've got plenty of clothes."

"The white will be gorgeous against your skin."

I open my mouth to protest. He's done too much already.

"Seeing you in that dress is going to be *your* gift to *me*. We'll call it a bonus payment."

I laugh.

"Go get your size, baby. I want you to wear it for me tonight."

I'm giddy. The dress really is stunning. "Thank you." I have to admit, I'm thrilled. I trot over to the dress rack to look at the sizes while he hones in on a rack filled with jewelry and key chains.

"And pick out a pair of earrings, too," he calls over to me.

"No, Jonas, that's too much. Just the dress."

"Well, then, I'll just have to pick out a pair for you," he says.

I flash him a huge smile and turn my attention back to the dress rack. I hold the dress up. The embroidered trim is breathtaking.

Behind my back, I hear Jonas talking to the old woman behind the cash register. "We'll take the dress—the white one she's holding," he says. "Plus these earrings. And both of these, too. *Gracias.*"

"*Están ustedes de luna de miel?*" the woman asks him.

"*Sí,*" Jonas replies, smiling.

"*Felicitaciones.*"

I whip my head to look at Jonas. He's nodding and smiling at the old woman, but clearly he didn't catch what she said. Based on that Americano accent of his, I gather Spanish isn't his strong suit—but even if he understands a bit, he clearly misunderstood what the old woman asked him. Oh boy, when I translate for him later, he's going to laugh that he replied yes to her question.

Outside the store, Jonas shows me the earrings he picked out for me. They're silver and turquoise—a lovely complement to the dress.

"They're perfect," I gush. "Thank you."

"I thought they'd look pretty with the dress." There it is again—that I'm-treating-you-like-my-girlfriend look. It melts me.

"I love them, Jonas." I kiss him. "Thank you. For everything. You're so generous."

"You're welcome." He takes a big breath. "And there's just one more thing." He reaches into his plastic bag and pulls out two handmade bracelets, identically woven with multi-colored yarn. They're friendship bracelets, basically—the kind of thing crafty teenage girls might make for each other back home. He grabs my wrist and starts fastening my bracelet around it, a shy smile on his face. How cute is this man to give me a Belizian friendship bracelet? One minute he's talking about his hard-on and the next minute he's a fourth grader with a crush.

"You're so adorable," I say, feeling rather fourth-grader-ish myself.

He fastens the other bracelet on his own wrist. "As a member of the Jonas Faraday Club—the sole member—you need a color-coded bracelet."

"Oh yeah." I laugh. "To designate my freaky-ass 'sexual preferences.'" I look at the multi-colored bracelet on my arm. "I'm not a purple?"

"No, you're not a purple." His tone just called me a big dummy. "Neither am I. We're a brand new color—a color designated for just the two of us." He holds his wrist right next to mine. "We're a perfect match."

Chapter 26
Jonas

Fucking finally.

I lick my lips.

As much as I thoroughly enjoyed seeing her in her new white sundress at dinner—and she was even more beautiful in it than I could have imagined—I'm not sad to see that pretty dress crumpled on the floor right now. I reach around her back and unclasp her bra. I love the way her breasts fall when freed from their cruel bondage.

She looks drunk—and not from the rum punch we drank at dinner. No, she's drunk with arousal. Damn, she's ready to go off like a rocket. And so am I.

I press play on the song I've cued up for this moment. "Madness" by Muse. There's no better song to express what I'm feeling. This song is telling her my truth with every word and note.

The minute we walked through the door after dinner, I ripped my clothes off unceremoniously, and she immediately followed suit, pulling her dress off and throwing it onto the floor with a loud whoop. It turned me on. But then again, everything she does turns me on.

"Lie down," I command, motioning to the bed.

She complies without hesitation, crawling on her hands and knees onto the bed like a cat. The sight of her white G-string disappearing up her delectable ass almost brings me to my knees.

"On your back," I order, barely able to breathe.

She complies and stretches herself out to her full length, her dark hair unfurling onto the pillow around her face. Her breathing is shallow. She's already twitching with excited anticipation about what's about to happen to her—oh man, anticipation is eating her alive right now. Well, guess what? Anticipation can move the fuck over—I'm the only one who gets to eat her alive from now on.

The singer from Muse is telling her my truth.

I crawl onto the bed, growling and spreading her legs as I approach. She arches her back, yearning for me. Without warning, I dive down and bite savagely at her G-string. She shrieks in surprise. I take the fabric in my teeth and shake my jaw like a dog with a chew toy, breaking the elastic waistband and ripping the remnants off her in one fell swoop.

She gasps.

I see my sweet target. It looks utterly delicious. But not yet.

I climb on top of her and kiss her mouth, my hard-on pressing insistently into her thigh. She wraps her arms around me, her pelvis reflexively tilting up and thrusting toward me, inviting me to enter her.

Madness.

I caress between her legs ever so gently, my fingers barely skimming the tip of her, and she moans softly. I dip my finger into her—oh God, she's so ready for me—and bring my finger to my mouth. "You taste so good," I whisper hoarsely. I dip my finger into her again and bring it to her mouth. She sucks it voraciously. "So good," I breathe again, and she nods, writhing under me.

My wet finger glides back down and finds her tip. It's erect— hard and slippery against my fingertip. I can barely breathe.

Madness.

My lips find her breasts as my fingers move in and out of her. Her nipples are hard and at full attention. I lick one of them for a moment and then let my mouth trail down to her belly. She moans softly.

My tongue finds the inside of her thigh.

"Jonas," she whispers, exhaling a shaky breath and arching her back.

I can't hold off anymore. My lips move to her sweet spot, to the glorious pussy I've been yearning to lick for half my life. I kiss her again and again and again, making love to her wetness with my lips and tongue.

"Yes," she breathes, arching her back into me. "Yes."

Madness.

I write the alphabet into her deliciousness, one distinct letter at a time, paying close attention to what her body's telling me to do. When I reach "H," a fierce growl escapes her, so I linger on that letter until her body is writhing and jolting.

When the time is right, when her body tells me to, I move on down the line. I ... J ... K ... L ... M.

Oh, wow, my baby likes "M." Oh yeah, she does.

M ... M ... M ... M ... M ... M.

M is for madness, or so the song keeps telling us.

With each and every letter, with each and every swirl of my tongue, with each and every kiss of my lips and mouth, I'm telling her the truth about my devotion to her. Emphatically.

N ... O ... P.

She's whimpering. Writhing vigorously.

Q ... R ... S.

"S" usually stands for "sure thing" or, sometimes, "secret weapon"—I can't remember the last time I even made it past "S"—but, no, not with Sarah. Because Sarah's not like anybody else. But I already knew that.

I move on to "T."

Bingo.

Oh yeah, my baby likes her some "T."

"T" is for Taser gun, apparently, because her body is jerking savagely like I've just jolted her with one.

T ... T ... T for My Magnificent Sarah.

T ... T ... T for my sweet baby.

She's gyrating wildly and gasping for air.

Oh yeah, she's losing her fucking mind.

And so am I.

She's unfurling.

Untethering.

Her pleasure is morphing into pain.

By the time I get to "Z," which I follow with a long string of zealous exclamation points, she's hanging on by the barest of threads.

The key is firmly in her lock—and now it's time to turn it.

My tongue teases her tip for a brief moment—but who am I kidding? We're way past the point of teasing. I take her hard cherry in my mouth and suck her like she's never been sucked before.

Lauren Rowe

She howls and thrashes like a wounded animal caught in a trap.

Oh, my baby. Come on.

She grabs the back of my head with both hands and shoves me into her with all her strength, screaming my name, spreading her legs forcefully.

Let go, baby.

Her mind is detaching from her body; I can feel it.

Madness.

I twirl my tongue around and around and around, over and over, grunting and groaning into her. Oh God, I'm either going to come, pass out, or have a fucking heart attack. I can't . . .

She's howling like a fucking monkey right now. She's not human.

I shudder. I'm so turned on, I can't . . .

But, no, no, no, I don't come 'til she does. I don't come 'til she does.

Come on, baby. Surrender.

I plunge my tongue into her, penetrating her as deep as my tongue will go, eating her alive, sucking her, devouring her, willing her to surrender.

I can't hang on much longer.

I skim my teeth across her engorged tip.

She screams.

Let go, baby. Please. Please. Please. Please. Please.

I nibble her, right on her sweet button.

Click.

She unlocks.

Thank God.

She reflexively shudders in my mouth like a window opening and closing in rapid succession. Over and over and over and over she shudders from the inside out, jolting and jerking and convulsing like she's having a seizure—and, oh my God, she's shrieking from the very depths of her soul through it all. She's laying herself bare to me, showing me everything. Oh God, yes, she's surrendering, finally—to the pleasure, to the truth, to me. Yes, to me.

She's pure beauty.

She's perfection.

She's my greatest creation.

268

My every God-given instinct is to plow into her and let her body constrict and tighten around me—the most delicious feeling known to mankind, the holy grail—but I'd sooner die right now than come without her, and I can't be one hundred percent sure.

Madness.

She twitches powerfully, one last time, and then she's done.

Her shrieking subsides. She's trembling. Moaning. Sweating.

"Jonas," she finally says, her voice catching in her throat. "Yes," she gasps. She puts her hand over her chest, calming her racing heart.

I look up at her from between her legs. Her chest is heaving.

I'm delirious.

"You did it," she whispers. Her eyes are wild. She's seen the light.

Madness.

"Make love to me," she purrs, gyrating. Her breasts are rising and falling.

I climb up to her face and lick her, claiming her. She returns the gesture, lapping at my lips and chin and tongue.

"Make love to me," she purrs again.

I plunge into her, desperate for my release. Her body receives me with a warm and hungry welcome.

"Sarah," I groan, making love to her—glorying in her. We fit together like no two people ever have. Her body was uniquely designed for mine.

She's the ideal form of beauty.

She's the divine original.

With every movement of my body, I'm telling her how I feel.

"Jonas," she whispers in my ear.

I'm gone.

I let go with a loud, deep growl, my entire body seizing and shuddering and releasing.

Sarah.

She's my religion.

I'm her devotee.

She's all-powerful.

I am but her supplicant.

I surrender.

Yes, I surrender.

Totally and completely.

"Madness," I breathe, collapsing on top of her. My body jerks violently again, apparently experiencing some sort of aftershock. "Oh my God, Sarah."

She laughs that gravelly laugh of hers.

"Holy fuck." I'm still shaking. My heart is still racing. "Madness."

Chapter 27
Sarah

"Sarah."

I whip my head up. The last thing I remember, I was tangled up in Jonas. When did I fall asleep? It's the dead of night. The jungle is alive around us.

The mosquito net is opened and Jonas is standing at the foot of the bed. His erection is enormous. Like, holy moly. His eyes are cut from steel. His chest is heaving.

Music blares from Jonas' laptop. This time the song is "Closer to God" by Nine Inch Nails. Every hair on my body stands at full attention. I know this dark song—and I know exactly what it means. The song is telling me exactly what he's going to do to me—how he's going to fuck me. My chest constricts.

Count me in.

This song has always, always turned me on at my very core in the most primal way, making me feel horny and naughty and fucktastic like no other song ever has. Every time I hear it, I secretly imagine myself getting fucked by some beast of a man, without mercy, in exactly the way the song describes. And now, finally, that day has arrived—and that beast of a man is the man of my dreams.

His eyes gleam at me. He reaches out, coaxing me out of the bed.

He's going to fuck me like a beast.

Yes, please. And thank you.

My entire body is pulsing along with the primal beat of the song. I'm already gyrating and Jonas hasn't even touched me yet.

Jonas leads me out into the warm night air on the deck, giving me an eyeful of his backside in the moonlight as he walks. Holy moly, that's quite a backside.

The dark jungle canopy looms beyond us in all directions. He leans my back against a wooden railing and spreads my legs apart like he's about to frisk me. His fingers touch between my legs, and he smiles when he feels how aroused I already am. The tip of his penis penetrates me briefly and I throw my head back in anticipation of being fucked—but he chuckles. He's just teasing me. Bastard.

He grabs a cushion from a deck chair, places it at my feet, and kneels before me like he's saying his prayers. He looks up at me and licks his lips.

I smile down at him. I'm ready.

He leans into me. I feel his warm breath on me.

My chest heaves. Holy crap, the anticipation is killing me.

What's he doing? He's not going in. He's skimming his lips, ever so gently across me, like he's taking in the aroma of a fine wine before swirling it in his mouth. My legs are trembling.

He leans forward and kisses me, lightly, reverently. No tongue. Just soft, adoring kisses, over and over. My knees instantly buckle.

And there it is. Oh God, yes, his warm, wet tongue. He laps at me like he's repeatedly licking an envelope closed. Within minutes, I'm already moaning and writhing like he's been down there pleasuring me for hours. Maybe it's muscle memory from earlier tonight, maybe it's a newfound confidence in knowing where this is headed, maybe it's having him kneeling humbly before me, or maybe he's just "learned me" so frickin' well that any form of resistance is futile, but in record speed I'm already going out of my mind. A guttural sound emerges from my throat as his tongue begins twirling and swirling and shifting my hard clit around. I throw my head back, enjoying the sudden intensity of the pleasure. When he begins sucking and swirling his tongue at the same time—something he's never done to me quite like this before—I grip the railing. I throw my head back again, but it doesn't relieve the pressure building inside me.

I slam myself into his mouth, grinding into his face, forcing him into me. I can't stop my hips from jerking and thrusting into him. I clutch the railing, digging my fingernails into the wood, trying to keep my legs underneath me, but my knees keep buckling.

Oh my God, I'm gonna come. Oh God, yes, holy fuck, I'm gonna come.

I throw my head back and howl. My insides are fluttering, undulating, warping as my knees buckle and melt. I'm practically squatting onto his face, thrusting and smashing myself into him over and over, yearning to take him into me. Oh God, I'm insane right now. Depraved. Ha! I am fucking this beautiful man's face right now. But I don't care. I'm standing on the edge of a deep, dark chasm, and oh God, oh God, oh God, I'm about to leap into the void. He grunts and grabs at my ass, pulling me even closer into his face, gnawing at me with his teeth as he does. I can't stay upright. I can't maintain control. I spread my legs to give him deeper access to me, my hips thrusting into him. This is pure ecstasy. Or agony. Or both. My hands are lost in his hair, pushing him into me. I'm shaking. I'm dizzy. Pain and pleasure have united. I'm ready to come. Right now. *Right fucking now.*

"Now!" I howl. "Jonas! Now!"

He leaps to standing, his erection glorious in the moonlight, and he turns my shuddering, shaking, frenzied body toward the railing. Without the slightest hesitation, he slams into me from behind, feverishly reaching around and touching me as he does so. Oh God, yes, yes, yes, yes, he's thrusting into me, fucking me like an animal, pounding into me, riding me deep and hard and without mercy, fondling me rhythmically all the while. I can't think. I can't breathe. I fondle my breasts, my hard nipples. I reach down and feel him sliding in and out of me, yes, yes, yes, yes, and then I bring my wet finger to my mouth and suck on it, aching to find some way to relieve the pressure inside me.

"Fuck me," I growl, my hips thrusting and tilting to receive him as deeply as possible. "Harder," I groan, and he complies. His fingers massaging me are magic. I'm falling, losing myself, going out of my fucking mind. This is even better than the last time.

"Baby," he grunts in my ear, and my body twitches violently, as surely as if he's just said "open *sesame*" and opened a darkened chamber at the farthest reaches of me. There's a moment of weightlessness, disorientation, like an ocean receding sharply just before a tsunami, and then, finally, finally, a warm wave of intense pleasure slams me from the inside out, seizing every muscle in my body and sending my heart racing.

The first wave is followed immediately by another and another and another and another and another and another, until my entire body is constricting and contracting violently. I begin to say "Jonas" but the only thing that escapes my lips is an animalistic shriek. My entire body tightens and tenses all at once with one final, epic seizure, then releases rhythmically into pulses of pleasure radiating throughout my core.

Jonas cries out savagely as he rams me, his hardness slicing into me one final, merciless time. "Sarah," he cries. "Oh God, Sarah."

He collapses onto my back and sighs, his sweat mingling with mine.

I turn around to look at him, and I'm instantly greeted with his voracious lips.

After a moment, he pulls away from me and laughs. "Wow."

But I can't laugh. I can't speak. My heart hasn't slowed to a normal rate yet. I'm light-headed. Disoriented. My knees are rubbery.

I wobble over to a deck chair and take a seat.

He sits across from me, sweat glistening on his brow.

"Wooh!" he says. "Epic." He's giddy.

I nod. I can't speak. Oh my God.

Several minutes pass as we catch our mutual breath.

"Twice in one night, baby," he finally says, smiling. "Mount Everest has officially been conquered."

Boom. Just like that, I've got a horrible pit in my stomach. I didn't allow myself to think about it, but now I can't help myself. *I'm Mount Everest.* I said so myself. *And Jonas is a climber.* So now what? Does he want to move on to a new challenge—Kilimanjaro or The Matterhorn, maybe? This is a man who wants to get women off more than anything else. No, he *needs* to get women off. I've known that from the start. And he just accomplished what he set out to do with me, and then some. What's left to keep him interested now?

He's still grinning, oblivious to the thoughts racing around inside my head.

"So admit it—you like chocolate a helluva lot better than green beans, don't you?"

I'm too tense to say anything.

"You still wanna lecture me about how sex for a woman is about so much more than coming, blah, blah, blah emotion, blah, blah, blah? Please, enlighten me."

I know he's teasing me, trying to be playful, but I can't deny the anxiety that just crashed down on me like a ton of bricks. He promised not to come 'til I did. And he's delivered on his end of the bargain. So is my climax the end of the road for us? Will he check the box marked "Big O" next to "Sarah Cruz" and move on? Does he even want to continue with the rest of my month-long membership? I look down at the bracelet on my wrist. I feel like crying. I don't want my time with Jonas to end. Ever.

"Well?" Jonas asks, smiling broadly, clearly oblivious to the panic threatening to overtake me.

I clear my throat. "Just because you love making women come more than anything, that doesn't mean it's the only thing." I jut my chin at him. "Not for me, anyway."

His smile vanishes. In fact, his face flashes anger.

"Jesus," he mutters, shaking his head. "Here we go again. Un-fucking-believable."

Wow, he's pissed. I don't understand the sudden rage contorting his features. I open my mouth but nothing comes out.

He leaps out of his chair and glowers at me. "I love 'making women come more than anything'? Fuck! I've had it with your daddy issues, Sarah—your fear of abandonment. I'm not gonna keep paying the emotional debts of your asswipe of a father."

I'm flabbergasted.

He leans down to me, placing his hands on the arms of my deck chair, making me shrink back. "I might be a cocky-son-of-a bitch-asshole, but I'm not a total and complete dick, okay? When are you finally going to trust me? Are you even *capable* of trust? If not, just tell me now, once and for all, so I don't keep banging my head against a fucking wall trying to make you see the *upside* to me."

My eyes are wide. What is happening? He's enraged. What did I say?

He pushes off from my chair in a huff and paces around the deck, his taut muscles tensing like a cat on the prowl. "What more can I do to prove myself to you?" He motions in frustration to the suite, to the jungle—to the entire expanse of Belize. "I'm running out of ideas, Sarah." He looks up to the sky, trying to contain his anguish. "You're so scared of being abandoned—you're turning it into a self-fulfilling prophecy." He grunts.

I shake my head. How did I screw this up so badly, and so suddenly? What did I say that set him off? "No," I begin.

But I can't find the words. Because he's right. He's absolutely right.

I've been gripped with fear from day one with him. I've been convinced he was going to own my heart and then shatter it into a million tiny pieces. Yes, I've been waiting for him to do it. And I still am.

He leaps back over to me and cups my face in his hands. He leans his face right into mine. "There's no more 'making *women* come' for me. Haven't I made that clear to you a thousand different ways?" He exhales in extreme exasperation. "There's only making *you* come. There's only getting *you* off. There's only *you*, My Magnificent Sarah. You're the one I want. You're the one I need. You fucking own me—you and your bossy bullshit and olive skin and gravelly voice and big ol' brain and delectable ass and adorable smile. *You, you, you.*" He brusquely grabs my arm like I'm a rag doll and yanks it up. He points to the bracelet around my wrist. "*You.*" He shows me his matching bracelet. "And me." He grunts loudly, like a gorilla. "For a smart girl, you can be such a dumbshit sometimes, I swear to God."

My mouth is hanging open.

He's pacing again. "Didn't you understand the Muse song? *Madness*?"

I shake my head. I guess not. I thought I'd understood it, but I must have missed something. I thought the song meant he planned to lick me into a frenzied state of madness, a temporary state of delirium—mind detached from body. What else could it have meant?

"Madness, Sarah. *Madness.*" He stares at me as if he's just made everything crystal clear.

I shake my head dumbly. Okay, madness.

His eyes are suddenly moist. "I lost my mind a long time ago, Sarah. Like, literally, lost it. And it was so painful." He chokes up. "I swore to myself, never again—no matter what."

He comes back over to me and grabs my shoulders roughly. I recoil instinctively.

His eyes flash and he releases me. "I thought Plato was scoffing at madness, telling me to avoid it at all costs. But I had it all wrong."

I shake my head. I don't understand.

"And then I met you, and I *wanted* to have a serious mental disease. I wanted to go mad." He shakes his head, brimming with emotion. "Plato wasn't telling me to *avoid* it. He was telling me to *embrace* it."

My eyes are wide. My heart is racing. Is he losing his mind, like, for real? "I don't understand."

He grits his teeth. "'*Love* is a serious mental disease,'" he says, making air quotes and drawing out the words. "That's what Plato said. *Love* is a fucking serious mental disease." He's shouting. I can't tell if he's angry or frustrated or passionate or all of the above. He glares at me, his hands gripping the arms of my chair again. "Why would anyone want a serious mental disease? It hurts. It's torture. It's *painful*." He grunts again. "He said love is *madness*, Sarah. And I thought that meant I needed to avoid it—because I've been avoiding it my whole life." He's losing the battle with his emotions.

I'm speechless.

"But you drive me crazy." His voice is cracking. "And I *want* you to."

I close my eyes, trying to keep my tears at bay. My heart is bursting.

"Do you understand what I'm saying to you?" he whispers.

I nod. I understand completely.

He leans his forehead onto mine. "There's no *women* to get off anymore, you big dummy. There's only *you*."

I blink and the tears that were pooling in my eyes streak down my cheeks. I nod profusely. I understand.

He clenches his jaw and lurches away from me. He's suddenly angry again. "But if you don't want me, if you don't feel the same way, just tell me now. Rip off the fucking Band-Aid. I can't take it anymore."

Is it even remotely possible he's not one hundred percent certain about my feelings?

"Jonas," I say, my emotions threatening to overwhelm me. "Jonas, look at me. *Look at me.* Yes, I want you. Of course, I want you. You drive me totally, completely, irreversibly crazy."

His chest is heaving.

"Insane in the membrane," I say softly.

He exhales sharply.

"Psychotic. Deranged. Out of my mind."

He twists his mouth.

"Sick in the head. Demented. *Loca.*"

He grins.

"I'm cuckoo for Cocoa Puffs."

He laughs, despite himself.

I stand and wrap my arms around his neck. "I've got a serious mental disease. It's madness."

He kisses me deeply.

"You big dummy," I whisper.

He beams at me. "I knew you wouldn't be able to resist me."

I laugh.

"So this is settled, then?"

I nod.

"No more crazy-ass trust issues?"

"No more."

"No more one step forward, two steps back?"

"Full steam ahead." I pause. "As long as you promise to let me talk about my beloved Maltese Kiki all day, every day."

He bursts out laughing. "Deal."

"But don't worry," I say, my lips hovering an inch from his. "I promise, absolutely no weekend trips to IKEA." I nuzzle my nose against his.

He cocks his head to the side and pulls back. "Well, hang on a second. Let's not be hasty."

I arch my eyebrows in surprise.

"I'm just saying, I mean, it *might* be tolerable, occasionally, to go to IKEA *if* we were to get some of those meatballs while we're there. Have you ever had IKEA meatballs? They're pretty good."

I beam at him. "Yeah, I like those meatballs."

He nods decisively. "Okay, so it's settled. We won't foreclose the *possibility* of going to IKEA, as long there are Swedish meatballs involved." He suddenly grabs my ass with gusto. "Or, maybe we'll just stay home and I'll nibble your *albóndigas,* instead." He laughs. "God, I love this ass."

Wait, how does he know the Spanish word for meatballs? I pull back from him, an epiphany hitting me like a thunderbolt. "You speak Spanish?"

"Yeah. Not fluently, but pretty well."

My heart lurches with my sudden, glorious, heart-melting epiphany.

"What?" He raises his eyebrows, not understanding the sudden flush to my cheeks. "It comes in handy when I travel. What?"

"Oh, Jonas." I kiss him.

Who would have thought the man who's allegedly allergic to "Valentine's Day bullshit" would turn out to be a diehard romantic, through and through? The woman in the souvenir shop asked him in Spanish, "Are you on your honeymoon?" and my metaphor-loving man replied that, yes, we were—while purchasing a flowing, white dress for his "bride" and matching bracelets for our wrists. Oh jeez. How could I have assumed he'd misunderstood her?

"Estamos de luna de miel," I say, kissing him. *We're on our honeymoon.*

He grins from ear to ear under my kiss. *"Claro que sí."* *Of course, we are.*

Madness.

"You're a poet," I murmur into his lips.

"Nah," he says. "Only with you."

I sigh. "Jonas."

"What?

"You're a cocky-asshole-motherfucker, you know that?"

"Yes."

"But you're also the man of my dreams."

Epilogue
Jonas

After a long travel day, we're finally back in Seattle and trudging up to her apartment door. I'm trailing behind her, holding her suitcase, admiring her backside as we walk.

What a trip.

What a woman.

What a life.

I'd planned so much for our second full day in Belize yesterday—rappelling down a three-hundred-foot sinkhole in the jungle, a late afternoon helicopter ride, swimming in Belize's famed Blue Hole. But that's how you make God laugh—you make plans. As it turned out, we didn't leave our tree house once yesterday, not even to eat. And it was the best day of my life. Well, the second best day.

From the minute we woke up this morning to when the limo pulled up to her apartment building thirty seconds ago, we've been like giddy kids. At breakfast this morning on the deck, when I looked across the table at her, the jungle alive all around us, I felt a kind of happiness surge up inside me that almost took my breath away.

"You're the divine original form of *woman*," I told her. "You're *woman-ness* in the ideal realm."

She gave me that look—the look I'd move mountains to see—the look that makes me want to be a better man.

"You're man-ness," she replied matter-of-factly. "My manly man-ness-y manly man."

I laughed.

And our giddiness didn't end after breakfast.

Through the van ride to the airport and hours of waiting around and two flights, we haven't stopped laughing and sighing and gazing at each other and cooing sweet nothings into each other's ears and stroking each other's skin and laying soft kisses on each other's lips and cheeks—all the while marveling that this is our life. We're on top of the world together—on top of an ideal world inhabited by just the two of us.

We arrive at the front door to her apartment.

The door is slightly ajar.

"What the . . .?" she mutters as she pushes the door wide open. "Oh my God," she gasps.

The place is wrecked—top to bottom, absolutely trashed.

I put my arm in front of her to keep her from venturing inside.

"Stay here," I say, stepping forward.

I can't believe my eyes. When I came to pick her up for the airport four days ago, this place was as neat as a pin. And now it's in shambles. Whatever used to be on the walls and on her shelves and in her drawers now litters the floor. Holy shit, the place is a total disaster area. What the hell is this? Some kind of hate crime?

I feel her body heat right behind me. I reach back and pull her into me. She's shaking.

"Oh no," she gasps.

I whip my head to look at her.

She's pale as a ghost. "My laptop," she says, grimacing. Tears are pricking her eyes. "It's gone."

Oh, Jesus. I suddenly know exactly what this is all about. Damn, how did I not understand instantly?

I grab her suitcase in one hand and her arm in the other and pull her out the door, back to the limo.

"Come on," I command. "You're coming home with me."

She doesn't put up a fight.

She's shaking like a leaf as I guide her into the backseat of the limo. My heart is racing like a bullet train.

I don't even want to think about what might have happened if she'd been home when they came. They couldn't possibly have known she'd be away, could they? Were they planning on her being home when they showed up, or did they come in her absence on purpose, intending to give her a spine-chilling warning?

I should have known when she told me about her encounter with Stacy that she was in danger. Clearly, we're dealing with a sophisticated, global operation with *a lot* of money at stake. They're not going to let some law student in Seattle put their entire organization at risk. I'd bet there are some seriously bad motherfuckers running this whole operation—motherfuckers who'd do just about anything to protect their cash cow.

I put my arms around her in the backseat. "I've got you."

She nods.

They've got her computer. They've got all our communications. All her personal information.

Kat.

"Call Kat," I say, louder than I'd intended. "Make sure she's okay."

She looks at me, confounded.

"Stacy obviously went on a rant to whomever she reports to about some brunette and blonde horning in on her territory, right?"

Her eyes are wide.

"How many other intake agents are there in Seattle?"

"I'm it, I'm pretty sure."

"Okay, then they know the brunette is you; and now that they've got your computer, they know who the blonde is, too."

She looks like she's having trouble processing what I'm telling her.

"There are pictures of you and Kat on your computer?"

She nods. "Tons."

"Emails with her?"

She nods again.

"And she's in your contacts, right?"

Her face bursts into utter panic.

"Call her right now. Tell her we're coming to get her. She's gonna stay with us at my house 'til we get this worked out."

She pulls her phone out with a shaking hand.

"Have any of your emails with Kat ever mentioned The Club?"

She thinks for a minute. She shakes her head. "Never."

"Okay, that's good. But Kat was with you at both bars, so they must figure you told her everything."

"Oh my God."

I take her hand in mine. "I'm not gonna let them hurt you." I squeeze her hand. "This shit stops right here, with me."

Sarah nods at me, but her attention is immediately drawn to her phone. Kat has picked up.

"Kat," Sarah breathes into her phone, relieved to hear Kat's voice. "Are you okay?"

I dial Josh on my phone. He picks up right away.

"Hey, how was Belize?"

"Josh, you gotta come to Seattle. Right now. We've got a situation."

"Something with the deal?"

"No, something else. It's an emergency."

"Are you okay? Is Sarah okay?"

"Yeah, I'm okay. The trip was incredible—Sarah's incredible. She's with me right now. It's The Club. It's total bullshit, Josh. A fucking scam. I'll tell you everything when you get here." I lower my voice and cup my hand to my phone so Sarah won't hear the next thing I say. "I think Sarah's in danger. Like, maybe serious danger."

He pauses briefly. "I'll be able to catch the last flight out if I hightail it to LAX right now. If not, I'll charter something. I'll see you soon."

"Hey, and tell your hacker buddy to clear his calendar. I've got a big job for him starting immediately."

"Will do. See you soon."

We hang up.

Sarah's winding up her phone call with Kat.

"Just get out of there," she says. "We'll pick you up in fifteen minutes. I love you, too."

She hangs up and wipes her eyes. "Her place was ransacked while she was at work. Same as mine—completely trashed. And they took her computer, too." Her voice catches in her throat. "What have I gotten her mixed up in?"

I pull her toward me, but she's too amped up to be comforted.

"The police just left her place. They think it was a burglary—because that's all she thought it was. But now that she knows about my place, she's scared to death."

"You told her we're coming to get her?"

She nods. "She's meeting us at the gas station down the street from her place in fifteen minutes."

"Josh is on his way, too. He'll be at my house later tonight." I kiss the back of her hand. "I don't want you going back there, you understand?"

She nods.

"Ever again. You're staying with me now." I pause. "Indefinitely."

She nods again. No fight at all. I'm surprised. And relieved. And secretly thrilled, even in the midst of my acute agitation. She's really going to be mine now. Every day and every night. Well, damn, I guess there's a silver lining in everything, no matter how horrible.

"Is there anything you need from your apartment? I'll go back later with Josh and get it."

"Some clothes, maybe."

"I'll buy you new clothes."

She doesn't fight me on that, either. Wow, she must really be freaking out.

"My text books," she says.

"Okay. I'll get them." If they're missing or destroyed, I'll buy her new ones.

She sighs. "The only other things I care about are on my laptop." Her voice quavers.

"This is my fault," I say, my stomach somersaulting. "You wanted to take your computer to Belize, and I wouldn't let you." A familiar darkness is welling up inside me. "If it wasn't for me, they wouldn't have your laptop right now." And they wouldn't have been able to identify Kat—or at least not so quickly. Goddammit. Sarah's been mine all of three days and I've already put her and her best friend in danger and probably put a target on my own back, too. Why did I make her leave her laptop behind? And why the hell did I ever fuck Stacy? I knew I was making a massive mistake when I did it—I *knew* it—and I did it anyway. But Stacy's a red herring. The real question is why I applied to The Club in the first place? Was I following my father's path to hell? Was I having another nervous breakdown?

I run my hand through my hair.

Unwanted images are invading my brain—flashes, snapshots, incomplete impressions—all of them unbidden and savage. Blood streaming out of her nose. Her hand grasping and flailing at the rope around her wrist. His hairy ass. The gleam of the knife.

I close my eyes.

I see her glancing frantically over at the closet, pleading with me to stay put. I see the look of fear in her eyes. I see the look of desperation. But for the first time ever, for the first time in twenty-three years, it's not her blue eyes pleading with me—it's Sarah's big, brown eyes.

My stomach lurches violently. I rub at my eyes, trying to erase the pictures in my head. I'm going to protect her this time. Or die trying. I'm not going to fail her this time. I'm not going to let him hurt her again. I'll kill him if I have to—with my bare hands if I have to, before I let him hurt her.

"No," Sarah says sternly. "Jonas, no." She grabs my arm and shakes it. "Jonas, look at me." Her voice is surprisingly forceful. She tugs on my arm.

I comply.

"This is not your fault. Don't say that—don't even think it."

I exhale.

She squeezes my hand. "We're in this together," she says. "Okay? I need you to keep focused. There's no blame here. There's only what we're gonna do about it. No more fucking around. That means both of us."

She's right. What the hell am I doing? This is not the time to give free reign to my demons. I feel like punching myself in the face I'm acting like such a pussy. Right now is about one thing—protecting my baby. At all costs. There's no time to waste thinking about anything else.

Okay, my head is back in the game.

"Was everything backed up on your laptop?" I ask.

She cringes. "No, none of it." She's thinking. "But I shared all my course outlines with my study group just the other day, so I can get those. Oh my God, thank God I did that. Nothing else matters right now except those study outlines. Oh, and my photos—but my mom and Kat have the ones that matter." She sighs. "Crap. I can't believe this is happening."

I look out the window of the limo, watching parked cars whiz by.

Nobody hurts my baby. Nobody even *threatens* to hurt my baby.

I was willing to kiss my money goodbye in karmic exchange for finding my Sarah. I was willing to let bygones be bygones, to chalk it all up to me getting the comeuppance I deserve in the grand scheme of things. Damn, I was willing to walk away and never look back and let those bastards keep shilling their global brothel with no one the wiser. Maybe all the guys joining The Club subconsciously (or even consciously?) know what they're really getting, for all I know. Or if not, maybe they don't want to know. Who am I to make that decision for all of them, I figured? But, oh no, hell no, all bets are off now. Those bastards fucked with my woman—the woman I *love,* goddammit—and now they're going down.

I look over at Sarah, at her elegant profile. She's pursing that beautiful mouth of hers, deep in thought. She senses me looking at her and turns her gaze on me. Her cheeks are stained with dried tears, but she's strong now. She's ready for a fight.

"I'm gonna protect you," I say.

"I know you are," she says.

"I'd never let anything happen to you," I clarify, just in case she doesn't fully understand.

One corner of her mouth tilts up. She nods. She knows.

"I need you, Sarah," I say, my heart pounding.

"I need you, too," she says softly, a lovely grin unfurling across her face.

But that's not what I meant to say just then, not at all. I mean I *do* need her, of course, yes, that's clear to me now. I need her. I want her. I can't get enough of her. But I meant to say something else. Something else entirely. I shift in my seat.

"I'm not going anywhere," I whisper.

Her smile widens. Her eyes crinkle. She's not going anywhere, either.

But that wasn't what I wanted to say, either. I exhale.

I look out the window again. She leans against my shoulder, apparently content. She doesn't need me to say anything more. She knows.

But, no, there's still more to say.

I take a deep breath. "Madness," I whisper in her ear.

She nods. "Madness," she repeats back to me. She squeezes my hand. Yes, she understands. She always understands. *Love is a serious mental disease.* Yeah, she knows. There's nothing more I need to say. I've already told her a thousand different ways.

You're everything I never knew I always wanted. That's the quote I selected for my Valentine's card to her—and I really thought I meant it when I chose it for her. But, damn, I didn't even know her back then—I only knew who I *hoped* she'd be. So that time doesn't count. But, wait, when she called me a poet in the cave, I said, *"At the touch of love everyone becomes a poet."* How much clearer could I have been? That was pretty damned clear. And then, of course, I told her the biggie, *"Love is a serious mental disease."* And I played the Muse song for her, too. I exhale. Yeah, I've definitely told her. There's nothing more I need to say.

I've said enough. More than enough.

I gaze out the window again, my fingers woven into hers.

She shifts her head on my shoulder and sighs.

Fuck.

I haven't said enough.

Fuck.

I don't want to speak in riddles anymore. I don't want to quote Plato or fucking Matthew Perry to tell her how I feel. I want to tell her in my own words, as clearly and as simply as a man can say it.

"Sarah."

She looks up at me.

But the words don't come out of my mouth. I'm tongue-tied.

My heart is racing.

I've never uttered those three little words to a woman before, except to my mother—never even been tempted—but I want to say them now. I want to say them to my Sarah.

I look into her eyes.

My Magnificent Sarah. I'd die before I let anything happen to her. Or kill.

I don't want anyone else.

I love her. I do. I love her.

I love Sarah Cruz.

I need to tell her. I know I do. Right now. She deserves to hear those exact words, especially now.

My heart pounds in my ears.

I look into her big, brown eyes.

She's looking at me with a kind of unadulterated adoration, an unconditional acceptance I didn't even know existed in the world, at least not for someone like me. The look on her face makes me want to throw myself at her feet.

There's a long beat as I struggle to form the words on the tip of my tongue. I want to tell her, I do, but we're racing to pick up Kat. I don't want to share this moment with Kat. I want to say those words for the very first time when it's going to be just Sarah and me, when I can say them to her and *show* her how much I love her at the same time.

My chest heaves.

She squeezes my hand and smiles at me. Her eyes are warm. Kind. "Oh, my sweet Jonas," she sighs. She puts her hand on my cheek. "You're all upside, do you know that?"

I sigh and close my eyes. I'm blowing it. I know I am.

I press my cheek into her hand. God, I love this woman.

"You're nothing but upside, my sweet Jonas," she whispers. She squeezes my hand and puts her other hand over her heart. "It's madness."

The Reclamation (The Club Trilogy Book 2) and *The Redemption* (Book 3) are both available now. Here's the synopsis of The Reclamation:

The second installment of Jonas and Sarah's epic and addictive love story picks up right where *The Club* left off, hurtling to a heart-stopping conclusion that will leave readers breathless and screaming for the final installment of the trilogy. What starts out as an innocent exploration of attraction quickly spirals into a steamy story of unbridled passion, obsession, heartbreak, and, ultimately, redemption.

Here's an excerpt from *The Reclamation*:

Chapter 1
Jonas

There are two twitching, trembling women standing in my living room right now—and I'm not talking about the good kind of twitching, trembling women. Sarah and Kat are scared shitless right now, freaking out about their places being ransacked and their computers stolen (undoubtedly by the motherfuckers at the Club), and wondering if today's events represent the sum total of the iceberg slamming into them, or just the tip of it. And I can't blame them for being scared. Now that Sarah knows the truth about The Club—and The Club *knows* she knows their secret—what might those fuckers be willing to do to protect their global cash-cow-prostitution-ring? Well, I'm not going to wait to find out. I'm taking these motherfuckers down.

And here's what readers are saying about *The Reclamation* (Book 2):

"I could not put this book [*The Reclamation*] down. Loved it!"—Amazon reviewer

"This book [*The Reclamation*] left me needing more! What an awesome story. I almost want to delay reading 3. Not ready for the story to end."—Amazon reviewer

"The author has her hooks in us and is twisting to see just how cruel she can be. And with this said I just downloaded the last book in this series to my phone. I can't wait a moment longer to know what happens next."—Amazon Reviewer

"... beautifully written, just rips your heart out cuts it up and then pours that acid spit from Alien on it..."—Amazon reviewer

"I have to say that *The Reclamation* is my favorite book of the trilogy."—Amazon Reviewer

And here's what readers are saying about *The Redemption* (Book 3) and *The Club Trilogy*:

"This series is the 'Divine Original' of awesome-ness!"—Amazon reviewer

"In a word? Transcendent!"—Amazon reviewer

"The emotional journey that Jonas continues has to be one of the most heartbreakingly beautiful things I have ever read..."—Amazon reviewer

"Book 3 is by far my favorite of the series..."—Goodreads reviewer

"... a beautiful conclusion to the BEST love story I've read."—Amazon Reviewer

"Thank you Lauren Rowe for the BEST trilogy I've ever read!!!"—Goodreads reviewer

"This has to be one of the most satisfying endings for a book series that I have read in a while. The best really was saved for last in this case. It was hit straight out of the park."—Goodreads reviewer

"I cried so much while reading this book [*The* Redemption] and I must say, this is my favorite part of The Club trilogy."—Amazon Reviewer

"What a conclusion to a mind blowing trilogy!! I couldn't put this book down until I read the last word!! Makes me sad it's ended!"—Amazon Reviewer

"Lauren Rowe has conquered Mount Everest with this one!"—Amazon Reviewer

About the Author

Lauren Rowe is the pen name of a USA Today best-selling author, performer, audio book narrator, songwriter and media host/personality who decided to unleash her alter ego to write The Club Trilogy to ensure she didn't hold back or self-censor in writing the story. Lauren Rowe lives in San Diego, California where she lives with her family, sings with her band, hosts a show, and writes at all hours of the night. Find out more about The Club Trilogy and Lauren Rowe at www.LaurenRoweBooks.com and be sure to sign up for her emails to find out about new releases and exclusive giveaways.

Dedication

This book is dedicated to the wonderful ladies who read this book first and responded with a hearty "hot damn and hell yeah": Nicki, Marnie, Lesley, Tiffanie, Colleen, and Holly, plus, my mom, mother-in-law, and aunt. I was thrilled but not surprised when my best girlfriends loved the book—but when my mom, mother-in-law and aunt loved it, too? "We old ladies like the sexy stuff, too," my aunt explained to me. So effing awesome. Thank you, ladies, all of you. I love you all.

Additional Books by Lauren Rowe

All books by Lauren Rowe are available in ebook, paperback, and audiobook formats.

The Club Series (The Faraday Brothers Books)

The Club Series is seven books about two brothers, Jonas and Josh Faraday, and the feisty, fierce, smart, funny women who eventually take complete ownership of their hearts: Sarah Cruz and Kat Morgan. *The Club Series* books are to be read in order*, as follows:

-*The Club* #1 (Jonas and Sarah)

-*The Reclamation* #2 (Jonas and Sarah)

-*The Redemption* #3 (Jonas and Sarah)

-*The Culmination* #4 (Jonas and Sarah with Josh and Kat)*
    *Note Lauren intended *The Club Series* to be read in order, 1-7. However, some readers have preferred skipping over book four and heading straight to Josh and Kat's story in *The Infatuation* (Book #5) and then looping back around after Book 7 to read Book 4. This is perfectly fine because *The Culmination* is set three years after the end of the series. It's up to individual preference if you prefer chronological storytelling, go for it. If you wish to read the books as Lauren intended, then read in order 1-4.

-*The Infatuation* #5 (Josh and Kat, Part I)

-*The Revelation* #6 (Josh and Kat, Part II)

-*The Consummation* #7 (Josh and Kat, Part III)

In *The Consummation* (The Club #7), we meet Kat Morgan's family, including her four brothers, Colby, Ryan, Keane, and Dax. If you wish to read more about the Morgans, check out The Morgan Brothers Books. A series of complete standalones, they are set in the same universe as *The Club Series* with numerous cross-over scenes and characters. You do *not* need to read *The Club Series* first to enjoy The Morgan Brothers Books. **And all Morgan Brothers books are standalones to be read in *any* order.**

The Morgan Brothers Books:

Enjoy the Morgan Brothers books before or after or alongside *The Club Series,* in any order:

1. *Hero.* Coming March 12, 2018! This is the epic love story of heroic firefighter, **Colby Morgan,** Kat Morgan's oldest brother. After the worst catastrophe of Colby Morgan's life, will physical therapist Lydia save him... or will he save her? This story takes place alongside Josh and Kat's love story from books 5 to 7 of *The Club Series* and also parallel to Ryan Morgan's love story in *Captain.*

2. *Captain.* A steamy, funny, heartfelt, heart-palpitating insta-love-to-enemies-to-lovers romance. This is the love story of tattooed sex god, **Ryan Morgan**, and the woman he'd move heaven and earth to claim. Note this story takes place alongside *Hero* and The Josh and Kat books from *The Club Series* (Books 5-7). For fans of *The Club Series,* this book brings back not only Josh Faraday and Kat Morgan and the entire Morgan family, but we also get to see in detail Jonas Faraday and Sarah Cruz, Henn and Hannah, and Josh's friend, the music mogul, Reed Rivers, too.

3. *Ball Peen Hammer.* A steamy, hilarious enemies-to-friends-to-lovers romantic comedy. This is the story of cocky as hell male stripper, **Keane Morgan**, and the sassy, smart young woman who brings him to his knees on a road trip. The story begins after *Hero* and *Captain* in time but is intended to be read as a true standalone in *any* order.

4. *Rock Star.* Do you love rock star romances? Then you'll want to read the love story of the youngest Morgan brother, **Dax Morgan,** and the woman who rocked his world, coming in 2018 (TBA)! Note Dax's story is set in time after *Ball Peen Hammer*. Please sign up for Lauren's newsletter at www.laurenrowebooks.com to make sure you don't miss any news about this release and all other upcoming releases and giveaways and behind the scenes scoops!

5. If you've started Lauren's books with The Morgan Brothers Books and you're intrigued about the Morgan brothers' feisty and fabulous sister, **Kat Morgan** (aka The Party Girl) and the sexy billionaire who falls head over heels for her, then it's time to enter the addicting world of the internationally bestselling series, *The Club Series.* Seven books about two brothers (**Jonas Faraday** and **Josh Faraday**) and the witty, sassy women who bring them to their knees (**Sarah Cruz** and **Kat Morgan**), *The Club Series* has been translated all over the world and hit multiple bestseller lists. Find out why readers call it one of their favorite series of all time, addicting, and unforgettable! The series begins with the story of Jonas and Sarah and ends with the story of Josh and Kat.

Does Lauren have standalone books outside the Faraday-Morgan universe? Yes! They are:

1. *Countdown to Killing Kurtis* – This is a sexy psychological thriller with twists and turns, dark humor, and an unconventional love story (not a traditional romance). When a seemingly naive Marilyn-Monroe-wanna-be from Texas discovers her porno-king husband has thwarted her lifelong Hollywood dreams, she hatches a surefire plan to kill him in exactly one year, in order to fulfill what she swears is her sacred destiny.

2. *Misadventures on the Night Shift* – a sexy, funny, scorching bad-boy-rock-star romance with a hint of angst. This is a quick read and Lauren's steamiest book by far, but filled with Lauren's trademark heart, wit, and depth of emotion and character development. Part of Waterhouse Press's Misadventures series featuring standalone works by a roster of kick-ass authors. Look for the first round of

Misadventures books, including Lauren's, in fall 2017. For more, visit misadventures.com.

3. *Misadventures of a College Girl* – a sexy, funny romance with tons of heart, wit, steam, and truly unforgettable characters. Part of Waterhouse Press's Misadventures series featuring standalone works by a roster of kick-ass authors. Look for the first second of Misadventures books, including Lauren's, in spring 2018. For more visit misadventures.com.

4. Look for Lauren's third *Misadventures* title, coming in 2018.

Be sure to sign up for Lauren's newsletter at www.laurenrowe books.com to make sure you don't miss any news about releases and giveaways. Also, join Lauren on Facebook on her page and in her group, Lauren Rowe Books! And if you're an audiobook lover, all of Lauren's books are available in that format, too, narrated or co-narrated by Lauren Rowe, so check them out!

Made in the USA
San Bernardino, CA
02 September 2018